Praise f

The Lawyer and the Laundress is a sweet and historically
rich romance set against the unique backdrop of the Upper
Canada Rebellion. Christine Hill Suntz skillfully conjures
the era, while grounding her story with themes of faith,
friendship, and the healing power of love. A beautiful read.

MIMI MATTHEWS, *USA Today* bestselling author of *The Muse of
Maiden Lane*

Suntz weaves a rich tale of second chances, hope, and faith set
during a unique and unsettled time in Canada's history. This
story will surely capture your heart from start to finish.

J'NELL CIESIELSKI, bestselling author of *The Socialite*

I was completely swept away by this debut! The spunky
laundress and her "upstairs/downstairs" courtship hooked
me right away. Beautiful prose and lovable characters make
this marriage-of-convenience story a can't-miss romance, set
during a little-known time in Canadian history. Perfect for
fans of Sarah Ladd, Laura Frantz, and Julie Klassen. Christine
Hill Suntz is a stunning new voice in historical fiction!

ASHLEY CLARK, acclaimed author of the Heirloom Secrets series

Christine Suntz shines in her debut novel filled with beautiful
prose and engaging characters, set in a little-known slice of
history. *The Lawyer and the Laundress* is the perfect addition
to the historical romance genre. Fans of Tamera Alexander and
Tracie Peterson are sure to enjoy this delightful new offering.

SARAH MONZON, author of *An Overdue Match*

The Lawyer and the Laundress

the

LAWYER

and the

LAUNDRESS

CHRISTINE HILL SUNTZ

Tyndale House Publishers
Carol Stream, Illinois

Visit Tyndale online at tyndale.com.

Visit Christine Hill Suntz's website at christinehillsuntz.com.

Tyndale and Tyndale's quill logo are registered trademarks of Tyndale House Ministries.

The Lawyer and the Laundress

Cover designed by Libby Dykstra

Edited by Kathryn S. Olson

Published in association with the literary agency of Rachel McMillan.

Scripture quotations are taken from the *Holy Bible*, King James Version.

The Lawyer and the Laundress is a work of fiction. Where real people, events, establishments, organizations, or locales appear, they are used fictitiously. All other elements of the novel are drawn from the author's imagination.

The URLs in this book were verified prior to publication. The publisher is not responsible for content in the links, links that have expired, or websites that have changed ownership after that time.

For information about special discounts for bulk purchases, please contact Tyndale House Publishers at csresponse@tyndale.com, or call 1-855-277-9400.

Library of Congress Cataloging-in-Publication Data

A catalog record for this book is available from the Library of Congress.

ISBN 979-8-4005-0775-5 (HC)
ISBN 979-8-4005-0776-2 (SC)

Printed in the United States of America

31	30	29	28	27	26	25
7	6	5	4	3	2	1

~

But oft, in lonely rooms, and 'mid the din
Of towns and cities, I have owed to them,
In hours of weariness, sensations sweet,
Felt in the blood, and felt along the heart;
And passing even into my purer mind
With tranquil restoration:—feelings too
Of unremembered pleasure: such, perhaps,
As have no slight or trivial influence
On that best portion of a good man's life,
His little, nameless, unremembered, acts
Of kindness and of love.

WILLIAM WORDSWORTH
"Lines Composed a Few Miles above Tintern Abbey"

Chapter 1

TORONTO, 1837

She hadn't thought a person could be so hungry that just the sound of cooking could make a mouth water. *Thump. Flip.* The cook was kneading bread. Sara O'Connor took a tentative step across the courtyard toward the broad clapboard building in front of her.

She closed her eyes, picturing the soft dough stretching and rising to fill the bread box. For a moment, she forgot about the uneven cobblestones poking through the worn soles of her shoes and the earthy smell of the stables behind her. If Mrs. Cooper took her on, she'd have fresh bread to eat.

At the sound of footsteps, Sara's eyes flew open. A woman, tall and raw-boned, emerged from the back of Cooper's Inn. She marched in Sara's direction, her full skirts a garish slash of color amid the drab gray and brown of the courtyard.

Mrs. Cooper herself. The woman's eyes swept over Sara, lingering on the frayed hem of her gown. She frowned.

There'd been a day when this would have bothered Sara. When she would have straightened her shoulders and put the woman in her place with a cool look and a few well-placed words. But not anymore.

Sara lowered her eyes and reminded herself to start with a curtsy. Above all, keep her words to a minimum. "Good morning, ma'am."

The woman ignored her greeting. "Awful young to be a washerwoman, aren't you?" She reached out and circled Sara's forearm with two meaty fingers. "Awful scrawny, too."

Forgetting her resolutions, Sara twisted her arm and shook off the older woman's touch. "I'm twenty-nine. I've taken in laundry for years."

Mrs. Cooper's eyes narrowed. "Don't you put on airs with me."

Sara bit her lip and dropped her gaze. Her voice always gave her away. "No, ma'am."

"Hmmm. What's your name?"

"Sara O'Connor." She willed herself to stay still under the woman's scrutiny.

"Well, beggars can't be choosers."

Their eyes met. Did this mean—?

"Start on that." Mrs. Cooper gestured to a heaping basket of linens next to a shed in the back of the courtyard. "You get all that hung out by the time dinner is over, and I'll consider taking you on."

Even the mountain of soiled laundry couldn't stem the rush of relief. Maybe tonight she'd have food to fill her stomach, and some left over to bring home for Granny. She wouldn't have to avoid Granny's questions or see the worried frown the old woman tried to hide.

The thought gave her strength, and she strode to a wash kettle tipped on its side next to the remnants of a fire. A search of the shed yielded a tub of soap and a washboard, but not the chains that would hang her kettle from the tripod.

She glanced at the kitchen. The noon meal was well underway. Delicious wafts of something savory—beef stew, she was sure of it—drifted across the courtyard. What would Mrs. Cooper say if she returned, and Sara hadn't even started?

Returning to the shed, she scanned the barrels that lined the wall. She tugged at one, but it didn't budge. Maybe if she tilted it up and rolled it to the side—

"Reckon you won't find the chains there."

Sara jumped, her face heating. The voice belonged to a boy, perhaps ten or eleven years old. He leaned in the doorway, a long stalk of hay between his teeth, dressed in a ragged shirt and a pair of trousers held up with rope. Sara winced at the hollow look on his face that spoke of hunger and wondered if she looked the same. She focused on his eyes, clear and sharp. Knowing.

"Where are the chains then?" she asked with studied disinterest. He nodded toward the stable, adjusting the stalk of hay between his teeth. Sara considered marching into the stable herself, but this boy could save precious minutes. If he told the truth. "Would you fetch them for me?"

"I might."

Sara shrugged and looked around the courtyard as though his answer didn't matter to her. "I suppose I can ask the groom—"

"I'll get 'em. If . . ." The boy took in her clothing, almost as worn as his own, and sent an uncertain glance to her pockets.

"If?"

"You make it worth my while."

Sara held back a smile. Streetwise boys who'd grown old before their time were nothing new to her now. "I've got nothing to offer you, not even a scrap of bread." His face fell. "But I could mend your trousers. Make them fit right, too."

The boy tugged at the rope around his waist. "Nothing wrong with my trousers." A dull red flush crept up his face.

"Of course not." Sara kept any trace of pity out of her voice. "But you look like a sharp one. A boy who wants to move up in the world. How are you ever going to get a position as a groom in trousers like that?"

The boy assessed her. "You'd kit me out proper? Like a real groom?"

"I'd do my best. I can sew." One of the few useful skills she'd learned as a girl.

The boy nodded and scampered off. Sara started the fire, crossing her fingers that he'd come back with the chains as promised. He did. Helped her hang the cauldron, too, and carry over buckets of water from the pump.

Sara opened her mouth to thank him when a bellow echoed across the courtyard.

"Henry, you good-for-nothing idler, get back here."

Sara sent Henry an apprehensive glance.

"Not to worry, miss," the boy said with a cheeky grin. "Ol' Rawley's bark is worse'n his bite. Mrs. Cooper, on the other hand . . ." He looked over his shoulders at the inn and grimaced. "Well, if I was you, I'd get the wash done right proper."

He trotted back to the stable and Sara bent to her task, putting the linens in to soak. She searched for stains that demanded extra attention and soon lost herself in the methodical movement of fabric over the ridges of the washboard. Granny had taught her well and she'd come to enjoy the work. At the very least, it left her so tired at the end of the day that she had no time for worries . . . or regrets.

By the time Mrs. Cooper approached her corner of the courtyard, her arms ached, but she'd filled two lines with gleaming linens.

"Could be whiter." Sara peeked around the clothesline. Mrs. Cooper examined the linens, her mouth turned down in a frown. "Next time, boil them longer."

Sara nodded, pressing her palms together. *Next time.* She cleared her throat. "Does that mean—"

"There's more wash to be done. You'll collect the dirty linens after the guests eat."

Sara was too relieved to be daunted by the woman's words. She'd found work, all on her own. No longer would she be under Molly's thumb, doing the laundry in exchange for veiled insults and rations that couldn't possibly sustain her. In a few months, she might have enough saved to pay for better rooms for Granny and a hot meal once a day that would bring the color back to Granny's cheeks.

A young woman in a starched apron approached as Sara hung the last of the sheets. "Mrs. Cooper says you're to follow me. Servants eat in the kitchen." She turned back to the inn without another look in Sara's direction.

The maid's dismissal didn't bother her. Unlike other servants, the washerwoman worked on the fringes of the household with no pretensions of moving up. Sara wouldn't join in the kitchen gossip nor walk to the lake or the park with the others on their half day off.

She'd be alone. Exactly where she wanted to be.

~~~

The coffee was cold. Never a good sign.

James Kinney set his cup on the table. Mrs. Hobbes governed his row house on Duke Street to the highest standards of efficiency. Cold coffee was no accident.

He rose and paced to the window. An early frost dusted the small square of grass that separated his house from the muddy road, empty but for a few servants bent on errands. A crisp breeze brought golden leaves tumbling from the maple tree and swept away the smoke and dust that usually hung in the air above the city streets.

James contemplated his escape. He could avoid whatever bee was in his housekeeper's bonnet, head to his chambers, and attack the mountain of work involved in his latest case. Taking on the Canada Land Company required delicate maneuvering. One misstep and he'd be branded a rebel and lose the standing he'd spent a decade building.

But he never left without saying goodbye to Evie.

Mrs. Hobbes returned with breakfast, her shoulders stiff with unsaid words. He recognized the signs. She wouldn't be put off.

"Was there something you needed, Mrs. Hobbes?"

The older woman faced him. "Me, Mr. Kinney?" Her eyebrows lifted.

She wanted him to pry it out of her. Well, he wasn't a barrister for nothing. "The new maid isn't working out?"

"Betsy's able to handle things while I'm away." Mrs. Hobbes drew up her formidable bosom and swept her hands down the front of her black serge dress, smoothing an imaginary wrinkle. "But now that you mention it, I've had my worries about Evie lately. She seems . . . unhappy."

James straightened. Here was something new. "Unhappy?"

"I hardly see hide nor hair of your girl these days. Curled up with a book or writing those stories of hers."

James thought of the composition she'd written the day before, the stack of books she'd finished last month. "She's ready for more challenging lessons." He took a bite of breakfast. "I'll work on a new case for her tonight."

"Pardon me, Mr. Kinney, but it's not more lessons she needs. She's lonely, sir, and that's the truth."

"Lonely." His stomach clenched at the word. James claimed a long acquaintance with the state, but Evie? "What evidence do you have?"

The older woman crossed her arms. "I won't submit to interrogation like one of your criminals, Mr. Kinney, that I won't." She sniffed. "But since you ask, the only other children she sees are across the aisle at service. On Sunday she wouldn't even look up when Charlotte Cooper's girls spoke to her."

Evie seemed fine to him. Last month she'd presented the best argument against the Poor Law he'd heard yet. "Nonsense. You should have heard her debating Andrew."

Her lips pressed together in a disapproving line. "A young lady hasn't much need for debating."

Young lady? Since when had his little fairy become a young

lady? "She's not even ten. She has plenty of time to learn about balls and fashions."

"Mark my words, Mr. Kinney. You keep her here all alone and she won't be fit for society." Her voice was sharp, insistent. Unrelenting.

Fit for society. Fit for assemblies and gossip and a world of artifice that he'd come to despise. James's hand clenched around the handle of his coffee cup as he lifted it to his lips. A drop of dark brown liquid sloshed over the edge, landing with a plop on the elegant carpet of twining roses Amelia had ordered all the way from France. He let out a long breath and lowered the cup. "I'm not going to send Evie away to school."

Her chin quivered. "Mr. Kinney. To think I would make such a suggestion to a man in your position." James suppressed a smile. He'd yet to see anything that would come between his redoubtable housekeeper and speaking her mind. "However, I've often said young ladies need someone to show them how to get on in company. Why, Charlotte Cooper's engaged a governess for her daughters, one come all the way from England." Mrs. Hobbes crossed her arms with a meaningful lift of her brows, and he resisted the urge to roll his eyes.

"Not everything that comes from England is all it—" He paused. "Charlotte Cooper's hired a governess?" His fingers drummed a rhythm on the table. James hadn't been inside Cooper's Inn for a decade, not since Andrew had steered him away from the ramshackle lodgings at the wharf and introduced him to the comfortable, well-ordered respectability of Cooper's Inn.

"I wonder if Evie could join in the lessons." His words came faster as the idea took shape. "I could take her on my way to the courts and fetch her on my way home." The next few months promised to be eventful. Dangerous, even, if the rumors of rebellion were to be believed. Lessons would keep Evie too busy to ask questions. "Capital idea, Mrs. Hobbes."

Mrs. Hobbes opened and closed her mouth without a sound. James grinned. He'd solved Evie's boredom and silenced Mrs. Hobbes in one go. He rose, eager to put his plan into action. "I'll speak to Mrs. Cooper today. With any luck, Evie can start by the end of the week."

"No, Papa!"

James and Mrs. Hobbes turned to the figure in the doorway. Evie stood, her brown eyes huge in her pointed face, her hair sticking out in all directions, staring at him with a mixture of accusation and fear.

"I don't want to have lessons with those girls. They don't like me." She crossed her skinny arms over her chest. "You can teach me everything I need to know."

James's stomach tightened, just as it did when an opponent brought forward an unexpected argument in the courtroom. Usually, the challenge put him on his mettle. He waited for his whirling mind to stop and the perfect counterargument to click into place. Nothing. Apparently, his analytical skills deserted him when it came to his daughter.

"Nonsense, Evangeline." Mrs. Hobbes bustled over to Evie's side and put an arm around her shoulders, smoothing down the flyaway strands of hair with her other hand. "Don't you want to learn to be a fine lady?"

"I want to be a barrister, like Papa. I have a legal mind. Papa said so."

Mrs. Hobbes sent James an accusing glance over his

daughter's head, and he quickly turned his attention to Evie. If he could face Allan MacNab across the courtroom, then he should be able to handle one little girl. "Wouldn't you like to play with the Cooper girls?"

"I'm fine here. I like helping Mrs. Hobbes."

"Fine, are we? Why don't we tell Papa what you were up to yesterday?"

Evie froze. Her eyes darted to Mrs. Hobbes with a look of entreaty.

"What happened?" James stepped closer, his heart sinking.

Mrs. Hobbes crossed her arms over her chest and gave Evie a hard stare. Evie took a breath and straightened her shoulders. She wasn't short on courage.

"I went to the livery to see the puppies."

The tension drained out of his shoulders. Little harm could come to her in this neighborhood where everyone knew her by sight.

"And?" prompted Mrs. Hobbes.

"And Sproule's."

"Sproule's?" James repeated, his heart pounding. The store was on the other side of town. "By yourself?"

Evie shrugged. "It wasn't hard to find. I remembered it from the last time we were there."

"You can't be running around Toronto on your own. It's not safe!" James knelt in front of her and put his hands on her shoulders. "What would possess you to go so far?"

"I thought they might have new books. I needed to find out what happened to Ivanhoe," she said in a small voice.

"Uncle Andrew said he'd bring you the next volume."

"It's been *weeks*. I think he forgot." Her wide brown eyes

sent a prickle of guilt through him. He'd been so busy, he hadn't even noticed how much time had passed. "I'm sorry, Papa."

James struggled against the pull of those eyes and the instinct to gather her close and assure her all was forgiven. But such deliberate disobedience required consequences. He cleared his throat. "*Ivanhoe* will stay on my shelf until I feel you can be trusted again." He met Mrs. Hobbes's eyes over the top of Evie's head. "And you'll start lessons this week."

"No! I won't go. You can't make me."

Her vehemence startled him. She'd never refused his bidding before. His eyes skittered over her head to land on the maple in the yard, its leaves a burst of bronze and gold in the morning sun. The tree was the reason Amelia had chosen this house. *Gives an air of stately elegance, don't you think, James?* He hadn't thought any such thing, but he'd bought whatever kept the sparkle in her eyes.

He looked at Evie, suddenly seeing her as Amelia might: arms akimbo, hair sticking up every which way, chin tilted at a defiant angle. His stomach clenched as he acknowledged the truth in Mrs. Hobbes's warning. He delighted in Evie's sharp mind, but a young lady as a barrister? She'd be a social pariah. Amelia would have been horrified.

"It's time you learned to be a young lady." He should have approached the idea gradually, planned his arguments and counterarguments, but it was too late for nuance. "It's what your mother would want." Although he didn't raise his voice, the words seemed to float in the air between them, echoing in the sudden stillness.

Evie slowly raised her eyes to his. "My mama?" There was a note of longing in her voice.

"Your mother was every inch a lady." He forced the words out past the tightness in his throat. He'd tried to be father and mother to her, but he still felt so inadequate to the task. *Show me the path forward. Help me to do what's right for her.*

Evie chewed her lip, a sure sign she had doubts. It was time to push his advantage. "It would've made her proud."

Evie was silent for a long moment. "All right, Papa. I'll go."

Chapter 2

The morning stage swept out of the courtyard, the cries of the ostler mingling with the rumble of carriage wheels on the hard-packed macadam road. Sara didn't look up from her cauldron of bubbling linens. In the weeks since she'd started at Cooper's Inn, she'd grown used to the bustle of the courtyard, even found it comforting.

Often the best place to hide was in plain sight.

"You seen the new girl?" Henry leaned against the woodpile, chewing on the hunk of dark bread Sara had slipped into her pocket at breakfast. Since she'd mended his clothes, he was a frequent visitor to her corner of the yard.

Sara nodded. She'd spied the child, following behind the Cooper girls like a sober shadow. "Who is she?"

"Takes lessons with Cressida and Sophronia." He looked up, gauging Sara's interest. "Always coming to the stables to see the horses. Not that I blame her." He gave a theatrical shudder. "Imagine being cooped up with the Goblin all day."

"Henry, you shouldn't say that." She repressed a smile. "I'm sure Miss *Giblin* is a fine teacher." She scanned Henry's face. For all his bravado, he lived a lonely life, with only the disdainful grooms and taciturn Rawley for company. "If she likes horses so much, perhaps she could be a friend for you."

Henry snorted. "Not likely. Her father's some kind of fancy law man. A bar . . . barter . . ."

"Barrister." Sara looked down, stirring the clothes with forceful strokes of the washing paddle. She felt a sudden pang of sympathy for the girl. Lawyers didn't make the best fathers.

Henry's head shot up at her sharp tone. "Aye, that's the word. How do you—?"

She had no intention of satisfying Henry's curiosity. "Best get back to the stable before Mrs. Cooper comes to inspect the laundry."

The warning was enough to send him scurrying back to his post. Sara fished out a steaming shirt and dropped it in the basin. She knelt, scrubbing the soiled collar and cuffs against the washboard, the acrid scent of lye burning her nose. Losing herself in the rhythmic movement, it was several moments before an unfamiliar sound penetrated her concentration. Her hands stilled. It was coming from the shed.

A child. Sobbing?

Perhaps Miss Sophronia Cooper had been denied a sweet-meat. Sara resumed her scrubbing, but soon put that idea to rest. The Cooper girls snatched treats from the kitchens or played tag in the drying lines of laundry, but they never took refuge here.

Sara sighed and wrung out the shirt, placing it in the rinse water before rising. She had no trouble keeping her distance from adults, but a child in difficulty was another story. Stepping inside the shed, she gave her eyes a moment to adjust to the gloom.

It was the girl Henry had told her about, huddled next to a barrel of flour, her shoulders shaking with deep, wrenching sobs. Sara took a step closer and crouched in front of her.

"Whatever is the matter?"

The girl paid her no notice. Sara slid to the ground beside her, leaning back against the rough wooden wall and drawing her knees up to her chest.

"Sometimes it helps to talk about it," Sara said, after a while. "I'm Sara. The laundress."

The girl sucked in a shuddering breath and peeked out at Sara between her fingers. Her face was thin and pointed, and her hair stood up in all directions where it had come loose from its braids.

"Evangeline! Evangeline Kinney, you come back to the schoolroom this instant."

Sara recognized the high-pitched, nasal tones of the governess echoing across the courtyard. The girl tensed, the fine lace trim on her gown brushing Sara's arm. A wealthy girl. Sara grimaced. Riches didn't bring happiness. She didn't need this little one to remind her of that. The girl turned to Sara, her brown eyes wide.

"Please don't tell anyone I'm here."

Sara hesitated. Mrs. Cooper would probably fire her on sight if she thought she'd come between the girl and her governess. Yet the pull of those dark, sad eyes was hard to resist.

"All right," Sara finally answered. The girl's shoulders relaxed.

"But you think about what I said. There's nothing so bad that doesn't get better by talking it through." Sara almost laughed at the platitude. Maybe she should learn to take her own advice. "I've got to get back to work."

Sara rose and returned to the boiling kettle of sheets, wondering what would make the girl weep with such abandon. Her muscles tensed, remembering the girl's eyes, stormy with grief and fear. Water sloshed out of the pot and hissed on the hot rocks, calling Sara's attention back to her work. She stared at the boiling laundry and tried to put the child out of her mind. The little girl wasn't her business, and there was precious little a washerwoman could do to help.

"Are you *cooking* the clothes?"

Sara started. There were still traces of tears on the girl's cheeks, but her voice was clear, her eyes fixed on the boiling cauldron with unabashed curiosity.

The girl approached and Sara held up a restraining hand. "Watch out, or you'll get burned. The water splashes up." She stopped but continued to watch Sara's movements with interest. "Haven't you ever seen anyone do laundry before?" Of course, she hadn't. Neither had Sara, at her age.

The girl shook her head. "Can I stir it?"

"Certainly not." Mrs. Cooper would be horrified if she saw the little girl doing Sara's work.

"Oh." The girl's shoulders drooped, and Sara was sorry she'd been so hasty. But what girl of nine or ten *wanted* to do laundry? At her age, Sara had been dressing her dolls and stitching samplers. When she wasn't sneaking into her father's library.

"It's about time to get them out of the wash water anyway," Sara continued. "Evangeline, is it?"

"Evie," she said, her eyes following Sara's movements. "What's that for?" She pointed to a tub of cold water standing a few feet from the fire.

"It's the rinse water." Sara smiled. It was hard to resist the look of earnest interest on the girl's face. It had been so long since anyone besides Granny noticed her at all, never mind asking a question or offering help.

Don't get involved, Sara. She's not your child. The pain hit, sharp and familiar. Her arms would always be empty. She should be over the sting by now.

Sara hefted the basket to her hip and pointed to the empty lines. "I've got to hang these out. Shouldn't you return to your lessons?"

The smile faded from Evie's face. "She said I'm naughty and deceitful." Evie straightened, a militant look in her eyes. "I'm not. I don't lie like Cressida and Sophronia." Sara could well believe that. Even buried in the laundry as she was, she'd heard enough of the Cooper girls' mischief to make her wary of their pranks. "Please, let me stay here with you. Just a little longer."

Tears filled Evie's eyes and Sara's resolution to keep her distance washed away like the water over the cobblestones. She slid an arm around Evie's shoulders, pulling her in so the girl's head rested against her chest.

"I told you I'd listen if you need to talk. The offer still stands, you know."

Evie clasped both arms around Sara's waist in a hug so tight it threatened to cut off her breath. After a few moments of silence, Evie started to speak, her voice muffled against the rough fabric of Sara's apron. "They make up stories about me. That I steal biscuits from the kitchens and break their toys." She looked up, her eyes shooting sparks. "I don't. *They* do. But Miss Giblin never listens to me."

Sara swallowed. She knew what it felt like to be ignored. Unheard. She sighed. "No one listens to me, either." She looked down at Evie and waggled her eyebrows. "Sometimes I tell them what I really think."

"You do?" Evie looked at her in awe. "Even Mrs. Cooper?"

"Oh, not to her face. She'd never stand for that." Sara winked. "I say it inside. To myself. Makes me feel better." Sara looked down at Evie's thoughtful face and smiled. "Come, there's work to do. Would you pass me the pins while I get these on the line?"

Evie scooped up the bucket and skipped after her, the heartache of earlier seemingly forgotten. An hour slipped by in easy camaraderie as they worked together, Sara guiding Evie's arms to pin the sheets to the line and laughing as Evie darted between the billowing linens.

"This must be what it's like to float in the clouds, don't you think?" Evie's eyes were dreamy.

"Clouds would be a lot softer than Mrs. Cooper's sheets."

Evie giggled and Sara felt a pang at the bright smile on the girl's face. She'd had flights of fancy like that herself, once upon a time. Her future had been full of promise, her imagination nourished by every novel she could get her hands on.

"Are you hungry?" Sara asked as they hung the last sheet. "It smells like Mrs. Cooper is about to serve the guests their supper."

Evie's slight frame tensed. "It's time for supper already?"

"Likely." Sara sniffed. "Beef pies, that's my guess. What do you think?"

The girl ignored Sara's question, busy smoothing her hair and straightening her dress. "I've got to go. Papa collects me on his way home."

Before Sara could thank Evie for her help, the girl was gone, darting around the lines of laundry, and heading to the front of the inn.

Sara returned the empty basket to the shed, her thoughts full of the strange little girl. She seemed familiar, but not because they'd met before. Because she reminded Sara of herself at that age. Right down to her fear of her papa.

A slim book caught her eye, nestled against a barrel. She picked it up, flipping to the first page. *Ivanhoe.* Her fingers tightened around the volume as a wave of longing swept through her. Once upon a time, *Ivanhoe* had fueled her dreams of adventure and the beautiful Rowena had been her model. She swallowed, tracing the title with her finger. She had more in common with practical, persecuted Rebecca now.

Perhaps she could keep the book and find a way to get it back to Evie tomorrow. She cast the thought aside as soon as it entered her mind. She'd be accused of stealing if anyone found it among her things. Hurrying inside, she ignored the curious glance of the scullery maid as she darted through the dark, warm depths of the kitchen. She slipped through a side door that led to the front hall where Evie waited, shawl and bonnet in hand.

Sara bit her lip. If Mrs. Cooper caught her here, she'd be accused of shirking her work. Evie jammed her bonnet on her head and tied a lopsided bow as she stood on tiptoes to see out the window that flanked the wide front door. Sara's heart contracted, propelling her forward.

"Evie," she whispered. The little girl tensed, then relaxed when she turned and saw Sara's face. "You forgot your book." Evie bit her lip, her gaze sliding sideways. "It *is* your book, isn't it?" Sara searched Evie's face, wondering at her reluctance.

Evie tucked *Ivanhoe* under her arm, hidden from sight in the folds of her shawl. "Thank you," she muttered.

"Mind if I fix your bonnet?" Sara motioned to the haphazard bow and Evie shrugged and returned her gaze to the street. "He walks, does he?"

"Oh yes, his chambers aren't far from here. And we live just around the corner, on Duke Street."

Sara recognized the respectable address. As Evie described their walk home, Sara straightened her bonnet and tucked in the flyaway strands of hair. She should get back to the laundry before she was seen, but . . .

"Evie, have you told your father?"

Evie's eyes flew to her face and Sara held her gaze until the girl shook her head. "I don't want him to worry. I'll say it to myself, just like you said."

She'd wanted to help and only made a mess of things. "There are times when you shouldn't keep things in. If you aren't happy—"

"It will only make him feel bad," she said with a fierce frown. "I'll show Papa I don't need these silly lessons. I just have to prove I know how to be a lady. It can't be that hard."

Sara almost smiled. It seemed Evie didn't need her help after all.

"There he is!" Evie squealed and gave a little hop.

Sara peeked out the window over Evie's head. A man approached the inn with long, purposeful strides, his fine suit setting him in contrast to the farmers plodding down King Street on their way home from market. Her stomach tightened with wariness. She knew enough of barristers and fathers to keep her distance.

Sara stepped back into a dark, deserted parlor as he bent his head to enter through the massive oak door. He tucked his fine beaver hat under his arm, revealing a faint sprinkling of gray in his close-cropped brown hair. His nose was too long for fashion and his sharp jawline gave him a fierce look that reminded her of his little girl.

Then his gaze fell on Evie and a smile lit his face, softening the sharp angles. Sara's breath caught as the stern father transformed into a tender papa before her eyes.

"Hello, poppet." He placed a swift kiss on her forehead. "All done with your lessons for today?" His voice was deep with a hint of Scots in its lilting cadence.

Evie looked down. "I'm ready to go." Her voice was wooden, and though she didn't lie outright, Sara saw the smile fade from her father's face, as though he knew she was hiding something.

Ask her. Take the time to find out what's going on. The man's lips thinned, but he said nothing. He gripped Evie's elbow to guide her to the door and *Ivanhoe* tumbled out from beneath her shawl.

Evie froze. Sara could read the panic in every tense line of her body. Her father bent down and picked up the book.

"*Ivanhoe?*" He didn't raise his voice, but the word cracked like thunder through the front hall.

Sara pushed her hand against her roiling stomach. She recognized his tone. Disapproval. Judgment.

Evie shuffled her feet. "I needed to see how it ended."

"I forbade you to read this book." His voice hardened, each word slicing through the air and making Evie's shoulders slump until her head hung low. "How could you disobey me?"

Evie's back was to her, but Sara was close enough to see the tear that balanced on the edge of her chin before dropping to the floor. Couldn't the man see that Evie didn't need censure? Someone needed to tell him how unhappy his little girl was at Cooper's Inn. *Someone, yes,* her mind told her heart, *but it doesn't have to be you.*

Sara checked an unconscious step forward, biting back the words that bubbled to the surface and stifling the urge to barge into the entry and force this man to show his daughter compassion. She needed to keep her head down and get her work done. She needed to take care of Granny, not a poor little rich girl who would probably be just fine on her own. Besides, she was the laundrywoman. Why would he listen to her?

A group of men entered the hall from the noisy common room. Sara knew a moment of panic. What if they were headed *here*? A frantic glance around the parlor revealed a table and chairs. A hearth. No place to hide.

She gave her head a shake as the men moved to the front door. A group of farmers wouldn't pay for a private parlor, which she would have known at a glance if she hadn't let panic take over. Just as her heart rate slowed, she caught a glimpse of fine wool amid the homespun. Silver-blond hair. There was something familiar about the man that made her retreat further into the shadows.

He stopped to talk to Evie and her father, turning so she had a view of his profile. Pale, chalky skin, strangely smooth. Her hand came up to cover her mouth, stifling her gasp.

"Kinney? Didn't know Cooper's Inn was one of your haunts." It *was* him. She recognized the mocking challenge in the man's voice, though she hadn't heard it in years.

"Didn't realize it was one of your haunts either, Mr. Osgoode."

Heart racing, Sara pressed her back against the wall of the darkened parlor. She stood, scarcely daring to breath as the men took their leave. The cool draft from the opening and closing of the door ruffled her skirt and woke her from her terror. She couldn't stay here, frozen against the wall.

After a peek to assure herself the hall was deserted, she scurried back to the laundry, willing her galloping mind to focus. It would be dark soon. She needed to get the clothes off the line. Fingers trembling, she reached for the first pin.

She didn't know how a man of Osgoode's fastidious standards ended up at a simple coaching inn, nor how he came to know Evie's father, but her vulnerability struck her anew. Whatever security she thought she'd found at Cooper's Inn was an illusion that could come tumbling down at any moment.

~~~

James sighed, surveying his desk. He'd stacked unanswered letters and half-finished arguments in two tidy, intimidating piles, yet he still couldn't focus on his work. Something was wrong with Evie.

She didn't chatter his ear off at the supper table, nor try to debate court cases with him as he tucked her in at night. Lessons at Cooper's Inn were supposed to make her happier. He rubbed his eyes. Perhaps he'd been too hard on her about *Ivanhoe*.

He picked up the first letter on the pile, recognizing his

brother-in-law's scrawling, extravagant hand at once. He turned the letter over. *Surely Andrew wouldn't*— He ripped open the page, his stomach clenching as he read the note. Andrew had to leave the city. Could James handle the case alone?

James crumpled the note in his hand. It was the second time Andrew had left him in the lurch this month.

He'd handle the trial. He owed his brother-in-law that much, but covering up his absence from the keen eyes of others was another matter. As though James conjured him with his thoughts, a knock sounded at the door and a clerk ducked his head in, his curious eyes darting around the office. James braced himself for a question about his absent partner, but the clerk had another mission.

"Mr. Ballantine is here to see you, sir."

"Ballantine?" James stared. The richest man in the colony was an old family friend of Andrew's, but he'd never called on James before. "Of . . . of course. See him up."

James rose and paced to the window, wracking his brain for what might have prompted the visit. Ballantine certainly didn't seek a lawyer, for Stephen Osgoode had handled his affairs for years.

Thomas Ballantine didn't keep him wondering long. He strode in a moment later, closing the door with a firm shove of his hand and turning to face James. His countenance, always serious, was drawn in forbidding lines and his crisp silver side-burns quivered.

James greeted the older man and invited him to take a seat, indicating the simple straight-backed chair in front of his desk.

Ballantine hesitated, and James suppressed the inclination to offer him his own larger, padded chair. He didn't often have guests with the prestige and wealth of Thomas Ballantine, but that didn't mean he had to grovel. Ballantine removed his elegant top hat and, after a moment's hesitation, sat. James breathed a sigh of relief and joined him on the other side of the desk. Although he was nearing sixty, Ballantine was still a tall, imposing man. Seated, he was less intimidating.

James waited for the man to bring up the reason for his visit. The silence stretched, Ballantine seeming fascinated by a fresh drop of ink that beaded on the worn desk. James surreptitiously moved his blotter to soak up the stain. "How can I help you, Mr. Ballantine?"

The question seemed to jolt Ballantine back to the moment and he cleared his throat. "I came hoping to find my godson." His eyes moved around the room. "Though I'm not surprised to find him absent."

"Ah." James subsided into silence. Better see what the man wanted before he said too much.

"Do you know where Andrew is?" Despite the casual posture, legs crossed and arms resting loosely at his sides, Ballantine's eyes were sharp, pinning James in place.

Sweat trickled from beneath James's wig. If he'd known he'd be up for interrogation, he'd have taken the time to remove his heavy court robes. "I . . . no. I don't."

Ballantine ran a hand over his chin as though he were deciding what to say. "His father was a great friend of mine." He shot James a keen glance. "Promised him I'd look after the boy."

James kept his face carefully blank. "Yes, I'm aware there is a connection."

Ballantine braced his hands on the edge of James's desk, as though he were getting to the point of the matter. "I haven't seen him in weeks," he said. "He hasn't answered my letters, either."

"We have been quite busy," James said, still unwilling to expose his friend. "I'm afraid I'm not certain what could have kept him—"

Ballantine pushed aside James's words with a swipe of his hand. "Nonsense. You and Andrew are thick as thieves."

James avoided Ballantine's gaze, picking up his penknife to sharpen his quill. Andrew Ridley was the first man he'd met when he stepped foot in Upper Canada with nothing but a law degree and fifty pounds he'd inherited from an uncle in Edinburgh. He'd never be where he was today if Andrew hadn't taken him under his wing and introduced him to the law society. Introduced him to Andrew's beautiful sister, too.

"We were thick as thieves," James said, meeting Ballantine's eyes and dropping all pretense of ignorance. The older man clearly knew as well as James that Andrew wasn't traveling for business or pleasure. The younger man had formed an unhealthy interest in the hothead William Lyon Mackenzie and his plans to liberate Upper Canada from British rule. "If you think I can curb what he means to do, you overestimate my influence."

"He must be made to see reason." Ballantine's hands slammed down on the desk, upsetting the stack of letters. "If his father were alive, he'd have something to say about it, I can tell you. The Ridley name was one of the most respected in Upper Canada. Always loyal to the crown."

Under the bluster, James saw regret and loss in Ballantine's eyes. "Are you certain he's joined the rebels? He was investigating our case against the Canada Land Company. Perhaps . . ."

Ballantine shook his head. "Osgoode mentioned to me that he's been seen at rebel meetings. Recognized."

"Osgoode?" Just the name of the barrister raised James's hackles. The man jealously guarded his position as the colony's premier barrister and he'd take any opportunity to discredit James and Andrew. "How would he know?"

Ballantine's gaze slid sideways. "Osgoode has connections all over the colony."

James thought of his encounter with Osgoode at Cooper's Inn the day before. Yes, the man did have some unusual connections. He still hadn't figured out how a snob like Osgoode had found himself in the company of farmers and laborers.

Ballantine rose and took a restless turn about the small room. "You know as well as I that a rebellion would come to nothing. A bunch of hotheads and disgruntled yokels. But the damage to Andrew's reputation . . . to his family's reputation . . ." He planted his hands on the desk. "The son of one of the foremost families in Toronto joining the rebellion. Imagine the scandal. It will ruin everything we stand for."

Ruin their profits was more like it. James grimaced. Andrew was right about one thing. A few wealthy families stifled Upper Canada, lining their pockets while limiting growth and opportunities for newcomers. Change was needed, but not through a violent rebellion the rebels couldn't hope to win.

James sighed, his forehead creasing in worry. There had to be a better way. "I don't know if he'll listen, but I'll try to talk some sense into him."

Ballantine nodded his approval. "You're a good lad, James. You've more influence than you realize." He looked out the window at the lowering sun. "Why don't you leave early today and track Andrew down? He's awfully fond of that daughter of yours. Don't imagine he'd turn down an invitation to supper if it came from her."

James gave a reluctant nod. Ballantine wasn't above using Andrew's affection for his niece for his own ends. Neither was James, in this case. Andrew was more than a friend. He was Amelia's brother and Evie's beloved uncle. James would do everything he could to save the man from ruin.

Ballantine paused with one hand on the doorknob. He looked back at James, his rigid posture giving way to an uncharacteristic slump. "Thank you, James. The lad is the closest thing I have to family left. Don't fancy seeing him dangle at the end of a hangman's noose."

Chapter 3

"Sara?"

Sara started, almost dropping the heavy iron. Three days had passed since she'd found the little girl in tears, and Sara figured Evie had forgotten about her. A relief, she assured herself. But at the oddest moments, she'd catch sight of the girl and wonder if she'd settled in. She wondered about that stern father of Evie's, too. Had he brushed aside Evie's worries, or would he take the time to understand his little girl?

Not that she'd try to find out. She still hadn't recovered from the fleeting glimpse of Stephen Osgoode in the front hall. Exactly the reminder she needed to keep her distance from this little girl and stay in the servants' quarters where she belonged.

"Could I stay here for a while?" Evie was already perched on top of a barrel, her eyes wide and pleading. "I won't be any trouble."

It was a risk. She finally had the promise of wages and work to fill her days and numb her mind. But she couldn't bring herself to refuse those sad eyes. They brought back memories of another lonely little girl, a girl Sara had been trying for ten years to forget.

"Don't you think you ought to return to the parlor for your lessons?"

"I can't do my lessons." Evie looked up and met Sara's eyes, her lip curled. "It's *French*. Miss Giblin says I have no ear for languages. I'm hopeless."

"Nonsense," Sara replied. *"Tout le monde peut apprendre le français."*

Evie's eyes widened. "What does that mean?"

"Anyone can learn French." Sara held up her hand when Evie opened her mouth to protest. "Repeat after me: *Je parle français.*"

"Je parle français."

"See, you're speaking French."

"Really?" Evie bounced her seat.

"Yes, really. Are you ready for more?"

As she pushed the heavy iron across the sheets, Sara taught Evie the basic greetings, surprising herself at how much she remembered. How long had it been since she'd practiced French? Ten years? Longer?

Far from being hopeless, Evie soon could introduce herself and ask after the weather. Sara shook her head in wonder. The girl remembered everything, watching Sara with fierce concentration. No ear for languages, indeed. She resisted the urge to march right into the parlor and give that snobby Miss Giblin a piece of her mind. What a sight that would be. The laundress come to teach the governess a lesson.

Evie's brow wrinkled in concentration as she repeated the French words to describe her favorite place. She spread her arms with a flourish to show Sara the breadth of the lake, only to cry in pain when her hand knocked against the rough planks of the wall.

"What is it, Evie? A splinter?" Sara set the iron on the rack.

"*C'est rien.*" Evie tucked her hand under her skirt.

"It can't be nothing if it hurts that much." Sara looked for a loose nail or a bit of rough wood, then grabbed Evie's hand to look for a splinter. The girl jerked her hand away, but not before Sara saw the red welts along her palm.

"You're hurt," Sara said. "What happened?"

Evie pressed her lips shut. Sara sent a panicked glance to the irons, heating in the fire in the courtyard. "Did you burn yourself?"

Evie shook her head. "It's nothing. I wasn't listening, so—"

"I've had worse."

Sara and Evie jumped at Henry's voice from the doorway. He peered over Sara's shoulder to examine Evie's hand with a practiced eye. "Then again, I'm older than you." He patted Evie's shoulder in a gesture of sympathy. "Got a temper, does he? Need to learn to stay out of his way."

Sara turned horrified eyes to Evie. "Your father did this?"

Evie's head jerked up. "Papa? Of course not."

Not her father. Sara felt a surge of relief. Whatever his shortcomings, she could absolve James Kinney of this crime. Still, those welts were no accident. She opened her mouth to question Evie further, but Henry jumped in before she could speak.

"You said you were going to tell me more of that story." Henry crossed his arms with an accusing stare at Evie.

"I will, but I need to practice French first. Or I'll be in big trouble with the Gob—" She sent a guilty look in Sara's direction.

Henry leaned back against the wall and crossed his arms with a disgruntled snort. "Hurry up. I want to find out what happens to that Saxon fellow."

Sara turned to Evie. "Cedric the Saxon?" A character straight out of *Ivanhoe*. She raised her brows, remembering the scene in the front hall. "I thought your father forbade that book."

Evie ducked her head. "He only took it away because I disobeyed him. If I have a good report from Miss Giblin, he'll let me have it back. That's why I need to practice French." She elbowed Henry. "Why don't you learn it, too?"

Henry scoffed at the idea, but he perched on a sack of potatoes, his body tight and alert, interjecting questions and dry comments into Sara's lesson that had them all giggling. He had a quick mind and an uncanny ability to mimic voices. If he weren't stuck in a world of grinding poverty, he'd make something of himself. Perhaps she should—

Stop, Sara. You can't save anyone. You can barely keep yourself and Granny alive.

"Henry!" Rawley's voice bellowed across the courtyard. "You think these stalls will clean themselves?"

Henry straightened. "Better go."

Evie reached out and grabbed his sleeve. "I'll find you—"

Henry shook his head. "If you come to the stable now, I'll get it for sure."

Evie released her hold on him. "I'm sorry. I don't mean to get you in trouble."

Henry's eyes softened, the hardness in his face disappearing for a moment. "Rawley'll be taking his nap after lunch. You . . . you can come and pet the horses then if you want." He shuffled his feet.

Evie smiled. "All right." Her smile faded as Henry darted out the door. She avoided Sara's eyes as though she knew what was coming next.

"Tell me what happened." Sara moved to stand in front of Evie and crossed her arms.

"To Cedric the Saxon?" Evie studied her hands, her voice carefully neutral.

Sara narrowed her eyes. The girl was clever, she'd give her that much. "To your hand."

Evie opened her mouth, then shut it again, and shook her head.

"Evie, no one has the right to hurt you." Sara softened, moving closer to wrap an arm around Evie's shoulders. "No one. You need to tell your Papa."

"No. I can't tell him. He'll be so disappointed."

Sara sighed. Fathers were so difficult to please. "He loves you. He'll want to know." She hoped the words were true.

Evie looked down, her lower lip wobbling. "I don't do it on purpose. I just . . . can't seem to care about stitches and parties and how to curtsy." The words burst from her in a torrent, her voice raw and aching. "Miss Giblin gets so mad when I don't pay attention."

Sara tipped up Evie's chin. "And?"

"She hits me." Evie's voice was thick with tears. "With the stick."

"Oh, Evie," Sara said, brushing the wild flyaway hair off Evie's forehead. "Oh, my poor sweet girl."

~~~

James glanced down at Evie as they walked to Cooper's Inn the next morning. She skipped beside him, oblivious to the cold bite of the wind.

"What do you suppose you'll learn about today?" he asked, only half expecting a response. These days he got little more than monosyllables in answer to his careful probing.

To his surprise, she sent him a look under her lashes so full of her old mischievous spirit that he took heart.

"*Nous parlons français. Comment ça va, Papa?*"

"*Ça va bien, ma petite. Et toi?*" he responded.

Her mouth hung open in surprise for a moment. She tugged his arm, bringing them both to a stop in the middle of the boardwalk. "You can speak French?"

"Enough to get by."

"Why didn't you teach me?"

"I'm not fluent. Your mama, on the other hand, was proficient." Amelia loved more than just the language. She ordered furniture from Paris and carpets from Aubusson that they could ill afford. Not that he'd stopped her, of course. In those first, heady months of marriage, he'd never thought to refuse her anything.

Evie was staring at him, her eyes wide and serious. "My mama spoke French?"

"Yes, of course. Ladies learn French and your mama was most definitely a lady."

They resumed their progress down the street to Cooper's Inn. Evie was quiet, her brow furrowed in thought. He'd long pushed memories of Amelia away, as if not mentioning her would protect Evie from feeling the loss of a mother. No wonder Evie was surprised when he brought her up now.

"Papa, do you know the verb *être*?"

James scratched his head. "Hmmmm . . . *je sommes, tu êtes* . . . Is that the one?"

Evie giggled. "No, that's all wrong. Now, pay attention."

Warmth spread through his chest as he listened to Evie recite her conjugations. She was happy. Excited at the chance to teach Papa instead of the other way around. His respect for the stern Miss Giblin went up a few notches.

When they arrived at the inn, he followed Evie into the parlor. She stopped at the threshold and sent him a questioning glance.

"Go ahead," he urged. "Get ready for your lessons. I just want to have a word with Miss Giblin."

Evie's eyes widened. "But she likes to start promptly at eight."

"I won't take but a moment. Go on."

He gave her a shove in the door and followed her into the room. She removed her bonnet and headed over to the table where the Misses Cooper sat. Evie's eyes followed his progress into the room.

Miss Giblin rose at his appearance, her movements slow and precise. A faint smile curved her thin mouth but didn't reach her eyes. When he'd first met her, he worried she would take all the joy of learning from his daughter, for she seemed singularly lacking in any humor or enthusiasm. Now, he knew better.

"Mr. Kinney," she began. "I'm sure you're here to discuss Evangeline."

"Indeed, I am." He smiled. "And to commend you on the

excellent work you are doing. I can scarcely credit all that she's learned."

Miss Giblin opened and closed her mouth, as though he'd just pulled the rug out from under her. "Well," she said finally, looking back at Evangeline.

"I can see you take great pains to educate your pupils," he continued. "Evie spoke French all the way here."

Miss Giblin's eyes widened, and she darted a glance at Evie. "Oh, well, I'm glad she acquitted herself well."

James smiled. "Very well." Miss Giblin didn't betray a flicker of warmth. A stern woman, but what did that matter, if she knew how to inspire her students? "Well, I'd best be on my way." He bowed and turned to leave the parlor, glancing at his pocket watch. Blast, he was running late, and he'd hoped to go over his arguments once more before the morning session began. He strode into the corridor—and ran straight into a mound of linens.

White fabric splayed in all directions. His arms shot up to fight for balance, taking hold of the woman behind the linens on instinct to keep her from toppling. "I beg your pardon, miss," he said, releasing her arms with a hasty step back. "I should watch where I'm walking." He bent to pick up a handful of cloth that had fallen at his feet.

"Not at all," she replied. "I didn't look where I was going."

Her voice, smooth and low, brought him up short. What kind of servant spoke like that? His eyes traveled up, over the coarse fabric of her gown to the mobcap that hid all but a few strands of curling blond hair.

The woman held herself like a lady, shoulders straight, chin high, with none of the deference he might expect from a servant.

His eyes came to rest on her face, tracing the delicate line of her jaw. He averted his gaze. Now was not the time to notice *that*.

She stood back for him to pass, but his feet refused to obey his command. Instead, he stooped to pick up more linens. "I do apologize," he said, stuffing the last sheet into her basket, his eyes returning to her face.

"Thank you for your help, sir." Instead of the curtsy he might expect from a servant, she inclined her head in a graceful sweep. He found himself bowing in return.

"Permit me to introduce myself. James Kinney. My daughter takes lessons here." Her eyes met his as he straightened, deep blue and clear. He was struck again with her calm, the way she held his gaze without deference or confusion.

"Yes. Evie is a delightful child. So curious and eager to learn."

James couldn't help but smile at this praise of his daughter, though her words made him even more curious about the woman before him. "You help with the young charges, do you?"

A flush spread over her cheeks and she averted her gaze. "No, no, nothing like that. I just—" She paused. "I'm just the washerwoman." Her voice lowered until he could barely hear her words.

"O'Connor!" Mrs. Cooper's shrill voice rang out across the entry. "What are you doing loitering about the public rooms? You've fetched the linens. Now get back to the laundry." Mrs. Cooper strode forward, her hard eyes on the woman.

"Entirely my fault," James said, battling a startling need to put himself between the woman and her irate employer. The laundress swung about without a word, ducking behind Mrs. Cooper, and scurrying across the common room.

Mrs. Cooper glided over to James, all vestiges of annoyance

replaced with a serene smile. "I do apologize, Mr. Kinney. Can't think what that woman was about to linger in the front rooms."

"Indeed," he murmured, his mind still on the laundress who spoke like a lady. There was a puzzle there that he wanted to solve.

Out of the corner of his eye, James saw the woman pause on her way to the kitchens. She looked back, her gaze meeting his for a fleeting moment. An expression crossed her face that James could only describe as . . . hurt. As though he'd betrayed her somehow.

He realized his absent response to Mrs. Cooper made it sound like he agreed with the woman. He took a half step forward to—what? Explain himself? Defend her? What was the matter with him? The watch in his hand told him there was no time for a delay, for he was expected in the courtroom in half an hour. Besides, he knew nothing about her.

He turned to catch a final glimpse of the woman and realized his explanations would have been futile in any case, for she was gone.

Chapter 4

Sara darted through the kitchen, her face hot with humiliation. She ought to be used to this by now. She was a servant.

Yet it had shamed her when his gaze had traveled up from her worn boots, over her old dress, and came to rest on the oversized cap she wore to keep her hair away from her face. She'd suddenly become aware of the frizzy curls sticking to her neck and forehead, the damp splotches on her gown, and the caustic scent of lye that hung about her like a cloud.

Making her way across the courtyard, she began to sort the linens, throwing them into piles with unnecessary force. She'd accepted the reversal in her position years ago. Why would she care how James Kinney saw her? He was probably a snob in any case, and just because he happened to be a *handsome* snob shouldn't matter in the least.

Evie snuck into the laundry shed again that afternoon. Sara knew she ought to send her back to the schoolroom, but she couldn't bring herself to do it. The girl's warm acceptance was a balm to her wounded spirit, her cheerful questions a welcome distraction from the memories that plagued her. *Just a few minutes,* she promised herself.

A few minutes turned into a French lesson and a recitation of their favorite poems. They might have continued an hour or more if a shaggy red head hadn't poked through the window of the shed. "If I were you two, I'd consider shutting my trap and getting back to work. The Goblin's on the prowl." He nodded in Evie's direction. "She come snooping around the stable, asking where you was."

Evie shot a fearful look at the door before her gaze moved to Sara.

"You'd best get back to the schoolroom," Sara said to Evie, "before she finds you here."

"Quick," Henry said with a glance over his shoulder. "She's crossing the courtyard right now."

"What?" Sara gasped. She peeked out the door. Miss Giblin was picking her way across the cobblestones, her eyes darting from side to side and two high spots of color in her cheeks.

Evie blanched, squeezing her eyes shut. "She'll tell Papa for sure."

The sound of Mrs. Cooper's strident voice, joining the search and calling Evie's name, had Sara moving in front of the girl, as though she'd protect her from punishment. "Don't worry, my love. It's me who kept you here, rambling on about poems. I'll tell her so."

Henry shook his head. "You'd be in for it then, Sara." He grabbed Evie's arm and pulled her toward the window. "C'mon, Evie. We'll jump out here and cut through the mews." He gestured to the laneway behind the inn. "Mayhap we can get you inside through the front door without anyone the wiser." He grabbed the windowsill and pulled himself up. "But you can't cry or make a fuss."

"I won't." Evie looked outraged. She stretched her hands up for a boost.

Henry's eyes narrowed at the sight of the welts on Evie's palm. "Do what I tells you, and move fast." He reached down for Evie's uninjured hand and pulled her up on a crate, then he jumped out the back window.

Evie moved to follow him, but something held her back. "Sara, help me!"

She balanced precariously in the narrow windowsill, yanking at her skirt where a flounce had snagged on a nail.

"Stop," Sara called, rushing to her side. "You'll rip it, pulling like that." She held on to Evie with one hand while the other felt for the place the fabric was caught and worked the fine wool off the nail.

"Rip it, Sara." Evie's voice was frantic now, her little body straining against Sara's hold. "We're running out of time."

"O'Connor! What is the meaning of this?"

With a sinking heart, Sara looked over her shoulder. Mrs. Cooper stood in the doorway, her hands on her hips.

Evie was right. They'd run out of time.

~~~

"The court rules in favor of the defendant. Case dismissed." Judge Roper followed his pronouncement with the heavy thud of his gavel.

James sunk to his seat, scarcely able to meet the eyes of his client. Wilkie's face hid none of his despair. The land company had swindled the man, but they'd see no justice today. Andrew was supposed to hunt down the witness they needed. But Andrew wasn't here.

"If the squatter isn't out by spring, I'll put in another injunction," James told the man. "At no charge."

Mr. Wilkie nodded, though every drooping line of his body said he'd given up. From the corner of his eye, James saw Stephen Osgoode rise from his seat at the back of the room, and he steeled himself. Osgoode headed the most successful firm in the city, but that didn't stop him from keeping a close eye on his competition. He was probably thrilled with James's loss and would favor him with a round of patronizing and fabricated commiseration.

Osgoode approached, his narrow gaze assessing Wilkie before deciding the farmer was beneath his notice and addressing himself to James.

"Don't know why you took this case on," he began, looking quite satisfied with himself. "Buyer beware. Any fool could tell you that." He glanced over at the defense and gave a friendly nod to the opposing barrister. "Besides, no profit in it."

James looked away. Osgoode would never believe that there was more to practicing law than protecting the interests of the wealthy.

Weariness settled over James as the courtroom emptied. He cleared the table of notes and correspondence, wishing he could organize and dismiss all his worries so easily. He'd had no luck tracking Andrew down and now he'd lost the case they'd been working on for a month. Picking up his papers, he rose to return to his office, taking a last glance out the window. A fine carriage pulled up in front of the courthouse and a man emerged. James caught sight of a familiar profile. Ballantine, here to check on his sorry progress at finding Andrew.

James glanced at the sky. It was a fine day for October, sunny and dry. A day to stroll along the beach or drive in the country. Perhaps he'd escape out the back door and fetch Evie early. They'd go to their favorite spot on the lake. Ballantine could save his tongue-lashing for another day.

When he arrived at Cooper's Inn, the parlor was deserted. Upon inquiry, he discovered the girls retired upstairs in the afternoons to draw and stitch. He stifled a smile, imagining Evie bent over a sampler. She'd jump at the chance to escape a few minutes early.

"Very well," he told the maid in the entry. "Could you fetch Miss Evangeline? Tell her to bring her things and wait here. I'll walk to the livery and order the carriage."

When he returned, he expected to see Evie bouncing out the door, but there wasn't a flicker of movement from within.

"Hello?" he called. "Mrs. Cooper?"

Rapid footsteps sounded on the landing. "Mr. Kinney." Mrs. Cooper sailed down the stairs with a bright smile. "What brings you here so early? No trouble, I hope?" She glanced outside at the street as though a band of rioters might be trailing him.

"No, nothing like that," he assured her. "But it's such a fine day, I'm taking Evie on a drive. I already asked a maid to fetch her."

Mrs. Cooper sent a harried glance over her shoulder. "I'll see what's keeping her."

James paced the length of the front hall, poking his head

into the private parlor. Empty. He suppressed a flicker of worry. What harm could come to her here?

Then he heard Mrs. Cooper's shrill voice calling Evie from somewhere behind the inn. James bolted around the tables in the front room, through the kitchen, and past a startled scullery maid to emerge into the courtyard. He squinted against the sudden brightness, making out several figures in the far corner, Mrs. Cooper and the stern-faced governess among them. His eyes lit on Evie's flyaway braids with a rush of relief, and he strode forward.

"She does no harm here, Mrs. Cooper. Only practices her lessons and gets a bit of fresh air."

James recognized the low, measured tones. *The laundress again.* She stepped into the sunlight, her chin thrust forward. Her eyes, as direct as ever, met her employer's without a hint of hesitation. She was truly the most unusual servant he'd ever come across.

Mrs. Cooper reached out and grabbed Evie's arm, her face red with anger. "Do you see the trouble you've caused?" she said, giving Evie a shake.

James surged forward, his only thought to separate that woman from his daughter. "What's going on?" he said, jogging up to Evie's side. Mrs. Cooper took one look at his face and stepped back, dropping Evie's arm.

"Mr. Kinney. I didn't see you there."

"Papa," Evie said, her voice equal parts fear and relief. She crowded close and James ran a comforting hand over her hair. He inhaled, unclenching his jaw and biting back the words that boiled to the surface. Evie was nervous enough without his anger adding to her tension.

"What happened?" He worked to keep his voice level.

"It's not my fault, Mr. Kinney." The governess stepped forward, her face pinched and flushed. "I do my best but when a child is determined to disappear . . ."

Disappear? He'd thought Evie safe under the supervision of Miss Giblin, and she'd disappeared?

Mrs. Cooper summoned a serene smile. "What a naughty little miss, not to come when she's called. We were worried. I'm sure your Papa will have something to say about it." There was an edge in the woman's voice, but James refused to rise to her unspoken challenge.

"Come, poppet," he said, turning away from the gathered group. "You can tell me about it on the way home." He would have to take Evie to task, of course, but he had no intention of doing so in front of this audience.

It might have ended there, but for Miss Giblin, who blocked their path. "Mr. Kinney, if I am to maintain order in the schoolroom, there must be repercussions for insubordination."

"I think there've been *repercussions* enough, wouldn't you agree, Miss Giblin?" The laundress spoke, her voice clear and sharp.

For a moment, Miss Giblin looked taken aback but she quickly rallied. "What have *you* to say to anything?" She sent Mrs. Cooper a look full of challenge. "In England servants are dismissed for talking out of turn."

Evie stopped midstride and turned to face the women, her little body tense with outrage. "It wasn't her fault," she said.

It was all the motivation James needed to follow his instincts. He'd failed in the courtroom today. Power and wealth had won over justice. He wouldn't let it happen here.

He sent Evie a reassuring smile and stepped back into the fray. "Repercussions, you say?" He sent the laundress a keen glance before focusing his attention on Miss Giblin. "Do explain."

Miss Giblin wasn't easily cowed. "Your daughter refuses to stay in the schoolroom. Disappears for hours at a time. It's untenable."

James sent his daughter a swift glance and caught her guilty expression. "Evie should certainly ask permission before leaving the room." Miss Giblin sent Evie a triumphant smile. "But," he continued, "surely the children are allowed some time to play in the afternoon, once lessons are done?"

Miss Giblin's smile disappeared. "I was not hired to watch children *play*, Mr. Kinney." Her chest swelled in indignation. "The children are to stay in the schoolroom and work on their lessons and samplers."

No wonder Evie had sought out other company. Stitching all afternoon was her idea of a nightmare. "Perhaps I ought to have Evie fetched home for the afternoon. I'm sure she could stitch just as easily there as here." His gaze swung back to Mrs. Cooper. "Of course, in that case, I'd expect to pay half the fees."

"No need to be hasty." Mrs. Cooper tripped over her words in her hurry to reassure him. "I'm sure this is a simple misunderstanding. Rest assured, the children will have time to play."

Miss Giblin made a sound as though she would protest, but Mrs. Cooper raised a hand, and she was silent.

"Excellent," James said. He sent an impersonal smile around the circle of women, his eyes resting on the laundress for a long moment. Her head was bent, her shoulders slumped. He felt a strange surge of disappointment that she didn't seem to approve of his maneuvering. "I will talk with Evangeline," he continued. "She certainly shouldn't be slipping away so that no one knows where she is." Evie drew in a quivering breath, and he squeezed her hand in reassurance. "Now, if you'll excuse us, my carriage is waiting." James turned Evie around and steered her away, blocking out the babble of voices that erupted behind him. He lowered his head to murmur into her ear. "How about going on a drive today?"

Evie didn't pay any heed to the offered treat. Instead, she craned her neck around to look at the women still arguing in the courtyard behind them.

The ringing sound of a slap, followed by a sharp cry brought him to a halt. Evie sent him a wide glance and he turned to see the washerwoman leaning against the shed, a hand cradling her cheek.

"*Sara!*" Evie cried. She ripped her hand out of his grasp and ran to the woman's side.

Chapter 5

Sara cupped her stinging cheek and questioned her sanity. She'd kept her head down and her mouth shut for years now. Why, today, had she needed to get involved?

"Sara, are you hurt?" Evie came pelting up to her and grabbed her hand.

"I'm fine," she said, wishing she could fade into the building behind her.

Evie swung about to look at Mrs. Cooper. "You hit Sara. Why did you do that?" Her little voice was outraged.

Mrs. Cooper's mouth dropped open for a second. "Young ladies do not question their elders," she said, her shoulders stiff with disapproval.

"Evie." James Kinney approached, eyes flashing. He drew his daughter to his side, and her hand slipped from Sara's grasp. Sara braced herself for another recrimination.

"Mrs. Cooper." James's voice was sharp. "That was unnecessary."

Sara risked lifting her gaze, surprise making the breath catch in her throat. Was James Kinney defending her?

Mrs. Cooper's mouth opened and closed without a sound.

"Servants and children must be controlled with an iron hand, Mr. Kinney," Miss Giblin said, coming to her employer's aid. In the governess's thin, reedy voice, the words sounded more like a whine than a defense.

"There's no need for physical blows." James stepped closer to Sara, his eyes on her cheek and his body forming a safeguard and blocking her from view. "Are you—" He raised his hand as though he would cup her cheek. Their eyes met and he checked the movement, dropping his hand back to his side. "Are you injured?"

For a moment, she was tempted to step closer and take shelter behind the solid wall of his shoulders. Foolishness. When had a man ever provided security she could rely on? She clenched her fists, stepping away from the protection he seemed to offer. If she didn't defuse the situation and find a way for Mrs. Cooper to save face, she could lose her job.

"I'm fine, sir," she murmured, ducking her chin. "I'd best get back to work." She took a cautious step to the washing shed.

James Kinney turned to Mrs. Cooper. "I must ask you to reconsider your methods of punishment."

Mrs. Cooper crossed her arms. "I'm within my rights. I can manage my servants how I want. I don't tolerate no sloppy work nor disrespect, neither." The woman's polished accent slipped a fraction.

Her strident voice garnered the attention of a passing maid

who stopped to listen. From the corner of her eye, Sara saw the grooms gathered in the door of the stable and her face burned. She'd be the talk of the inn that night.

"I am well aware you are within your rights." James's voice was cold and clipped. "Still, I would rather my daughter see rational discussion and compassion than violence."

That was why he'd intervened on her behalf. She was an object lesson, not a person. Heat washed over Sara's cheeks at how she'd misread his words and the expression in his eyes. She'd thought he'd wanted to protect *her*. She'd been away from common decency so long, she'd forgotten what it looked like.

Mrs. Cooper seemed to collect herself, the skin of her face smoothing. "Yes, Mr. Kinney, I'm sure you have the right of it," she said, her voice gracious again. "A lady always shows restraint." She shooed away the circle of servants who'd gathered to witness the little drama. "Back to work, everyone."

The group in the courtyard broke up. Sara kept her head down and hurried to her laundry shed with a sigh of relief. If she could stay out of view for a few days, maybe this would blow over.

"Papa, make sure she doesn't hit Sara again." Evie's voice floated across the open space, clear for anyone to hear.

Then again, maybe not. As much as Sara dreaded the attention, Evie's defense warmed a frozen place in her heart.

A shadow fell across the dirt floor of the shed. "Listen here, O'Connor." Sara flinched at Mrs. Cooper's voice. "No more chances. You keep yourself out of my business or you'll be back out on the street where you belong."

"Yes, ma'am," Sara answered, not daring to look up.

"Never trusted you. Putting on airs, talking as if you was

a lady." Mrs. Cooper grabbed her ear, forcing her about with a vicious twist so she could stare down at her. "You stay away from that girl. A friend like her could open doors for my daughters. I'll not have some serving wench putting a spoke in my wheel. Got it?"

A hundred replies flew to mind, but Sara bit her tongue. How easy it would have been for the old Sara to put this woman in her place. She'd never appreciated the power of her name and standing until she lost it. But this Sara needed to work. Granny depended on her.

"I understand," she whispered.

~~~

James turned the carriage down Front Street and prepared himself for the inevitable questions. When Evie encountered injustice in the world, she'd take it up with him. The kittens about to be drowned at the livery. Mr. Sinclair arrested for debt, even though everyone knew the fire that destroyed his business hadn't been his fault.

But Evie was strangely silent as they left the city and wound their way to the shore. The surrounding land was uncleared, with patches of thick forest broken up by marshes and streams. The wind blew cold off the lake, carrying with it the dry, icy smell of winter. He reached down and pulled out a carriage blanket for Evie, pointing out the dark sheen of a muskrat as it disappeared into the marsh.

She didn't respond, her eyes trained on two gulls that soared above them in the clear blue sky.

He cleared his throat. "I'm sure it won't happen again."

Evie's head swung around. "Are you?" Her eyes were bright, challenging. "Mrs. Cooper said she was within her rights. She's *allowed* to hit Sara?"

James sighed, scrubbing a hand over his face. He knew better than to try to comfort her with platitudes. "Well, I don't know about *allowed*, but it's not a crime."

"Sara was just trying to help."

"I know it seems wrong." He moved the reins to one hand and wrapped his free arm around her shoulders. "It *is* wrong, but Mrs. Cooper owns that inn, and she runs things as she sees fit. If Miss O'Connor doesn't like how they treat her, she is free to seek work elsewhere."

Evie's eyes filled with tears. "It's my fault she got hit."

Sara O'Connor had risked a lot to defend his daughter. No wonder Evie was drawn to the woman. "No," James said firmly. "It's Mrs. Cooper's fault." He'd had a glimpse beneath the woman's sugary smiles and veneer of gentility. She wasn't the warmhearted widow he'd thought her. "But she assured me it won't happen again."

James hoped the woman spoke the truth. Every time he closed his eyes, he saw the angry welt on Sara O'Connor's face. He'd wanted to step between the women, and force Mrs. Cooper to back down. Tuck Sara O'Connor under his arm and steer her right out of that ugly scene. He sighed. There was precious little he could do for a woman in Sara's position. Any interest he showed was bound to cause gossip and make her situation more difficult. Yet he couldn't dismiss her from his thoughts.

"Sara is an unusual laundress." He hadn't meant to say the words aloud.

Evie swiveled her head to stare at him, her eyes bright. "What do you mean? She works hard. Her linens are really clean."

"Well, I just—" Why was a woman so poised and intelligent, so . . . *beautiful* stuck in the laundry? He had a thousand questions about her. About the education and refinement clear in every word she uttered. The fire of conviction and courage in her eyes. He sighed. Not one of his questions Evie could answer. "Never mind."

The carriage path turned, revealing their first view of the lake, glinting deep blue in the afternoon sun. He tied the horses to a tree, marveling again at the expanse, as broad as the North Sea of his youth. The sound of the waves lapping the shore calmed him, settling his swirling emotions. Evie, too, relaxed, running along the beach and squealing as the icy water threatened to soak her boots.

They found their favorite inlet along the rocky shore and collected smooth skipping stones. Evie went first, holding the stone with the tips of her fingers and accomplishing nothing more than a solid plop.

"You've lost your touch," he teased as his stone made seven jumps across the water.

Evie shrugged. "I'll just watch."

"Here, try this one," he said, grabbing her hand to shape her fingers around a perfect flat oval. She flinched and jerked her hand back. "Hold on. What's this?" He uncurled her fingers to display two red welts across her palm. James searched her face, but she avoided his gaze. "Evie. What happened?"

"I—it happened yesterday. At the inn."

He pictured the courtyard of the inn and the fire rimmed

with heating irons. His fingers tensed, gripping her wrist. "Were you playing near the fire?"

Evie kicked the loose pebbles at her feet. "Sometimes I help Sara. I like her."

It seemed he and Evie had that in common. James thought back to the scene in the courtyard when Sara O'Connor had flung back her shoulders to defend his little girl like an avenging angel. No wonder Evie was drawn to her. But doing laundry instead of lessons? "The wash is Miss O'Connor's job, not yours. You are there to learn."

"But Papa, you said servants are people just like us. That we should help them and appreciate what they do."

James sighed, running his fingers through his close-cropped hair. "Yes, yes, that's true, but—" But he'd meant Mrs. Hobbes, not the laundrywoman at Cooper's Inn. As usual, Evie had gone straight to the crux of the matter, finding the inconsistencies most adults overlooked. He cast his eyes up to the deep blue, flawless sky. *I could use some wisdom here. How do I reach her?*

Scooping her up, James sat on a wide flat boulder and settled her on his lap. Evie opened her mouth, but James spoke before she could intervene. "There are things you need to learn that I can't teach you." He pulled his head back to look into her eyes. "Things your mama wanted you to know. You are there to learn and make friends. Soon you'll need to go to assemblies and balls—" These supposed treats only made her draw back, and James changed tacks. "And the theater. You can attend lectures, too." Evie chewed her lip and James pushed his advantage. "But first you must learn how to go on in society. You'll need some friends your age. That's why you're in classes with Miss Giblin in the first place."

Her face took on a mulish look that he suspected she'd inherited from him. He hated to threaten, but—"There's always Miss Strachan's school in Kingston." He let the thought hang between them.

Evie looked up at him, aghast. "You'd send me away?"

He hugged her. "I would *hate* to do that. But I need to do what's best for you. You can't stay here with me forever." Her eyes filled with tears and his heart cracked. "I'm sure it won't come to that. You've learned so much from Miss Giblin. Do your best and all will be well, you'll see."

"Yes, Papa." Evie tucked her head under his chin.

He relished the warmth of her little, trusting body curled up in his arms. Would that he could keep her here forever. "Listen, Evie. One more thing. I don't want you helping Sara—er, Miss O'Connor anymore." He hated the feel of the words in his mouth, hated the wounded confusion on Evie's face. But Evie needed to establish herself among her peers. Learn about society, not laundry.

"But—"

"No buts. You don't want her to get in trouble again, do you?" Evie shook her head. "Then you stay in the schoolroom and let Miss O'Connor tend to the laundry."

Chapter 6

A dozen punishments followed the scene in the courtyard. No slaps, nothing so obvious, but subtle challenges meant to remind Sara of her place. Twice Mrs. Cooper returned the linens to wash again. *Not nearly clean enough. Do you think I don't have eyes in my head?* Instead of arguing, Sara recalled Granny's pale, pinched face, and worked harder.

Yesterday when Sara approached the kitchen for dinner, Cook handed her a bowl of cold porridge. "Stew's all gone," was all Cook said, but she couldn't meet Sara's eyes.

These small cruelties Sara could endure, but Evie's absence hurt. As much as she tried to convince herself that it was better this way, she missed her.

"*Sara.*"

The whisper made Sara jump. She paused in the upper hall, her arms full of dirty linens.

"Over here, in the blue room."

She should tell her to leave straight away before they both ended up in hot water. But Sara found herself moving to the open doorway, longing for a glimpse of her little friend. Evie stood inside, out of sight of anyone who might walk by.

"You should get back to the parlor before anyone sees you here."

"I need to talk to you. Just this once." Evie's brown eyes were huge with a mute appeal that melted Sara's resistance.

Sara glanced down the hallway. Empty. For now. "Very well, but quickly."

"I can't come and see you anymore." Evie looked down, her hands twisting in the fabric of her skirt. "I promised Papa."

Sara felt a foolish pang at this. James Kinney thought her a bad influence? She set her basket down and sanity returned. Of course, he did, and he wasn't wrong. The more time Evie spent with Sara, the more likely they'd have a repeat of the scene in the courtyard.

"He's right." Sara fought to keep her voice matter-of-fact.

Evie gave a jerky nod. "I—I'll miss you, Sara."

Sara softened. "I'll miss you, too. Promise me you'll stay out of trouble. Do what Miss Giblin says?" At the thought, Sara's eyes flew to Evie's hands. "She hasn't hurt you again, has she?"

Evie shook her head. "I'm fine."

The faint sound of voices came from the landing, girlish giggles, and the distinctive cadence of Miss Giblin's recitations. Evie's head jerked up, her braids bouncing. "I've got to go. She hardly ever lets me out of her sight these days." She took a step forward and put her arms around Sara in a fierce hug. "Goodbye, Sara. You were the best teacher I ever had." The voices grew louder, and Evie darted out the door and down the hallway.

"Goodbye," Sara whispered. She followed more slowly, collecting the last of the dirty sheets. At the top of the stairs, she paused, straining to hear the voices drifting up from the parlor.

"First you disappear, then you can't even answer a simple question."

"I—I'm sorry, Miss Giblin. Could you repeat it?" There was panic in Evie's voice.

"I most certainly will not. Come here."

There was an ominous silence, then the sound of Evie's footsteps moving slowly across the floor. *Thwack.* A ruler hitting flesh.

Sara didn't think. She dropped the linens and rushed down the stairs and into the room.

"Stop." The occupants of the room turned as one, staring at her. Sara advanced, her steps long and deliberate. "Miss Giblin, I must protest. You have no right to hit this child."

Miss Giblin's mouth had drawn into a fierce frown. "How dare you question my methods?" She pointed a bony finger at Sara, her body stiff with outrage. "Return to the laundry at once."

Sara pushed between Evie and the governess. "I think Mr. Kinney made his feelings about corporal punishment perfectly clear." Evie leaned into Sara, her hand finding hers with a sigh of relief.

Miss Giblin's lips quivered in indecision. "Well, I—" Her eyes lit on Evie's hand in Sara's and her eyes narrowed. "It's not your place to interfere. Don't think Mrs. Cooper won't hear about this. Your days are numbered here, I can assure you."

Sara deflated with each word, all the indignation that had

propelled her replaced with defeat until her shoulders hunched. Why couldn't she hold her tongue when it came to this little girl? She was Sara O'Connor now. Her opinion counted for naught. Her eyes found Evie, silently begging her forgiveness.

Evie managed a shaky smile. "It's okay, Sara. I'll be all right."

Miss Giblin turned her icy stare on Evie. "Don't speak unless you're spoken to," she barked. "Haven't you caused enough uproar?"

Evie's face crumpled and Sara took an unconscious step closer, only to have Miss Giblin turn on her. "Out. Or I'll call Mrs. Cooper and have you removed."

Sara turned, her steps heavy. Gathering up the mass of soiled linens, she reflected on her options. There was only one person who could protect Evie. Her father.

She thought back to the moment in the courtyard when he'd stepped in to defend her from Mrs. Cooper's blow, and a tiny thrill went through her. But he'd since told Evie to avoid her company. Would he listen to what she had to say?

She set the linens to soak and trudged to the shed to refill her bowl of soap. Henry bolted upright when she entered, banging his elbow on the barrel of apples and hiding a rough burlap sack behind his back. Sara froze.

"Please tell me this isn't what it seems." She couldn't lose Henry, too. If Mrs. Cooper caught him stealing, she'd have him hauled before the magistrate without a second thought.

"I'm not stealing. Leastways, not for me."

"It's still stealing."

Henry's chin jutted out. "I've got to do something."

"About what?"

"About Evie."

Sara looked back and forth between the sack of apples and Henry's face, tenser than she'd ever seen it. "What are you talking about?"

"I'm taking Evie away from here. She can't take it anymore, the way the Goblin picks on her. Promised I'd do something. And I will."

Since when had Henry proclaimed himself Evie's protector? Sara's heart melted at the look of fierce determination on his face.

"Listen, Henry, you can't do this. Evie's father would find her, quick as anything, and you'd be off to the workhouse. Or worse."

Henry paled at her words, but his hands tightened into fists where they clasped the sack. "I'm willing to take the risk. Don't know much about fathers but seems to me she'd be better off without him if he's going to leave her to the Goblin every day."

"He doesn't know." Henry shot her a skeptical glance. "She's hiding it from him." Sara stepped forward and put her hand over his to release his grip on the sack. "Let me talk to him before you do something rash."

Henry's eyes narrowed. "Not going to tell him our plan, are you?"

Sara fought a brief battle with her conscience. "No," she said finally. "I won't need to, because once he knows, I'm sure he'll put a stop to Miss Giblin's punishments." At least, Sara hoped he would. He was a reasonable man. He loved his daughter. He wasn't like *her* father.

Henry chewed his lower lip, looking far from convinced, but he dropped the apples back into the bin and stuck out a grubby hand for her to shake. "Deal. You'll talk to him soon?"

Sara nodded, her heart failing at the task before her. She'd been able to confront Miss Giblin without hesitation, but the thought of searching out Evie's father had her wanting to hide. She sent Henry back to the stables and hurried to her kettle of laundry. Picking up the long washing stick, she pounded the linens. He was just a man. The worst he could do was ignore her, and she was plenty used to that.

But James Kinney wouldn't ignore her. She'd seen him defend his daughter and watched Evie's face glow with love for him. He would want to know. Her racing heart settled as she began to plan.

~~

James picked his way across the street, dodging horse patties and a sluggish stream of filth that meandered down the side of the road. The inn came into sight, and he quickened his pace. Maybe he'd take Evie to the lake again. It was the last time he'd seen her happy.

"Mr. Kinney. I must speak with you." A voice, vaguely familiar, whispered from the narrow alley on his right.

James stopped and peered into the passageway where a woman stood, her face obscured by shadow. He cleared his throat. "If you seek legal counsel, please come to my chambers tomorrow morning. A clerk will hear your case and tell you if there's anything to be done." It wasn't the first time a woman in desperate straits sought him out. He'd heard enough stories of abandonment and trickery to last a lifetime. Usually, there was nothing the law could do but he could sometimes steer them in the way of work or shelter.

"It's about your daughter."

His daughter. A bolt of panic sent his heart racing. "What about my daughter?"

"She's safe," the woman hurried to add. "But there's something you should know."

The woman moved into the light and a bolt of recognition sent every nerve in his body tingling with awareness. Sara O'Connor. His eyes traced her face, searching for any sign of the slap she'd received but the angry red marks had faded. He stifled the urge to reach up and touch the smooth velvet skin of her cheek.

"Well, what is it, then?" He heard the impatience in his voice. She shrank back, biting her lip, unaware it was his own wayward thoughts that lent an edge to his voice.

Her shoulders straightened. "Based on your reaction the other day, I thought you would want to know. It's about Miss Giblin. She uses a ruler to . . . punish Evie. When she doesn't pay attention, when she gets an answer wrong." She looked him full in the face and continued, her voice rushed. "I—I know it's not my place, but I must speak."

James clenched his hands, stifling the immediate urge to storm into the inn and demand to see his daughter. There was a core of truth about Sara O'Connor that compelled him, but a lawyer knew there were two sides to every story. She could be bent on revenge after that scene last week.

"Evie would have told me."

"Would she?" The woman drew herself up, a challenge in her eyes. "Check her hands."

Her words sent a spiral of dread through him. The welts. How had he missed something so obvious? Without a word, he turned and rushed to the inn. No sign of Evie waiting at her usual place just inside the door.

He pushed open the door to the parlor. The Cooper girls

sewed demurely by the hearth while Evie stood in the middle of the room, reciting from a slate. At his appearance, all eyes turned to him. Evie paused and took a step toward him.

Miss Giblin sent him a cool smile from her position at the window. "We aren't finished yet, Mr. Kinney. Perhaps you would take a seat?" She indicated a hard wooden chair in the corner and turned back to Evie. "Start again."

Evie darted a fearful glance at the woman. "West of Prussia is Saxony."

"Wrong." Miss Giblin turned to James, her lips curved in a faint, superior smile. "Perhaps now you see, Mr. Kinney, what comes of daydreaming in class. Sophronia and Cressida finished a half hour ago."

The girls at the hearth lifted wide eyes from their samplers, their glossy black curls bobbing. The eldest sent Evie a sideways glance and something like a smirk crossed her features. A wave of red swept up Evie's thin cheeks and she lowered her chin.

James stood frozen for a long moment as the full force of what his daughter experienced hit him square in the gut. No wonder Evie was miserable. Rage churned inside him, but he knew it wasn't only Miss Giblin who was at fault. He'd been blind. Unwilling to see beyond what he wanted to see.

"Come, Evie. It's time to go." Evie flinched at the bite in his voice. James forced himself to relax. "Maybe we'll have time to go by the lake before supper." He held out his hand and Evie walked to him.

"Mr. Kinney, I must protest. I am the one to dismiss students, and Evie well knows she cannot leave until she finishes her lessons."

How had he ever thought it right to put his daughter's

education in such hard and inflexible hands? James put a hand on Evie's shoulder and gave her a gentle push. "Run and put on your bonnet, my love." Evie wasted no time darting out the door. He spun around to face Miss Giblin, and the woman took a hasty step back.

"I sent my daughter here for an education," he said sharply. "Not to be humiliated." He let his eyes roam about the room, coming to rest on the Misses Cooper, who had given up any pretense of sewing and watched the adults with avid interest.

"You sent her here to become a lady," Miss Giblin replied, finding her voice. She lifted her chin, her eyes hard. "Let me assure you, Mr. Kinney, that is no simple task."

"Then you will be relieved to know it is no longer your concern."

Chapter 7

Sara watched from the alley as Evie left with her father, wondering if James Kinney had put a stop to his daughter's torment. Something about the angry set of his shoulders told her he had.

She might never see Evie again. Or her father. A hot rush of longing swept through her, and she allowed herself a moment to imagine walking at their side. Leaving the humiliation of Cooper's Inn with a little girl's trusting hand clasped in hers and a pair of broad shoulders she could lean on.

Stifling the sharp ache, she comforted herself with the reminder that she'd helped this motherless little girl. Evie had a father who cared about more than society's dictates. What happened to Sara would never happen to her.

Sara squared her shoulders. She'd throw herself into her work and let her heart go back to its dormant state. In a few months she'd have enough money to move Granny to new lodgings. She darted around to the mews, and made her way to the courtyard, hoping her absence hadn't been missed.

"Sara." Henry's whisper hissed out from the stable door as she passed. "Cooper's looking for you. Don't look happy." His thin face was pinched with worry.

Before Sara could thank him, the innkeeper's voice boomed across the courtyard. "Just where have you been, O'Connor?"

Sara's heart dropped. Mrs. Cooper came out of the laundry shed, hands on hips. "I just stepped out for a moment, ma'am."

"What for? A man? Should've known you were loose, coming with no references and all."

Sara forced her eyes down. "I did nothing improper, I assure you."

Mrs. Cooper took a step closer, her eyes narrowing. "It's too late for putting on airs. I warned you, O'Connor, that your next false step would be your last. Jennie saw you filling Mr. Kinney's ears with lies."

"It's not lies," Sara said, forgetting caution, forgetting everything that kept her safe. "Miss Giblin is too harsh with Evie. She'll kill the girl's spirit."

"Spirit? What use has a lady for spirit? James Kinney ought to be thanking us for taking that odd thing in hand."

"Evie ain't odd." Henry darted to Sara's side, hands on hips. "She's smarter than all of you lot put together."

Mrs. Cooper cut off Henry's words with a cuff to the side of the head. "Get back to the stable." Henry's dirty hands fisted at his side and his eyes narrowed to slits.

Sara put a restraining arm around his shoulders. "It's all right, Henry. Run along, before you get into more trouble." He hesitated, his wiry frame pulsing with tension. She leaned to whisper in his ear. "She could send you back to the workhouse."

At her words, the fight drained out of him. His shoulders sagged and he took one step back, then another.

Mrs. Cooper ignored him, reaching to grab Sara's arm with a painful twist. The woman stood a few inches taller and many pounds heavier than Sara. "Get out." She released Sara with a shove.

Sara stumbled. Why couldn't she have held her tongue? She clenched her hands, clammy with panic. "Please let me stay. You can dock my pay."

The older woman's lip curled. "If you imagine I'd keep a lying, sneaking servant in my employ, you're not as clever as you think you are."

Dread filled her in a cold wave. What would she and Granny do without this job? "A reference." Her voice came out like a croak, and she cleared her throat and started again. "I need a reference, Mrs. Cooper. Surely you can't fault the work I did."

Mrs. Cooper stepped forward, her narrow gaze boring into Sara. "If you're not off this property in ten minutes, I'll call the magistrate."

Sara stemmed the rush of tears. No new lodgings for Granny, no restorative broth or warm fire in winter. Granny had given her a home and the love of a family, and she'd repaid her with failure.

"I'll collect my things."

"No need. The maid fetched them." With a snap of Mrs. Cooper's fingers, Jennie hurried out of the kitchen and shoved a sack into Sara's hands with a triumphant smirk. "Now get out."

The fog in her mind cleared. "But my wages . . . I'm owed this month still."

"Says who? I'd like to see you prove it."

Except for Henry and Evie, she'd avoided others in her month at the inn, but the isolation she'd sought in the laundry had come at a price. Not likely any of the staff here would risk their positions to defend her. But how could she go back to Granny with nothing?

"I—I'll go to the magistrate." Sara swallowed her panic and forced confidence into her voice.

Mrs. Cooper snorted. "And drag your name through the courts? There wouldn't be an establishment in Toronto that'd hire you after that." Sara shrank back, clutching her sack of belongings to her chest. Not a chance she would risk the notoriety of court, even if she could afford it. "Go," Mrs. Cooper said, sensing victory, "before *I* go to the magistrate and have you arrested for trespassing."

Sara turned to the mews, her throat aching with suppressed tears. Her feet dragged across the cobblestones, the days of work and worry hitting her in a wave of exhaustion and despair. No money, no work. No future. She'd been here before, but that didn't mean it hurt any less.

~~~

"James Kinney. I'm here to see Mr. Ballantine."

Ballantine's butler inclined his head and opened the door, indicating James should precede him into the spacious front hall. It was a formal home, built along the lines of an English country estate. The dark walnut wainscoting and heavy side table reminded James of his childhood home. The same eerie quiet, the same sense of suppressed mourning that his grandparents had maintained after his parents' early deaths.

"I'll let Mr. Ballantine know you're here." The butler took James's hat and indicated a straight chair pushed against the wall.

James opted to pace. A summons from Ballantine was rare, and the invitation to meet at his private residence in the middle of the day even rarer. He didn't dare refuse, even though he knew it would mean an uncomfortable interview at the very least. Ballantine must have seen Andrew's fiery open letter in the *Correspondent and Advocate*. They wouldn't be able to hide his involvement with the rebels much longer.

The door to the nearest room stood slightly ajar, permitting James a glimpse into the library. A wide stone fireplace filled his line of view, topped by a portrait. A young woman looked down on him, dressed in the high-waisted fashions of twenty years earlier, her blond ringlets falling over her shoulders. Her eyes were blue and her gaze so direct, it felt as though she were looking at him. James suppressed a shiver. There was something almost familiar about her, though he knew Ballantine's wife had died years before.

"James, my boy, good to see you." Ballantine swept past him, opening wide the door to the library.

He took a seat behind an ornate desk, surrounded by bookshelves. Dark draperies hung from the tall windows behind him, completing the look of an English country squire holding court. He waved to the seat across from him with a careless flick of his hand. "Well? Have you read it?"

James gave a reluctant nod. "The letter was unsigned. We can't be sure . . ."

Ballantine snorted. "Got his fingerprints all over it." He picked up the sheet of newsprint on his desk. *"One need only look at the practices of the Canada Land Company to see this injustice in action,"* he quoted, throwing down the paper in disgust. "Every man in the city knows the two of you took on the company. They'll figure out it's him." He sent James a hard stare. "Or you. He must be stopped."

"I've made inquiries. Andrew's been out of town." He winced. He had nothing but excuses for Ballantine. No wonder the man was out of patience with him.

"You must find him. He still won't answer me." Ballantine's stern facade slipped, permitting James a glimpse of the helpless worry underneath the bluster.

Ballantine could be conservative and unbending, yes, but he had Andrew's interests at heart. "I—I will. I'll find him."

Ballantine sat back in the chair with a satisfied smile. "Good, good. Osgoode offered to go." James straightened, biting back a protest. "But I thought he'd take it best coming from you," Ballantine continued. "You must impress upon him the danger he faces. The governor has no patience for reformers these days."

James nodded. Ballantine's fears weren't overstated. Just last week, the authorities had arrested a man for publishing what amounted to little more than a mild rebuke of British oversight in the Canadian colonies. If they discovered the proof that Andrew had written that letter, he'd be behind bars.

"My secretary will be happy to book you passage on the stagecoach." Ballantine reached for the bell, then paused, his hand hovering over the silver handle. "On second thought, it's faster to ride. You have a mount, don't you?"

James nodded, his unease building. "But I can't—"

Ballantine clapped his hands together in satisfaction. "Excellent. There's no time to be lost."

"Sir, I can't leave right away." One of Ballantine's magnificent silver-gray eyebrows rose, making James swallow. "I must make arrangements for Evangeline."

The older man dismissed Evie with a wave of his hand. "She can stay with that Cooper woman for a time, can't she? Heard she was taking lessons there."

Warmth crept up James's cheeks. The man must have eyes everywhere. "Not any longer."

"Eh?"

"The governess's methods weren't to my liking."

Ballantine snorted. "Nonsense. You coddle that girl." He shook his head. "Mark my words, no good can come of indulging her."

James bit his lip. Ballantine hadn't taken an interest in his personal life in years, and now the man was dispensing child-rearing advice. "I don't like leaving Evie. Mrs. Hobbes is away at her daughter's confinement. There's only the new maid, and she's not much older than Evie."

Ballantine reached over and gave James an awkward pat on the shoulder. "You know what I think? It's about time you marry again." James shook his head, but the man held up his hand and forged ahead. "No, hear me out. Your loyalty to dear Amelia's memory does you credit, but a man in your position needs a wife."

At the mention of Amelia's name, a rush of emotion swept through James, equal parts longing and failure. Emotions he couldn't even understand himself, much less explain to a man like Ballantine. "Sir, I don't feel—"

"Trust me. That girl of yours needs a mother. And if you've any aspirations to advancement, you need a proper hostess at your table."

If that's the case, why haven't you married again? James bit back the impudent question. "I've no aptitude for politics."

Ballantine rose, and James followed suit. "Aye, so you've said. Thought Andrew would make a name for himself, but . . ." The older man moved to the door and motioned for the butler to bring James's hat. "Well, I suppose I've said too much, but don't be forgetting what I called you here for." He turned and grasped James's hand. "Don't fail me, James. You've a good head on your shoulders. You could have some influence, and not only with Andrew."

With this parting shot, Ballantine retreated into his library. The butler opened the front door and James found himself outside the mansion, his mind spinning. *How can I make a difference, God? I'm no statesman.* Yet if he might prevent bloodshed, he had to try.

He mounted, his thoughts spinning back to Osgoode. Ballantine was ever blind when it came to that man. Osgoode offering to help? The idea was laughable. If Andrew had done anything incriminating, Osgoode would be certain to make it known to every Tory in Toronto. Unless James stopped Andrew before it could get that far.

But he couldn't imagine leaving Evie even one night, never mind the days required to track Andrew down. He'd thought, perhaps naively, that Evie would settle back to her old routine, working through her lessons in the mornings, and helping the new maid in the kitchen in the afternoons. Each night he set out a passage for her to read and a composition to write, but it wasn't enough. She was bored and listless, responding to his conversation at supper with monosyllables, though she assured him she learned more from him than she ever had with Miss Giblin.

Was marriage the answer? His fingers tightened on the reins, causing his horse to toss her head in protest. A face flashed through his mind, but it wasn't Amelia's round cheeks and dimples. For a moment, he saw Sara O'Connor, as clearly as if she stood in front of him, her chin tilted at a defiant angle, her eyes clear and knowing. He shook his head. The least likely candidate for a wife he could imagine.

A wife. A surge of longing gripped him. He remembered laughter and the weight of a hand curled about his arm. The warmth of a woman's shape lying next to him at night.

On the heels of the longing came darker memories. Tears and accusations and that suffocating sense that he would never get things right.

Marriage he couldn't do. But peacekeeping? Perhaps.

He turned his mare onto Duke Street. Before he reached the gate, Betsy came running from the front step.

"Oh, Mr. Kinney. Thank God you're home."

James jumped down and bolted to where Betsy stood, tears running down her face. "What's happened?"

"I didn't mean to, sir. I did exactly as you said, put her to work in the parlor this morning." She started to wail, lifting her apron up to hide her face.

"Come, now." He tried to keep his voice calm, though he wanted to take the girl by the shoulders and shake the story out of her. "Where's Evie?"

"Weren't no sign of her when I called her for lunch." She wiped her face and dropped the apron. "She's gone."

Chapter 8

The row house was like dozens of others in Irish Town, a worn, flimsy building made of rough-hewn timbers, intended as a temporary lodging for settlers moving on to the bush. But once a family entered Irish Town, they could rarely scrape together the wherewithal to leave.

Sara paused at the back door. Molly, the landlady, was in the middle of one of her rants, and Sara had the sinking feeling she was today's topic.

"You want to tell me why a fancy-talkin' lady like her can't get a job?"

"She's looking." It sounded like Molly's sister Peg was visiting. "Give 'er another week. For Granny's sake."

"Bah—she could be a lady's maid or housekeeper, with all her learnin'. You ask me, she don't want to work."

Sara squeezed her eyes shut. It wouldn't be any use trying to convince Molly she was trying. She was three months behind on room and board as it was. The only thing keeping a roof over their heads was Granny's position as the healer and midwife of Irish Town.

Sara had paced the streets of the city all morning and had more doors slammed in her face than she cared to remember. A fresh wave of illness raged through the slums, and no one wanted contact with contagion. Even if they talked to her, there was a slim chance they'd employ a washerwoman who spoke like a lady. She was a figure of suspicion, especially without reference or recommendation.

Sara turned and crept back through the alley to the front door, stepping over a stream of filth and the remains of a very large rat. She'd check on Granny and get a drink of water for her hollow stomach. Then, she'd try again.

The front door opened into a tiny foyer with a narrow set of stairs for the upstairs tenant and a hall that led back to the kitchen and Molly's room. When Granny was well, the bare wood had been scrubbed clean, but now the corners were full of cobwebs and the stale air was heavy with the lingering odors of cabbage and human filth. A door on the left opened into the small front room where Granny spent her days.

She pushed open the door and froze, unprepared for the sight that met her eyes. Evie—her Evie—was curled up at Granny's feet, her face creased in a wide smile while Granny spoke.

"Evie?" Sara said, as soon as she caught her breath.

Evie jumped up. "Sara. I found you."

When Evie sprang forward, wrapping her slender arms around Sara's waist, it was the most natural thing in the world to return the embrace, to tuck her chin and press a kiss onto

Evie's flyaway hair and inhale her warm child scent of sunshine and soap.

Evie squirmed and Sara released her. "What brings you here, my love?" The enormity of the situation dawned on her. Evie had no business in this part of town, much less alone. "Does your father know where you are?"

A flush spread up Evie's cheeks. "Well, not exactly."

"Evie."

"He doesn't know. Henry told me how to get here. Then I asked some children down the street. They pointed to this house."

Sara closed her eyes for a moment. "Evie, we've got to get you home. They'll be so worried. It's not safe here."

Evie dismissed Sara's worries with a swipe of her hand. "Papa won't be home from the courts for hours still."

Granny leaned forward in her chair, her eyes bright. "A few more minutes won't make a difference. Make us a pot of tea, Sara, there's a good lass. Not every day I get company." Sara hadn't seen her so animated in months.

"Yes, Sara, please. I want to hear the end of the story."

Sara weakened. "Fine, just a cup of tea, and then I must get you safely home."

Molly was alone in the kitchen.

"Granny wants tea," Sara said, hesitating at the door.

Molly shrugged and picked up a basket of clothes. "I'm off to the creek with the laundry." She sent Sara a narrow glance. "Don't think I won't know what you've taken from my kitchen."

Sara let out a slow breath as the back door closed and she was alone. She took a precious pinch of tea from the tin box high on the shelf and set the water to boil. There was no milk or sugar, of course. She hoped Evie wouldn't turn up her nose at such fare. And she hoped she could somehow get the girl safely home again with James Kinney none the wiser.

~~

James stood in the street, worry growing like a vine in his chest, threatening to cut off his breath. He'd checked the livery and then Sproule's before racing home again to see if she'd returned. Nothing. Where could she be?

A flash of movement caught his eye and he paused. A closer look revealed it was only the edge of a shirt on the neighbor's clothesline, blowing up over the fence.

Laundry. The inn. Sara O'Connor.

He jogged to King Street and slipped down the alley to enter the inn from the back, pausing a moment to catch his breath outside the carriage entrance. The courtyard was quiet. There was no sign of the washerwoman . . . or Evie.

"Somethin' I can help you with, sir?"

James started, looking down to find a grubby stable boy at his side.

"Name's Henry." The boy sketched a bow.

"I'm looking for the laundress. Miss O'Connor?"

The boy took his cap off and scratched his scalp. "Don't work here no more."

"What?" He hadn't reckoned on never seeing Sara O'Connor again. He'd been so certain she held the key to Evie's where-abouts, too. "Have you seen my daughter, Evie? You might remember her. She took lessons here."

"I remember her right enough, sir." The boy rocked back on his heels. "She come by. Looking for Sara, too, she was." The boy looked him up and down, giving James the curious feeling that this urchin was sizing him up.

James curbed his impatience. "Where is she?"

"Headed out about an hour ago."

His stomach dropped. *Please, let her be safe. Let me find her.* "Headed where?"

Henry chewed his lip, looking away.

"Tell me." James's voice was hard, the tone he used for criminals under investigation. "I'll make it worth your while."

"No call to get tetchy now, sir." James reached out as though to grab the boy and the lad hurried on. "I told Evie what I know. The washerwoman walked east. To Irish Town, I reckon. She has people there."

James hadn't thought the washerwoman sounded in the least Irish, but with a name like O'Connor, it stood to reason. "What has this to do with Evie?"

"Went to find her."

James's heart sank. Irish Town was the poorest area of the city, a slum full of crime and disease. "You sent my daughter off to Irish Town on a wild goose chase?" James's voice was deceptively smooth, but some instinct of self-preservation must have alerted Henry to danger, for he took a step back, holding his hands out in front of him.

"I meant to go with her, only Rawley wouldn't let me." He sent James a look of entreaty. "You don't know how determined she was, sir. I tried to get her to wait, but she just . . ."

James swallowed his anger. He knew exactly how determined Evie could be. "How well do you know Irish Town? Think you could find her for me?"

Henry's chest swelled. "Ain't no corner I don't know, sir."

"Well, then, let's be off." Henry sent an anxious glance to the stable. "Don't worry. I'll make it right with the stable master when I return. You'd stand to earn a shilling. Or two."

Henry needed no further encouragement. They zigzagged through a warren of mews and alleys, the tidy yards and storefronts of the upper town giving way to rows of dreary homes in various states of disrepair, some little more than sheds. The stench grew overwhelming, for there were no ditches here to carry away the filth.

"She can't be much ahead of us." Henry attempted to assure him. "She don't know these shortcuts like I do."

"There are hundreds of people in Irish Town. How could Evie think she'd even find Sara?" James spoke mostly to himself, but Henry answered, certain enough of his importance now to risk further displeasure.

"Sara's different. Kind of woman people remember, you know?"

James nodded. He did know. Scarcely a day had passed when the woman's face hadn't flashed through his mind.

The closer they got to the heart of Irish Town, the greater his panic. Groups of ragged, dirty children crept out of alleys as he strode past. Evie wouldn't have the slightest clue how to go about finding her friend and she was bound to stand out in her fine dress. A prime target. His stomach clenched, and he strained his eyes for a glimpse of her straw bonnet.

Finally, they stopped in front of a corner house so dilapidated it seemed in danger of collapsing into its neighbor. Henry spoke to a boy out front and sent James a nod. "She's here all right. In with Granny O'Connor right now."

A rush of relief carried James up the steps. The front door

opened into a narrow front hall. The door to his left was ajar and he peered inside to find a tidy room that belied its surroundings. And Evie.

She was perched on a stool in front of a rocking chair, speaking confidingly to an old woman. A small table and a sagging bedstead were the only other furniture in the room. Under her feet, a braided rug provided a splash of color.

Evie sprang up when James entered, her happy exclamation of "Papa!" silenced as soon as she saw his face.

"Evie," he said, between relief and anger. "What possessed you to disappear like that?"

"I'm sorry, Papa. I went to Cooper's Inn, but Sara was gone. I had to find her. I never said goodbye."

She spoke as though her actions were reasonable. Logical, even. James bit back the reprimand on the tip of his tongue, aware they had an audience. "It was dangerous, Evie."

"Well, she didn't come to no harm," the old woman said.

James remembered his manners, swept off his hat, and directed a bow in the old woman's direction.

She was small, her form almost swallowed up in shawls and wraps. A cap, worn but clean, was tied under her chin. Though her face was wrinkled, her eyes sparkled with life, and he found himself being sized up under a shrewd gaze that left him slightly uncomfortable.

"She been no trouble, sir," the woman said. "Right nice young girl, she is." The old woman frowned. "Ought not to've come, though." She reached down and lifted Evie's chin. "No young lady ought to be seen careening around the city on her own."

"I'm in complete agreement with you there." James shot a severe glance at Evie, and she colored and hung her head.

"I—I'm sorry."

"Well, come along then. We've taken up enough of this good woman's time as it is."

The old woman let out a cackle. "Time's all I've got these days. Did me good to have a bit of a visit. And besides—" She studied him, her knowing eyes seeming to see right into his heart. "I've been waiting for you."

"For me?"

She nodded. "Been praying for years. Lately, I've had a sense my prayers would be answered."

James took an unconscious step back. He wasn't sure what the old woman was talking about, but he was certain about one thing. He wasn't the answer to any woman's prayers. "I don't understand. Perhaps you're confusing me with someone else?"

The old woman swept his words aside with an impatient motion of her hand. "No, I'm not that far gone yet. You're the one."

Before James could answer, the door at the back of the room swung open. Sara appeared, carrying a tray of sorts, with a chipped teapot and an assortment of tin cups. James froze for a long moment, his eyes roaming over her, soaking in her presence. A knot in his stomach relaxed, seeing her, knowing she was well and safe. He felt like . . . smiling. He frowned instead. Sara O'Connor had caused him no end of trouble. There was nothing to smile about.

"Here we are then," she began. She looked up and her eyes met James's. "Oh—you." The tray wobbled.

"Yes, indeed," James replied. "Me."

Chapter 9

The sight of James Kinney robbed Sara of speech. He seemed to fill the tiny room, his face a stern mask that gave little doubt of his displeasure at finding his daughter in the slums. With her.

"Pull up a stool and join us." Granny's cheerful voice broke into the tense silence. "Put that tray down, Sara, and fetch a chair from the kitchen."

Sara turned, glad for the excuse to escape James's accusing gaze.

"My apologies, but we must leave at once." James's tone, clipped and icy, made her spine straighten. He could blame Evie's actions on her all he wanted, but she'd done nothing wrong.

"Come, now, surely you've a moment to spare for a lonely old woman." Granny seemed impervious to his tone. "I promised this girl of yours the rest of the story of Tír na nÓg, I did."

"Yes, Papa, please say we may stay. Just a few minutes."

He opened his mouth to protest, then closed it again as Evie pulled over the stool and patted it. Sara suppressed a smile at the sight of James, no more able to deny the two of them than she was.

Safe in the kitchen, she paused and gripped the back of the chair with unsteady fingers. The sight of James Kinney did strange things to her. Part of her wanted to rush back in and defend herself. Explain Evie's arrival and how she'd planned to ensure Evie got home safely. The rest of her wanted to never leave the kitchen again.

Sweeping aside her hesitation, she lifted the chair and returned to the room with measured steps. James Kinney was nothing to her. Not an employer, not a friend. His opinion shouldn't matter in the least.

Sara poured the tea at the rickety side table while Granny told her story. Although she forced her eyes to stay on the cups in front of her, she knew exactly the moment his shoulders relaxed and James leaned forward, captivated by Granny's story, as Sara would be herself if she hadn't heard it countless times before.

Granny paused so Evie could pass the cups around, and Sara took a seat further back, taking in the scene before her. Evie perched on her father's knee, and he had one arm around her waist. With the other hand, he sipped weak tea from a battered tin mug, not betraying by a flicker of an eyelid that it was any less than he was used to. Father and daughter leaned forward as Granny concluded the haunting story of Oisín, the man caught between two worlds.

"Why didn't he stay with Niamh in Tír na nÓg?" Evie asked.

"He missed his home too much. Doesn't work, trying to leave your world, you ken. Ought to have stayed where he was born."

Sara bit her lip and looked down. Granny always chose her stories with purpose. Perhaps she wanted to warn Evie of the dangers of wandering too far from home. Then again, her message might be directed at Sara as well.

James sat back with a smile, taking another sip of his tea. "A grand story, Mrs. O'Connor. I fancy I'll keep my eyes open for fairies next time I drive through the woods."

The chill had melted from his voice, leaving a warmth that gave Sara pause. She tried to imagine any other man of his position in this room and found she could not. He might disapprove of her, but he'd made himself at home with Granny. She hadn't expected that.

"Aye, well, I doubt there's fairies here in Canada. Left them all behind in Ireland, I did."

Evie straightened, casting off her father's embrace to lean closer to Granny. "Are you sure, Granny? Have you ever looked?"

"Where would I be finding fairies in Irish Town, my dear? Now, if a body had a chance to get to the woods . . . well, there's no telling what you might find."

Evie turned to her father, her face alight. "Papa, do you think we might see some, next time we drive to the lake?"

"Fairies are mighty shy creatures, I've heard. But it wouldn't hurt to look." James rose, pulling Evie to her feet. "Thank you for your hospitality, ma'am, but it is time we were on our way." He shook the old lady's hand with a warm smile, then turned to Sara. The smile faded, replaced with the stern lines she recognized. "Might I have a word with you, Miss O'Connor?"

Sara inclined her head. "Certainly." What else could she say? He followed her into the kitchen, still blessedly deserted.

"I am not sure what prompted this foolish start of Evie's," he began. "She seems uncommonly fond of you." He sent her a sharp glance, as though she, and not Evie, had planned the meeting. "I would ask . . . don't encourage her in this attachment."

Sara forced down her ire. Fostering the bond that had sprung up between her and Evie would only cause them both pain in the end, she knew that just as well as he did. "Of course, sir," she said, her eyes on the floor.

"I should have seen how it would be." James paced the length of the room in three strides. "She never knew her mother. Natural she'd latch on to you when you showed her kindness." He paused, looking straight into her eyes. "I didn't realize until today how lonely she must be. But it won't do, you know. For her to get attached to you."

Sara wished she knew how to stop the words. They pierced the soft corner of her heart that Evie had warmed, each one hurting more than the last. "Of course not," she managed. "Children get over things quickly. I'm sure now she's seen I'm all right, she won't give me another thought." She wouldn't stop thinking about the Kinneys, though. They'd given her a glimpse into a world she thought she'd put behind her. A world of family, of books and learning. But it wasn't her world, not anymore.

James studied her for a moment, his gaze so intense a flush of heat rose in her cheeks. "You're nothing like any washerwoman I've ever come across, Miss O'Connor."

"Indeed? How many laundresses have you come to know, Mr. Kinney?" Her chin rose, the sharp words spilling out before she could hold them back.

James smiled ruefully. "That's exactly what I'm talking about. What other servant would put me in my place so neatly?"

Sara's lips twisted. "You might be surprised." Servants were cleverer than their employers gave them credit for, she knew that now.

Instead of taking offense, James laughed. Warmth bloomed around her heart, a sense of shared humor that she hadn't felt in a very long time.

"Papa, come back. I think you'll like this story, too." Evie called from the other room.

The smile faded from James's face. "You do agree, though?" He spoke in an undertone, moving to the door. "To keep your distance?"

Sara straightened her shoulders. A moment of shared humor meant nothing. He still didn't want his daughter near a laundress. "I didn't lure Evie here today, nor have I made any effort to contact her." She made a show of tucking the mismatched chairs around the table. "The problem might be better remedied by your keeping a closer eye on your daughter." She was instantly ashamed of her words. They'd slipped out, a visceral impulse to get back at him. To hurt him with words the way he'd hurt her. Childish. She sneaked a glance at his face. He wasn't smiling now.

His eyes narrowed. "Quite right, Miss O'Connor." He gave her a stiff bow before turning on his heel and leaving the kitchen.

Sara forced her feet to follow him into the front room where James bowed over Granny's hand in farewell.

"Goodbye, Sara," Evie said, coming to her side. "Now that I've found where you live, I'm sure we can visit."

Sara refused to look up, but she felt the weight of James's silent expectation all the same. It was better this way, she consoled herself. Easier for them both to make a clean break.

"I'll be starting a new job soon, my dear," Sara said. "You mustn't come looking for me here. It isn't safe."

"Aye, lovey, you listen to Sara now," Granny chimed in. "Ain't the neighborhood for a young thing like you."

Evie chewed her lip. "Well, then you can come to my house. For tea. Mrs. Hobbes makes the best lemon biscuits. Bring Granny, too." Evie went to Granny's side and picked up her hand. "You'll love the lemon biscuits, Granny."

Sara's heart cracked. She glanced at James, expecting to see him frown or pull Evie away. But he smiled a soft, sad smile and smoothed his hand over Evie's head.

"Come, my dear, it's time we were leaving." He put his arm around Evie's shoulder and guided her to the door. His eyes met Sara's over Evie's head for a fleeting moment. He hesitated, then sent a brisk nod in her direction before they both disappeared out the door.

Sara stood in the front room, staring after them until the creak of Granny's rocker recalled her to the present.

"Well, that's what I call a gentleman," Granny said, almost to herself. "Mighty attached to that daughter of his, too." Granny sent Sara a shrewd glance. "Mayhap that's not all he's attached to."

Sara gasped. "Granny, where on earth do you get such thoughts. I'll never see them again."

"Hmph." Granny rocked with renewed vigor, muttering about young people who couldn't see for looking.

Sometimes it was a trial that Granny knew her so well. Sara

gathered the teacups, avoiding Granny's eyes. "Besides, he is a fine gentleman, just as you said. What would he want with a washerwoman?"

"Yer not a washerwoman, no more than I'm the Queen of England." Granny shook her head. "God isn't only a God of blessings. He's the Man of Sorrows, too, ye ken. He knows how it feels."

Sara lifted the tray, her eyes lowered so Granny couldn't read her thoughts. What good was a God who led you into sorrow?

"There's a time to mourn and a time to rejoice, says so right in the Scriptures. Mayhap your time of mourning is done. Might be time to live again."

Sara took the tray to the kitchen, unwilling to hear more. Colin had promised her joy, too, once upon a time. *I don't think you've ever really lived in that stuffy mansion. Come with me, Sara. We're going to live, and I'll make you happier than you've ever been before.*

She'd followed him, away from everything she'd ever known. Only he'd been wrong. Three years in the lumber camps had broken his health and his dreams. The year after that, he'd died in her arms.

Granny O'Connor was wrong, too. She'd never be rejoicing again.

~~

Henry materialized out of an alley as they left Irish Town. Evie turned to the boy with the familiarity of an old friend.

"Henry, have you heard of Tír na nÓg?" Evie trotted up to Henry's side.

"Nope," Henry said.

It was all the encouragement Evie needed. She started in on a version of Granny's fairy story that had Henry at turns fascinated and incredulous.

"You must be loopy if you think I believe in fairies."

"Well, if you don't believe me, ask Granny yourself." Evie stuck her nose in the air and turned to face the front.

"All right, I s'pose it might happen." Evie didn't spare him a glance. "C'mon, Evie. Tell me the rest."

"Fine, I will. But don't interrupt this time."

Evie prattled on, leaving James to wonder at their easy rapport. He wouldn't encourage a friendship with a street-smart stable boy, but at least Evie was absorbed enough to put Sara O'Connor out of her mind.

Henry gave them a cheerful wave when they reached Cooper's Inn. "Reckon I'll see you 'round," he said to Evie.

"Maybe." Evie shrugged, her eyes darting to James. Perhaps she thought he would put a stop to this friendship, too. Maybe he should.

Silence stretched between them as they headed home. James glanced down at Evie, who seemed deep in thought. Or deep in resentment. He searched for something that would cheer her up. "You can write to Sara if you like."

Her chin shot up and she grabbed his hand, bringing them to a stop on the boardwalk. "Papa, listen. I've thought of something even better."

"What is it?" James wasn't sure he wanted to hear the answer, especially if it had something to do with Sara O'Connor.

"Well, Sara needs work and I need a teacher." Evie's voice grew animated as the idea took shape. "Why can't *we* hire her?"

James shook his head. How could he make her see that Sara

wasn't the answer? She'd set the laundress up on a pedestal. "Sara was a good friend to you when you were in a difficult spot, but a teacher needs certain . . . qualifications." He put his hands on her shoulders to steer her home.

"Sara is qualified. More qualified than Miss Giblin." Evie's chin jutted out in a way that warned James he had a battle on his hands. "She speaks French, she can name every capital of Europe and she knows all about the kings and queens. And the Magna Carta," she finished with relish, as though that fact alone should end all discussion.

"I know I made a mistake with Miss Giblin, but there are other teachers. We'll do better this time."

Evie lifted her eyes to his and James inhaled sharply at the ferocity of her expression. "You think she's just a washerwoman. She's not good enough to be my teacher, but you're wrong."

"I don't think it. I know it," James said, his calm beginning to unravel. He hadn't realized how much she wanted a younger woman in her life. A mother. Today's dangerous venture into Irish Town only confirmed what she would do to get it, and it sent a chill down his spine. "A laundress from Irish Town cannot teach you what you need to know." He pushed her down the street, her feet dragging with every step.

"You don't understand." Evie's toe caught on the edge of a board, bringing her to a stop once again. "Sara *was* my teacher. The best teacher in Upper Canada. She—"

"Evangeline Amelia Kinney." James cut her off with a slice of his hand. "We will not discuss this any further."

Evie's face crumpled, and James draped an arm around her shoulders and guided her through the gate and up the steps of their home. It killed him to say no to her, even for something as patently impractical as hiring a laundress as her teacher. *Men have no business raising a child on their own.* He could almost hear Mrs. Hobbes's knowing sniffs of disapproval. Maybe she was right. Evie was vulnerable to a friendly face and Sara O'Connor was a kind woman. Clever, too, for she'd picked up a little learning somewhere.

But a woman like Sara O'Connor couldn't teach Evie how to dress and dance and take her place in Toronto society. A laundress as her governess? Evie would be a laughingstock. As soon as they reached the front hall, Evie slid out from under his arm and sent him a stormy glance before pounding up the stairs to her room. He didn't try to stop her.

There was no future in this friendship and nothing to be gained by prolonging it. The sooner Evie came to terms with this truth, the better off she'd be.

Chapter 10

"Come, Granny, just one more sip." Sara held a steaming cup of tea, a special blend of herbs she'd mixed to Granny's exacting instructions.

Granny gave her a wan smile but didn't lift her head from the pillow. "I've had enough, dearie. I do hate to miss the Sabbath service, but it can't be helped."

Sara chewed her lip, worry gnawing at her. Granny's energy had always seemed boundless.

"Why don't you go?" Granny reached out and grabbed her hand. "You can tell me about the sermon when you get home."

"I . . . I don't usually attend." Sara picked up a basket of mending, hoping Granny would let the matter drop.

"You should."

Sara sighed. She avoided church whenever possible. "I don't get any comfort from it, so why should I go?"

Granny snorted. "It's not about hearing what you want to hear. You go to hear what you *need* to hear."

"What about the Learys' youngest? You said you'd come look in on his fever today," Sara said, hoping Granny would drop the subject of church. Besides, if anything could get Granny out of bed, it would be a sick child. "Maybe this afternoon, if you have a rest this morning?"

Granny made a noncommittal sound and closed her eyes, as though their brief discussion had sapped all her strength. Fear rushed at Sara as her eyes traced the thin form on the bed. Granny was the only person she had left. She'd picked Sara up when Colin died and taught her how to live again. She couldn't lose her.

Granny's decline was so gradual that Sara hadn't noticed it at first. She'd lost weight and slept more, but this was the first day she hadn't gotten out of bed.

"You go," Granny said, her eyes still shut.

It took Sara a moment to comprehend Granny's words. "To the Learys? Without you?"

"You've come with me scores of times. You know what to do."

"They want *you*. You're the healer."

Granny's hand slid across the worn squares of the quilt to grasp Sara's arm. "You're a healer, too."

Sara's heart pounded, a familiar wave of panic rising in her throat. She never wanted to hold another life in her hands. Once was enough. "No, I'm not."

"Ye are." Granny's voice took on something of its former astringency.

Sara turned away to tidy the breakfast tray. Granny didn't know what she was asking. Sara accompanied Granny on sick visits whenever she could, partly to help the older woman, and because it fascinated her. But she wasn't a healer. Colin's death was proof of that.

"I've seen you with the sick." Granny was nothing if not persistent. "You've a sense about you—you know what they'll be needing."

Sara swung around to face Granny. "What if I go and he doesn't get better?"

"What if ye don't go and he dies?" The tray tilted in Sara's hands at Granny's blunt words. "The herbs you mixed for me'll work as well as anything. It's fluids they need for a fever." Granny raised her head off the pillow, her eyes refusing to leave Sara's. "It's time you were using the gifts God gave you. Now, go." She collapsed back on the pillow, closing her eyes.

In the kitchen, Sara stood for a moment, staring at the collection of dried herbs that hung from the ceiling. *I can't do this.* She reached up and grasped a brown leaf, her hands unsteady. It turned to powder between her fingers. *But what if it were Evie?* She snapped off a few sprigs of feverfew and put them in a small cloth sack.

"Where're you off to?"

Sara jumped and turned. Molly stood at the back door, her eyes darting from the herbs to the sack in Sara's hand.

Sara cleared her throat. "The Learys. The youngest has taken sick."

Molly snorted. "They've more where that one came from."

Her cruel words erased the last of Sara's hesitation. If she refused to help, she'd be no better than Molly. She scooped out a handful of elderberry flowers from the tin in the cupboard.

"They'll have nothing to pay you with, you know. Don't know why Granny bothers."

"Granny's not going. Just me." Granny wouldn't accept payment, in any case. Not from a family as poor as the Learys.

"She still feeling poorly?"

There was no worry or compassion in Molly's voice. Just a curiosity bordering on eagerness that turned Sara's stomach. Sara jammed her cap on her head, pushed past Molly, and out the back door. If something happened to Granny, Molly would kick Sara to the curb. There were plenty of tenants who could pay more.

It wouldn't come to that. She'd find another position and get Granny out of Irish Town. She'd pay for a doctor, too.

Sara arrived at the Learys to find the front room awash with mourners. She was too late. Two-year-old Sean's pale form was laid out in the living room. His mother sat beside him, her eyes wide and vacant and her body swaying back and forth in time to a funeral dirge only she could hear. Sara looked away, tears of sympathy springing to her eyes. No mother should face this.

The Learys' older children stood around their mother, their faces gaunt with loss and hunger. Sara scanned their faces for signs of illness. It was certain to spread when people lived so close together, in a home meant for one family that now housed five. If only the people of Irish Town could earn a decent living. Clear a farm and create a life for their families. All they needed was what they'd been promised when they'd boarded a ship to leave everything familiar. All they got was the same grinding poverty they left behind.

Her eyes landed on Mr. Leary, standing stern and tense

across the room. He took one look at Sara and strode to her side.

"Where's Granny O'Connor?" he said, cutting off her words of consolation.

"She's ill. She sent me . . . I—I'm sorry I'm too late."

"Not too late for Jennie. She's in there." Mr. Leary waved a weary hand toward the dingy kitchen where a five-year-old Jennie lay on a mat on the floor. A bright red rash spread up her swollen neck.

Sara made tea, then bathed the little girl with cool water. At first, her movements were slow and hesitant, and her hands trembled as she wiped the cloth over Jennie's forehead. What if she somehow made it worse? When the tea cooled, she managed to get the little girl to swallow small sips. *Keep them cool and drinking every chance you get.* Sara repeated Granny's rules to herself as she got to work. She could do this.

As the hours slipped by, Sara was dimly aware of the songs of the mourners in the next room and Mr. Leary's restless pacing. By evening, Jennie rested comfortably, her fever down. Sara let out a long breath as the girl slipped into a natural slumber. Her color was better. She'd even opened her eyes and asked for her rag doll. All signs pointed to an improvement.

"Bless you, Sara O'Connor."

Sara looked up to where Mr. Leary had joined her. He looked down at his sleeping daughter and a tear slid down his cheek.

"I don't figure we could bear to lose her. Not after little Sean." He flexed his hand and reached down to smooth the hair back from his daughter's face. "I reckon it'll help Maudie, too," he said. "Would you go tell her Jennie's on the mend? She'll believe it better from you."

Maud was alone in the front room, staring down at her hands. As Sara approached, she saw the woman held a small cap that she twisted round her fingers. Her pain was almost palpable.

"Maud?" The woman gave no response, though her hands stilled, the knuckles growing white as she clutched the child's hat. "Jennie's better."

Maud's head jerked up. "Better?" Her voice was a low rasp. She stood and took two quick steps forward. "She's better?"

Sara nodded. "She's sleeping now. I think she'll be all right."

Maud's face crumpled. "Oh, thank God. I . . . I couldn't have *borne* to lose another baby."

She rushed to Jennie's side, her relief seeming to snap her out of her paralysis. Sara saw Mr. Leary curve his arm around his wife's shoulders. Saw Maud lean her head on his chest. Despite the tragedy of this day, Sara felt a flicker of hope. *You're a healer, too.* For the first time, Granny's words didn't feel impossible.

It was late by the time Sara crept back into her makeshift bed in the corner of Granny's room. She was so tired that she only removed her shoes before stretching out on her pallet.

"Well?" Granny's voice carried across the room, making Sara jump.

"He was already gone."

"Oh, the poor little mite." There was a moment of silence, heavy with loss.

"But his sister will recover, I think. The rash hadn't spread far, and she could still swallow."

In the gloom, Sara saw Granny's head lift from the pillow. "The rash, was it red?"

"Yes." Sara didn't elaborate. She didn't need to. Granny knew as well as she did what that rash meant.

Sara had a feeling she'd better sleep while she could. She'd seen scarlatina before and she knew one thing for certain. Where there was one case, there would soon be more.

~~~

"Still no word from your young partner?" Osgoode leaned through the doorway into James's office. Most barristers in Toronto kept their offices above the courthouse. It was convenient, but James couldn't help but wish for more privacy.

James looked up from the notes he was making for his next case, his body tense. "No." He didn't elaborate. The less Osgoode knew of Andrew's whereabouts the better. Besides, none of James's inquiries had yielded answers.

"I hear Ballantine paid you a visit." James heard the antagonism in Osgoode's voice, though he tried to mask it. "I know what he was after. He's my client, after all." He nudged an uneven floorboard with the toe of his boot, studying the rough edge. "I could take a trip up to Holland Landing. Just to get the lay of the land, so to speak." Osgoode's voice was deceptively innocent. Holland Landing was rumored to be the hub of rebel activity. James could only imagine the damage Osgoode could do to Andrew's reputation if he found hard evidence of his involvement.

James forced a smile that probably matched Osgoode's in its insincerity. "No, no, I'll take care of it."

Osgoode lingered a moment longer. "Well, do let me know if there is anything I can do to help."

James sighed once the man had finally taken his leave. He needed to give Andrew his serious attention. Yet he couldn't leave Evie with only Betsy for company. Especially not now, when she wasn't feeling well.

He'd noticed the first symptoms at breakfast today. Evie winced as she swallowed her porridge, pushing away the bowl after a few bites. Her eyes were heavy, and her cheeks flushed. He sent her back to bed with assurances from Betsy that her Mam's mustard plaster and a cup of tea would have the girl better in no time.

But when James returned home from the courts that day, Evie was fevered and miserable. A worried frown replaced Betsy's former confidence. He sent for the doctor and spent a restless hour at Evie's bedside, coaxing her to drink her tea.

"Putrid sore throat," the doctor pronounced later that evening, looking grave. He felt along her swollen neck and shook his head, gesturing for James to follow him out into the hall. "Keep an eye out for a rash. Could be scarlatina."

James looked back at his daughter with a sickening flash of fear. He'd nursed her through several colds and fevers, but he'd never seen her so sick she wouldn't talk. Wouldn't swallow her tea or beg him to read her a story. He didn't know much about the illness, only that it was often fatal. Especially in children.

"The scarlatina?" Betsy spoke from the landing, her voice filled with horror.

The doctor nodded. "Heard there was an outbreak. Haven't seen any cases among my patients, but you can't be too careful."

"What can we do?" James said.

He handed James a small bottle of laudanum. "Give her a few drops in water if she should grow too restless. I'll return in a day or two. Maybe bleed her then."

After seeing the doctor out, James went back to Evie's side. She opened her eyes. "Oh, Papa, I feel so awful."

"I know, my love. Here, take some more tea." Evie drank, her forehead crinkling in pain as she swallowed. "I can't imagine how you caught this. Unless—" He paused, remembering Evie's disappearance three days earlier with a flash of dread. "When you went to find Sara, was anyone sick? Did you go anywhere else besides Granny's home?"

Her chin wobbled. "It was a long walk. I stopped . . . some children gave me a drink."

James let the panic wash over him, leaving him cold. He'd kept her safe for ten years and now—his hands clenched with a burst of anger. *First, Evie has her heart broken, and now she ends up sick. And somehow Sara O'Connor is in the middle of it.* His logic told him he couldn't blame it on the laundress. But at this moment, logic wasn't ruling his thoughts. Fear was.

"Come, let's say our prayers." Prayer was the only antidote to fear he'd ever found. He repeated the familiar words with her, but his soul cried out its own lament. *Please, God, see us through this. Make her well.*

"Rest now. Betsy will have you on the mend in no time."

But the next morning when he entered the kitchen, Betsy was tying her bonnet. "My mam's sent for me," she announced, avoiding his eyes. "I'm needed at home."

James stood for a moment, speechless. "You're leaving? For how long?" James's mind felt scrambled. It was hard enough without Mrs. Hobbes. If Betsy left them . . .

"I left broth on the stove and two mustard plasters there." She gestured to a cloth-draped plate on the counter.

"You ready?" A boy with Betsy's dark eyes stood at the back

door. The wind was cold today, rife with the threat of snow, but he seemed loath to enter the kitchen. "Mam said I was to get you home right quick. Didn't want me catching—" He broke off with a self-conscious glance at James.

Betsy hustled him out the door and James sat down at the table with a thud. He was alone, holding his daughter's life in his hands. He bowed his head. *Be with me, Lord. Show me what to do.*

Betsy's broth and plasters proved no match for the march of Evie's illness. She grew hot and restless, refusing to eat or drink and a bright red rash spread up her neck, announcing scarlatina. The doctor came in the afternoon and bled her, leaving James with only the dubious assurance that time would tell.

James sent a hasty note to Andrew, but he wasn't surprised when the messenger returned with a scribbled note from Andrew's manservant explaining the younger man hadn't been home in days.

James ran his fingers through his hair. He didn't have time to worry about Andrew now. His mind spun in ever-widening circles, following the doctor's vague instructions to the letter, although the laudanum and heavy covers he prescribed only seemed to make her more restless. James sat by her side through another night, seeing no improvement. *Please. Don't let her die.*

The delirium that came next was the most terrifying symptom yet. She didn't respond to him, though she cried out in pain whenever he lifted her to drink. Then her mutterings took a definite form, one which had his heart sinking.

"Sara," she cried out, over and over. "I need you. Come back."

He soon grew so sick of the woman's name that he wished he had cotton to stuff in his ears.

"Who is this Sara?" Dr. Whittaker asked at his next visit. James sighed. "Just a friend she had at Cooper's Inn."

"Hmmm. Too risky to bring another child in."

"Not a child—a servant."

"A servant?" The doctor paused, seeming to weigh the information. "Well, you need help with the nursing, Kinney." He returned to packing his implements. "I've made inquiries, but most won't come when they hear it's scarlatina. Terrifies people, that one does. You think this Sara would help?"

James shrugged. Sara O'Connor was many things, but a coward wasn't one of them. He could hardly send for her, though, seeing as how he'd all but forbidden her to see Evie again. Besides, what could she do that they weren't already trying?

"If you could get someone who's had some experience with the disease . . ." The doctor shook his head. "Well, that's neither here nor there." He gave James's shoulder an awkward pat, his worried eyes on Evie's still form. "A few more days and we'll know."

Know what? James was too terrified of the answer to ask. Instead, he watched the doctor leave, his hand holding tight to the doorjamb.

Oh, God, what am I supposed to do now?

A flicker of movement outside the front gate caught his eye, followed a moment later by a shaggy red head that popped up over the fence.

"Henry?" The boy froze, as though he wasn't sure whether to answer James or bolt. "Is that you?"

"Heard about Evie." His hands came up to grip the fence. "I was wondering how she was."

"She's very sick." James stepped outside and motioned Henry closer. The boy vaulted over the fence and trotted up to the porch. "How are you feeling?"

"Fit as a fiddle," Henry said, but his cocky smile didn't reach his eyes. "What's wrong with Evie?"

There was no point hiding the truth. "Scarlatina."

Henry didn't flinch. A child from the slums had probably seen more than his share of disease. "Too bad we can't fetch Granny."

"Granny?" James repeated.

"Granny O'Connor's the best healer in Irish Town. One of the grooms told me her tea saved his little sister."

"Her tea?"

Henry nodded. "Got a special blend."

A week ago, James would have no more thought of inviting Granny O'Connor to nurse his daughter than the Queen of England. But today was different. He was desperate. Today he faced the specter of life without Evie.

He dug in his pocket for a handful of coins. "Hire a carriage and bring Granny back. With her tea."

Henry eyed the coins with interest but shook his head. "Can't. Last I heard, she ain't left her bed in days."

His spark of hope fizzled out. "Ah."

Henry tilted his head. "Sara might come, though."

The name sent a jolt through him. "Sara O'Connor is a healer, too?"

Henry nodded. "She helps Granny."

Evie wanted Sara. And if Sara brought the miracle tea with her, wasn't it worth a try? He didn't give his mind a chance to question the impulse. "Can you find Sara right now?"

"Aye guv, that I can." Henry shifted his weight back and forth, looking like he was ready to sprint into action.

"Go. Tell her my daughter is ill and wishes to see her."

Henry cocked an eyebrow. "You reckon she'll come?"

James closed his eyes for a moment. "I hope so, Henry. I hope so."

Chapter 11

A knock startled Sara from a light sleep. She jumped up from her pallet and rushed to the door before the sound could wake Granny. Since the wave of illness hit Irish Town, she slept in her clothes, her sack of supplies at her side. Her services were in demand, probably because she wasn't afraid to approach the sick.

She was one of the few who had nothing to lose.

Henry stood on the doorstep. "Been sent to fetch you. Got the sickness and they need a nurse."

Sara stared at Henry, nonplussed. She hadn't thought scarlatina had reached the other parts of town. Even if it had, she wouldn't be welcome at Cooper's Inn. "I don't understand—"

"Best get going," Henry urged. "Powerful sick, she is."

"But I'm needed here." Mrs. Cooper could hire a doctor. Why would she trust her daughter to Sara's nursing?

"C'mon, Sara." Henry tugged her arm. "Before it's too late."

"Too late?" Her hesitation wavered. The girl must be very ill.

Molly bustled out from the back room to add her voice to the discussion. She craned her neck to see over Sara's shoulder. "Sent a carriage? No doubt they'll pay right well for a nurse."

There was no way to ignore the summons now that Molly had sniffed out the source of next month's rent. Swallowing her reluctance, Sara followed Henry outside. He helped her into the carriage, jumped up with the coachman, and they were off.

By the time they'd reached King Street, Sara was no closer to understanding the strange request. Then the carriage turned right onto a sleepy side street. Sara stuck her head out of the window.

"Why are we turning here, Henry? The inn is two blocks on."

Henry looked down at her. "Brought you straight to Mr. Kinney's house, just like he said."

"Mr. Kinney?" Sara collapsed back against the worn leather seat, thinking over her conversation with Henry. He'd never actually *said* Cooper's Inn. Still, James Kinney seemed even less likely to summon her than Mrs. Cooper.

The carriage rolled to a stop in front of a tasteful rowhouse with a small square of green in front. Henry jumped down and opened her door.

Sara didn't budge. "You're sure it was Mr. Kinney?"

"Law, Sara, used to think you was a sharp one. Of course, I'm sure. She's in an awful bad way, I heard."

Evie. He must be talking about Evie. Sara sat bolt upright, her throat tightening at the thought. "Evie's sick?"

Henry held the door and motioned her to descend. "Been asking for you day and night."

Sara hurried up the walk, her reluctance to see James Kinney again vanishing in the face of her worry for Evie. No one answered her knock, but the faint glow in an upstairs window assured her the house wasn't yet to bed. She knocked again, louder this time, and heard a heavy tread on the stairs.

The door opened and Sara found herself face-to-face with James Kinney. In shirtsleeves, unshaven, with lines of exhaustion around his eyes, he was hardly recognizable as the same man who'd dismissed her from his life just a week ago. She took an unconscious step back at the torment in his eyes.

"You came. Thank God." His voice was hoarse. "Please, come in."

She quickened her pace to follow him up the stairs. "What happened?"

"She took ill a few days ago." He rubbed a hand over his face. "Doctor says it's scarlatina."

Sara stopped midstep and grasped the banister, picturing the ravages of the illness on Evie's small form. She wasn't strong enough for this. What if—

"Sara?" James looked over his shoulder.

"Yes." She inhaled, resuming her steps. "Scarlatina is everywhere in Irish Town."

He stopped at the first door, his hand on the knob. "I figured that must be where she picked it up." He didn't look at her, but she felt the weight of blame. "Henry said you've nursed the ill with much success. If there's anything you can do—" His voice broke.

In the face of his distress, she forgot the words he'd spoken the last time they met and her determination to put this family out of her mind. "I . . ." Her voice cracked. "I'll do everything I know how."

He nodded once and reached for a doorknob. He paused, straightening his shoulders as though he were about to face an opponent.

The sour smell of sickness pervaded Evie's room. A lamp burned low on a table by the bed, illuminating her small form. She was pale, her eyes closed. Sara stood in the doorway, her throat swelling with emotion.

At the bedside, James lifted Evie's head and held a cup to her dry, cracked lips. She sealed her mouth and turned away.

Sara moved to the other side of the bed and picked up Evie's hand. "Evie. It's Sara. You must have a drink. Open up, now." She tried to infuse all of Granny's calm confidence into her voice.

Evie stilled, then opened her mouth a fraction, just enough for a trickle of water to enter. Her throat worked as she swallowed. James lowered her back to the pillow.

"Amazing."

Sara lifted her eyes from Evie's pale face to find him watching her.

"I've been trying to get her to drink all day." He gave a rueful shake of his head. "She doesn't seem to hear me. I can't do anything to help her." He looked down at his fists, the knuckles white with tension.

She felt a strange impulse to squeeze his clenched hands and assure him Evie would be fine, but she couldn't promise anything of the kind. "She'll need fluids, and lots of them, to recover." Sara forced a calm cheer into her voice that she was far from feeling. "Did the doctor leave anything?"

James waved to a bottle on the bedside table. "He left

laudanum, but I can't get it down her." He turned to her, his eyes wide with hope. "Maybe you can get her to take it."

"I can try." She reached out and felt Evie's forehead. Hot. She grasped her wrist and found the pulse faint and uneven. "What she needs is willow bark tea." She reached to remove the sack she'd slung over her shoulder. "I brought some."

Sara expected him to argue with her and insist on the doctor's remedies. Instead, he nodded. "I'll boil water."

She set to work, mechanically tending Evie as she had a score of other children, mixing Granny's special blend of herbs and coaxing the tea down Evie's throat, drop by painstaking drop. James stayed by her side, lifting Evie as needed and watching the slow progress with barely restrained fear. After an hour he straightened and released a slow breath.

"She looks better." James leaned over the bed, resting the back of his hand against Evie's forehead. "I think the fever's down. That tea did the trick."

Sara stilled, the cup in her hands suspended over the bed. She remembered the ebb of hope and despair, how she'd searched for the smallest sign of improvement to convince herself Colin would get well.

"Tell me the truth," he said suddenly, his voice harsh in the quiet room.

Sara put the cup and spoon down on the bedside table with precision, her fingers lingering on the nightstand.

"You've seen this before," he said. "You must have a sense of her progress. If she's going to—"

Sara rested her hand on Evie's forehead, debating what to say. She smoothed back the damp strands of hair, then motioned James to follow her to the hall. He joined her, standing so close

Sara could see his bloodshot eyes and the deep groves of worry across his brow. If only she had words to comfort him. But she didn't. She only had the truth.

"It's serious," Sara said. "The crisis will be tonight if I'm not mistaken."

"The crisis?"

"The turning point. Her fever might break, and she'll recover. Or—"

"Don't say it." For a moment, his eyes blazed, and she took a step back at the ferocity of his anger. It left him as quickly as it came. "Sorry." He cleared his throat. "It's just . . . I can't lose her."

His eyes closed for a moment, his dark lashes sweeping down over the shadows of his unshaven face. How could days without sleep make him *more* handsome? Without thinking, Sara reached up, her fingers hovering inches from his rough cheek. She understood his agony.

A muffled cry from inside the room had them jumping apart and flying to Evie's side. Heat emanated from her fevered body. The tea wasn't working fast enough.

"We need to get her temperature down." Sara's mind switched to the lessons she'd learned at Granny's side. "Cold water."

"There's a block of ice in the cellar."

She'd forgotten about the luxury of ice at any time of year. "Yes, that would help."

James sprang into action, returning with a bowl of ice chips. They worked steadily, sponging her body, and slipping tiny shards of ice into her mouth. Finally, she seemed cooler. The restless movement of her arms and legs stilled and she seemed closer to natural sleep. Sara sank to her chair, her arms quivering with exhaustion.

James sat across from her, holding Evie's hand, eyes closed. His lips moved, and although she couldn't hear his words, she knew he was praying. There'd been a time when she'd begged God for Colin's life, expecting an answer. She hoped James Kinney wasn't destined for the same disappointment.

He opened his eyes and caught her staring. Flushing, he looked away. "We are told to cry to the Lord in trouble," he murmured.

She recognized the psalm. One of Granny's favorites. "Well, it can't hurt."

"You think prayer ineffective?" There was no censure in his voice, only curiosity, and it prompted her to answer more openly than she might otherwise have done.

"In my experience, it has been."

James was silent for a moment. "I'm sorry," he said finally. "I've long sensed you are, like me, not unacquainted with sorrow."

"My husband." Sara hadn't intended to tell him more, but the openness of his expression lowered her guard and loosened her tongue.

James looked up, surprised. "You were married?"

"Yes." Sara folded the cloth in her hand into a tiny square. "He died from cholera. Back in '30."

James leaned forward across the bed with a soft murmur of sympathy. His eyes were serious, conveying sympathy without pity and loosening the last of the tight hold she kept on her memories.

"I tried to save him, but I didn't know then what I know now. I'd never nursed anyone before. I couldn't get him to drink. I couldn't help him." Emotion crept into her voice, the terror and loneliness of those last days when she'd been unable to save Colin.

James stared at her. "But surely you weren't alone. What about your family?"

Family. The word still sent a pang through her. "No. No one could come near the sickroom, not even Granny."

"You didn't catch it?"

Sara shook her head. "Winters he worked at a lumber camp, trying to save up enough to set up his trade. He wanted to be a smithy." She could still see Colin when he'd returned from camp. He'd lifted her up and swung her in a circle and promised they'd never be parted again. "The work was hard on him. When cholera came through that summer, he just . . ."

James's eyes filled with compassion. "I'm so sorry. That must have been horrible."

Scenes flashed through Sara's mind. The long night spent washing and dressing his lifeless body. The cart that came to fetch the dead. Three days alone in their room, staring out the window and wondering why she couldn't seem to die as well. She would have, if Granny hadn't come and pulled her back into life.

"It was . . ." She swallowed, uncertain how to put the tumble of grief and loss into words. "It was hard."

~~~

A widow. That was pain he knew something about. He looked at Sara, wondering if she'd say more, but she kept her eyes trained on Evie's still form on the bed.

Throughout the night they battled the fever, bathing her

with cool water and coaxing her to swallow sips of tea. Her temperature rose again, and she grew more restless, each hoarse cry hitting him like a physical blow. *Don't take her, too. I can't bear it. Please.* He rose and paced to the window.

The first hints of dawn lightened the horizon with streaks of violet and crimson. How could a day promise to be so beautiful when his daughter suffered? It was preposterous that the city continued its regular rhythm when Evie's life hung in the balance.

Sara didn't leave Evie's side. As before, her voice seemed to pierce the delirium and bring Evie some level of peace. She never hurried her words, nor did a trace of worry or fear enter her voice. He could bask in that tone all night, for it soothed him as much as it did Evie. As soon as Sara had taken charge of the sickroom, a load lifted.

"Thank you for coming," he said, suddenly needing her to know what her presence meant to him. "It's a blessing to have someone with experience. I . . . I never seem to know what to do."

She turned her eyes to him, her expression conveying so much kindness that his chest constricted. "It can't be easy," she murmured. "Raising a little girl on your own."

"Sometimes I wonder if her mother would've done things differently. Maybe she would have caught the signs earlier, never let her get this sick." He broke off. What was happening to him? He *never* talked about Amelia.

"Evie told me she doesn't remember her mother," Sara said. There was a question in her words, as though she expected an answer.

He almost didn't give her one. He'd never told anyone of

those dark days after Evie's birth. Yet tonight, with Sara in the circle of candlelight, he finally found the words.

"She had a hard time with Evie's delivery. I was worried, but the doctor assured me it was normal." He broke off. "The birth was horrible, but the fever after was even worse. She grew weaker by the day. A week later, she was gone." He clasped one of Evie's restless hands against the bed covers. "It's been just the two of us ever since."

"I'm sorry," she whispered. After a moment, she cleared her throat. "For what it's worth, I think you've done a wonderful job raising Evie."

Her words warmed him. It was the first time anyone had said he'd done something right as a father. He gave a rueful smile, thinking of Ballantine's advice. "Universal opinion seems to be that I should marry again. But I—I can't." There he was, spilling his heart again. What was it about this woman that loosened his tongue?

"I understand." His shoulders relaxed at her quiet words, spoken so softly he almost missed them. He looked up to find her watching him with compassion. "Sometimes it's just not worth the risk."

Evie moaned and Sara rose and picked up the cup on the side table. "One more sip, my love," she murmured. Evie screwed her lips shut and turned her head to the side.

"Here, let me help." James stood, lifting Evie higher so the liquid didn't run out of her mouth.

Sara leaned closer and her hair brushed his chin. She'd long ago abandoned her cap and the soft strands glinted with gold and honey in the lamp's glow. He caught a whiff of her scent. Warm and sweet with a hint of roses.

Sara's head shot up, jolting him out of his thoughts. "Mr. Kinney?"

He realized he'd lowered Evie's head, making it difficult for Sara to reach her mouth. He straightened, hoping the dim light would mask the faint warmth in his cheeks.

"I'm sorry," he blurted out.

"Pardon me?" Sara stared at him, her eyebrows raised.

"About what I said. That day with Granny. I didn't realize—" James paused. He hadn't planned to apologize, not yet at least, and his exhausted brain couldn't seem to form the words he needed. "I didn't know how close you were. What you meant to her." He risked a glance at her face and found her staring at him, her eyes wide in surprise. "The things I said to you—Well, I was wrong, and I'm sorry. Evie clearly needs you." *And I do, too.* Where had that ridiculous thought come from?

"You were right," Sara replied. "There was no point in prolonging our friendship." She set the cup down and set about straightening the bedclothes. "But I'm glad you asked me to come."

"So am I."

At his words, her hands stilled on the bedclothes and her eyes locked with his. She was the first to break their gaze, her eyes darting to the rocking chair in the corner. "She's quieter now. Why don't you rest for a few minutes?"

He felt his daughter's forehead, searching for any sign she was better. She did seem to rest easier. On impulse, he reached across the bed and took Sara's hand in his. It was rough, the nails short and the skin cracked. "Do you really think she's better?"

"I think so. I promise I'll wake you if there's any change."

She returned the pressure of his hand, and he felt the strength in her, the competence. Felt a shot of awareness flow up his arm, too, that set his heart pounding. He dropped her hand.

He settled back in the chair, pushing aside his confusing reaction to Sara O'Connor. Instead, he focused on Evie, comforted by the sight of her chest moving up and down in a regular rhythm. His eyes grew heavy in the dark room, and he allowed the exhaustion of the past days to overwhelm him.

A hand on his shoulder shook him awake. He opened his eyes, squinting at the bright sun that flooded the room.

"There's a change," came Sara's excited voice beside him. He jumped to his feet, almost knocking her sideways. He reached out to steady her, looking deep into her eyes.

"What kind of change?" His voice was hoarse.

She smiled. "Look for yourself."

He crowded next to Sara at the bedside. Evie was still, her breathing deep and even. He touched her forehead. Cool. Her face was no longer flushed an unnatural red. "She's better?"

"The fever's broken."

He glanced at Sara's smile and felt a rush of relief so deep, his knees weakened. He bowed his head. *Thank you for sparing my girl. For bringing me through this time of trial. For bringing Sara into our lives.*

When he opened his eyes, she was staring at him. "God answered your prayers." There was a hint of accusation in her voice that he understood.

"This time." James held her gaze. "Prayer isn't magic or wish fulfillment, I've learned that the hard way. Evie is better and I'm grateful. I felt a presence with me through it all." James shrugged. "More than that I can't explain."

She shifted beside him, and their arms brushed. A tingling awareness sizzled up his side. His fingers reached for hers without conscious thought. She smiled up at him, her fingers tightening around his. There were dark circles under her eyes, and wild curls escaping the knot of hair at the base of her neck. Yet at that moment, she was the most beautiful woman he'd ever seen.

Chapter 12

Sara sipped a cup of tea, staring unseeing out the kitchen window. The long night was a blur. Her world had centered on saving Evie's life . . . and erasing the look of torment from James Kinney's face. Now that the crisis was over, she had the sense she was coming back to reality. A reality she wasn't sure she wanted to face.

She drained her cup and smoothed her rumpled skirt, stifling the longing for something pretty to wear. Something other than coarse linen, stained from years of washing other people's clothes. Something that would make a man like James Kinney sit up and notice. She dragged her fingers through her tangled curls and twisted them under her cap, pushing away foolish yearnings. Placing Evie's tea and broth on a tray, she hurried from the kitchen, almost running into James.

"Oh—"

"Pardon me—" James reached out to steady the tray and hot liquid sloshed onto his hand. He winced.

"I'm so sorry," Sara said. "Are you hurt?"

"It's nothing." He cleared his throat but didn't move. She could see the slight curl in his hair, still damp from a wash, and smell the faint bergamot scent of his shaving soap.

Her eyes dropped to his hand, remembering the moment last night when his fingers, warm and gentle, had wrapped around hers. She'd felt that touch down to her toes. Could still feel it.

She took a step back, needing more space between them. "How is Evie?"

He cleared his throat. "Better. Much better." His smile and the relief in his voice warmed her. "She's asking for you."

James was close on her heels as she headed up the stairs. Probably assessing the frayed fabric of her skirt and the cracked leather of her boots. She straightened her shoulders. She'd long ago accepted her circumstances. So why did James Kinney make her long for things she'd thought forgotten?

"Sara," Evie said as soon as Sara crossed the threshold. "Papa said you were here. I thought I dreamed it."

"I'm very real," Sara said, bending over to press a kiss to Evie's brow. "How are you feeling?"

Evie grimaced. "I'm a little bored. Can you tell me a story?"

Sara smiled. The little girl was feeling better. "Yes, my love, but first you must take some broth." Sara set the tray down and took up the bowl of broth while James lifted Evie to sitting.

Evie shook her head. "I'm not hungry."

Sara paused, the spoon halfway to Evie's lips. "You need to eat if you are to regain your strength."

James met her eyes over Evie's head. "Perhaps Miss O'Connor could tell you a bit of the story each time you take a spoonful," he said, with a half smile that was more of a challenge.

Miss O'Connor again, when last night she'd been Sara. Probably for the best. A little distance between them was a good thing. "Splendid idea, Mr. Kinney."

"All right," Evie said, her eyes brightening. "The one about Lochinvar."

Sara loved the poem and had taught it to Evie in the laundry shed. She sent a self-conscious glance at James. Would he disapprove of such a wild, romantic tale for a young girl? But his eyes were as alive with anticipation as Evie's. She cleared her throat and dove in before she could think better of it. "O, young Lochinvar is come out of the west!" She paused and raised an eyebrow until Evie swallowed a spoonful of broth. "Through all the wide Border his steed was the best." Evie's eyes glowed and she swallowed another spoonful, then another. They emptied the bowl as fearless Lochinvar spirited fair Ellen to safety.

Sara made the mistake of looking up as they reached the last stanza. James's eyes were still fixed on her, curious and intent. Studying her face in a way that made her aware of his nearness. "So daring in love, and so dauntless in war . . ." Her voice faltered.

Every word of Scott's poem left her. James was no impetuous Lochinvar, but his careful concern for his daughter held an attraction all its own, spinning a web around her that froze the words in her throat.

"I'm ready for the next line." Evie said, breaking the silence that had descended. "It's the best one!"

"Have ye e'er heard of gallant like young Lochinvar?" James

finished the stanza, his voice resonant with the faint Scottish lilt she'd come to recognize.

James lowered Evie back to her pillow. "I see you are a devotee of Scott, Miss O'Connor."

It wasn't a question, but Sara sensed his probing all the same. She'd been fortunate to grow up with a governess who loved novels and read her Scott and Burney in the evenings instead of sermons. But how would a servant know Sir Walter Scott? She hurried to turn the focus away from herself before he could ask.

"You, as well? You're from Scotland, I believe."

"Papa was born in Edinburgh," Evie said.

"Really? My fam—" Just in time she stopped herself from blurting out more than he needed to know. "Your family, that is, you must miss them." She set down the empty bowl and busied herself straightening the sheets around Evie's small form.

"I was orphaned young. Raised by my grandparents, who've since passed away." His voice was clipped as he adjusted Evie's pillow. He seemed just as reluctant to share his past as she was. "Come, poppet, you're tired. You should sleep."

Evie ignored him, turning her attention to Sara. "Do you have family far away?"

James raised his head, looking at her with a faint lift to his brows. Sara picked up the tray and retreated from the curious eyes of father and daughter. "There's only Granny." Only Granny who loved her, anyway. Her father had washed his hands of her years ago. To her relief, James turned the topic.

"I meant to tell you both that I've sent word to Mrs. Hobbes to ask her to return as soon as she's able." James glanced at Sara. "She's our housekeeper." His eyes dropped to the tray in her arms. "She'll take some of the load off you."

Sara swallowed. Was this James's way of telling her to leave?

Evie sent a worried look between Sara and James. "But you'll stay, right, Sara?"

The little girl's eyes pleaded with her to agree. Half of her wished more than anything to stay. The other half knew she'd be better off leaving now, before she grew more attached.

Sara moved to the door. "You're so much better already, Evie. You won't need a nurse much longer."

"But I need you, Sara." Evie's voice rose with each word. She pushed aside the covers Sara had just straightened, as though she would get out of bed.

"Hush now," James said, guiding her shoulders back to the pillow. He looked at Sara with entreaty just as potent as his daughter's. "Please stay. At least until Evie is fully recovered."

Sara nodded, giving in to the temptation. A few more days couldn't hurt. It wasn't like she had a job to return to.

James smiled and came to take the tray from her hands. He leaned forward and she felt again the distracting pull of his nearness. What was the matter with her? "I must finish my correspondence," he said, his voice low. "Would you stay here with her?"

"Yes, of course." He left and Sara breathed a sigh of relief, the tension leaving her shoulders. She couldn't think straight when James Kinney was in the room.

She washed Evie from head to toe and helped her change into a fresh nightdress. By the time they finished, Evie was drooping with fatigue and Sara tucked her in with the admonition to take a nap.

"*Non. Je ne . . .* How do you say *want* again?"

"*Veux.*"

"Je ne veux pas."

Sara smiled. Evie's curious mind was still grasping for knowledge, even when she must be exhausted. "How about another poem while you rest?"

Evie brightened. "'Lochinvar' again?"

Sara smiled. "If you like."

Evie reached out her hand to clasp Sara's with surprising strength. "I love you, Sara."

Sara felt a rush of emotion, bittersweet. When Colin died, she'd accepted she'd never be a mother. Then Evie came along, her love ripping the scab from old wounds and leaving Sara raw and aching. Now she knew what she was missing.

"I love you, too, Evie." Sara leaned forward and pressed a kiss to Evie's forehead, now cool to the touch.

Evie settled back into her pillow and closed her eyes. "Is this what it feels like?"

"Pardon me?"

Evie yawned. "What it feels like to have a mother."

~~

Outside Evie's room, James released a long breath and leaned against the wall. Evie's words hit him with the force of a blow.

He'd done his best to be father and mother both, but it wasn't enough. Evie needed more, and she'd found it in Sara O'Connor, who recited poetry, spoke French and seemed to know on instinct how to love his daughter best. Was there anything Miss O'Connor couldn't do? He shook his head. *Sara was my teacher. The best teacher in Upper Canada.* Evie had tried to tell him, but he hadn't wanted to listen.

He crept downstairs to the makeshift office he'd set up in the dining room and collapsed in his chair. His correspondence was spread out before him, reminding him of the responsibilities he'd put off during Evie's illness. It was time for things to return to normal. For Sara O'Connor to leave before Evie grew so attached that the parting broke her heart all over again. Before *he* grew attached.

He opened the letter at the top of his pile, a note from Ballantine that verged on the hysterical, claiming Andrew was still in the company of Mackenzie. James sighed, rubbing his eyes. Was Osgoode the source of Ballantine's information? He needed to track down the truth, but how could he leave Evie when her health was still so fragile?

Evie. Andrew. In his weary mind, the problems mounted with no solution in sight. Unless—

Unless he could convince Sara O'Connor to stay.

Chapter 13

Sara stretched to loosen the crick in her neck that inevitably followed a night spent sleeping in a chair. A glance at Evie assured her the child continued to improve. Her breathing was deep and even, her forehead cool to the touch.

She washed and straightened her clothes as best she could before heading downstairs. They'd finished off all the food in the pantry, and she'd need to cook if they were to eat before Mrs. Hobbes returned. The thought filled her with dismay. She'd managed to teach herself how to make tea and boil vegetables, but her bread always turned out hard and dry, even though she'd tried for months to perfect her loaves. Colin had never complained, but she'd sensed his frustration as they'd battled to make a future. Having a wife without a single useful skill couldn't have helped.

Sara entered the kitchen and stopped short. A woman stood at the stove, stirring a pot of what smelled like porridge. She was built along ample lines, with a snowy white apron that enveloped the stiff folds of her black gown. This must be Mrs. Hobbes, back from her daughter's confinement and ready to resume charge of the household. A warmhearted woman from the sound of it. Fond of Evie.

The older woman turned at the sound of Sara's steps. Her eyes narrowed, traveling over Sara and the smile died on Sara's face.

"You must be the nurse," she said, her voice clipped. "Well, I'm back. We won't need your services anymore."

The older woman's dismissive tone set fire to the pride that still burned low inside her. Sara raised her chin. "Mr. Kinney hasn't said anything to me about leaving."

A faint flush rose in the woman's cheeks. "If you're waiting for your wage, you can sit on the back step until Mr. Kinney has finished his breakfast." She turned back to the stove, effectively dismissing Sara.

Sara's flash of spirit evaporated. She blinked and swallowed back a sudden rush of tears. It was time to return to reality. This wasn't her home.

"Very well," she said, her voice wooden.

"The porridge is ready. You might as well eat before you go." Mrs. Hobbes plopped a bowl on the table, her voice gentler now. "I'm sure Mr. Kinney won't be long."

Sara didn't want to wait for James Kinney to drop a few coins in her hand. She'd nursed Evie because she wanted to, because Evie was the closest thing to a daughter she'd ever have.

But that porridge might be all she ate today. Pride was a luxury she couldn't afford. Instead of striding out the door with her dignity intact, Sara pulled out a chair and ate her breakfast.

~~~

Pounding at the front door woke James where he'd fallen asleep, his head on the table. It was morning, judging by the light streaming through the east window. He stretched his aching shoulders, noting the distant clatter of dishes and the faint smell of coffee and sizzling sausage. Mrs. Hobbes had returned.

The knock sounded again, louder now, and he lurched to the front hall, running a hand through his tousled hair before opening the door.

Andrew Ridley stood on the front stoop, his clothes rumpled, face unshaven. "I saw your message as soon as I returned. How is Evie?"

James stepped aside and motioned for Andrew to enter. They about the same height, though the younger man was slimmer, with a natural elegance to his posture and an easy, engaging manner that drew people to him.

"She's much improved." James permitted himself a smile. "I think she's over the worst of it."

Andrew's shoulders slumped in relief. "Thank God. She's all of Amelia I have left." His eyes met James's. "All *we* have left."

James nodded once, a silent acknowledgment of the pain they shared.

"How did she catch it?" Andrew took off his tall beaver hat and shrugged out of his coat.

"She . . ." James hesitated. If he didn't tell Andrew the truth, Evie would. "She ran away last week. Ended up in Irish Town where the fever's running rampant. I brought her back straight-away, but . . ."

Andrew snorted. "I told you something like this would hap-pen." Now that his initial panic had subsided, Andrew fell back on his old confidence. "The girl runs wild. Evie should be at school."

"Evie belongs with me." James inhaled, praying for calm. "I haven't seen hide nor hair of you for weeks," he said, turning the topic. "Where have you been?"

A spark of excitement lit Andrew's face. "I've been traveling with Mackenzie."

James's stomach dropped. He hadn't expected such an open admission that the rumors were true. He gestured for Andrew to follow him into the dining room. "To what purpose?" he asked, once the door was shut.

"They've formed vigilance committees in every settlement. Dozens—hundreds of men have signed up. They're willing to do whatever it takes to form responsible government."

James shook his head. "Whatever it takes? Short of rebellion, I hope. That would be madness."

"It's not madness. It's the only way forward. There won't be a colony left for Evie's generation if things continue as they are. The governor and his cronies won't listen to reason, not when their profits are at stake."

"This is the path to ruin." James ran his fingers through his hair, searching for the words that would sway Andrew. "You know it as well as I do. Calmer heads must prevail."

"Calmer heads?" Andrew threw up his hands. "Where has that gotten us?"

"You helped me draft a letter of complaint to the House of Lords just last month. Colonel Fitzgibbon assured us it would get into the right hands in London. Surely that's a sign that Britain will listen."

Andrew snorted. "No one in the House of Lords is going to read that letter." He shook his head. "James, this is the time for action, not letters. For once in your life, stop prevaricating and take a stand. Join us."

James considered himself a calm, careful man, not given to bursts of temper. Andrew could get under his skin with a few well-chosen words. Amelia had been just the same, prodding and poking at his weaknesses until he gave in or retreated into icy silence.

Now he wondered if Andrew had a point. Perhaps what he thought was caution and good sense was a cover for his inability to act. He'd been unable to decide Evie's future for weeks and look where it got them.

He thought of Irish Town, of the poverty and despair that had followed those immigrants halfway around the world. Change *was* needed. Still, the thought of rebellion and the bloodshed that would follow sickened him. "I can't leave Evie," he muttered. "She's not well."

"You said she's better. Mrs. Hobbes can watch her for a few days." Andrew stepped closer, his eyes refusing to let James retreat. "I have supported you since you first stepped foot in this colony. We need your help."

"We?"

"I've made some friends." Andrew's chin tilted at a proud

angle. "They sought me out. Said they needed a legal mind on their side."

James bit his lip to mask his skepticism. "They know of your ties to Ballantine and the others?"

"Of course," Andrew said, his voice defensive. "I've nothing to hide."

"You don't think they could be using you to—"

"Don't be ridiculous. These are honorable men, not spies." There wasn't a flicker of doubt on Andrew's face. "Join us, James. Together, we could do so much good."

James paced to the window, staring unseeing at the street. "I *want* to do good." He turned his head to look at Andrew over his shoulder. "That's why I caution you to think this through. Rebellion . . . it's treason."

"Now is not the time for caution—" Andrew broke off, inhaling deeply. "Is that sausage?"

James suppressed a smile. For all that Andrew was a grown man of seven and twenty, he still reminded James of an impetuous boy. Perhaps a meal could mellow him when James's careful reasoning could not.

"I don't suppose you'd like to join me for breakfast?" James said.

Andrew sent him a sheepish grin. "Haven't eaten yet."

James couldn't repress an answering smile. "I'll ask Mrs. Hobbes to set another place."

He strode to the kitchen, the welcome for Mrs. Hobbes on his lips dying at the sight of Sara at the table, a bowl of porridge in front of her. She didn't look up when he entered. Instead, she seemed to shrink into her chair, her shoulders bowed down in a way he'd never seen before.

"Ah, Mr. Kinney," Mrs. Hobbes said. "I told the nurse you'd be along with her wages. She'll be leaving now that I'm back."

James froze, his eyes traveling between the two women. Mrs. Hobbes stood confident, a faint challenge in her stance while Sara O'Connor kept her chin down and her eyes trained on her breakfast.

"I see," James said, though he didn't at all. He needed to talk to Sara. Alone. "Mrs. Hobbes, welcome back. Would you set a place for Mr. Ridley? He'll be joining us for breakfast."

Mrs. Hobbes nodded and bustled off to the dining room, leaving James and Sara alone. Sara rose and carried her bowl to the sink.

"You're leaving?" he said, finding his voice.

Her brows knitted together. "I thought you wanted me to go. Mrs. Hobbes said—"

"I told Mrs. Hobbes I'd hired a nurse for Evie, nothing more." Perhaps she didn't *want* to go. He still could convince her to stay.

"Oh." Sara dropped her eyes. "Well, Evie is better. I thought I'd spare her a long farewell that would be painful to us both." She raised her eyes from the ground slowly, as though lifting something heavy. "Now that she's better, everything can go back to the way it was."

James swallowed, his throat dry as dust. She was probably right, so why did her leaving feel so wrong? "Don't you think you should wait? Just to be sure all is well?" He wondered if she heard the desperation in his voice. Sara couldn't leave, not yet, not like this. He *needed* her.

Footsteps sounded behind him. Sara glanced over his shoulder, her eyes widening a moment before she dropped her chin, hiding her expression beneath her mobcap.

"Who's this?" Andrew said from behind him.

"This is Evie's nurse, Miss O'Connor."

Andrew's gaze raked Sara from head to foot before he turned back to James with raised brows.

"You couldn't find a doctor?"

"Andrew," James said, a warning in his voice. "I owe Miss O'Connor a great debt. She saved Evie's life."

Andrew signaled his disbelief with a snort. "I very much doubt that." He turned his gaze back to Sara, assessing her in a way that made James long to knock his teeth down his throat. "Well, I suppose she'll be on her way, now that Evie's better." He motioned to the door with a faint frown of distaste.

In that moment James saw Sara through Andrew's eyes. Worn, shapeless dress, her beautiful, creamy skin and intelligent eyes hidden by a floppy mobcap in need of starch.

James had made the same hasty judgments when he'd first met Sara. Now he saw her gentle wisdom, her capable intelligence. The warmth in her eyes that drew Evie to her. Drew him closer, too.

But she was leaving, and they might never see her again. Loss, as bitter as bile, pressed on him.

"You mistake the situation, Andrew," he blurted out, his voice loud in the silent kitchen. Sara and Andrew both turned and stared at him. A trickle of sweat slid down his neck. He wasn't an impulsive man. He mulled over new cases for days. Yet now he spoke without sparing a moment to consider the consequences.

"Miss O'Connor isn't just the nurse. She's Evie's governess."

Chapter 14

Sara froze. What new turn was this? His eyes were serious, his tone as unyielding as a judge delivering a sentence. As though it had all been decided.

"James, surely not." Andrew Ridley spoke, his voice filled with horror.

Sara dragged her eyes away from James to the man beside him. The initial panic she'd felt on seeing Andrew Ridley had subsided once it became clear that he didn't recognize her. Perhaps not surprising, since the last time she'd seen him, she'd been spying on her father's guests from the upstairs landing of her home.

He was still handsome. Certainly, as a girl of fifteen, she'd thought him so. His soulful eyes and the overlong dark hair that flowed across his brow recalled every romantic hero. Today she saw another side of him, an icy disdain that judged and dismissed her on sight.

He was right, of course. The role of governess wasn't for her. Sara rose, intending to say just that until Andrew's next words froze her in her tracks.

"You don't need a governess. Evie should go to Miss Strachan's academy, just like Amelia did."

A wave of sick panic washed over Sara at the name of the school. Her year with Miss Strachan had been a nightmare. She imagined Evie under the care of that strict, supercilious woman, her actions critiqued, and her creativity and joy squashed. Even more soul-shattering than the criticism of Miss Giblin, for at least then Evie had returned to her father's love every day.

Mrs. Hobbes returned to the kitchen and sent a curious glance at the occupants. "I'll have your breakfast out in a moment, Mr. Kinney." She stopped in front of Sara. "I thought you were leaving."

Leave. Yes, she had to leave, no matter how much Evie's uncertain future might tear her heart in two.

"Wait." James grasped her elbow just as she would have turned to go. The contact shocked her into stillness. She searched James's face for a sign of his intentions. "Please, just a moment of your time, Miss O'Connor." He sent a harried glance at Mrs. Hobbes and Andrew who watched the tableau with avid curiosity, then tugged her out the back door onto the stoop.

Once they were alone, he didn't seem to know where to start. He grasped the back of his neck, his eyes searching the backyard as though the answer to his problems lay somewhere in the kitchen garden.

"I can't neglect my work much longer," he finally burst out. "I need someone to teach Evie. Keep a close eye on her. Someone who understands her."

Sara searched his face. Did he really want to hire her? It seemed unbelievable. "But before you said—"

He reached for her hands, squeezing them gently. "I didn't understand how much you meant to her until she was sick. She called your name." He shook his head. "Then you spoke French, and the poems, and . . . I realized how wrong I'd been about you."

She looked down where James's capable hands cradled hers. His long, ink-stained fingers were light as a butterfly's wing, yet they seared her right down to her toes. She felt the pull of him, drawing her in until she wanted to lean her head against his shoulder and forget her worries. There were a dozen reasons why staying was a bad idea. She was already too attached to Evie . . . and her father.

"Unless, of course," James continued, "you have another situation." He released her hands to run his fingers through his short brown hair, making it stick up in all directions and reminding Sara of his daughter. "I'm sorry. I didn't even think of that. Is your employer expecting you back?"

The thought would be laughable if it wasn't so terrifying. "No, I—I haven't found a position yet."

"Then take this one. You'd be well paid."

It was tempting, but life in the Kinney home held its dangers, too. She'd live so close to the world she once knew. What if she were recognized? Just because Andrew Ridley hadn't a clue who she was didn't mean she was safe.

"I know you're worried about Granny," he continued. "I

could send over a package every week. Meat, tea, whatever she needs."

His thoughtfulness took her breath away. They hadn't had fresh meat in years. "That's very kind, but—"

"I'm in a difficult position," he said, his voice stronger and more persuasive, as though he sensed her weakening. "A governess is hard to come by and Evie has become quite a handful. Miss Strachan's seems like my only option. Unless . . ." His eyes searched hers. "Unless you'll stay, Sara O'Connor. Please."

All her attention focused on the man in front of her, the warmth pouring out of him and the answering rush of tenderness that bubbled up inside her.

"Yes. I'll stay." She bit her lip against the rush of happiness the words unleashed.

The tension left James's body, and his smile broke out. "Thank you." He reached out for her hands again.

She tucked her hands behind her, avoiding his clasp, her joy already giving way to foreboding. The man in front of her could destroy whatever peace and contentment remained in her life and she scrambled for a way to protect her heart. "I'll need my evenings to myself, and a half day to visit Granny. And . . . and it's only until you find a proper governess. I won't promise anything beyond that."

His smile dimmed. "Very well." His voice was earnest, his eyes serious and steady on her. "But I hope you'll decide to stay."

She had to get away from the warmth radiating out of James Kinney. He was handsome enough when he was cool and logical. Smiling, he threatened to chase every coherent thought from her mind.

"I'll just go put my things away." She lifted her bag and

gestured to the back of the house. James followed her into the kitchen.

Mrs. Hobbes paused, her hand hovering over a half-filled platter of sausage.

"It's decided. Miss O'Connor will stay on as Evie's governess," James said.

"What?" Andrew Ridley's voice was incredulous.

James held up a staying hand. "Not now, Andrew."

He turned to Sara, his voice apologetic. "There's a maid's room in the attic. It's quite small, but I'm sure Mrs. Hobbes can make it comfortable."

"It will be fine." Sara wondered at her choice of words. Very little about this situation felt fine. Not Mrs. Hobbes's sidelong glances, nor Andrew Ridley's open hostility. Even James's strange about-face left her mind spinning. A week ago, he'd demanded she stay away from his daughter. Now he invited her into his home.

James gestured to the dining room as though he invited her to precede him. Sara's eyes widened. She was an employee, destined to take her meals in the kitchen, or perhaps upstairs with Evie. Not with the guests. She shook her head and stepped back until she felt the solid weight of the kitchen table behind her.

His hand dropped to his side and a frown formed on his brow. Sara turned to the housekeeper before he could protest. "Please tell me what I can do to assist you, Mrs. Hobbes." There. That ought to make her position clear to him.

Mrs. Hobbes picked up a platter loaded with sausage and eggs. "Watch the toast there." She nodded in the direction of the toasting rack and Sara hurried to the stove. From the corner of her eye, she saw James hesitate a moment longer before he followed the food into the dining room.

Sara released a long breath, knowing she'd made the right choice. If she had any hope of protecting herself, James Kinney needed to go back to his world. She'd stay here in hers.

Mrs. Hobbes returned to the kitchen. Sara risked a glance at her face, expecting to see disdain, but the woman's eyes were thoughtful. Curious, even.

Sara gave her a tentative smile. "Is my room up there?" She gestured to the narrow stairs that dropped down from the attic above the kitchen.

Her question set Mrs. Hobbes into motion. "Needs a good dusting, I imagine. It's become a storage room of sorts, but it should do." Her voice wasn't exactly warm, but Sara took heart that her open hostility had mellowed.

"I'm sure it will suit me admirably," Sara said, climbing the stairs. The ceilings were low, the air thick with the lingering smell of smoked meat. Shelves of preserves lined one wall and a bedstead sat opposite, stacked with linens. She set to work, moving the piles of fabric to a shelf. In the process, she uncovered a slim, paper-wrapped rectangle, tucked between the wall and the bed. She lifted it out, feeling the thick carved frame in her hands. A picture?

Curiosity won and she peeled back the brown paper to reveal the portrait of a woman with dark ringlets and creamy skin. She recognized Amelia Ridley from their school days, though she'd had little to do with the girls in the upper classes at Miss Strachan's. The woman in the painting was just as beautiful as Sara remembered. James Kinney had married the belle of Toronto.

If she hadn't left home, she might have become friends with Amelia. Perhaps even gone to her wedding. But by then, of course, she'd left her father's world for good.

Sara stared at the haughty tilt to the woman's chin, searching for a resemblance to Evie. It wasn't obvious, but it was there in the line of her brows and the soulful depths of her dark eyes.

Is this what it feels like to have a mother?

Evie had no sense of the woman who'd given birth to her and that broke Sara's heart. It wasn't right to keep this likeness hidden away. Sara hadn't known her mother, either, but she'd spent hours staring up at her portrait in the library and confiding all her girlish heartaches.

Sara tucked the portrait away and sat down on the bed. The emotions of the past days had left her drained and uncertain. Was she right to stay? There was Granny to consider, of course. Food, shelter, security for the coming winter. But there was another reason she'd accepted James's offer. She'd once been a lonely, motherless girl like Evie, trying to find her place in the world. For her, it had all gone horribly wrong.

But it didn't have to be that way for Evie.

~~

James came home from the courts the next day and bounded up the stairs to Evie's room. She sat in bed, her knees drawn up to support her book. As he entered, she looked up with an absent smile.

"Papa, do you know why Queen Elizabeth never married?"

He couldn't suppress his grin. It had been days since she'd

greeted him with an unanswerable question at the end of the day. His Evie was back.

"Ah, no, poppet. I'm not sure."

"Sara didn't know either." She looked up. "But she can name the reigns of all the King Henrys." Evie lifted her brows, clearly impressed. "I'm going to memorize them, too."

"Excellent." He breathed easier. For a moment, lying awake in the deep of night, he'd wondered what had come over him, handing his daughter into the charge of a woman he scarcely knew. But Evie was already happier than he'd seen her in weeks.

"I'm ready to get out of bed." Evie uttered the words like a challenge, pulling his attention back to her.

"Really?" James looked at her pale face and stalled. "What does Miss O'Connor think?"

"She said I had to ask you." Evie's lower lip jutted out in a stubborn gesture that told him more clearly than anything else that she was on the mend.

"Perhaps you can dress tomorrow if you promise to nap in the afternoon. And then the next day, you can try coming down for supper. Provided Miss O'Connor agrees."

Evie crossed her arms, none too pleased. "That's what she said, too."

"Where is your governess, by the way?"

"I'm here, sir."

A skitter of warmth shot through him at the sound of her low voice. He whirled to see her standing in the doorway, hands folded in front.

"Was there something you wished to speak to me about?" She didn't raise her eyes.

James found himself suddenly, irrationally, annoyed at her

formality, at the way she spoke to him like she was a servant, instead of a—a what? A friend? She was the governess, and if he wasn't such a fool, he'd thank her for keeping a distance. That night when they had been partners, saving Evie's life, was past.

"Yes, as a matter of fact. Evie has been telling me she'd like to get out of bed. Perhaps we can discuss this further. Downstairs."

"Very well, sir." She disappeared down the hall.

"Papa, are you mad at Sara?" Evie's anxious voice stopped him at the door.

"Of course not."

"Then why do you talk to her like that? In your courtroom voice?"

This child noticed everything. "Well, I *am* a barrister. I guess I just talk like that."

Sara waited in the front hall. Her eyes shot up for a moment, colliding with his before darting back down to her feet.

"Come to the parlor," he said.

"Couldn't you just tell me here?" The words rushed out of her, and she bit her lip.

"It will only take a moment." He heard the return of his barrister's voice.

She flushed and followed him into the room. He motioned to the settee and took a seat on the chair furthest from her. "How is Evie's recovery? Do you think she's ready to be up and about?"

She smiled, some of the tension leaving her shoulders. "It never ceases to amaze me, how quickly children recover. I don't see any harm in her getting up tomorrow." She glanced at him uncertainly. "Of course, you could have the doctor come, if you want to be sure."

"Dr. Whittaker will come when he is able." He willed her to meet his eyes. "Until then, I trust your opinion, Sa—" He cleared his throat to cover his slip. "Miss O'Connor."

She smiled, and he glimpsed the woman beneath the formal facade. His breath caught. When they let their guard down, when concern for Evie outweighed all the barriers, there was a thread of connection between them that tightened every time she was near. His legs itched to rise and join her on the settee, his fingers burned with the need to hold her hand and make the connection something tangible.

She cleared her throat and looked down, breaking the spell. James took a shaky breath. This was insanity.

"Mr. Kinney?"

He looked up, his heart starting to pound at the hesitation in her voice. Was there something she wasn't telling him about Evie's recovery? "What is it?"

"Nothing serious," she assured him. "It's just . . . well, I found something. Something Evie might like, and I was wondering . . ."

James nodded, urging her to continue. If he'd overlooked something Evie needed, he wouldn't hesitate to supply it. Surely, she knew that.

"There was a picture in my room. A portrait of Evie's mother, I think. Would you consider hanging it—"

"No." Though he hadn't raised his voice, the word echoed in the room. "I don't want her growing up with painful reminders all around her."

She straightened, her chin taking on a stubborn tilt. "I never knew my mother, but any mention of her gave me a great deal of comfort."

"The painting will only remind Evie of what she doesn't

have." He crossed his arms. His memories of Amelia were a blend of love, loss, and regret that he didn't want to relive every time he saw the painting.

She crossed her arms. "I disagree. It will give her a connection to her past." Apparently, she only played the role of servant when it suited her.

Feelings he'd buried for years rose, tightening his chest. He'd loved Amelia, once upon a time. Thought she loved him in return. It took him months to realize the woman he'd married was more concerned with impressing her society friends than the love he offered. He'd foolishly thought a baby would make her happy. But the birth of the child he'd desperately wanted had killed her.

He swallowed down the memories and focused on anger, a much more manageable state of mind. "Miss O'Connor, I beg you to remember your place. You are her governess, not mistress of this home." He winced at the ice in his voice, but it was better he stopped her now. "I know what's best for my daughter."

Silence reigned for a long moment before she ducked her head in a gesture he was coming to detest. "I'm sorry, sir. I didn't mean to speak out of turn."

Her voice was wooden, as though his anger hadn't affected her, but her hands told another story, clutching the skirt of her gown until her knuckles were white and drawing his attention to the worn fabric. He remembered the reason he'd wanted to speak to her in the first place and he cleared his throat, glad for an excuse to change the topic.

"There's something else. I'd like to give you an advance on your salary. You ought to have a new gown. Something more fitting for a governess."

Her chin shot up and a slow wave of red washed up her cheeks. He realized in an instant he'd gone about the thing all wrong. Shamed her.

He fished in his pocket for a coin, searching for the words that would mend his error. "Not that there's anything wrong with your . . ." He gestured helplessly at her worn gown. It was clean, but threadbare, with no pretensions to cut or style.

Pressing his lips shut, he held out the coin.

She hesitated. He watched her fingers clench as she drew in a breath. With a visible effort, she raised her hand for the coin.

"Thank you, sir," she said, bobbing a curtsy.

The curtsy bothered him more than anything else. "It's the least I can do. You saved my daughter's life." Emotion roughened his voice. Did she think about that night as often as he did?

She tucked the coin in her pocket and lifted her chin.

"You didn't have to pay me for that."

Chapter 15

"My dear Miss Kinney, what a pleasure it is to see you again." Sara stood in the doorway to the parlor as though she had just arrived for a social call. They'd been practicing social graces all week and it was time to put Evie to the test.

Evie giggled, then swept Sara a curtsy. "How kind of you to call, Miss O'Connor."

She plunked herself down on her chair and reached for a biscuit from the tray. Sara cleared her throat. Evie froze, her eyes rushing to Sara's face. Sara nodded meaningfully to the settee.

Evie jumped up. "Won't you sit down?"

Sara inclined her head and swept into the room. Evie's eyes strayed to the treats once again, but she resolutely turned her head to Sara.

"We are having very fine weather today," Evie said.

Sara's lips twitched at the earnest expression on Evie's face. "Indeed. Quite warm for November."

"I trust you've continued in good health?" Evie infused just enough boredom into her voice to mimic the haughtiest debutante.

Sara tried unsuccessfully to stifle a snort of amusement. Evie's face broke into a smile, and they dissolved into giggles.

"It must be so boring to be a lady," Evie said after they caught their breath. "Don't they ever talk about anything real?"

Sara thought about the conversation last week in this room. With James. She'd tried to talk about something real, but James Kinney hadn't wanted to hear it. She looked down at her hands, folded in her lap. "Not often. Though once you get good at it, you can say a lot without any words at all."

"What a waste of time." Evie flopped against the settee. "Why can't I just say what I mean?"

Because she'd be vulnerable. She'd get hurt. "Well, we must be mindful of others' feelings, of course."

"I wouldn't say anything *mean*. But why can't I talk about laws or history or the books I like?"

Sara couldn't meet the look of entreaty in her charge's eyes. "I don't know," she answered finally. "Young ladies can't talk about things like that, at least not with acquaintances. But you'll meet girls who will become friends. You'll be able to talk to them."

"Will I?" Evie toyed with her sash, twisting the loose ribbon around her finger. "Is that what happened to you? You found friends?"

"Uh—well, not exactly." She ducked her head, avoiding Evie's searching eyes until she could recover her poise. "That is, I'm just a laundress. I don't need to make social calls."

"Then how do you know how to do it?"

She'd prepared herself for a question like this, knowing Evie would eventually wonder. "I lived in a grand house when I was . . . younger. I heard many such conversations." That much, at least, was true.

"Well, I think it's stupid. Talking all day about nothing."

The front door opened, and Sara tensed. James must be home early from his chambers. She'd managed to avoid him the past few days, slipping away to help in the kitchen as soon as she heard his tread in the hall.

There was no escaping him now. She smoothed the front of her new dress, a blue brushed cotton with a high neck and long, narrow sleeves. Simple to the point of severity, but it fit her well. In this dress, she became a lady again.

Mrs. Hobbes had surprised her by offering to help when she'd come across Sara attempting to draw out a pattern on the kitchen table. With the two of them sewing every spare minute, they'd finished the gown faster than Sara had dared to hope. Mrs. Hobbes had waved aside her thanks, muttering darkly about the unsuitability of a governess who dressed like a scullery maid.

The parlor door swung open. "If you'll just wait here, Mr. Ridley, I'm sure it won't be long before Mr. Kinney is—oh." Mrs. Hobbes spoke over her shoulder, coming to an abrupt stop when she saw the occupants of the parlor. "Excuse me, Miss O'Connor. No one informed me the front parlor was occupied." Her tone indicated this was an unforgivable oversight. Sara rose to her feet and tried to look repentant.

"I'm sorry, Mrs. Hobbes. Evie and I were just finishing our tea. We'll be on our way." She'd crawl out a window rather than be stuck with Andrew Ridley.

"Uncle Andrew!" Evie squealed and darted around Mrs. Hobbes to embrace the tall figure. "I haven't seen you in so long."

Andrew Ridley bent over her hand in a courtly bow. "How's my little princess?"

Evie giggled and tugged him to Sara.

"This is my governess, Sa—Miss O'Connor."

"We've met," he said, not sparing a glance for Sara.

Sara cast her eyes about, wishing there was a discreet way to disappear from Andrew Ridley's presence. For his part, he ignored Sara and allowed Evie to lead him to an empty chair.

"Come and have some tea. And cakes," Evie said. He paused in front of the chair, long enough for Sara to realize he had no intention of sitting while Sara stood, poised for flight. She slid into a corner of the settee, wishing the ground would swallow her up.

"You're looking pale, princess. Shouldn't you be resting?" He spoke to Evie, but the words were directed at Sara. Questioning her competence.

"Evie has been improving by leaps and bounds, sir," she said. "And she's careful to rest every afternoon."

Andrew Ridley's eyes met hers and he lifted an eyebrow. "Indeed?"

Sara flushed and straightened her spine. Let the man see for himself what Evie was capable of. "Evie, why don't you prepare the tea?"

She regretted the words as soon as they left her mouth. She ought to have made some excuse to leave the room and avoid the man. Instead, she'd drawn his scrutiny down on them both.

His cool gaze swept over her before turning to Evie. "Yes, Evie, please, do the honors."

Evie's lips firmed with determination as she began the lengthy ritual. Sara bit her tongue more than once, contenting herself with encouraging smiles and nods when Evie sent panicked glances her way. None of the interplay was lost on Andrew Ridley.

Evie dribbled splotches of tea twice across the pristine tablecloth, but she managed the process well. Very well. Andrew leaned back in his chair with his cup.

"Well done, Evie," he said with a warm smile to his niece. "Where did you learn to pour? Did Mrs. Hobbes teach you?"

Evie's forehead wrinkled in confusion. "Sara—er, Miss O'Connor taught me."

"Really?" Andrew Ridley's attention turned to Sara, examining her like a specimen in a jar. "Miss O'Connor is full of surprises."

"Indeed, she is." James stood in the doorway, arms crossed. His narrow gaze settled on Andrew.

"Papa!" Evie rushed over to her father, and he bent down and pressed a kiss to her forehead.

"Hello, poppet. Having a tea party, are we?" His eyes scanned the tableau in front of him and came to rest on Sara.

She forced herself to meet his gaze with a bland smile, refusing to speculate on his reaction to her new gown. Sensing Andrew Ridley watching them, her eyes dropped to the cup in her hands, but not before she saw James's gaze shift to Andrew with a frown. She had the fleeting impression he was ready to slay all her dragons, even Andrew Ridley.

"Papa," Evie called, turning their attention back to her. "I'm learning how to pour." Her expression turned serious. "Will you join us?"

"Now that you mention it, I could use a cup of tea." James turned to his daughter, a smile softening his face.

His eyes settled on the only empty seat, beside Sara on the settee. He took a step forward and Sara braced herself. She hadn't been this close to him all week, not since he'd dropped a coin into her hand and told her to make herself presentable. She forced her shoulders to face straight ahead. But her body was only too aware that James Kinney was going to sit beside her.

And she wanted him to.

~~~

The settee wasn't large enough for two adults determined to keep a safe distance between them. James angled his body away from Sara, training his eyes on his daughter.

"How do you like your tea, Mr. Kinney?" Evie asked, as though she didn't know he only took a splash of milk.

James answered absently, his mind still reeling at the sight of Sara in her new gown, minus her mobcap. It was a simple dress, without an inch of ruffle or lace. Exactly what a governess would wear. So why did his eyes slide back to her and linger on the elegant line of her throat and the graceful curve of her hand resting on the arm of the settee? He'd only ever seen her wearing a shapeless sack and a dowdy mobcap. This woman beside him seemed someone else altogether. A lady.

"Evie, why don't you tell your Papa about your day?" Sara said suddenly. "Trade seats with me. I'll finish the tea."

Sara was already rising out of her seat as though she couldn't get away from him fast enough. Evie swooped in beside him, curling to his side and jabbering on about her lessons. Andrew peppered her with questions and the two were soon off in a lively debate about the merits of Oliver Cromwell. James watched Sara, the conversation fading into the background.

She prepared the tea with an efficiency of movement that was beautiful to behold, all the while listening to Evie with an indulgent smile. Even Andrew stopped midsentence to watch her, his eyes widening in disbelief.

James had long suspected there was more to Sara than she let on, but to be so well-versed in such a ritual bespoke more than just a talent for mimicking her betters. She'd prepared tea, and often, though such a task was usually reserved for the lady of the house.

"Mr. Kinney?" Sara's voice recalled him to his senses. She held out the cup.

"Thank you," he murmured, taking the saucer.

"Do you like Sara's new dress, Papa?" Evie asked. Sara's cup clattered in its saucer. Evie sent her a guilty glance. "Miss O'Connor, I mean."

"I—it's a very nice dress," he muttered, taking a gulp of tea and burning his tongue in the process. He felt the weight of Andrew's gaze on him, searching and suspicious.

"Well, it's time I must be leaving," Andrew announced, rising to his feet. "James, if you'll see me out, there are a few things I'd like to discuss."

"Certainly."

It wasn't until they were at the front door that Andrew turned to face him, his eyes piercing. "I don't know what is going on in this house, James Kinney, but you'd best watch yourself."

He was used to Andrew's hyperbole, but his words still took

James aback. "I can't imagine what you mean," he said, his voice bland.

"You know exactly what I mean. I see the way you watch her. To think I'd live to see Amelia's place usurped by a—" He pressed his lips together. "It doesn't bear thinking."

James was caught between denial and mortification that his attraction to Sara had been so obvious. "Your suspicions do you a discredit, Andrew," he said, opting for denial. "I have no intentions toward Miss O'Connor. If that is indeed what you are referring to."

His words seemed to placate his friend. Andrew's eyes searched his face. "See that you don't forget it." He edged closer as they walked down the path to where he'd tethered his horse. "Listen, I didn't come here today to lecture you on governesses." His eyes began to crackle with excitement. "There's a meeting tomorrow. I want you to come with me." James's heart started to pound. It was the opportunity he'd been waiting for. A chance to find out what was really going on. "We could leave as soon as the afternoon trial is done," Andrew continued. "It's not far. Just north of here at Montgomery's Tavern."

James wanted to shake some sense into his friend. Reasoned letters and careful maneuvering were the ways to effect change, not a meeting of hotheads filled with alcohol and fueled by a sense of injustice. But he needed to show Andrew he was open to change and willing to hear every side to the story. He nodded. "Yes, I'll come."

Andrew grinned, and James caught a glimpse of the open, generous young man who'd welcomed a newcomer into his life. Who'd given James a family again.

"Excellent. I knew you'd change your mind." He rolled his

eyes with the familiarity of a longtime friend. "You've always needed time to think things through." With a smooth motion, Andrew mounted his horse and spurred him down the street, as impatient as ever, weaving his way between the carts and pedestrians.

Filled with misgivings, James made his way back to the parlor. He paused a moment to observe Evie and Sara undetected. Evie giggled as Sara drank an exaggerated sip of tea, her pinky finger in the air, and took the tiniest bite of a biscuit.

"Why can't I just eat as many biscuits as I want? There are lots on the plate."

The smile left Sara's face. "Indeed, my love, but you wouldn't feel well after a whole plate of biscuits. Besides, many children have never tasted a biscuit. Doesn't seem fair that you should eat so many, does it?"

"Why haven't they any biscuits?"

"Sugar is expensive."

"Oh." Evie sank back in her chair, her face thoughtful.

"Come, let's take the tea things to the kitchen. I'm sure Mrs. Hobbes could use some help with supper, too."

James backed away from the parlor before either occupant noticed him. One minute she poured tea like a countess, the next she championed the poor. Who was this woman?

Chapter 16

"Higher, Sara!"

Sara gave Evie a final push and she went sailing on her swing with a whoop of joy. The sun was bright, warming the chilly air and prompting Sara and Evie to head outside to the maple in the front yard.

Sara kept an eye on the street, ready to duck inside as soon as James came into view. It wasn't that she was afraid to face him. Quite the opposite. She wanted to share her thoughts and bask in his conversation, as they'd done by Evie's bedside.

But she couldn't allow the comfort of her situation to lull her into complacency. One misstep and she'd be out on the street again.

A horse trotted up to the front gate and a man dismounted. She saw at a glance it wasn't James, but the man seemed familiar.

His elegant wool suit was immaculate despite the dust of the road, a languid grace in his stance that reminded her of—

"Good afternoon. Is Kinney here?" He finished tying his horse to the hitching post and opened the gate.

She shuddered as she saw his face. The marble-smooth skin and odd, pale eyes hadn't changed a whit. Twelve years ago, Stephen Osgoode had destroyed her life. Broken her father's trust and pushed her out of her home forever.

All because she'd refused to marry him.

"You, there." He motioned them closer. Evie skipped to the fence, but Sara didn't budge, pressing her back into the tree.

Osgoode looked down at Evie. "Where is your papa?" He spoke with the forced joviality of one who wasn't comfortable with children.

"I . . . He's at the courthouse, I think." Evie took a step back, eyes wary.

"Really?" He didn't sound convinced. "He didn't go to a meeting today?" His voice was unrelenting. Sara could well imagine the power he wielded in the courtroom.

"I don't know." Evie shrugged, her usually open expression closed. Sara understood her reluctance. There was a narrow focus to Osgoode's questions that had nothing to do with casual curiosity. Was Osgoode a threat to James in some way? She shivered. He was a dangerous man to cross.

Osgoode pointed his riding crop in Sara's direction. "Who's that?" Sara's heart stuttered.

"She's my governess."

"Ah, the governess."

Sara ducked her head, praying the distance and the shadow of the maple tree would obscure her. Thank God she'd been too afraid of grass stains to wear her new gown outside. She released a slow breath as his attention switched back to Evie. He didn't recognize her.

Osgoode twirled his riding crop, his eyes scanning the yard as though searching for clues. His focus suddenly shifted back to Evie. "When do you expect him home?"

"I don't know." Evie paused, her head tilting to the side. "Would you push me on the swing?"

For a heart-stopping moment, Sara wondered if he would. Osgoode sent a horrified glance at the swing. "No, I . . . I've things to do. I must—good day." He backed away to where his mount was tethered and swung up into the saddle without a backward glance. Evie, bright girl that she was, said the one thing guaranteed to get rid of him.

She trotted to Sara's side. "I don't like that man," she said once he'd ridden away. "He reminds me of Brian de Bois-Guilbert."

Sara made a noncommittal sound in her throat at the mention of the villain of *Ivanhoe*. Evie didn't know the half of it. She took a breath to quiet her still-racing heart. "Does he work with your Papa?"

Evie shrugged, wrinkling up her nose. "I don't know. He's never come to our house before."

Sara's shoulders relaxed. Not a close connection. From the few clues he'd let drop, she'd pictured James a reformer while Stephen Osgoode had been a Tory through and through. She couldn't imagine that had changed. It was part of what her father had admired in him.

She bit her lip, realizing the delicate line she was treading. Toronto society was small. James Kinney would have never hired her if he'd known the scandal she carried. A wellborn woman who'd run off with a stable boy was not governess material.

Evie yawned. She was still recovering, though she considered any time spent resting in bed a sort of punishment. In lieu of a nap, Sara spread an old quilt in the sun and forced enthusiasm into her voice. "Now, what shall we read, my love?"

Instead of pouncing on her favorite from the stack, Evie plopped down on the ground, absently tracing the pattern of the quilt with her finger.

"I don't care. You pick," she said, lying back on the blanket.

"Are you feeling well?" Sara studied Evie's face, feeling a twinge of concern. "Perhaps you should lie down."

Evie's head jerked up. "I'm fine."

"Well, are you sure you don't want to pick the book? You usually have an opinion."

"How 'bout that bloke Ivanhoe?" A loud whisper floated across the yard.

"What on earth?" Sara scanned the fence along the side of the property. A dark shadow was curled up on the other side, barely perceptible through the iron slats. "Henry, is that you?"

There was a long pause while the shadow through the fence was motionless. "Aye," he said finally.

"What are you doing here?"

"Coming every day for nigh on a week, I have."

Sara glanced at Evie. She sat up straight, her little body crackling with excitement—but not surprise. She shot a hesitant look at Sara, one that spoke volumes about what her charge had been keeping from her.

"You knew he came?"

Evie looked down with a reluctant nod. "I saw him through the window. Brought him out some biscuits."

Sara thought back to the many times Evie had asked to be excused. To visit the privy, or so Sara thought.

"Look," Henry continued, finally giving up any attempt to keep his voice down, "there ain't much time left before Rawley wakes up from his nap and takes to wondering where I be. Can't you just read?"

Sara hesitated. James Kinney might not like it. Then again, it wasn't as though she'd invited the boy. One more look at Evie's face, eager and hopeful, and she made up her mind and opened *Ivanhoe*. "Where were we?" she said, flipping through the pages.

"About to start the tournament," Henry said.

"I've been telling him all about it," Evie explained. She turned to Henry. "Come over here with us."

"I be just fine here."

"Please?" Evie changed tacks, her voice cajoling. "I'll share my biscuits with you."

Henry made no response. Sara motioned Evie closer with a conspiratorial wink. She began to read in a low voice, ensuring Henry couldn't catch every word. He soon stood up and placed his hands on the pickets. In one fluid motion, he vaulted over the fence and came to lean against the tree behind them.

Sara finished the tournament scene with a flourish and Henry forgot himself enough to let out a whoop of approval when the mysterious Desdichado arrived to rescue Ivanhoe and vanquish every knight in evil Prince John's retinue. He dropped to the quilt and helped himself to a biscuit, listening while Evie prattled on about Desdichado's probable identity.

Henry's presence enlivened the little girl. As much as Sara

worked to make lessons interesting, she was no replacement for a friend Evie's age. But what would James Kinney think of a stable boy befriending his daughter? The gate slammed shut and Sara realized she was about to find out.

James made his way toward the group on the quilt, his serious gaze moving from Evie to Sara and coming to rest on Henry. "We have a visitor, I see."

"I's just leaving, sir." Henry doffed his dusty cap and darted around James to the front gate.

"Wait," Evie called. "Come back tomorrow. Sara can read us the next chapter."

Henry froze midstep and looked back over his shoulder. "Rawley keeps me hopping most days. Not sure if I'll be back." He spoke slowly, as though he were testing the response.

"I'm surprised he ever lets you out of his sight." James's voice held a question.

"Well, he do like his naps. He don't care what I do then, as long as my stalls are clean."

"Hmmm, I see." James rubbed his chin, staring down the street in the direction of Cooper's Inn.

Sara bent to pick up the blanket and began to fold it with careful precision. Henry was just a little boy who needed love and companionship. Not so different from Evie, but she wasn't certain if James Kinney would see it that way.

"He really likes *Ivanhoe*, Papa." Evie's voice broke into the tension. "He could help me learn my lessons, too, right, Sara?"

"Well, I—" Sara darted a glance at James, but his face gave nothing away. She'd need to get him alone and explain how this friendship benefitted Evie. From the corner of her eye, she saw Henry creep toward the gate.

"Henry!" James called, stopping the boy in his tracks before he could make his escape. Evie looked up at her father in surprise. Sara, too, held her breath.

James jogged to Henry's side, bending over to say a few words in the boy's ear. Henry nodded, looking up into James's face for a long moment. Then he slipped through the gate with a final pat on the back from James.

"Evie," James said, returning to where they stood under the tree. "Do you suppose Mrs. Hobbes has any more biscuits?" He looked down at the empty plate in Evie's hand with a meaningful lift to his brows.

Evie nodded, sending Sara an encouraging smile as though she knew what the adults were about to discuss, then darted to the kitchen. Sara lifted her chin, holding the folded blanket to her like a shield. She'd calmly explain the advantages Henry's friendship brought Evie and let James make his decision. It was as simple as that.

"Henry came uninvited?" James's question came quick and sharp as soon as Evie was out of earshot.

Her hackles rose at the skepticism in his voice. "I had nothing to do with it, if that's what you're asking. Neither did I discourage him from joining us." She took a breath. "Evie needs to be around children her age," she continued, softening her tone. "Henry is good for her."

"I wouldn't have chosen Henry as an ideal companion for my daughter."

No daughter of mine will join herself to a common stable boy. What's his name? What's his family? What, no answer for me? He's nothing, that's why. You associate with him, and you'll be nothing to me as well. As if you've never been born.

Sara swallowed. The words were as sharp and poisonous now as they'd been years ago. In that moment, Sara forgot all about keeping her head down and minding her place. "So, Henry is a fine lad when he helps you out of a tricky spot, but not good enough to associate with your daughter?"

"That's not—

"Yes, I understand. Blood will tell, and all that." She didn't try to stem the sarcasm in her voice. "It's a wonder you let your daughter within ten yards of *me*." Sara turned on her heel and marched to the door. Through the haze of anger, she registered that James was following her, but she refused to slow her steps.

"Miss O'Connor. Sara. Wait—" He reached out, his fingers encircling her wrist, bringing her to a stop. He swung her about to face him. "You misunderstand me. Perhaps a few months ago, I would have judged and dismissed Henry on sight. But I've talked to the boy. He's clever. Cares about Evie, too, more than those Cooper girls ever did." He released her to run his fingers through his hair. "I thought it over these past few days, all the mistakes I've made. I tried to do what was right, what I thought her mother would have wanted." James stepped closer, all but forcing her to look him in the face. "But I went about it all wrong. Look what happened at the inn."

Sara swallowed, the rush of anger evaporating in the face of James's admission. "Well . . . I heard the Goblin did come highly recommended."

A tentative smile curled the corners of his mouth. "She was a tyrant. And I might never have figured it out if it weren't for you."

Sara was speechless. James Kinney, successful barrister, was admitting he'd been *wrong*?

James cleared his throat. "I told Henry he was welcome here, as long as he didn't shirk his responsibilities. I might drop a word in Rawley's ear, too. Make sure the lad doesn't get himself in trouble. That is, if you don't mind another student?"

"No," she said. A funny warmth bloomed in her chest. "I don't mind."

When they'd first met, she'd thought James Kinney was as much a snob as Andrew Ridley or Stephen Osgoode. Yet he surprised her at every turn with openness and generosity that she'd not expected from a barrister.

The thought left her shaky and uncertain. James Kinney was still part of the world that had rejected her and made no room for Colin. Only time would tell if he were truly a man she could trust.

~~~

"Papa," Evie said over supper. "Might we play a game tonight?"

James looked up from his pudding, surprised. Parlor games were usually Uncle Andrew's territory.

"A game?"

"From my girl's book. You said we could try the handker-chief game the next time Uncle Andrew came."

"Uncle Andrew's not—"

But she'd already darted from the table. James sat back, taking a sip of his tea. Evie was right. There was no sense waiting for Andrew.

He'd ridden to Montgomery's Tavern that afternoon only to find it deserted. No word from Andrew, no sign of a meeting anywhere. He couldn't believe Andrew had deliberately misled him, but there was no other explanation, was there?

Two sets of footsteps soon came down the hall. A moment later, Evie peeked her head into the dining room. "Come to the parlor, Papa. We're ready."

James jumped up and pulled a clean handkerchief from his pocket, ignoring the way his heart gave a leap. He entered the parlor, remembering at the last moment to slow his steps to a natural pace, his eyes seeking Sara out. She sat on the settee, all her concentration focused on the book on her lap. She looked up at him in surprise.

"Evie, I thought you said—" She broke off, looking away and biting her lip. He brushed aside the spurt of disappoint-ment. She hadn't thought he would come. Well, that explained how Evie got her to agree to a parlor game when she so rarely left the kitchen in the evenings.

"Papa, you must stand here while we hold the corners of the handkerchief. When you say, 'Hold fast,' we let go. And when you say, 'Let go,' we hold on." Evie shrugged. "Doesn't sound that hard."

But it turned out to be harder than she thought, doing exactly the opposite of what he told them. Evie soon collapsed into giggles.

"You win, Sara. Now it's my turn to give the orders," she announced, catching her breath. "Papa, you hold two corners."

As James edged closer, the smile on Sara's face faded. She kept her eyes glued to her hands. They stood only the width of a handkerchief apart. So close, he could smell the hint of roses in her hair and count the faint sprinkle of freckles across her nose. He must have been mad to agree to this game.

A crease formed between her brows, and it soon became apparent she'd lost her former concentration. He would certainly be winning if he weren't too distracted by her nearness to focus on Evie's commands.

"Let go," Evie said.

They both released the cloth. James bent to catch a corner at the same time Sara reached down. Their fingers tangled together as they grabbed for the falling square of fabric. A jolt of awareness shot up his arm and spread through his body, leaving his heart pounding and all his attention centered on the feel of her fingers entwined with his.

He commanded his hand to let go. Instead, his fingers curled around hers and his thumb rubbed across the smooth skin on the back of her hand. Her breath caught and she looked up, her eyes wide and wary. He had a sudden wild urge to pull her closer, wrap his arms around her and lose himself in her softness. Sara tugged harder and James dropped her hand and took a hasty step back.

"You two are so slow," Evie said in exasperation. "We'd better try a different game." Evie darted to the door. "Could you pick it out? I'm going to fetch a plate of biscuits."

"Oh, but I—" Sara's hesitation was lost in the flurry of Evie's movement as she darted off to the kitchen, leaving the two of them standing in an uncomfortable silence.

Sara moved to the hearth and stood with her back to him, staring into the flames. He remembered another evening when they'd worked together in the glow of the fire. Shared their lives. Now there was a distance between them he didn't like. He wanted the laundress Sara O'Connor back.

"James," she said, turning suddenly. After days of avoiding him, the intensity of her direct gaze made his breath catch. He wondered if she realized she'd used his given name. "A man came here today."

Her words brought an abrupt end to his wandering thoughts. "What did he want?" He took a step closer, scanning her face as his heart pumped. "Did something happen?"

"No, no, nothing like that. He . . . he wanted to know your whereabouts. Seemed quite insistent on it." She paused but he kept his lips sealed. The less she knew of rebellions and Andrew Ridley, the better.

"Did he leave a name?"

She seemed on the verge of speaking, but then closed her mouth and shook her head. "What did he look like?"

"Tall," she muttered. "Pale hair and eyes . . ." She gave a tiny shudder, the movement so slight he wouldn't have noticed if he hadn't had all his attention trained on her.

Osgoode. If the man had dared to—"You're certain he didn't harm you in any way?"

"No. He . . . I just—I didn't like the look of him. I was worried." She shrugged, looking down as a hint of color tinted her cheeks. "I just thought you should know."

He wondered how much he should share with her. "Probably just an anxious client," he said, opting for caution. "I'm sure it's nothing to worry about."

She was completely still for a long moment. Then she raised her chin and looked at him. He almost took a step back at the raw emotion in her eyes. "Be careful. He's a dangerous man." She bit her lip, turning to stare at the fire. "That is, he seemed like a man you wouldn't want to cross."

James tilted his head. Most people couldn't see past Stephen

Osgoode's suave exterior, but Sara was perceptive. A good woman to have in his corner.

"I'll be fine," he said. "I'm a barrister, remember? I'm good at getting out of trouble."

Their eyes met, hers soft and luminous in the evening shadows. He watched the tremulous smile on her lips and felt the answering smile stretch his face. She tilted her chin up and drew closer. Or was he drawing closer to her?

They sprang apart at the sound of Evie's footsteps in the hall. James ran a hand through his hair.

Beside him, Sara expelled a shaky breath. "I—I don't think I'll play again, after all. Good night. I'll see you in the morning," she said as she passed Evie in the hall, disappearing into the kitchen before he could respond.

Good thing, because he still didn't trust his voice. Sara's presence in his life upended all his certainties. It wasn't only Evie who came alive in her presence. He should be worrying about Andrew Ridley's whereabouts and threats of violence. But all he could think of was her.

He was drawn to her, that was clear. He wanted to follow the thread of connection between them and see where it led, but that was a fool's errand. She was his daughter's governess. Pursuing her would bring scandal down upon them all. Besides, he wasn't husband material. His marriage to Amelia had taught him that much.

He'd controlled himself before, buckled down and buried his passions. Learned how to live without the love or companionship of a partner. He could do it again.

Chapter 17

Church was a mistake. Sara realized it as soon as they came through the doors.

It was Mrs. Hobbes who had all but herded her out the door. "It's the Sabbath," she'd said when Sara attempted to sneak back to her room after breakfast.

"Oh, but I don't think—"

"We all go to Sunday service." Mrs. Hobbes's voice brooked no argument.

Sara fetched her bonnet and set off beside Mrs. Hobbes, a few steps behind James and Evie. That disastrous moment in the parlor yesterday evening had only reinforced the need to keep her distance. Her heart had been frozen so long, she'd foolishly thought herself impervious to attraction. It was humbling to realize how susceptible she was to a handsome face and a few kind words. Another minute alone with James and she might have been tempted to step into the circle of his arms.

St. Andrew's was smaller than the imposing church she'd attended with her father, the facade a warm plastered brick instead of towering limestone. She let out a long breath. She was unlikely to see anyone who would recognize her.

The glare of curious eyes burned into her back as she sat in James's pew, Evie between them. She kept her eyes on the ground in front of her and her face shielded by the straw brim of her bonnet. The reverend rose and began the service, the words so familiar, they were part of her very bones.

"The Lord also will be a refuge for the oppressed, a refuge in times of trouble." The minister's voice pierced her fog, the words calling back to another time, a time she'd prayed expecting an answer. "And they that know thy name will put their trust in thee: for thou, Lord, hast not forsaken them that seek thee."

Church had once been her refuge. Outside of books, it was the only place her child's heart had found love and comfort. But she'd turned her back on this place when Colin died. When God had turned his back on her.

Sara inhaled sharply, earning a glance from Evie. She forced a smile and turned her attention back to the sermon. She shouldn't put her trust in anyone. Not God. Not even a sweet little girl named Evie.

Her only thought after the service was escape, but they were hemmed in by congregants greeting each other and catching up on the news of the week.

"I heard he'd taken her on." A familiar voice slid across the aisle, chilling Sara.

Mrs. Cooper.

There was no way to avoid her. Sara was trapped between Mrs. Hobbes, who waited for her turn to shake the minister's hand, and James, deep in conversation with the man in the next pew.

Mrs. Cooper leaned closer to the woman beside her. "Can you imagine, putting your child's life in the hands of a laundress?"

Evie's hand slipped into hers. Sara looked down. Evie smiled up at her and rolled her eyes. Warmth entered Sara's frozen limbs, warmth that started where her hand connected to Evie's and spread to lodge somewhere in her chest, rich and sweet.

"Don't know what they would have done without her, and that's the truth." Mrs. Hobbes directed her words across the aisle where Mrs. Cooper and her cronies stood. The curious eyes of the ladies turned to Sara as Mrs. Hobbes told the story of Evie's near brush with death.

Sara gripped the back of the pew in front of her, unable to credit what she was hearing. Evie's support was endearing but hardly surprising. But to have the suspicious Mrs. Hobbes defend her was something else entirely.

Finally, they made it to the street. Evie turned to Sara. "Are you hungry? Mrs. Hobbes gets a half day today, so we go to the Inn for dinner. Come on." She set off in the direction of Cooper's Inn, pulling Sara behind her.

"Oh, no, I couldn't possibly . . ." Her stomach tightened just thinking of the gossip if she were seen sitting down to dinner with Evie and James. And in Cooper's Inn, of all places.

"Evie." The edge of warning in James's deep voice brought Evie to a stop. "It's also Sara's half day. She no doubt has things she'd like to do."

Sara grasped the excuse like a lifeline. "Yes, indeed." She was planning to visit Granny, but she hesitated to mention it lest Evie would want to come. She couldn't picture James Kinney allowing that. "I'll . . . see you later. Enjoy your dinner."

She fetched the sack of supplies she'd purchased with the money left over from her dress. Tea and biscuits, soft bread and a wheel of cheese.

Mrs. Hobbes looked up from her seat at the hearth as Sara entered, her gaze as guarded and assessing as ever.

"Thank you . . . for what you did." Sara surprised herself at the words that burst out of her mouth. A frozen part of Sara's heart had thawed at Mrs. Hobbes's defense. Friendship. She'd almost forgotten what it felt like.

No smile softened the woman's features. "I won't have gossip about my lamb. She's got a hard enough go as it is."

"Well, I appreciated your words."

"To think, we trusted that woman with our Evie." Mrs. Hobbes continued as though Sara hadn't spoken. "I encouraged it, you know, her taking classes there." Sara eased into a chair, not taking her eyes from Mrs. Hobbes. "Almost broke her spirit." The housekeeper paused, turning her attention back to her tea. "It doesn't look right, a young thing like you staying with no mistress in the house, but I'll do my best to put a good face on it." She sent Sara a fierce glare. "I've never seen Evie as happy as she is now. I don't want her heart broken." There was a warning in her voice, a reserve in her manner that didn't offend Sara. In a way, it drew her closer, this shared desire to protect one lovable, motherless girl.

"I don't want that either," Sara managed, her throat clogged with emotion.

"I'm not a fool," Mrs. Hobbes continued. "You're no more a poor washerwoman than I'm a duchess." Sara's grip tightened around the sack in her hands. "I suppose you've your reasons for keeping mum, and I won't push." She drained her cup of tea, then rose with a smooth motion to face Sara. "I'm glad we understand each other."

Sara smiled uncertainly and nodded, her mind spinning. Just what exactly did Mrs. Hobbes understand about her? She wished she were brave enough to ask. But that could lead to a conversation she had no intention of having, to memories of her father and a glittering world she didn't believe in anymore. She was Sara O'Connor now. Sally Ballantine was dead and buried and destined to stay that way.

～～

The house was quiet without Sara. He and Evie read in front of the parlor fire, waiting for the sound of her return. At least, that's what it seemed, for they both started at every noise and Evie rose more than once to peek out the window.

"She's back," Evie said finally, running to the door.

But Sara wasn't the same woman who'd left three hours earlier. Her eyes were wide with distress, her mouth trembling.

"What's wrong?" He couldn't mask the panic in his voice.

"I . . . I'm sorry, sir. I'd have given more notice, but—"

She was leaving them. "You can't give notice." His voice rose. Didn't she know how much Evie—how much they needed her?

"Mr. Kinney, please. Granny's sick. I need to go back."

Evie ducked in front of him. "Oh, no. Does Granny have what I had?"

"No, no." Sara sent Evie a reassuring smile that didn't reach her eyes. "She hasn't been well for months now." She took a shuddering breath and her eyes flew back to James, filled with worry and fear. "It's her heart. I only came back to get the doctor. And to tell you."

"What did he say?"

Her throat worked. "He won't come."

James ran a distracted hand through his hair, his mind fixated on one point. "It's not safe. It will be dark soon."

"I've lived in Irish Town for years. I know how to watch out for myself." Her lips firmed.

"You can't go there alone at night." Even to his own ears, he sounded harsh. His smooth-spoken ways seemed to desert him around her.

Sara let out a sigh that was more like a shudder. "I must. She was so weak . . . I've never seen her like this." Her eyes grew bright with unshed tears. "I don't know how much time I have, but I need to go. She's all I have left of Colin."

Colin. Her husband. James cursed himself for being an insensitive clod. She was hurting and he was snapping orders as though she were a clerk in the courthouse.

"Mrs. Hobbes," he called down the hall to the kitchen. "Would you pack some bread and cheese we can eat on the way?"

Sara followed him. "Mr. Kinney, what are you about?"

"I'm taking you, of course." He bent down to peer into Evie's bright, curious eyes that were following every development. "Run to the livery and order the carriage, poppet."

Evie nodded and dashed out the door.

"There is no need to put yourself to so much trouble, sir. I can walk."

"You'll get there twice as fast in the carriage."

She looked down. "I know how you feel about Irish Town. There's no need to expose yourself to it."

He took a step closer, crossing his arms. "You know precious little about me, Sara O'Connor, if you think that." Maybe once he'd avoided Irish Town, but he'd learned to see past the dirt and stench to the good people who lived there. Sara had taught him that. "I'm coming."

For a moment Sara stared, her mouth slightly open as though she didn't know how to answer him. "Well. I . . . Thank you."

Evie darted in the door. "I told them to hurry," she said, catching her breath. Her eyes were hopeful. "May I—"

"No." James took one look at her and shook his head. "You'll stay here with Mrs. Hobbes."

"But Papa—"

"Evangeline Kinney, you will do as I say." He saw the mulish tilt to her chin and bent to whisper into her ear. "Sara will worry about you if you come along. She'll be afraid you'll take sick again. She's already upset, you can see that for yourself."

They both looked at Sara, who paced the front porch, her eyes trained for the first sight of the carriage.

Evie nodded. "All right, Papa." Evie held up her arms and he hugged her tightly. She tugged his head down to her level and whispered into his ear. "Make sure you bring her back."

James nodded. "I will." He'd make sure Sara got safely to Granny, ensure everything possible was done to help her. Then, he'd make sure Sara came back here where she belonged.

His carriage turned out of the mews and stopped in front of the gate. James tossed the stable boy a coin and held out his hand to help Sara up.

She paused with one foot on the step and her eyes met his, full of an emotion he couldn't name, half worry, half relief. Her fingers tightened around his for a moment before she took her seat. After all she'd done for him, he was finally able to do something for her and it made him . . . happy.

Daylight was beginning to fade as they set off and the wind was sharp with the smell of snow. She must be cold in her bonnet and shawl, though she gave no sign of it. She sat perched on the edge of the seat, as though she could urge the horses faster with the momentum of her body.

"Is she your mother-in-law?" he asked, unable to curb his curiosity any longer.

Sara's face was serious, the corners of her mouth turned down in sadness. "My grandmother-in-law, though she was more like a mother to Colin than his own." She bit her lip and James primed himself to ask another prying question. Thankfully, she continued. "She raised the grandchildren while the parents worked. When Colin and I married, she was the only one who supported us." Sara paused, clearing her throat. "My family didn't . . . approve of the match."

James sat back, letting her words sink in. "But after your husband died, surely you could have gone back . . . ?"

"They cast me off, said I was dead to them."

James imagined never seeing Evie again. Impossible. What sort of family would make a pronouncement like that?

"Granny O'Connor is the only reason I survived. She gave me a home and taught me her trade." Sara's voice broke and he fought the urge to put an arm around her.

"I'm sorry." He was conscious of the inadequacy of the words, but they were true, nonetheless. He was sorry her family had rejected her, sorry she'd had to work so hard just to stay alive. He was sorry she'd been working for him instead of caring for Granny.

He flicked the reins, urging the mare forward. He couldn't go back and change the past, but he could do everything in his power to get her to Granny O'Connor in time.

Chapter 18

Sara jumped down as soon as James brought the carriage to a stop, resisting the temptation to hold her handkerchief over her nose. She must have been out of Irish Town too long, for the stench of the open sewers almost overpowered her.

Inside, the tiny landing was dark, the only light coming from a lamp burning low beside Granny's bed. Granny lay, still and pale, her cheeks sunken and her skin an unnatural gray. She looked small and frail, and the sight brought a lump to Sara's throat.

"Granny? It's Sara."

Granny's eyes opened a fraction and the corners of her mouth lifted. "Sara, my dearie. Come all this way back just for me?"

"Of course," Sara answered, her eyes taking careful inventory of Granny's face, looking for a symptom she might have missed. She had no idea what was wrong, or what she could do to make Granny better.

Granny's eyes lit on James where he hesitated in the doorway, and some of her old spark returned. "Brought company, did ye?"

Sara looked over her shoulder. "He insisted on escorting me. Forgets I've spent more time in Irish Town than he ever did."

James held her gaze and crossed his arms as if to confirm that he wasn't going anywhere.

"Only proper, accompanying you." Granny sent him a nod of approval. "I told ye he were a gentleman."

Sara knelt beside the bed, taking Granny's small, wrinkled hand in hers.

"How are you now, Granny? Did the tea help?"

Granny squeezed her hand, so lightly she could barely feel it. "As well as can be expected."

"I'll have you better in no time."

Granny's smile was gentle, as though she were comforting Sara instead of the other way around. "Never mind that."

"But there must be something we can do." Sara wanted to stand up and stomp her feet. Force Granny to get better.

"Hush now. I'm ready to go."

But I'm not ready to lose you. The ache of unshed tears clogged Sara's throat. She heard James retreat into the entry and softly close the door.

"You're a good lass, Sara." Granny's hand crept from under the quilt to cover hers. "I never had a daughter until you."

Sara swallowed. "If it hadn't been for you, I don't think I would have survived after Colin died. You saved me."

Granny smiled. "'Twas the Lord who saved you, dearie. Has

kept his hand on you all these years, too. And now you've a new life before you. Where you belong."

"Oh, we're not—that is, it was only temporary. Mr. Kinney will find a real governess now. I've come back to nurse you. You'll be better in no time with me to care for you."

"Don't even think of it." Granny's voice was sharp and her hand squeezed Sara's with surprising strength. "It's my time to go. I'm ready. I'll see Colin again, and Sean, too. That's Colin's grandfather. You never knew him, but he was a good man. Like Colin. Wild for horses, too."

Sara squeezed her eyes shut, picturing Colin as she'd first seen him in her father's stable, his blue eyes aglow with laughter. He'd wanted to own a livery. A tear slipped down her cheek. He'd been so young, so full of hope and energy.

"I miss him," Sara murmured.

Granny nodded. "Reckon you'll always miss him. But now it's time to look ahead to your future. Ye've a life before you, one God planned better than you or I ever could." Granny paused for a moment, to catch her breath.

Sara opened her eyes. "Granny, you should rest. Don't worry about me, I'll be fine."

Granny snorted, sounding so much like her former self that Sara hoped for a moment she might recover after all. "Fine, is that what ye call it? Hiding away, too afraid to care about anyone again?" Granny's wise eyes pierced through her defenses, seeing everything she'd thought she'd hidden.

"I'm doing well. Working, taking care of myself."

"Living separate from others 'tain't living, Sara. I hope ye'll realize that before it's too late."

Sara kept her lips sealed. She wouldn't argue with Granny. Not today.

Granny sighed. "Come, give me a kiss then. I love you, girl, like you were me own."

"I love you, too." Sara kissed her cheek, letting the silent tears flow. It felt like losing Colin all over again. Her last connection to his family, the last person in the world who cared what became of her.

"Ye mustn't carry on so," Granny said. "I'm going to a better place."

"But I . . . I need you."

"Child, you've got everything you need right here." She tapped Sara's chest, right over her heart. "You're not alone."

Sara's eyes darted to the door where James had stood minutes before. Granny gave an impatient shake of her head. "I'm not talking about him, though if you both weren't so stubborn . . . but that's another story. I'm talking about faith. Hope. All those things you pretend you don't need. You figure God abandoned you, but you know deep down that's not true. He was there all along, holding you up until you was ready to stand again."

Sara's heart burned in her chest at Granny's words. She didn't want to stand again. She wanted to hide in Irish Town with Granny, safe from the world that had turned its back on her. Yet she couldn't deny that something had changed. *Holding you up until you were ready to stand.* Was that what had kept her going through the dark years? Was it God who'd led her to the love of a little girl and helped her feet find bedrock again?

"Ye'll do just fine, dearie." Granny dropped her hands, her body sagging back into the pillows.

"Is there anything I can get you?" Sara straightened Granny's blanket with trembling fingers. Whatever bedrock she'd found was still mighty shaky, for she didn't think she had the strength to face another loss.

"Come to mention it, I could do with a cup of tea," Granny said.

Sara stood. Tea she could do. "Of course."

~

James retreated to the quiet of the front hall and soon realized he wasn't alone. He found himself under the scrutiny of a woman of indeterminate years. Her hair was dark brown and her face unlined, yet her body was bent with years of work that had aged her before her time.

"Got an eye on Sara, do you?"

James drew himself up and infused every bit of lawyerly condescension he could muster into his tone. "I can't imagine to what you are referring."

The woman was undeterred. "Can't you?" She gave a hoarse burst of laughter. "Don't think I'd be against it, that's not why I'm here."

"Well, then I cannot imagine why you linger."

Any other woman would have retreated before the ice in his tone, but this one only smirked. "You can't scare me with all your fine talk, no more than Sara can." She took a few steps forward and lowered her voice. "She ain't coming back here to sponge off me, not once Granny is gone. I'll let out the front room."

"I see." James raised his brows. "And who, pray tell, are you?"

"Her landlady." She crossed her arms, seeming to run out of patience. "Look, you'd be doing her a favor, taking her on, so to speak. Might be all she's good for now."

"I have already taken her on, so you need have no fear," James answered haughtily. "She is my daughter's governess."

"Is that what you fancy gents call it?"

If she were a man, he'd be at her throat, demanding satisfaction. He contented himself with a growl. "Sara is a lady."

"Lot of good that does her." The woman gave another burst of her strange, gruff laughter. James spun away before he said something he'd regret, backing into Granny's room. How had Granny and Sara come to be under the thumb of such a woman?

Granny was alone, her eyes bright and watching. She gestured to James. "Come here."

He moved into the room and sat on the stool at her side.

Granny lifted her head off the pillow. "I've got some things I need to say." She paused, her eyes drifting to the kitchen. "I hate to leave her. I know she be a woman grown, but she'll never survive here in Irish Town, not without me. She needs to be among her own folk." Her hand came out and grasped his arm, her grip surprising for one so feeble. "You'll take care of her, keep her safe, won't you?"

James didn't hesitate. "Of course. She has a position with me for as long as she wants it."

"A position, you say?" Granny regarded him with somber eyes, and he couldn't help but feel he'd disappointed her.

"I pay her well. She's happy with us." He wasn't sure whom he was trying to convince.

"What Sara needs is a family." Granny stared at him for a long moment, and he had the uncomfortable feeling she could see right down into his soul. "I reckon that's what you need, too."

The words hit him like a gavel, sharp and hard. He had a daughter. That was all the family he needed. "She—she's made Evie happy. We want her to stay." He swallowed. "I'll keep her safe, Granny. I promise." Security was all he had to offer, but suddenly, it didn't feel like it was enough. Granny's sharp eyes watched him, waiting. Expecting declarations he couldn't give.

Granny's face softened and she let her head rest once again on the pillow. "Aye," she said finally with a satisfied nod. "I believe you will."

She closed her eyes, the lines of pain and exhaustion once again prominent on her face. James rose and paced the room, letting out a jagged sigh. How had he ended up so embroiled in Sara's life that he couldn't think straight?

He stopped short at the sight of Sara in the doorway, holding a steaming cup of tea.

"Thank you," she whispered, a faint flush in her cheeks. "I would never hold you to a promise given in such circumstances, but it was kind of you to comfort her."

James grasped her elbow as she would have slipped past him. She looked up and met his eyes and he realized his words weren't merely to placate an old woman. He would protect Sara with every tool at his disposal.

"Make no mistake, Sara O'Connor. I meant it. I meant every word."

Chapter 19

Granny lingered another hour, her breathing increasingly slow and labored. Sara listened for each inhalation, her heart in her throat, wondering if it would be the last. When the end came, it was peaceful. Granny didn't open her eyes, didn't speak, but the lines of pain disappeared from her face.

Sara buried her face in the blankets, letting the tears fall as she rested her head against Granny's side. She didn't want to let go. James stood back, a silent presence that was strangely comforting. He reminded her she wasn't completely alone. Evie needed her.

James's hand touched her shoulder, tentative and warm.

Sara turned, drying her face and avoiding his eyes, afraid to see sympathy that would crack her composure again.

"Would you . . . would you like me to make arrangements for the funeral?" he asked.

Sara tensed. The funeral. She'd hadn't even thought that far. Her eyes flew to his face. "I'm not sure. I haven't thought—" The thought of arrangements and plots made her head spin. Not to mention fees she had no way of paying.

"You pack Granny's things. Say a final goodbye. I'll take care of it." He squeezed her shoulder, calm and steady. A rock when she was adrift.

"Thank you."

In the hall, he spoke with Molly in a low murmur. From the corner of her eye, she saw him press a coin into Molly's hand, saw the woman nod with alacrity. She ought to refuse his help. Granny wasn't his responsibility. Yet she was so weary, so heartsore, she couldn't rouse herself to protest. He could deduct it from her wage.

It was past midnight by the time she'd packed Granny's meager belongings into a crate to be delivered to the widow next door, keeping only a quilt and the family Bible for herself. James led her to the carriage, putting a steadying hand under her elbow. He seemed to understand her state of mind, for he didn't pester her with questions. She needed the quiet of the drive home to examine her sorrow.

Alone. She was alone again. The control she'd kept over her emotions loosened and the tears began. Soon her shoulders shuddered with suppressed sobs. He didn't utter any calming platitudes but let her linger in her grief. The only sign he heard her was the clean handkerchief he pressed into her hand with a gentle squeeze.

The house was abed when they returned. Sara lit a taper from the table in the front hall, illuminating a letter addressed to James. He scanned the note, his lips tightening. Sara turned to head to the kitchen. She felt raw, her heart aching with loss. She wanted to curl up in her attic and block out the world, yet she dreaded being alone.

To her surprise, James dropped the letter on the hall table and followed her. "Are you hungry? I'm sure there's something in the larder." His voice was gentle, coaxing. He lifted his candle to better illuminate their faces.

"Won't we wake Mrs. Hobbes?"

He shook his head. "She sleeps with Evie when I'm from home. Come, a cup of tea wouldn't go amiss, I'm guessing."

Tenderness lit his features, so unlike the formal expression she was used to that it took her a moment to comprehend his words. And by then, she was following him down the hall to the kitchen, his hand grasping her elbow. It felt easy and natural. Too natural. When he looked at her like that, as though her well-being were paramount, it was hard to remember that he was her employer.

In the kitchen, he surprised her again, setting the kettle on to boil and slicing bread for toast. She watched him, her brows raised in question, and he shrugged, a sheepish smile tugging at his lips.

"I wasn't always a useless lawyer, you know. When I first arrived in Upper Canada, I had rooms with some other bachelors. We had a maid come in, but I had to learn my way about the kitchen." He buttered the toast and set a slice on a plate in front of her, then rummaged in the pantry for the jam. "I'm afraid tea and toast are about the extent of my capabilities though." He sat down across from her, his smile lighting up his features and drawing her in, making her want to smile back.

"I had to learn the hard way, too," she found herself saying.

"Granny taught me a bit, but it was mostly a trial by fire." James took a sip of his tea, his eyes roaming over her face, all his attention focused on her. It was delightful and terrifying all at once.

"What was your worst disaster in the kitchen?" he asked. "I'll tell you mine, but you go first."

To her surprise, she did just that, recalling that first failed loaf of bread she'd made in the bake kettle, black on the bottom and mushy on top.

"You'd never made bread before?" James stared at her, his chin tilted in question.

"Ah, no, never." She hurried on before he could ask another question about her past. "My bread was unrecognizable. Like a blob of paste in a bowl made of charcoal. Colin ate it anyway, though he couldn't manage to look like he enjoyed it."

The smile faded from James's face. "You miss him still."

Sara nodded, looking away. What was it about this man that brought down all her defenses? "He was ever patient with me."

"I'm sorry," James said, clearing his throat. "I shouldn't bring up the past. No sense remembering old wounds."

His words brought her eyes back to his face. "Don't apologize. I . . . I want to talk about him. When I remember him, it's like I still have some connection with the love we once shared." His eyes widened, and she bit her lip, wishing the words unsaid. It usually made others uncomfortable when she shared her grief. She turned the topic. "Now tell me your cooking story. Let me guess . . . burnt toast?"

"How did you know?"

Sara found her eyes glued to James's face as he recounted a mishap with flaming toast. She'd never seen his expression so open and animated.

"I just forgot about it, there's no excuse. But by the time I'd doused the flames, the street was full of neighbors about to organize a fire brigade." He gave a self-deprecating shrug. "You should have seen the looks on their faces when I came out and had to explain how I'd managed to set the kitchen curtains on fire."

She laughed and he joined her and neither of them could seem to stop. She couldn't remember when last she'd laughed this hard. Maybe during those first few heady days of her courtship with Colin. Maybe never.

Colin. What a strange joy it was to simply remember the happy times. She drained the last of her tea and put her cup down to find James watching her intently.

The kitchen shrank until it was only the two of them, close together in the gentle glow of the candle. His gaze slid lower to rest on her mouth and her heart lurched. The room was unaccountably warm. Her tongue darted out to moisten her lips, and she heard his sharp intake of breath.

"Sara, I—"

She jumped up, breaking the spell between them. "It's late."

"Wait. I just want to ask you something." She paused in the act of picking up her dishes. "I'm going away."

Sara fixated on one word. "Away?"

His eyes slid away from hers, down to a crumb on the table. He pinched it between his fingers, depositing it on his plate. "Yes. That letter . . . I'll need to go north by Friday. There's a meeting in Holland Landing I must attend."

Holland Landing. The tiny town was a hotbed for radicals from all she'd heard. "You're a rebel?" The words left her in a rush of surprise. James struck her as serious and law-abiding. Far from a rabble-rouser.

If she closed her eyes, she could picture her father, pacing around the parlor, denouncing the rebel leader, Mackenzie. *The way he sees it, any common lout who can answer yay or nay ought to decide the future of this colony. Can you imagine what would befall us if those men had their way?*

James flushed. "Not a rebel exactly. But things need to change." His lips firmed. "We're strangling in a morass of regulations that only benefit a few families." His hand slid across the table, coming to rest on top of hers. "You've seen how the poor spend their savings to come here and then are trapped in the same poverty they thought to leave behind. It's not right."

"I know," Sara whispered. Colin worked fourteen hours a day, she'd taken in laundry, yet they'd been trapped in a dingy lodging with no hope of anything more. Poverty drove him to the lumber camps. And ultimately killed him.

James fought against the control of old money and old-world hierarchies. The thought warmed her. She'd grown up in that world and fought against it, too, in her own way.

"But it's dangerous. I mean, rebellion . . . it's treason."

He gave his head an impatient shake. "I'm not talking about an armed rebellion. I'm talking about change. The Whigs did it in England. There's no reason we can't have those same reforms. I feel better knowing you're here."

She wondered if he was aware of his thumb, slowly brushing across the back of her hand. She couldn't seem to focus on anything other than the warmth of that movement, each sweep sending a shower of sparks up her arm.

Granny told her she wasn't alone and maybe she'd been

right. Here were two people she'd come to care about who needed her.

She gave a short, jerky nod. "Don't worry about Evie. I'll take good care of her. We'll be right here waiting when you get back."

~~~

James closed his eyes for a moment. *We'll be right here waiting.* Sara had included herself in the promise. He hadn't realized how much he'd wanted to hear that, even as he recognized the danger it presented. He was attracted to her. He wanted to be with her, talk to her . . . *touch* her. But she was his governess. Whatever this was between them was impossible. Wasn't it?

As though she heard his question, she tugged her hand out from under his, looking pensive. He couldn't bear to see the worry on her face. He reached out to grasp her hand again as she would have tucked it under her skirt. "Sara, remember my promise to Granny. You have a home here for as long as you need it."

Instead of comforting her, his words seemed to distress her further. Her lips trembled. Tears wet her lashes and trickled down her cheeks.

"Don't cry," he said, brushing away a tear with his thumb. "I hate to see you upset." He knew how sorrow built, how each new loss brought old wounds sweeping back, stronger than ever. Something at once sweet and painful shifted inside him. He'd walk through burning coals if it would take this pain away from her.

"Don't cry?" Her lips twisted in a brief, humorless smile. "After Colin died, I didn't shed a tear. It was like I was afraid if I started crying, I would never stop."

James closed his eyes, allowing himself a moment to feel the grief he'd bottled up for so long. Amelia's death was fraught with guilt and horror and . . . powerlessness. He tried never to think of it.

"I needed to cry," she said, squeezing his hand. "Granny knew that. She wore me down, talking about Colin, mourning him with her Scriptures and songs until I finally cracked and sobbed in her arms for hours. After that, well, I wasn't happy, but I could finally sleep through the night again."

He hadn't slept well for five years after Amelia died. He still often woke in the night, though lately, since Sara O'Connor had come, it was better. He'd thought it was because his worry for Evie had eased. But perhaps—

"I-I beg your pardon," she said, rising suddenly. "I've been rambling on when you must wish me long gone to bed."

James straightened, realizing she'd read his continued silence as disinterest. "No. Please stay. I just—" It was intoxicating, being with her like this. Feeling things he'd bottled up for years while he soaked in the play of emotions across her face. She turned away, her hand slipping from his grasp.

He didn't want her to leave. Not yet.

"I was the same," he said, rising. She froze, turning back to him. "I never cried. Thought I had to be strong for Evie. Now I'm wondering if that wasn't . . . good for me." The words spilled out, each one releasing some of the tight control he clung to.

Her lips curved in a tremulous smile. "Well, that's why I'm crying now, you know. Because it's good for me."

James cupped her face in his hands. "And you, Sara O'Connor, are good for *me*."

For a long moment their eyes met, her gaze soft and

luminous. If he lowered his head just a few more inches, he could touch his lips to hers. Find out if they were as soft as they looked.

The taper on the table sputtered. Sara blinked and stiffened, and he dropped his hands as though he'd been stung. He hadn't kissed a woman in years. What was it about Sara O'Connor that had him thinking about kisses and romance and . . . loving again?

He tried to read her reaction, but she kept her face averted, pulling down the ladder that led to her room, her movements jerky and rushed.

"Sara, wait . . ."

She turned, her foot on the bottom rung, her brows raised in question. He struggled for words, his emotions in a tangled knot of hope and fear. He wanted to tell her how he admired her. How he'd never let anything hurt her again. But how could he promise such a thing? There were too many reasons why drawing closer to her would be a mistake.

"I . . . Good night," he finally said, his hands clenching at his sides.

She was still for a long moment before giving a jerky nod and turning her back to him.

"Good night, Mr. Kinney."

Chapter 20

James left for Holland Landing the day after he stood by her side at Granny's funeral. The weather had turned colder, freezing the mud into unyielding ruts in the road and sending down the first lazy flakes of snow. Sara handed him an extra muffler and a flask of tea and blinked away tears. Granny's loss hung about her like a heavy fog, but the sharp ache that flooded her heart as James rode away was something different. New.

After that hour together in the kitchen, she'd forced herself to acknowledge the truth. She was in the grip of an inconvenient and pointless attraction. James Kinney was a thoughtful, intelligent man and a loving father. No wonder she was drawn to him. But by his own admission, he had no intention of marrying again. Amelia Ridley was still enshrined in his heart.

She pushed aside the pang this thought gave her. She ought

to welcome this time away from his distracting presence to get her unruly emotions in order.

Sara threw herself into lessons, retreating with Evie to the warmth of the kitchen. Mrs. Hobbes listened to her favorite's progress with an indulgent eye, telling them stories of Evie's toddler years while they ate around the scarred wooden table.

On the second day, Henry joined them in the afternoon for the next chapter of *Ivanhoe*. Mrs. Hobbes took one look at his skinny frame and warmed up a plate of ham and mash that she claimed would go to waste otherwise with the master away.

That evening Sara built up the fire in the parlor and they set to work on a new duet. Though she'd filled every minute of the day, James was never far from her thoughts. She worried that he was caught up in dangerous currents. She wished he was home.

"Sara, aren't you going to correct me?" Evie stopped playing and looked at Sara.

"Sorry. I was woolgathering. Try those last five measures again."

Evie placed her fingers on the keyboard. "You don't have to worry about Papa."

"Pardon me?" Sara said, startled.

"He went to help Uncle Andrew. It's his duty, he told me so."

"His duty?" The temptation to probe was irresistible.

"To work within the law, to find peaceful solutions to problems. He says most of the trouble in the world would stop if people would sit down and talk. Make some rules and follow them. Papa's good at making rules."

He wasn't too shabby at breaking them, either. After all, he'd hired a washerwoman as his child's governess. "Come, let's practice this piece once more, and then we'll try the duet."

Evie wasn't a natural musician, no more than Sara was, but with regular practice, she would become proficient. They managed to get through two pages before they both dissolved into giggles.

"That was horrible," Evie sputtered.

"That was lovely," said a deep voice from the front hall.

Sara spun about on the piano bench while Evie squealed and bolted to her father. James swooped her into his arms. Sara's eyes took an inventory of his person, but besides ruddy cheeks and mud-spattered trousers, he seemed no worse for his travels.

His eyes met Sara's over Evie's shoulder, his wide smile surprising her. Of course, he was happy to see his daughter. But that didn't explain why his eyes sought hers, or why she smiled back like a fool at the sight of him. By the time he'd set Evie down on her feet again, Sara had schooled her features back to what she hoped was mere polite welcome.

"Why are you home so early, Papa?" Evie pulled him into the room. He'd only been away one night instead of three.

"I missed you, poppet, so I turned right around and came home as soon as I could."

There was more to the story, judging by the dark circles under his eyes. Sara rose, wiping her hands down the front of her skirt. It was time she left, before she asked questions that a governess had no business asking. "We're done with lessons for today. If you'll excuse me." She tried to walk past them, but his arm shot out, grasping hers.

"Wait. Will you play that again? With Evie?"

"Oh, well, it's not ready. We've got to practice—"

"Please. I haven't heard that piece in so long. And to see

my little girl playing . . ." He cleared his throat. "It would have made her mama happy."

Evie froze. "My mother?" she questioned. "Did she play the pianoforte?"

James nodded, avoiding Sara's eyes. "She loved to play."

Sara wondered if he'd say more, and for Evie's sake, she hoped he would. But he sealed his lips and settled into a chair in the corner, leaning his head back.

Evie tugged Sara to the piano, and they struggled through the new piece again, before settling on an easier duet. James clapped and although he professed interest, his expression grew more somber with each new song. He rose and paced to the window, his posture tight with tension. Sara glanced at him when the music permitted, but his face gave away no clues to his thoughts.

"I'll be back shortly," he announced as soon as the next song finished. His voice was grim, as though he set about some unpleasant task. Evie half rose as if to follow but he gestured her back to the piano bench. "Play that last one again."

He returned five minutes later carrying a large paper-wrapped rectangle that Sara recognized. Her stomach tightened.

"A present!" Evie jumped up from the piano bench to crowd close to him.

Sara searched his face, but his expression was solemn, betraying no sign of what prompted this change of heart. He released the string and pulled at the folded edges to reveal the portrait.

"Who's that?" Evie's voice was soft, as though she hesitated to ask.

James smoothed his hand over his daughter's head. From

her position at the piano, Sara could see the slight tremble in his fingers.

"It's your mother."

Evie studied the portrait of Amelia as a young lady, her dark hair parted in the center to cascade in ringlets around her face. Her gown was pink, a light, airy creation with a ruffled skirt and exaggerated leg-of-mutton sleeves that had been all the rage a decade earlier. She reached out a finger to trace one of Amelia's hands as it rested gracefully on the back of a chair.

"She was beautiful."

James tilted up her chin and looked into her eyes. "You look like her."

Evie's eyes widened. "I do?" She jerked out of his grasp to examine the portrait again.

It was true. Amelia Ridley lingered in the slant of Evie's eyebrows and the curve of her lips. Sara blinked back tears, knowing how much this connection would mean to Evie.

"We could hang it in your room," James said. "If you'd like that."

In response, Evie hugged him tight. James met Sara's eyes over her head. *Thank you*, he mouthed.

Sara smiled. Words floated about her mind and stuck on the tip of her tongue, words of approval that seemed presumptuous in a governess.

"Why don't you run ahead and pick a place for us to hang it," James said. "I'll get the hammer and a nail."

Evie dashed off. Sara busied herself tidying the piano books, surprised when James didn't immediately follow Evie out of the room.

He cleared his throat. "I had time to think about what you

said. I've blocked my grief. Trying to protect Evie, I suppose. But you're right. Evie should know her mother. It's painful but there are good memories, too. I need to share those with Evie."

Sara ducked her head. Of all the surprises the evening brought, James Kinney admitting she'd been right was the greatest. The knowledge brought no satisfaction, however. What a fraud she was, encouraging James to confront his memories when she had no intention of doing the same.

~~~

There was a smile on James's face as he finished the last of his correspondence. It was almost time to go home.

Evenings had become his favorite time of day. Evie and Sara joined him in the parlor, and he could watch the play of emotions over Sara's face while she helped Evie with her embroidery or at the pianoforte. He chuckled at the quiet, clever asides she interjected into Evie's dramatic retelling of the day's events. He liked having her nearby.

He liked it far too much.

It was taking his mind away from the tension growing around him, the letters he ought to answer, the debates that should take his attention.

He'd resented every mile he'd traveled away from them, every minute he'd wasted questioning men who had no intention of admitting a thing. Someone had tipped them off. The meeting in Holland Landing turned out to be a few old men reminiscing about the last war with nary a rebel in sight.

Still, he'd seen enough to make him worry. The smithy at Holland Landing was making pikestaffs instead of horseshoes. In the distance, he'd spotted men in the fields moving in a formation that resembled military drills. A turkey hunt, he'd been told, though he'd never seen men stand in columns to hunt before.

He was forced to admit it might be too late for peacemaking. The reformers had turned into rebels, and they were serious. The Tories needed to come to the table.

A clerk ducked his head into his office, his face flushed. "Mr. Ballantine is here to see you, sir."

James's heart sank. If Ballantine expected to hear a tidy report of Andrew's rescue from the hands of wild rabble-rousers, he was bound for disappointment.

"Hello, sir," James said, rising as Ballantine entered and reaching forward to shake his hand. "Pleasure to see you again."

Ballantine grunted, lowering slowly into the chair across from James. He mopped his face with a handkerchief and paused a moment to catch his breath. "Blasted stairs. Next time I'll have you come to me."

James ran a finger under his collar and leaned back in his chair, waiting for the hammer to fall. Ballantine wouldn't be impressed with James's lack of progress. James mentally scanned the evidence, organizing his arguments as fast as he could. This might be the time to impress upon the older man just how serious the situation was.

"Dash it, Kinney. An awkward business, this."

Ballantine was worried that things would get *awkward*? James resisted the temptation to pull his hair out. Why would he persist in ignoring the evidence in front of their eyes? "It will be a sight more than awkward if something isn't *done*," James said. "These men are in earnest, sir. Why, I read one of the tracts they're circulating, and it spells violence. If you'd only—"

"I don't mean that foolish rebel talk." He swiped his hand through the air, brushing aside James's concerns. "It's the other situation I'm here about, though I'd rather not be. Not an affair for men." He spread his hands with a helpless shrug.

"Situation?" James prompted, mystified.

"Heard it from a few sources now." Ballantine mopped his head once more, then took a breath as if to steal himself for an unpleasant task. "Doesn't look right, a governess, living in your pocket like that. You were seen at church together. Causing talk."

Shock and chagrin held James silent for a moment followed by a flash of anger. Finally, some happiness came into Evie's life. Stability. Acceptance. His mouth firmed. Rumors were not going to tear all that away.

"I can't imagine talk could come of hiring a governess," he replied, his voice cool. "Seems a fairly common practice."

Ballantine brought his hand down on the desk. "Don't play the fool! Heard she's a pretty one, and I don't blame you. Gets lonely."

Outrage, hot and tingling, coursed through him. It wasn't like Ballantine to talk about a woman as though she were just a pretty face. He sensed the influence of Stephen Osgoode. Again. "Sir, I assure you, I have the utmost respect for Miss O'Connor. If Osgoode has told you otherwise, he's wrong. I would never—"

"Need a wife, that's the ticket." Ballantine leaned back in his chair as though he'd solved the problem.

James gritted his teeth. Just when he thought the conversation couldn't get any more mortifying.

"I've decided to host a dinner tonight." The statement took

James aback. Ballantine never entertained. "I've invited some ladies," he continued. "Bound to be one that'll do. We'll see you at seven." Ballantine gave him a stare that was meant to remind him of his place. Instead, it sent him over the edge.

"Please accept my apologies," James said, rising. "I believe I have an engagement tonight."

"Skip it."

"Not possible."

"Some of the finest families in Toronto will be there." Ballantine sent a meaningful gaze around the tiny office, taking in the sparce furnishings and Andrew's empty desk. "It wouldn't hurt to make some connections. Never know when you might need them."

James tried to stare Ballantine down, but the man's words hit close, and he dropped his eyes. Was this the opportunity he'd been waiting for? He could talk to the most important men in Toronto. There might be one receptive to his warnings about Mackenzie's men. "All right," he said slowly. "I'll be there."

Ballantine gave a satisfied nod. "I thought you'd come around. We'll see you tonight."

Chapter 21

Sara wandered through the remains of the kitchen garden. At the front of the house, a door closed and she heard the clop of hooves. James had a dinner engagement tonight. He'd be with ladies and gentlemen of his own circle. Where he belonged.

So why did she feel so . . . bereft? She had to stop yearning for things that could never be. She flipped up the broad tattered leaves of the Brussels sprouts, one of the last traces of summer's bounty. Rows of sprouts lined the stem, fresh and green, protected from wind and ice. She was safe now. She had a family, of a sort. It was enough.

She pushed the spade into the ground with a mighty shove of her foot, turning over a massive clump of soil with a satisfying thud. Scraping away the mud, she uncovered a few straggly carrots that she put in a bucket for washing. She'd need to return to the house soon. But not yet.

She regretted lingering a moment later when a man appeared in the mews behind the house. It wasn't James nor Andrew Ridley. He stopped and looked over the fence, his pale, icy eyes intent. Stephen Osgoode.

Her legs tightened, urging her to run, but he'd already opened the gate and taken a step in her direction. "Good afternoon," he said. "Miss . . . O'Connor, is it?"

She ducked her head, wishing she had her mobcap to hide beneath. "Mr. Kinney just left, sir. Would you like to leave a message?"

He walked toward her, his steps leisurely. "It's not Mr. Kinney I'm here to see. To tell the truth, I've been waiting for him to leave."

At his words, Sara's head jerked up. There could only be one reason he wanted to see her. He knew.

He laughed softly at her expression. "Yes. I've figured it out." He moved forward and she took an unconscious step back, her shoes sinking into the mud of the garden. "Can't imagine how Andrew hasn't. Only . . ." He reached forward and lifted her chin with one long, elegant finger, his eyes roaming over her face and then down, skimming her body with insulting thoroughness. "Yes, I suppose you have changed a fair bit from that girl in the schoolroom."

Sara jerked her chin out of his grasp, resisting the urge to wipe away the traces of his touch. He reminded her of a reptile basking on a rock, his eyes flicking back and forth, taking in her every movement. As though he were looking for a place to strike.

"What do you want?" She forced calm into her voice.

"Ah, straight to the point. In that, you're like your father." Sara pressed her lips together, refusing to confirm his suspicions.

He sighed. "I see you're going to make this difficult. I thought we could . . . renew our acquaintance."

"We have no acquaintance."

"I beg to differ."

She darted a glance over her shoulder, contemplating the possibility of flight. But what if he followed her to the kitchen? Spoke to Mrs. Hobbes? "I'm needed inside," she said finally, deciding to risk it. "I shouldn't be out here, talking to a strange man."

"Worried about propriety?" He glanced at the house, then back at Sara. "I find that hard to believe. You wouldn't believe the rumors flying about James Kinney and his lovely new governess."

She gasped. "They're not true."

He held up his hand. "Come now, we both know the truth matters very little. It's what people think is true that counts." His voice lowered. "I'd be willing to wager Kinney doesn't know the truth about *you*."

Sara feigned nonchalance. "What does it matter to you?" Letting Osgoode know he'd got to her was a fatal mistake.

"It doesn't." His voice was smooth as silk and just as cold. "It's none of my affair if Kinney wants to discredit himself and bring disgrace upon his daughter." An insincere note of self-righteousness surfaced in his voice. "But as your father's friend, I would be remiss if I didn't try to effect a reconciliation between the two of you."

Reconciliation. She stuffed down the flicker of hope the word engendered. It wasn't possible. "If Papa wanted a reconciliation, he could have found me any time these past ten years."

Osgoode ignored her words. "I have a plan that will set everything to rights." He rested one foot on the seat of the garden bench, leaning on his knee with the confidence of a pirate who'd captured a ship. "We'll go to your father together. Tell him you're a widow now and seek his forgiveness." He waved a hand at the Kinney house. "No need to mention too much about all this."

"No." If she ever did face her father, it wouldn't be at Stephen Osgoode's side.

"Come now, Sally."

She inhaled sharply. She hadn't answered to that name in years.

Osgoode straightened, seeming to enjoy her discomfort. "Your father might be a strong, unforgiving sort of man, but with me at your side, I think he'll come around." He smiled, a cool, calculating curl of his lips that didn't reach his eyes. "Especially when we announce our engagement. The perfect joining of two Tory families. Just what this colony needs to stay strong."

Sara studied him beneath lowered lashes. It was like she'd gone back in time. Twelve years ago, he'd wormed his way into her father's good graces and warned him of the brewing romance between his daughter and the stable boy. Together, they'd decided she should marry Osgoode. She'd had no voice. No choice. No one to listen to her side of the story and trust her words.

Now, his eyes held the same hard gleam. He wasn't about to give up until her father's business and her inheritance were in his hands. But she was no naive seventeen-year-old. He wasn't going to destroy her life a second time.

She cocked her head, tilting her chin up to show she wasn't intimidated. "I'm not going anywhere with you, Osgoode. Goodbye."

He reached out his hand and gripped her shoulder, his fingers biting through her gown. "I wouldn't be so hasty."

She squashed a flash of fear, remembering the stinging slap she'd dealt him all those years ago, the look of frustrated rage on his face when she'd refused his unwelcome advances. He wouldn't forget that scene. He wasn't a forgiving man.

"Don't be afraid," he said, seeming to read her thoughts. His grip on her loosened, his hand sliding down her arm in what could only be called a caress. It made her skin crawl. "We'll be married, and all will be forgiven." His voice turned low, cajoling. "You'll live in comfort for the rest of your days."

She shook her head, jerking her hand away from his grasp. She was twenty-nine years old, she reminded herself. He couldn't force her into anything. "Go away." She hated the fear in her voice, the cold panic that swept over her at his touch.

Her words did nothing to dissuade him. "I'd think twice if I were you." He moved closer, his voice lowering to a hiss.

Sara shuddered. She knew from bitter experience how Osgoode made good on his threats. When she'd run away with Colin, Osgoode retaliated by turning Colin's dream of owning his own livery into ashes, bringing on years of frantic work and worry that pushed Colin into an early grave.

His eyes hardened. "You think you can worm your way back into society, but you can't. Not without me."

She shook her head, the movement so forceful that a few strands of hair loosened from her tight bun and fell forward over her face. "I have no intention of entering society. I just want to be left alone." She wished she could mask the note of pleading in her voice. There was no purpose hoping for Osgoode's compassion, for it was an emotion he didn't possess.

He ignored her protest. "I can destroy Kinney's reputation. It won't be hard. You've already done most of the work. A few well-placed remarks will turn speculation into scandal. That Scot is barely hanging on to the fringes of good society as it is." He reached out, wrapping one of the loose strands of hair around his finger with a painful twist. "You stay here, and you'll ruin him, and his daughter, too."

Osgoode was a powerful man in Toronto society. She didn't doubt he could sabotage James's career if he set his mind to it. She couldn't allow that to happen, not when she could prevent it. "You don't need to say anything. I'll . . . I'll go."

"Excellent." He looked down at her stained gown with a frown of distaste. "Run and change your dress and we'll be on our way."

Sara's anger flared hot and bright. "I didn't say I'd go with *you*." She'd never put herself in this man's power again. "I'd rather be on the street than wed to you." She'd go back to Irish Town, find some way to—

"Don't be such a martyr." Osgoode's voice was impatient, calling her back to the present like a slap. "Kinney has secrets of his own, you know." She looked at him. Did he mean Amelia? "He's considering marriage, has he told you that? No?" He sneered. "I heard your father has a lady picked out for him. A Miss Wilson. Highly eligible." He smiled then, a menacing curve of the lips that chilled her. "Though, whether she'll have him after I'm done with his reputation is another question."

The back door slammed. Sara jumped but Osgoode merely turned to the sound, his movements as unhurried as ever.

"Miss O'Connor?" Mrs. Hobbes moved out onto the back

stoop, her mouth set in a disapproving line. "Evie's ready for you to check her lesson."

"I'll give you a night to think it over. I'm sure once you have a chance to consider . . ." His voice trailed away, but he kept his gaze trained on her, his eyes as hard as diamonds. She shivered and he smiled. "I'll be back for you, Sally." He tipped his hat and strolled back down the mews as though he hadn't a care in the world.

A wave of nausea threatened to choke her. She knew more than anyone what Osgoode was capable of. James's reputation would be ruined. He'd would have no way of supporting himself. Or Evie. She'd destroy his life. Just as she'd done to Colin.

Sara leaned weakly against the spade, the sickening fear fading under a far stronger emotion. Loss. She would lose them both. Well, she'd known it was coming. It's not like she could stay here forever. Yet she'd forgotten, grown complacent.

Evie's voice drifted across the yard, high and sweet. Calling her. Her heart contracted. Evie had just found security and routine. What would it do to her if Sara left?

Stephen Osgoode's words came back to her, sharp and insistent. *You'll ruin him, and his daughter, too.*

How could she stay?

~~

James stifled a yawn, wondering how soon he could politely take his leave. He eyed the parade of servants entering Ballantine's dining room. Not anytime soon, judging by the size of the next course: lobster cream, chicken croquettes, and a saddle of mutton. Ballantine had spared no expense.

Ballantine caught his eye and raised his eyebrows. His gaze slid across the table to rest on the empty seat across from James. Andrew Ridley hadn't made an appearance tonight. Ballantine frowned, his eyes meeting James as his head tilted in question. James could only shrug.

"Quite a large party this evening," he said, attempting conversation with his dinner partner. He'd been paired with Miss Wilson, a simpering chit barely out of the schoolroom who couldn't seem to string a sentence together beyond "How diverting, to be sure."

"I don't think anyone would miss it. It's the first dinner he's hosted in years. Mama said he hasn't opened his doors to company since—" Her voice dropped to a whisper. "His daughter."

Heavens, had the girl no more sense than to gossip about her host at the table? "Yes, of course, that must be it." He had no intention of rehashing the old story of Ballantine's wayward daughter. It had happened months before he'd even arrived in Upper Canada. He busied himself with his plate for a moment, searching for an innocuous topic of conversation.

"Miss Wilson, have you read *Ivanhoe*?"

"I adore *Ivanhoe*. So diverting, to be sure."

James looked down at Miss Wilson in surprise. She was a reader, was she? Thanks to Sara, he had more than a passing knowledge of Scott's latest novel.

"A capital book," he said. "Tell me, do you prefer Rowena or Rebecca? It's a matter of some debate in my house."

"Oh, well I—" A look of confusion passed over her face. "Which one is the princess? She's my favorite."

"Rowena," James said dryly.

Some men might find her rosy cheeks and tiny bow mouth

attractive, but she reminded James of a china doll. No spark of intelligence in her eyes, no strength to the tilt of her chin or the set of her shoulders. Did Ballantine think he was the same man he'd been a decade ago, so bowled over by a pretty face that he wouldn't notice there was nothing of substance underneath?

He refused the footman's offer of more wine, only half listening to Miss Wilson's imperfect recollections of *Ivanhoe*. Amelia had been as beautiful, her smiles as encouraging. As a young man with barely a feather to fly with, he'd never been the recipient of such admiration before. He'd rushed headlong into love without a second thought, not realizing that Amelia had seen him more as a challenge than as a man.

She'd planned to remake him into a model gentleman, a pillar of the Tory elite. Only he wasn't the ambitious, biddable husband Amelia imagined. He liked quiet evenings at home and had no interest in political power. He wouldn't invest his money in dubious land claims that lined the pockets of the rich and misled newcomers about the value of their allotments. He refused to go into debt to maintain a lifestyle they couldn't yet afford.

He'd been nothing but a disappointment to Amelia. Judging by the relief on Miss Wilson's face when she turned to her other dinner partner, he was a disappointment to her, as well. Finally, the ladies rose to move to the parlor. He inhaled, running through his argument once again. Soon, he'd have his chance to sway the men in this room into action.

"Well, gentlemen." Old Colonel Fitzgibbon leaned forward as soon as the port was poured and sent his sharp gaze around the table. "I'd like to know what that fool Mackenzie is up to."

"It will come to nothing, mark my words. They wouldn't know a musket from a spade," said a grizzled man to his right.

James cleared his throat. It was exactly the opening he'd hoped for. "We'd do well to pay attention." Heads swivelled in his direction, and he sought the words that would make them take heed. "That last election was a shambles, surely you can admit that. Reforms are necessary."

"Come now, Kinney," the Colonel responded. "You're starting to sound like one of them."

James scanned the table, but there was no sign of support in the unsmiling faces around him. The injustice struck him anew. These men, born to privilege, couldn't spare a thought for policy that didn't benefit them. He doubted he could change their minds, but he had to try.

"Gentlemen," James said, trying for a conciliatory tone. "I'm only saying what we all know. We can't continue to ignore the needs of newcomers, not if we want to move this colony forward." He held up a hand to silence the immediate rebuttals. "Land grants are a case in point. How can it be that hardworking immigrants are denied land because they aren't members of the Church of England? It's not what they were promised when they uprooted their lives to come here."

"So, you think every man who steps off a boat should be granted a parcel of land?" The Colonel snorted. "They wouldn't know what to do with it."

"Not necessarily. But I do think the lawmakers are more concerned with providing themselves with cheap labor than the future of this colony."

"Oh, ho, now the knives come out." The Colonel bristled as murmurs of dissent grew around the table.

"James, my boy," Ballantine said, his eyes flashing a warning. "If changes are needed, you can trust the governor to bring our concerns to the attention of Britain. All in good time."

James's hands clenched. Not one of these men had any intention of listening. Of compromise. "But sir, that could take months. Years. The rebels are preparing to fight. I've seen it with my own eyes."

"Fight?" The colonel scoffed. "One good British regular could take on twenty farmers and win. We've nothing to fear from those fools."

"But the governor sent the militia to Montreal," James said. "If worst came to worst, we'd be defenseless. We need to negotiate. Compromise."

The word brought a chorus of objection from the men around the table. "You can't compromise with treasonous rebels." The colonel's voice rose, his face darkening.

"We have a new queen." Ballantine interjected before James could respond. "Now is not the time for petty squabbles. We need to demonstrate our loyalty. Britain has always acted in our best interest." There were murmurs of assent.

"In *our* best interest, perhaps, but lawmakers should represent the concerns of everyone." Even as he said the words, he knew he'd gone too far. The incredulous laughter that greeted his words only confirmed it. But who would speak for the families living in squalor in Irish Town?

I could.

For a moment, he thought he'd spoken the words aloud. He knew the law. He knew people in power. He could *do* something.

Ballantine rose to his feet, calling to order the unruly arguments that sprung up around the table. "A toast to the queen."

He raised his glass and waited for the others to join him. "To Her Majesty Queen Victoria."

James had no choice but to join them. If only he could make them see they could be loyal to the Crown and still work for change.

"To the queen." The men's voices joined as one and harmony was restored to the table.

Ballantine's eyes sought his as he lowered his glass, sending a fierce glare in his direction before turning back to his conversation with the man beside him. James sighed. He'd be in for a tongue-lashing later, and for what? If anything, his words only seemed to widen the divide.

"You've missed your mark with this crowd, James." Stephen Osgoode had moved from his place on the other side of the table and taken a seat next to James. "You'll never get anywhere if they think you're a radical."

"Hmmm." James waited. Osgoode wasn't here to drop a friendly word of advice in his ear. He always had an ulterior motive in conversation. Over the years, James had learned it was best to bide his time and force the man to show his hand.

"Lovely girl, Miss Wilson. If you were looking for a wife, you couldn't do any better."

It wasn't the political diatribe he'd expected, but then, that was typical of Osgoode. Keep your opponents guessing. Attack when their defenses are down. In the aftermath of his failed attempt to engage his colleagues, James couldn't find the cool logic he usually employed to fend off the older man. Instead, his ire built. The nerve of the man, to imagine James would discuss his private life with him. He held his tongue, hoping Osgoode would give up and seek out more interesting prey.

"Rumor was you were cozying up to your new governess."

"What do you know of Sara O'Connor?" The question burst out of him, sharp and angry like the crack of a whip. It did nothing to cow Osgoode, who merely gave his cool, feline smile. Blast. He'd wanted James to react, and James had walked right into his trap.

"I know enough." Osgoode draped a languid arm on the table and played with the stem of his glass. "Not the sort of woman to make you a good wife."

Every drop of blood in James's body urged him to defend Sara and wipe the smiling confidence off Osgoode's face. He forced himself to take a breath, to sit back in his chair and examine Osgoode impartially.

It didn't make sense.

Stephen Osgoode put his self-interest before everything and everyone. He would love nothing more than to discredit James because of his connection to a laundress. What could he possibly gain from warning James away from her?

A self-satisfied smile slid over Osgoode's face. The man was enjoying watching James's confusion. He leaned forward. "I'd be careful, if I were you. Rumors have a way of spreading out of control. It would be a pity to see an upstanding man like you brought low by a scheming woman like Sara O'Connor." The satisfaction in his voice said he wouldn't find it a pity at all.

"You will not speak of her." James half rose out of his seat, bringing his hand down on Osgoode's wrist. He couldn't take another moment of her name in Osgoode's mouth. He gripped hard, feeling the narrow bones start to bend together.

For once, Osgoode seemed rattled. He sat up, attempted to

pull his arm away, but James gave no quarter. "James, what the devil . . . ?"

James bent his head low, so he could mutter into Osgoode's ear. "Leave Sara O'Connor alone."

Osgoode was too wily to show surprise if he felt any. "Why, James," he drawled, a hint of amusement in his voice. "I had no idea you were so . . . attached."

"There's a lot about me you don't know." James sent him a final, seething glare and strode from the room.

Chapter 22

Sara had always avoided the squalid shoreline, a rough-and-tumble row of trading companies and warehouses full of rum, salt cod, lumber, and beaver pelts. Rickety taverns bordered the sprawling market on Front Street, taking over after dark to cater to another kind of trade altogether: cockfighting, gambling, and every vice imaginable.

It was a dangerous place for women.

She should have planned this next step. Saved up her wages, gotten a reference from James, and found another respectable position. Surveying the motley collection of establishments on the dock, she could see that now. But Stephen Osgoode hadn't left her a choice. She'd shoved her belongings into a sack and snuck out the front door as soon as Evie was distracted by a book.

Guilt and loss mingled, tightening her throat, and sending

a dull ache through her chest. She imagined the confusion and hurt on Evie's face when she realized Sara was gone.

She'd never answer one of Evie's questions again. She'd never see James again, either. She couldn't believe how quickly she'd grown used to the warmth of his attention, the comfort of knowing he was near. Her life with the Kinneys already took on the hazy quality of a dream.

The world of the wharf, on the other hand, was all too real.

Dragging in a rough breath, she turned to the first tavern on the block, run by a seedy-looking man with greasy hair and rotten teeth. He looked her over from head to foot in a way that made her skin crawl.

"You'll do." He jerked his chin in the direction of the kitchen behind him. "Go make yourself useful."

The cook wasn't much better. She took one look at Sara and snorted.

"He'll keep you busy, I have no doubt." After a generous sip from the brown jug on the table, the woman set Sara to work making bread, a task that consisted mainly of picking weevils out of the flour.

"Will it be busy tonight?" Sara asked. The more she knew, the more prepared she'd be for whatever the night would bring.

The cook nodded. "Big meeting over at Davies' Tavern. Probably come here after."

"Meeting?"

The cook looked over at Sara and her sagging face briefly came alive. "I heard Mackenzie himself is coming to speak tonight."

Sara bit her lip. The rebel. Well, at least if the men were all debating politics, she ought to be able to slip away early.

"Where do the servants sleep?" she asked.

The woman indicated a narrow servants' stair behind her. "Up in the loft there."

She turned to stir something on the stove and Sara caught sight of a dubious hunk of meat in a grisly gray broth. Her stomach turned. She already missed Mrs. Hobbes's cooking.

She made her way up the stairs to a small airless attic with a few lumpy straw pallets. Her lodgings at Cooper's Inn were palatial by comparison. In a corner was a pile of ragged wool blankets, and under this, she tucked the sack carrying her precious blue dress. She'd keep her head down and her fine dress hidden away until she could earn enough to leave this city. In a new place, Montreal perhaps, she could get a position as a maid without worrying someone would recognize her. There was nothing tying her to Toronto, now that Granny was gone. She could start a new life.

The thought made her want to curl up in a ball and give way to the tears that threatened. She didn't want a new life. She wanted to go back to Evie . . . and James.

The cook kept her busy the next hour, scrubbing the crusted pile of dishes. Then, she swept out the tavern and cleaned the tables. By the time she finished, her arms were aching. She'd grown soft, living at the Kinneys'. Good thing she got out before she forgot how to survive.

~~~

The snow that threatened earlier held off, but a cold wind blew off the lake as James turned up his collar and mounted his mare. A ride through chilly, deserted streets was just what he needed. His mind was in an uproar, anger still thundering through his veins. He wanted to smash something. He wanted to tear Osgoode apart for making a game of him, for daring to threaten Sara.

He was angry with himself, too. It was his fault Sara was in this position. He'd brought her into his house, and insisted she stay. Exposed her to the scrutiny of the world and the insinuations of Stephen Osgoode. In the past, Osgoode had never dared threaten him so directly. But now . . .

Now, James had disrupted Ballantine's dinner party and rejected the woman he'd chosen for him. Supported the rebels in front of the most influential men in the colony. Instead of reining Andrew in, he'd practically joined the movement alongside him. Ballantine would probably wash his hands of them.

He knew how Osgoode worked. He'd drop a few hints and enflame the gossip already swirling. Then he'd rush to Ballantine, full of pretend concern while representing James in the worst possible light. In a week, James would be discredited, and Sara a pariah.

James couldn't shield a governess, not completely. People would see what they wanted to see, no matter how he tried to stay away from her.

The only way to protect her would be . . . to marry her.

A man in your position needs a wife.

Of course, Sara wasn't the wife Ballantine had in mind. He pictured the faces around the table tonight. Proud, entitled. They wouldn't acknowledge Sara O'Connor and he realized he didn't care. High society had been Amelia's dream, not his. He didn't strive to be a part of that world and he certainly didn't want that for Evie.

Marriage to Sara would cause gossip, yes, but it wasn't unsurmountable. As his wife, Sara would be under his protection in the eyes of God . . . and the law. The thought was reassuring. While every other certainty in his life failed him, the law never did.

His wife.

He drew his first easy breath since arriving at the party. Instead of sending him into a panic, the thought of marriage to Sara soothed him. It wouldn't be like the first time, when he'd let romance cloud his vision and drive him to foolishness. She'd know from the start what he could give her. Loyalty. Protection. And what he couldn't.

James dug his heels into the mare's sides, trotting along the dark, cold streets, his eyes trained for a glimpse of lamplight in the window to welcome him home. He was so lost in his longing, he almost rode into the small form that came darting across the street, calling his name.

"Mr. Kinney." Henry waved his arms, causing the horse to shy.

"Henry? What on earth has you out so late?" His heart seemed to freeze in his chest. "Is it Evie?"

Henry shook his head. "Not her. Mrs. Hobbes sent me to find you." He looked up, his face white in the gloom of the street. "Sara's gone."

The air left his lungs. "What?" There must be a mistake. She couldn't leave them. She *wouldn't*.

"She told Mrs. Hobbes she was preparing lessons in her room. When they called her for supper, she wasn't there." His voice caught. "I checked Irish Town. No one has seen her."

James took a breath, forcing his mind to function. "Her room, was it searched?"

Henry nodded. "Mrs. Hobbes said all her things are gone and she left no note." Henry's eyes searched James's face. "But I can't figure why she'd go without telling us."

"I—" James had no answers. For him, the last few days had been a revelation. He'd named memories and emotions he'd always hidden from others, and he'd felt . . . accepted. For the first time, he could imagine sharing his life with a woman again. He thought she might feel the same, but . . .

"Only one clue, as far as I can figure," Henry continued, scratching his head. "Mrs. Hobbes said a man were there, just after you left. Out in the garden."

"A man?" James felt the bottom drop out of his stomach. Sara was involved with someone else?

"Pale fellow," Henry added, watching James's face. "Tall, fine clothes."

"Sara left with him?"

Henry shook his head. "Nope, came back inside, wouldn't say a word about it. But Evie was watching out the window and said he'd come before. Some lawyer man who'd been around, asking about you. She doesn't like him."

James's heart started to race as a horrible suspicion entered his mind. Had Stephen Osgoode threatened Sara? James wouldn't put it past him. The man had arrived at Ballantine's *after* all the other guests.

A tense knot formed low in his belly. She didn't have a job, and she hadn't taken anything beyond her clothes. She didn't even have the wages he owed her. He tried to flip through the facts available as he did before every trial, but an image of Sara, alone and in danger swamped his mind and prevented all logical thought. He needed—

"I need your help, Henry." He reached down and Henry clasped his hand with a grim nod. He set his foot in the stirrup and swung up behind James on the horse.

"I reckon you do," Henry said from behind him. "Until you learn to keep a closer eye on your womenfolk, sir."

James sighed. If—no, when—he got Sara in his sight again, he wasn't planning to let her go. "Where do you figure she's gone? She'll have to find work."

"Prob'ly down at the wharf.".

The wharf. Home of the worst sorts of depravity in the city. "Surely not."

"Worth a shot. Only place to find work, quick like."

"Well, let's go then." James turned his horse south.

"Got a pistol on you, guv?"

"What? Of course not."

"Any gent what looks like you had better go armed into the wharf at night. Unless you're handy with your fives?"

It took James a moment to work that one out. "I don't make a practice of engaging in fisticuffs. I'm a lawyer. I use my words to solve conflicts."

Henry snorted. "Lot of good those'll do you down there."

James pressed his lips together. "Enough. Time is wasting. Let's go."

James had never visited the wharf after dark. The bustling dock was silent, the gangplanks drawn up for the night. All the activity had shifted inside, the only lights coming from the taverns that were jammed willy-nilly between the tall warehouses. At Henry's insistence, they stuck to the shadows and kept their heads down. Even then, James could sense watchful, calculating eyes on them. How would Sara survive in such a place? He forced his whirling thoughts to still. He needed his wits about him.

Henry stopped at the entrance to a dark alley. "Stay here now, guv. Let me do the talking."

James peered down the sliver of space between two buildings. Small forms materialized out of a side door. Children. The thought of them growing up in the shadow of this world made James ill.

Henry returned a moment later, tucking the coin purse James had given him back under his shirt. "Who were those children? Orphans?"

Henry shrugged. "Not exactly. Got mothers at least, only they're most often . . . occupied in the evenings. Little ones got to stay out of sight."

"They ought to be in bed."

Henry snorted. "Don't even have a house, never mind a bed."

James shook his head. While he worried about his daughter's curriculum, these children didn't even have a roof over their heads. It wasn't right.

"One of 'em figures she might be in Davies' Tavern," Henry said. "Worth a shot."

They continued down the road. The stench of the harbor, the fetid water dotted with rotting cargo, lingered in every gust off the lake. Henry stopped just before a tavern. The rough, deep hum of male voices spilled out into the street. "This be it, guv. Davies' Tavern. I reckon I should have a peep before you walk in there, sticking out like a sore thumb."

"Not a chance, Henry." James reached down and tweaked the boy's cap. "Sara will have my hide if she finds out I let you go into a place like that on your own."

As it turned out, James didn't stand out at all. The common room was bursting at the seams with men from every walk of life. Fine wool suits mingled with the rough linen of the dock-workers and the farmers' brown homespun. The warm, heavy air was thick with tobacco smoke and suppressed excitement.

James paused on the threshold to let his eyes scan the crowd. Ducking into the shadows at the back of the room, he caught snatches of conversation.

"Didn't even address our complaints," a man said from the table to his right.

"They never will, either. We can't waste any more time sitting around, waiting for them to notice us," said the stout man at his side.

The other men around the table nodded their agreement. James stood motionless. Instead of a den of vice, he'd walked right into a rebel hotbed.

Henry materialized at his side, shrugging his shoulders and jerking his head to the door but James was only dimly aware of the boy's movements. Another figure had caught his attention. At the front of the room, a man stepped up onto an overturned box, his red wig askew. James had no trouble recognizing William Lyon Mackenzie, the most vociferous critic of the government and the leader of the rebels. And at his side, eyes glowing with fervor, stood Andrew Ridley.

James didn't need Henry's tug on his arm to know it was time to leave. If Andrew caught sight of him, he'd never get away. And as much as he should stay and figure out exactly what would transpire in the crowded tavern, there was only one thought paramount in his mind.

He still hadn't found Sara.

Chapter 23

The patrons arrived in waves over the supper hour, keeping Sara busy in the kitchen. First came the stevedores, refreshing themselves after a day's work on the wharf, then the farmers heading home from market. She added potatoes and turnips to stretch the dubious stew and sliced loaves of dark, heavy bread. As night fell, the noise in the tavern increased and Sara glanced longingly at the back stairs. How soon could she finish and slip away?

"He'll be wanting you out front soon." The cook sat at the table, sipping from her jug and watching Sara scrape plates into the slop pail.

Sara froze. "I was hired as kitchen help." She wanted no part of the raucous gathering on the other side of the kitchen door. Serving girls in taverns were exposed to the worst sorts of insults. She pictured the shifty eyes and oily smile of her employer. She couldn't depend on him to protect her.

"Fools always buy more from a pretty face." The older woman took a long swallow. She shrugged. "Who knows, maybe you'll catch some gent's eye and make yourself a shilling or two?"

Sara inhaled, fighting back the instinct to drop the dishes and run. The cook might be wrong. The innkeeper had left her alone this long. She forced her hands to move faster. As soon as the dishes were done, she'd climb up to the servants' loft. With any luck, she could hide away until morning.

"Where's that new wench?" The innkeeper's voice boomed from the other side of the tavern door.

Sara's heart sank. She'd never been lucky. Grabbing a bucket, she started for the back door. "I'd better get more water for the dishes." She didn't wait for the cook to answer.

Too late, she realized how Granny had sheltered her. Even when they'd struggled, she'd never been exposed to real danger.

"Well, where is she?" His voice trailed out the door behind her, deep and menacing.

Sara quickened her step, hurrying across the yard to the pump. There was a stack of firewood where she could hide.

Please, help me.

Hide me.

Let him forget about me.

She realized with a jolt of surprise that she was praying. She hadn't sent up such a desperate petition since Colin lay dying in her arms.

Ye've a life before you, one God planned better than you or I ever could. She hadn't believed Granny at the time, but now—

If you're there, God, if you care at all, help me get away from here. Let me have one more chance.

Behind her, the back door was flung open, casting an arc of light onto the courtyard.

"Hey, now, come back here!"

Sara broke into a run, but his heavy steps followed, drawing closer. Hiding was out of the question now, but the gate that led to the mews was just ahead. She'd make a run for it.

A hand grabbed her arm, tightening like a manacle. "Where d'you think you're off to, I'd like to know?" The innkeeper said between gasps, swinging her about. He gave her arm a vicious shake. "You're needed to serve."

He stood so close, she could see the red veins in his eyes and a white fleck of spittle at the corner of his mouth. Though he wasn't much taller than she was, the hand that held her arm felt as unmoving as steel.

A wave of hopelessness swept through her, leaving her limp. So much for prayers. She was on her own, just like she'd always been.

~~

James clenched his jaw in frustration. Imagining they could find her in the maze of buildings and alleys seemed incredible now. She could be tucked away in a kitchen, or fast asleep in servants' quarters, but he couldn't give up. Someone in this city knew where she was. *Please let us find her. It's my fault she's out here. Let me have the chance to make things right.*

"You'd best follow me, guv." Henry's murmur barely reached his ears, calling him back to the present.

James looked down with a flicker of a smile. "Very well. You haven't led me astray yet."

But instead of following him into the next tavern, Henry gave his arm a jerk and pulled him into the nearest alley.

"Henry? What on earth?"

Henry pressed a finger to his mouth and pushed them back against the rough wall of the building, his eyes trained on the street. After a long moment, he relaxed and looked up at James.

"Don't think they're coming after us."

"They?"

"Didn't you see those rough chaps, across the way?"

James was forced to admit he hadn't.

"I reckon they'll be waiting around, now they've got you in their sights." He sent a narrow glance at James's fine wool suit. "Told you you'd stick out, dressed like that."

"Let's cut through the mews then," James said, with a nod down the alley. "We'll come out a few blocks down. Might lose them."

Henry eyed him with dawning respect. "Now you're getting the hang of things."

James led the way down the dark alley. He glanced down at the boy trotting at his side in time to see him yawn. It was late. He needed to get Henry home to bed. He needed to get back to Evie. For the first time, he pondered the possibility of *not* finding Sara. The thought was so terrifying, it stole his breath. He must have made some sound, for Henry sent him a curious glance.

James tried to summon a smile or a reassuring word for the boy, but his hope was dwindling. *I won't insist that she come back, not even for Evie's sake. Just let her be safe.*

"Release me."

Only two words, but they stopped James in his tracks. He recognized that low, clear voice. Sara. Hope bloomed as he scanned the rough wooden fence that blocked his view of the yard on the other side. Where was she?

"Not likely." A man answered, his voice rough and insistent. "You get in there and smile pretty. Make sure every man buys another round. What do you think I hired you for?"

James's hands clenched at the man's tone. He crept forward and peered over the fence.

"Nice work, guv," Henry whispered at his side. "You found her."

James spared him a tight smile, his eyes riveted on the scene before him. Her back was to him, but James knew that faded dress and floppy mobcap. A wiry man in a dirty apron held her arm, standing far too close.

"You hired me to work in the kitchen."

"Well, that's not what I be paying you to do. Sooner you learn who rules the roost here, the better." The man jerked her arm and Sara stumbled.

James forced himself to take a breath and settle the rage coursing through his veins. He needed to keep his wits about him. If he went charging in like a bull, Sara could end up hurt. He crept to the gate and slowly lifted the latch. The yard was in almost complete darkness except for a circle of light that spilled out of the back door.

"Let go of her." James strode forward, his eyes trained on the man.

Both figures stilled in surprise at the sound of his voice.

"James." Sara turned her head, her eyes wide. Under the shock in Sara's voice was something warmer, a wash of relief and gladness that he couldn't dwell on. Not until he got rid of the man who held her arm.

"An' who might you be?" The man squinted but didn't back down.

"I am Miss O'Connor's employer."

"Oh, ho, are you now?" The man seemed to find this amusing. "Well, that be a mystery, for I'm rightly certain that this here woman works for me, and that you be trespassing."

James squelched the urge to level the man and be done with it. There were better ways to solve problems, wasn't that what he'd told Henry? "She might be working for you now, but I had her first and she left without finishing the month she was paid for." James forced himself to relax the hands that had formed into fists. He leaned toward the man conspiratorially. "Owes me, you see."

Sara gasped in outrage behind him, but James kept his attention trained on the man. He'd explain later.

The older man narrowed his eyes. "Seems you want her back awful bad."

"Left me in a bind." James shrugged, attempting to downplay his interest, though judging by the calculating look in the man's eye, he hadn't fooled him. "I'd be willing to pay you for any inconvenience."

The older man scratched his chin. "Well, I might be amenable to a negotiation, so to speak."

"Excellent. My assistant will agree to the terms." James jerked his head in Henry's direction. The boy straightened, catching on without a hitch.

"Eh, look here, I didn't mean you could take her straight

away." The man swung Sara about. "I figure I should get one night's work out of 'er for all my trouble."

James tossed aside his pretense at calm and lunged, grabbing the man and twisting his arm around his back. He was smaller than James but tough and wiry. He struggled, clearly not about to give up. James tightened his other hand into a fist. It had been years since the informal boxing matches at school, but he reckoned he still remembered. Before he lost his grip on the man's arm, he landed a solid punch to the side of his head. The man crumpled, leaving Sara standing before him, an empty bucket dangling from her hand.

Henry let out a low whistle of admiration. "Don't reckon I'll be worrying about you anymore, guv."

James ignored him, focused on Sara. "Are you all right? Unhurt?" He scanned her face, looking for any sign of injury.

"I'm fine."

She wasn't, if the pallor of her skin was anything to go by. James turned to Henry. "Do you suppose you can hire us a carriage at this time of night?"

The boy caught the bag of coins James lobbed at him and tested its weight. "I could fetch a coach and four with this lot."

"A cabby would be fine," James said dryly. Henry darted off, leaving James and Sara in silence.

"What were you thinking, running off like that?" he said. Relief gave sharpness to his voice that he didn't intend. "Don't you know the danger you were in?" He realized as soon as the words left his mouth that it was the wrong tack to take but his fear for her scrambled his brain, robbing him of his usual powers of speech.

She looked up, her eyes blazing. "I am well aware of the

danger." She gave a short, humorless huff of laughter. "I've discovered safety is a luxury I can't afford." She wrapped her hands around her middle, the tremor in her hands giving lie to her anger. She'd been alone. Scared.

"Oh, Sara," he whispered, stepping closer. "Don't ever scare me like that again." He raised his arms, his hands hovering for a moment near her shoulders. Giving her the chance to move away.

She sighed, a catch in her breath, and leaned forward. It was all the permission he needed to gather her close, smoothing his hands down her back and feeling the tense muscles relax. She buried her face in his shoulder with a shudder, melting against him. For a long moment, he stood perfectly still, savoring the feel of her in his arms. Safe. *Thank God.*

Slowly, almost imperceptibly, their embrace changed. She shifted against him, and he became aware of the shape of her through the layers of their clothing. A wave of heat rolled over him that blocked the icy November wind. His hands swept up, learning the contours of her back and coming up to play with the silky wisps of hair at the nape of her neck.

She melted beneath his touch, her body pressing even closer to his. He didn't understand the danger until he bent his head, and his lips brushed the velvety skin of her neck. The touch jolted him, and she gasped. He lifted his head to look into her eyes. Scanning her face, he saw the fear was gone from her eyes, replaced by a soft warmth that lingered in her gaze and the gentle curve of her mouth.

He didn't contemplate the consequences. Leaning forward, he touched his lips to hers for the space of a heartbeat. Hers were just as soft as he'd imagined, moving beneath his in a slow response that sent the blood pumping through his veins.

A moan from the unconscious figure a few feet away called him back to reality. He froze and Sara took a hasty step back, pulling out of his arms.

He looked down, seeing in her eyes the same shock he was feeling. What was he doing? They were in a dank mew in the seediest part of the city, her former assaulter at their feet. And with one kiss, he'd forgotten all of it.

"I . . . I apologize. I can't think—" James scrambled for words, her silent, searing gaze unnerving him. He cleared his throat, regrouping, just as he would after an unexpected counterargument. "Please, let us forget this happened."

The soft, warm look in her eyes faded, her chin taking on its former stubborn tilt. "Of course." Her eyes dropped to the ground, her voice so low he had to strain to hear it.

The sound of a carriage in the mews was a blessed distraction, as was Henry's spry form, high up on the seat with the driver.

"C'mon, guv. Better hoof it before he wakes up." Henry gestured to the crumpled form of the tavern keeper, who was beginning to stir.

James grabbed Sara's hand, pulling her to the narrow roadway. Somehow, Henry had managed to find them a covered carriage that was relatively clean. The boy was a wonder. James bundled Sara into the cab, jumping in behind her as soon as he'd given the driver his direction.

James sent her an uncertain glance. She sat upright, her back not touching the leather squabs, her hands clenched tight in her lap. The flush in her cheeks was the only sign of what had passed between them.

He cleared his throat. Should he apologize again? He couldn't say he was sorry for the most perfect kiss of his life.

Then again, he might have offended her. He tried to read her expression, but her chin was tucked low, her eyes stubbornly trained on her hands. Silence stretched between them as the carriage left the mews and joined the main thoroughfare north.

Suddenly, she gasped and turned to him. "I need to go back." There was a thread of panic in her voice.

James stared at her, trying to make sense of her words. "What? We're not going near that sorry excuse for an inn ever again."

Her eyes glistening with tears. "My new dress. It's back there."

"Your dress." He could scarcely believe his ears. After all this, she was worried about a dress?

"It's the only nice thing I own." Her tears fell faster.

He looked out the window of the coach. He couldn't think straight when she cried. "We'll buy a new one," he said. Her breath caught on a sob, and she pressed her hand to her mouth to stop the sound. He turned toward her, desperation entering his voice. "You must see the danger. Please, don't cry."

She inhaled, her hand stretching out to smooth her skirt. "I'm being foolish. It's fine."

He had to strain to hear her voice over the rumble of the wheels. She bowed her head, her lips pressed together, offering no further words of explanation. He wanted to pull her into his chest. Kiss every tear from her cheeks. Never let her out of his sight again. But . . . she'd left him once today. What would prevent her from doing so again? The thought brought panic rushing back.

"Why did you leave?" She flinched at the harshness in his voice, and he tried to soften his tone. "Did something happen?" He thought of Osgoode. "Did someone threaten you?"

She looked up sharply at this, fear flitting across her face before she could lower her eyes. She said nothing. He ground his teeth in frustration. Why wouldn't she trust him?

"Mrs. Hobbes told Henry a man came. He spoke to you." She remained stubbornly silent. "Was it Stephen Osgoode?" At the name, a quiver went through her. He wouldn't have noticed it, except that all his attention was focused on her, as though she were a witness in a courtroom. "Tell me."

He let the silence linger. Her hands twisted in her lap until he brought his own to rest on top of hers with a gentle squeeze. She sighed, the tension leaving her shoulders, and chewed her lip as though she were deciding what to say. He felt a tiny thrill beneath his worry. He'd gotten through her defenses. She was going to tell him.

She cleared her throat. "I—I came to realize my presence in your home . . . might hurt you and Evie. He has powerful friends," she said finally, her voice low. "He said he'd put it about that I was—" She broke off, burying her face in her hands. An unmanageable surge of anger hit him, something that happened with alarming frequency when Sara was threatened.

"Osgoode bears me a grudge. Several of them," he said. "But I still don't understand what he hoped to gain by talking to you."

Her head jerked up, her mouth opening as though she were about to answer. Then her lips snapped shut. "If I work for you, he is going to destroy your reputation. Evie's future, too."

None of this was news to James. Still, warning Sara off would seem to counteract Osgoode's goal. With Sara gone, he'd lose his ammunition. A horrifying thought occurred to him. What if Osgoode was interested in Sara himself? She was a beautiful woman. Vulnerable, too. An easy target for a man with no scruples in search of dalliance. For a wild moment he wanted to command the driver to take him to Osgoode's lodging where he could pound the idea right out of his head. Then Sara's voice, low and aching, pulled him back from the brink.

"He's—he seemed like an awful man." She shuddered. His hand slid sideways, grasping hers as he gave in to the need to comfort her. She clutched his fingers. "I'm sorry you were worried, but running away was the only way to stop him."

"Not the *only* way," he said. Was she thinking about their kiss as much as he was? Surely he hadn't imagined her response.

She looked up, an unspoken question drawing her brows together.

James took a breath. Marriage was risky. He told himself he'd never face the torment of love and wanting and rejection again, yet when it came to Sara O'Connor, he couldn't seem to stop himself. Over the past hours, one thought had overshadowed all the others. He never wanted to lose Sara O'Connor again.

He cleared his throat, jumping in before he lost his nerve. "You could marry me."

Chapter 24

Sara fell back against the squabs. "Pardon me?"

"I've thought the situation through, and it's the only solution."

"The solution to what?" A sinking embarrassment sent heat rushing to her cheeks. Did he feel obliged to offer marriage because of that kiss?

"Evie needs you. You need a home." He lifted his hands as though it was the most logical idea in the world. Apparently, he'd forgotten all about their embrace.

"Those are not reasons to marry." She ought to nip his proposal in the bud. She would, as soon as the world stopped spinning and she could make sense of his words.

"This is ridiculous. Stop the carriage at once." Sara leaned forward, putting her hand on the door latch. She had to escape before she succumbed to the lure of his words and did something foolish. Like agree to this wild suggestion.

He put his hand over hers, his thumb rubbing the back of

her hand and sending a shiver through her. Her eyes focused on his fingers, strong and capable, sheltering hers. The touch reminded her of the way his hands had slid up her back to embrace her. The way his lips had lowered to hers, warm and smooth, until she'd felt his kiss all the way to her toes. He'd kissed her. Now he wanted to *marry* her. What had happened to straightlaced, serious James Kinney?

"You can't stay on as Evie's governess. I see that now. You're too—" He waved a hand at her, and she became acutely aware of her stained dress.

She reached a hand up and straightened her mobcap that was, as she suspected, completely askew. "I'm a servant, is that what you mean?" He probably regretted that impulsive embrace and was doing his best to put a good face on it.

"You're too beautiful." He pressed his lips together as though he regretted the words.

A warm glow coursed through her. He thought she was beautiful. His kiss and his words spun a web around her until she didn't know which way was up. She shook her head. She didn't want this attraction, no matter how his touch reminded her of what it felt like to live again.

"Look," he said, sighing. "When I pulled Evie out of Miss Giblin's classes, she just . . . froze. Didn't cry, didn't even ask about you after that first time. She wouldn't talk to anyone. It's like she stepped back from life. I don't know how else to describe it."

Sara understood. It was exactly what she'd done when Colin died. She turned to stare out the dusty window. But she couldn't continue like that, not now. Now she couldn't stop feeling.

"Since you came, she's different. I've never seen her so happy. She needs you, Sara."

"But marriage?" Sara searched his face, looking for clues to his feelings. He spoke as though she were merely the solution to a problem, but she couldn't forget the way he'd held her or the heat in his eyes. There had been nothing practical about that.

"There are benefits for you, as well," James continued. She wondered if this was how he sounded in the courtroom. Logical. Persuasive. "You would be comfortable. No more scrubbing."

She looked at James, trying to see past his calm confidence. He could have married a new mother for Evie any time these past years. Why choose a servant?

James must have sensed her hesitation, for he continued, his tone more persuasive than ever. "Evie needs someone who understands and appreciates her for who she is. Loves her."

Her resolve weakened. "I do love her," she whispered. She'd known within a day of their meeting that Evie was the daughter she'd never have. If she were married to James, if she were Evie's mother, she'd never have to leave. She leaned back in her seat, her eyes searching James's face. "What about you? What do you want out of this marriage?"

At her words, he dropped his eyes. "I'd make no demands on you." A flush of color spread up his neck and she wondered if he was reliving their kiss. "I've apologized for my embrace. I won't force my . . . attentions on you." His face was red now, and his voice lost its clear, purposeful tone. Did he regret their kiss? Did she? Perhaps. Her feelings for James Kinney were more muddled than ever now. He cleared his throat. "This marriage isn't about the two of us. It's about family. Stability."

Family. The word brought back every reason she couldn't say yes. There was so much he didn't know. She'd defied her father. Run off with a stable boy. Osgoode might hold a grudge against James, but that was nothing compared with the vendetta he nurtured against her. "But . . . that man." She forced the words out past the lump in her throat. Would she never be free of Stephen Osgoode? "He said he'd ruin you."

"Osgoode?" James's lip curled. "I'd like to see him try." Sara opened her mouth to protest, but he placed a single finger over her lips, warm and smooth. "He can't spread rumors if you're my wife, Sara." His eyes dropped to her mouth, and he pulled away, his finger brushing her lower lip. His eyes snapped back to hers with a sharp intake of breath. "There might be gossip at first, but it will fade."

Her mind spun, weaving possibilities and hopes, trying desperately to piece together a future with James and Evie. Osgoode wanted her inheritance, not her. If she were married to James, it was in his best interest to keep her identity a secret. But there would be dinners, assemblies. There was still the danger that she'd be recognized, and her reputation would taint James and Evie. "I can't go out in society," she blurted out. "I'd be useless to you."

James shook his head. "That's not what I want. I've had enough of society to last a lifetime." He looked into her eyes. "The past is in the past. This will be a fresh start for both of us."

Her eyes closed for a long moment. A fresh start. Was it possible? She could stay in that haven on Duke Street and steer Evie to adulthood, never feeling hunger or cold again. Osgoode's threats and the heart-stopping terror she'd felt when that innkeeper had grabbed her arm would be a distant memory. She'd prayed for help. For another chance to live. Was this proposal her answer?

"Trust me, Sara. I'll keep you safe."

She felt again the rush of relief when she'd heard his voice behind that squalid inn, the warmth and security of his arms around her. She was seized by a sudden, reckless need to grasp the dream before it evaporated.

"Yes."

He was silent for a moment, his mouth opening slightly in surprise. "P-Pardon me?"

"I agree." Sara's throat was so tight, she could barely get the words out, hope and fear mingling in a tight knot that was almost painful. "I'll marry you."

He swallowed. "Thank you."

There was surprise in his voice and a question behind his words, but she wouldn't—couldn't—explain.

"When?" she managed.

"I'll get a special license." James answered immediately, as though he'd already worked out the details. He *was* a barrister. He probably had everything planned to the minute. "I don't think we should wait until Osgoode can work his mischief. We can be married by Monday, if I can manage it."

Osgoode. At the name, a sick feeling rose in her throat, but she forced it down. If she married James, she'd be free of the man. She breathed easier and attempted to return James's confident smile.

Her past was dead and buried, as cold and silent as a tomb. She only had to keep it that way.

~~~

James spent the next day securing the license and tracking Andrew down. Despite the distance between them lately,

Andrew was the closest he had to family. From the glimpse of him he'd had at Davies' Tavern, he knew Andrew was back in the city. James took up a position outside his lodgings until he saw his friend's tall, lanky form swing into view.

James stepped out of the shadows. "Andrew." Andrew swung about. There were dark circles under his eyes, and he looked as though he needed a wash and a shave. He must have been up all night at that meeting. "I've been looking for you."

He didn't meet James's eyes. "Ballantine sent you to rein me in, did he?"

James sighed, "No. But someone should talk sense into you."

"Bah. You're an old woman." Andrew dismissed his concerns with a swipe of his hand. "This is the time for action, James." He unlocked his door, his eyes sweeping the street before pulling James in after him.

James sighed, following Andrew up the stairs and into his rooms. They entered a snug sitting room overlooking the street, furnished with two armchairs and a small table. A fire crackled in the hearth, thanks to Andrew's manservant, who met them at the door to take Andrew's coat. James refused the courtesy and the offer of refreshments. He didn't intend to stay long, nor get embroiled in a political debate.

Andrew waved the man away and gestured for James to join him in the armchairs. "I'm sorry about that meeting at Montgomery's."

James almost smiled. *Now* he apologized? "Where were you?"

Andrew shrugged. "Mackenzie is unpredictable. He decided to go to Newmarket and there was no way to get word to you."

James's finger gripped the arms of his chair. Anger wouldn't serve his purpose today. "I see."

Andrew seemed unaware of his irritation. "Have you decided?" He sounded like a child encouraging his friend to join in a game. "Will you join us?"

"I'm not going to risk my family's future for some half-baked rebellion." James sighed, rubbing a weary hand over his face. "The kind of change we need doesn't come about with violence."

Before James had even finished speaking, Andrew started shaking his head. "Once they see our numbers, once they realize how serious we are, there won't be any need for violence."

"There's a better way." James leaned forward in his chair. It was the first time he'd articulated the idea that had been brewing in his head for days. "We're not military men. We don't know battle strategy . . . we know the law. We can bring change *through* the law, not by fighting against it."

"It's too late for that, James."

"It's never too late to do what's right. I've thought it through. We could challenge the power of the rich in this city. Represent cases that really mean something. Make people see that things could change."

Andrew squeezed his eyes shut. "No, I mean, it's too late for *me*. I've made a commitment. There are things you don't know." His eyes popped open. "Please, James. Come with me."

"I can't." James cleared his throat. There was no easy way to introduce the purpose of his visit. "I—I'm thinking about getting married."

"What?" Andrew's mouth dropped open. "To that Wilson chit?" His eyes grew wide, as well they should. Marriage to the simpering debutante of Ballantine's choosing would be nothing short of disastrous.

"Of course not." James paused. "To Sara O'Connor."

Andrew was silent for a long moment, his eyes searching James's face. "You're serious." His voice rose. "Are you out of your mind? You don't know anything about that woman."

James jumped out of his seat and paced to the window. Andrew hit a nerve. He didn't know everything about Sara, but he knew enough. She'd been hurt by a family who rejected her. In time, she'd open up and tell him everything. For now, he couldn't demand more, not when he had no intention of sharing every harrowing moment of his story with her. The past was in the past, wasn't that what he'd told her? "I know all I need to. She's a good, honorable woman. She loves Evie and Evie loves her."

"Evie's not marrying her. *You* are. She'll turn your life upside down. She could ruin your career. Don't underestimate the power a wife wields."

James gave a short bark of laughter. "I'm well aware of the power of a wife." He held Andrew's eye until the younger man looked away, a slight flush on his cheeks. He'd never said a word against Amelia, but Andrew was perceptive. He must have noticed the tensions between them in those final months. Amelia complained to anyone who would listen about the inadequate size of their parlor and planned parties they hadn't the means to host. "How would you know, anyway?" James attempted to lighten the mood. "Got a sweetheart hidden away that I don't know about?" A dull red color swept up Andrew's cheeks. Instead of the glib answer James had expected, his barb had found its mark.

"Of course not," Andrew said, glaring at James beneath lowered brows. "Don't try to change the topic. You're marrying a servant woman you know nothing about. She's bewitched you."

"Don't be ridiculous. This is a practical arrangement."

"Practical, eh? A long engagement, then. No need to rush things."

"As soon as possible."

"What? James, you must consider—"

"I've given my word. It's all set." He couldn't lose her, and if that meant a final break with the man who had once been his closest friend, so be it. But he hoped it wouldn't come to that. He cleared his throat. "I-I'd like you to stand up with me." Andrew pursed his lips, his face inscrutable. James went on, "If you just got to know her, you'd see why I—why Evie loves her so much." Andrew's gaze searched his face and James wondered what his expression gave away. He realized he was standing tense, his fists clenched, and forced himself to relax. "At least give her a chance. For Evie's sake."

At the mention of his niece, Andrew's face softened. He inhaled and nodded once. "Very well. I—I'll try. For Evie's sake."

A rush of relief brought a smile to James's face. "Thank you. The ceremony is Monday morning."

"Monday?" Andrew looked shocked.

"Yes." James drew out the word with a slight question at the end. There was nothing unusual in the choice. "Reverend Wilkie said he'll come at ten o'clock."

"I . . . I can't Monday." Andrew rose and paced to the decanter and glasses on the side table.

"There are no trials scheduled for Monday. I've already informed the clerks." James's words didn't placate Andrew in the least, who poured himself a brandy and paced to the window. "I need you there, Andrew. You're all the family I have."

Andrew's shoulders sagged. He tossed back his drink, then turned to James, his face grim. "Fine. I'll try to be there. Unless you change your mind before then." He shook his head, his eyes mocking. "I'm not sure I know who you are anymore, James Kinney. You always said I was the impulsive one."

Chapter 25

She couldn't marry James Kinney.

Last night fear, exhaustion, and a good dose of attraction had muddled her thinking. She'd grasped at the chance for a future. In the weak December sun of today, she knew better.

Bundled up against a cold north wind, Sara had trudged down King Street to the dry goods shops. James assured her he had an account at Sproule's. She'd need only mention his name and she could purchase whatever she needed.

She'd waited in line, next to crates of boots and bins of dried beans and rice. The scents of leather and whale oil wafted through the room from the harnesses and lanterns that hung overhead. Ready-made clothing and finer fabrics were behind the counter, but Sara couldn't seem to reach the front of the line. Whenever she was close, the shopkeeper would move down the counter to help another patron. One better dressed than Sara.

"Excuse me, sir," she said finally, stepping to the middle of the counter. "I believe I am next in line."

The man didn't look up from the ledger. "Indeed?"

"Yes." Sara put her hands on the counter, making it clear she wasn't about to leave.

"What can I get you?" he said, turning away to tidy an array of gloves.

Sara ground her teeth. He was far enough away that she'd have to raise her voice. She began to recite her modest list, but the man swung about, interrupting her right after she'd listed a pair of half boots and before she could mention the shawl.

"We don't accept credit."

"The items are to be charged to James Kinney." The two women behind her in line stopped talking. Sara could feel their eyes boring into her back.

The man's eyes widened. "I can't do that." He looked her up and down. "I do not charge to accounts based on the say-so of any person who walks off the street." His tone left little doubt about his opinion of her. Before she could refute his claim, he moved down the counter, looking around Sara to the women behind her. "Ladies, I'd be happy to assist you."

The women moved past Sara with sidelong glances. They were not much older than she was, in dark wool gowns with full skirts and fine pelisses, marking them as solid members of the merchant class. One of the women met Sara's eyes for a moment and Sara's heart dropped. The woman had once been her schoolmate, a year or two ahead of her at Miss Strachan's. Sara ducked her head and backed away, but not before she saw the puzzled look on the woman's face.

Sara turned and fled the store. It was hard being invisible

Sara O'Connor, but that was infinitely better than being an object of curiosity . . . or scandal. If she married James Kinney, she wouldn't be able to avoid running into people she knew. What a fool she'd been to think she could hide from her past. A bitter blend of anger and frustration brought hot tears to her eyes. She blinked them back, stumbling out the door.

Back on the street, she wiped her eyes. Proudfoot's Emporium was next door. She'd have to try there, though the selection wouldn't be as good. James had paid her wages. She'd have enough for something simple.

The navy cotton gown she purchased was suitable for a housemaid. The shopkeeper counted her coins one by one, examining each as though he suspected she were a counterfeiter. On the way home, she'd twice had to step off the boardwalk to make way for the wide skirts of a lady, causing half-frozen mud to ooze between the cracks in her old boots. She welcomed the discomfort. This was where she belonged.

How had she ever thought she could marry him? She'd always be worried about detection, about bringing shame on them both. Luckily, it wasn't too late to change her mind.

That evening, she waited until Evie and Mrs. Hobbes were abed, then crept from her room. Light glowed from under the parlor door. At her tap, James bade her enter. She slipped into the room. James came to his feet in a rush, the paper he was reading floating to the ground beside him. "Sara." He bent over to pick up the paper and stood before her with a boyish, eager smile that made her heart flip.

"I must speak with you," she said, her voice serious. James's smile faltered and she rushed on before she lost her nerve. "I can't marry you." The words had been building all evening and it was a relief to say them out loud.

The smile vanished. His fingers clenched, wrinkling the newsprint in his hands. "What brought this about?" His gaze sharpened. "Did something happen?"

"Sober reflection." She had no intention of telling him about the scene at Sproule's. It was too . . . humiliating.

He folded the paper into a precise square. "Please, sit down. Explain." His voice was cool, emotionless and she had the uncomfortable feeling he was grilling her like a witness again.

She took a breath. Best get this over with. "I'm a servant. I can't be the mother Evie needs."

His shoulders relaxed, as though her words eased his mind. "Nonsense." He dismissed her concerns with one word and a shrug. "Evie loves you."

"Nonsense?" Her voice rose. The humiliations of the day, the week, the years were suddenly too much. "So says a man. You can earn your place in society through hard work. Control your destiny. A woman's position will always be dependent on others' opinions. With me as her mother, Evie won't have a chance."

James leaned forward, his gaze pinning her to the chair. "A chance at what, exactly?"

The fierceness of his voice gave her pause. She hadn't expected anger. "A chance to . . . to be invited into the finest homes. To marry well." It was more than that, though. She wanted Evie to have a choice. To be happy.

"And you really think that is what is most important to me?" He stared at her as though she ought to know better.

Didn't he realize how vulnerable Evie would be if something were to happen to him? Her temper rose to match his. "If it isn't, it should be." Surely, she didn't have to explain how the world worked. "I don't want her to struggle. Not like I did."

He tossed the newspaper aside and reached for her hands, his face softening. "I'm sorry for what happened to you." He paused as though looking for words. "But I've tried for too long to fit into a society that had no place for truth. For compassion. It's not the life I want for her. We can do better, don't you think?" Sara nodded, feeling a flutter of hope. "You've opened my eyes, Sara. I was living with blinders on. Now I see what's around me." He spoke faster, the words pouring out of him as though they'd been building up in a logjam until one piece shifted and they rushed forward in a gush. "The odds are stacked against the poor. They come here looking for a better life and end up stuck in the same world they tried to leave behind." He ran a hand through his hair. "It's wrong and I'm in the position to do something about it."

"Wh-what are you planning to do?" Would he join Mackenzie's rebels? The thought terrified her. He couldn't risk his life like that. They needed him.

"I don't want to spend my life on financial contracts that benefit the rich." He searched her face. At her slow nod of understanding, he continued, sweeping a hand in a direction that approximated north. "There are hundreds of men out there, in the settlements, who feel they have no recourse but armed rebellion. I could help. Explain the law and get their concerns before the authorities, but . . ." He bit his lip, his eyes sliding to the floor. "We'd have to leave the city."

Sara could have laughed at the relief that swept through her. He didn't want to fight. He wanted to leave the place that held only bitter memories and the threat of discovery.

"I bought an allotment years ago. As an investment, I suppose." He gave a huff of laughter. "Amelia assured me no woman would ever want to live there, but . . ." He looked at her then, his eyes pleading. "Do you think you could be happy far from the city? It would be hard work, I imagine, setting up a practice there, but perhaps together . . ."

Sara reached out and touched his forearm. Was this the same man who'd looked down his nose at her at Cooper's Inn? It was hard to believe. "Yes, I could be happy there." He smiled, relief and hope lighting his face. "It sounds wonderful." Her voice was husky. She wasn't sure if she dared believe the picture he painted. Could they really start over, in a place where no one had heard of Sally Ballantine?

He looked down at her hand on his sleeve. She flushed and moved to pull it away, but he quickly covered it with his own, holding it in place. "It won't be as lucrative as what I do now," he warned. "I might not be able to provide—"

"I'm a laundress who faced a life on the streets," she said, rolling her eyes. "I don't mind living simply. It's high society I'm afraid of."

He looked down at her, his smile growing until it threatened to crack his face in two. "I'm beginning to think you could handle just about anything that's thrown your way." She started to protest such lavish praise, but he reached out and cupped her cheek before she could say more. "I've never met a woman like you. True to her convictions, intelligent. I won't ask you to be something you're not. We need you. Please don't leave." He grabbed her hands and raised them to his chest. She could feel the beat of his heart, steady and strong beneath her fingers.

No one had ever valued her like this. Not Papa, who tried

to marry her off to Stephen Osgoode. Not even Colin, who'd treated her like a delicate china figurine to be set up on a shelf and admired. James wanted a partner.

In the life he proposed, her social status, her past, wouldn't matter. Her experiences in Irish Town could even help. It seemed too good to be true. "Are you sure this is what you want?"

Instead of answering, he leaned forward and pressed a quick, firm kiss to her lips. It was different from the lingering kiss they'd shared at the wharf. This was over before she had a chance to respond. Yet she felt the heat of it like a shock through her body, making her gasp.

He pulled back and they stared at each other, eyes wide. "I'm sorry. I didn't intend to offend . . ."

"It's all right." She smiled, surprised to find that it *was* all right. The fleeting touch of his lips made her want to put her hands on either side of his head and bring him close for another kiss. "It's more than all right. I mean—" Heat rose in her cheeks. "We *are* going to be married." Now why would she bring that up? He'd said it was a marriage for Evie's sake. That probably meant—

"But we agreed it was a marriage of necessity." He took another step back, balling his hands into fists.

"Oh," she said, looking down. He didn't want her as a real wife. Well, she could live with that. Once she got over this embarrassing desire to throw herself into his arms. "Of course. I'm sorry."

He ran his fingers through his hair, looking everywhere except at her. "It's not that I don't want—that is, it's not you . . ."

"Then what is it?" They needed to clear the air. Establish

the boundaries so she could teach her heart to stop racing every time he came close.

James squeezed his eyes shut for a moment, as though he were concentrating on each word that came out of his mouth. "It's . . . me. I can't make you happy."

Sara moved her head back to look him full in the face. It wasn't what she expected him to say. "How do you know what will make me happy?"

"I don't, not exactly. But I know I don't have it in me. It's only a matter of time before I start disappointing you. I'm not good at being a husband. Amelia—" He ran his fingers under his collar where a flush of red spread up his neck. He cleared his throat, his voice recovering its calm authority. "Look, I think we could be excellent partners, Sara. Partners in raising Evie. Partners in bringing change to this country. But more than that . . . it wouldn't work."

Sara nodded. When he put it that way, it seemed so simple. The tangle of attraction and yearning she felt for him clouded her judgment, but . . . she *wanted* to believe the picture he painted. Wanted to be part of this family more than she'd ever wanted anything in her life. "If you're certain this is what you really want . . ."

"It is." He grabbed her hands, his expression serious. "You only have to be sure it's the life you want as well."

Sara nodded. It was more than she'd ever dared hope for. A blessing, even. *A blessing.* She'd all but given up on those.

"That's settled then." He kept a firm grip on her hands when she moved to step away. "Now you can tell me what happened at Sproule's today."

He caught her off guard. "Pardon me?"

"You didn't answer Evie's questions about your shopping trip at supper. Didn't offer to show her your purchases, either." He crossed his arms.

She sighed. There were drawbacks to living with a barrister. "I . . . couldn't access your credit." She saw the gathering frown on his face and hurried to explain. "It's fine. I bought a dress at Proudfoot's."

"Proudfoot's?" He looked doubtful. Perhaps he knew the kind of simple fare on offer there. Still, she had no desire to go back and face the humiliation of Sproule's again.

"It's fine. I needed a dress and now I have one."

He looked at her, his gaze intent and searching. "But Proudfoot's . . ." He let the thought trail off. "You're certain it's what you want?"

"I'm certain. I'm plain Sara O'Connor. A simple dress will suit me fine."

~

James left the courts the next day with his mind still full of Sara. Before her, he'd never considered changing the course of his career. Never considered marrying again, either. Now a new life opened before him, one richer and more purposeful than any he'd led before. True, there was that sizzling pull between them that muddled his thinking and threatened his equilibrium, but he had that well in hand now. They'd set the boundaries. As long as he kept his emotions in check and a healthy distance between them, it would work out just fine.

He turned the corner onto King Street, the late afternoon bustle fading into the background as he stopped in front of a small house of whitewashed clapboard. A simple sign hung over the door, one he'd passed hundreds of times. *Madame Cloutier—Dressmaker.*

A dress. He could still hear the humiliation in her voice when she admitted what happened at Sproule's. A dress from Madame Cloutier's could wipe that memory from her mind. Besides, he'd promised her a new dress. Whatever cheap gown she'd purchased at Proudfoot's didn't count.

Before he quite knew what he was about, he'd pushed open the door and entered the elegant foyer of Madame Cloutier's. His eyes scanned the elaborate floral wallpaper and the impossibly small settees on either side of the hall. Not much had changed, not even the sweet, cloying scent that hung in the over-warm air. Madame was still the finest dressmaker in Toronto, the only place women could get a dress cut in the latest style.

A woman emerged from the back in an understated yet elegant black gown. Her eyes assessed him, taking in the cut of his coat and the state of his shoes before apparently deciding he could stay. Her posture relaxed and a faint smile curled her lips.

"May I help you?"

James opened his mouth, but no words came out. It was a good question. Why was he here? "I'm looking for a dress," he blurted out.

"Yes, I imagined as much."

He flushed. It wasn't like Cloutier's offered anything else.

"For your . . . wife?" she prompted.

"Yes. Well, almost . . . That is, yes, it's for my wife." Worse and worse. He had to get himself in line.

The woman's eyebrows rose. "Very well. A day dress or an evening gown?" James was silent a moment too long, for she continued. "Perhaps you'd like to see some fashion plates? To get some ideas?"

"A day gown. It's for a wedding. And I need it now."

She sent him a pitying smile. "Sir, Cloutier's has a long list of clientele. We don't have . . ." She paused, her mouth turning down in distaste. "Ready-made."

"But surely you have something returned, or a sample. Anything." He sounded desperate. He swallowed and forced a smile. "Please. It's a special day. I want to surprise her."

This was the right thing to say, for a tender look came over the woman's face. "Each gown at Cloutier's is made to order. I'm most sorry, sir, but we have nothing."

"I'd like to speak with Madame," he said, letting a trace of command enter his voice.

"Impossible. She's with a client."

He took a step forward. "Tell her Mr. Kinney is here. I believe she will recall my name." James had helped Madame Cloutier collect payment from a tardy client a few years back, and all without dragging anyone's name through the courts.

The woman stepped back, a flash of uncertainty in her eyes. She nodded once. "Very well. I'll return shortly."

James smiled, calling on every inch of charm he possessed. "Thank you. You are most kind."

She returned a moment later and motioned for him to follow her through a small door in the back that led to the workroom. Gowns in various states of completion were draped over tables and hung from the walls. She motioned to a pink gown hanging to his right.

"Considering your past help, Madame said you might have this one," she said. "Some of our clients live north of the city and Madame isn't sure . . ." She shrugged, a nervous gesture that James understood. Rebels and reformers lived north of the city. Lately, they'd had more on their minds than new dresses. "It's a lovely gown. Look at the detail here." The skirt opened down the front, the hem artfully pulled back to reveal layers of lace dotted with tiny rosettes.

"Ah, it's lovely, yes," he said, sensing she was expecting an answer. "But it's not exactly . . ." He paused. It was probably the height of fashion. The more ruffles the better, that's how Amelia had chosen her gowns. But it wasn't right. It wasn't Sara.

He scanned the room, his eyes taking in a rainbow of colors until they came to rest on a shimmer of gray in the corner. He took a step forward. It was a simple gown in a deep, rich silk, the only ornamentation a satin belt in a slightly darker shade with a gilt buckle at the front.

"That one," he said, pointing at the gown.

The woman paused. "Oh, but sir, if you want something special, I suggest—"

"That's the gown I want." His voice was firmer now.

She looked at the gown, then at James, before giving in with a nod. "Very well. But we must have the measurements. The cut is everything in a gown of that style. It must fit exactly right."

James nodded, his mind scrambling. "I'll have them sent over tomorrow morning." He'd have to enlist Mrs. Hobbes. "Can it be ready by Monday?"

The woman sighed. "Such short notice . . . there will be an extra charge."

James nodded. "Of course." He paused. "And include anything else a new bride might need."

The woman's eyes widened. "Sir?"

"A bonnet, wraps, shoes . . ." He waved uncomfortably at the collection of corsets and petticoats in the corner. "You get my meaning."

The woman nodded, a faint flush on her face. "Of course."

He left the store with a lightness to his step. The dress was meant for Sara, he'd known it on sight. Suddenly he couldn't wait for his wedding day.

Chapter 26

Sara flitted around the dining room, straightening the silver-ware and shining imaginary spots from the plates. She stood back, examining her handiwork with a critical eye. The delicate china she'd uncovered in the mahogany buffet gleamed, the edging of deep-blue flowers and elegant twining vines a splash of color amid the white table linen.

It was her wedding day.

The thought made her dizzy with panic. James would soon return with Andrew and the minister. Her eyes swept across the table one last time before a sudden thought had her scurrying back to the kitchen.

"Do we have fish forks? I think we'll need them for the stewed trout," she said, bursting into the room. A wave of heat hit her, the air heavy with the smell of roasting meat.

Mrs. Hobbes paused at the stove, lifting up the corner of her apron to dab at her forehead. "I'm sure we do, ma'am."

"I'll get them," Sara said hastily. "You're busy."

"You'll need the key," Mrs. Hobbes said.

Sara's eyes darted to the ring of keys that dangled from the housekeeper's apron.

Mrs. Hobbes followed Sara's gaze, her shoulders stiffening. She motioned for Sara to follow her into the dining room where an ornate rosewood box held the silver atop the buffet.

Instead of opening the box, Mrs. Hobbes held out the keys. "Perhaps you'd like to keep them now?" Her voice was cold and formal.

"No." Sara spoke more sharply than she'd intended. "Just because I'm marrying James—er, Mr. Kinney, doesn't mean anything will change."

Mrs. Hobbes gave a short, humorless laugh. "Of course, things will change. You're the mistress of this establishment now."

Sara chewed her lip. A wall had sprung up between her and the housekeeper ever since they'd announced their marriage. Now, when she entered the kitchen, Mrs. Hobbes stopped working to inquire what madam needed and how she might be of service. Sara missed the tentative bond of friendship between them.

"I know you must think I'm no fit wife for Mr. Kinney, but I'll be a good mother to Evie," Sara said finally, her voice throbbing with feeling. She searched the older woman's face, looking for any sign of softening. "I'll be a good wife, too." Her voice lowered, for she was less certain of herself here.

"You misunderstand me, ma'am." Mrs. Hobbes gave a sharp

shake of her head. "I don't doubt your fitness, not one bit. I've seen something of the world. Worked in a big house myself when I was younger. I know as well as you that you're no servant." She leveled a severe look at Sara. "You'll make Mr. Kinney a fine wife . . . if ever you find the courage to be yourself."

Sara inhaled sharply. "I don't know what you—"

Mrs. Hobbes held up a staying hand. "Never you mind. I've gone and said too much." She turned her attention back to the silverware and held up a set of thin silver forks. "Now, are these the ones you're looking for?"

Sara nodded, watching as Mrs. Hobbes bustled around the table and set out the forks. She made a futile effort to calm her racing heart. Mrs. Hobbes might have her suspicions, but that didn't mean she knew who Sara was. Or who she used to be.

"Perhaps you should be dressing, ma'am," Mrs. Hobbes said, pausing and looking at Sara's dress with a significant lift of her eyebrows.

Sara started and smoothed a self-conscious hand down her old skirt. "Yes. Of course." She turned and went up to Evie's room, her steps slow and heavy.

She'd had one dress fitting already with a seamstress Mrs. Hobbes recommended, but it would be two weeks or more before a gown was ready. Until then, she'd wear the navy calico. A far cry from a wedding dress, but it would have to do.

Evie met her at the top of the stairs, hopping from one foot to the other. "Is it time to get ready? I've got a surprise for you." Her eyes sparkled. "Well, Papa and I have a surprise for you."

At the mention of James, Sara raised her brows. "Really? What is it?"

"Close your eyes."

Evie grabbed her hand and tugged her into her room. "I hid it under my bed." She tripped over her words in excitement. "I promised not to say anything."

"Let me guess," Sara said with a smile. "The next volume of *Ivanhoe*."

"No." Evie giggled, putting her hands on Sara's arms to guide her into position. "Stand here. Now . . . open your eyes."

Hanging from the wardrobe was a gray dress, the silk shimmering pearly blue in the sunlight. The skirts were fashionably full, and the sleeves trimmed in rich braid a shade darker than the gown. Evie clapped her hands in approval.

"Do you like it?" Evie watched her face closely and Sara forced her frozen lips into a smile.

"It's . . . beautiful."

Evie clapped her hands. "I told Papa you'd love it. Try it on."

Sara complied, her movements slow, her mind still trying to grasp the gift. The soft folds fell around her, the fitted bodice forming to her figure. "I don't understand," she said, plucking at the sleeves. "It fits me perfectly."

Evie nodded, her eyes dancing. "Mrs. Hobbes got your measurements from the seamstress. Papa took them to Cloutier's." Her voice lowered to a reverent whisper as she mentioned the name of the most exclusive dressmaker in Toronto.

Cloutier's. The name brought back a host of memories. Interminable hours spent poring over fashion plates and standing for fittings. All for a wardrobe of dresses she would never wear.

"Look, Sara!" Evie was pulling a box out from under her bed. She opened it and lifted out gloves, a fine paisley shawl, and an elegant bonnet with a wide gray ribbon and a single silky ostrich feather that curled along the brim. Underneath, Sara caught a glimpse of fine lawn and the long, curving lines of a new corset.

She reached out a hand, running the heavy silk between her fingers. How long had it been since she'd worn something so beautiful? So . . . costly?

"I can't accept this," she said. An urgency gripped her. She couldn't go back to that life. She didn't want to be that girl who'd had every choice taken away, her future controlled by men who didn't understand her. "Unbutton me, Evie."

"What? No. You have to wear it. Papa—"

"Your Papa has no business buying me clothes."

"You like the dress," Evie said, her voice flat. "It must be Papa you don't like."

"No." Sara answered too quickly. "That's not it. It's just . . ."

"It's what?" Evie asked.

Sara looked down at the hurt and confusion on Evie's face. She was pushing away the child she loved because she was afraid. Afraid she'd be rejected anew by the world she once belonged to. Afraid to trust another man. She took a long, steadying breath. Her new life beckoned. She couldn't hide under her mobcap any longer.

"Never mind me," she said, reaching out to press a kiss to Evie's forehead. "I'm being foolish. Come, let's get your hair brushed." She guided Evie to the dressing table.

Evie sent her an uncertain glance in the mirror. Sara attempted a smile.

"After the wedding . . ."

Sara's hands stilled. "Yes?"

"After the wedding, will you be my mama?"

"I'd love that." *Mama.* She glanced up at the portrait of Amelia on Evie's wall. "But what about . . . ?"

"She's my mother." Evie's voice held no trace of doubt. "That's what I call her. In my head." Evie leaned back against Sara, tucking her head under Sara's chin. "But I call you Mama."

Sara pressed a kiss to Evie's head, her throat tight.

As soon as Sara finished the braids, Evie jumped off the stool and reached for a stack of papers. "Am I done getting ready? I want to finish my new story."

Henry's afternoon lessons had ground to a halt when he rebelled against the alphabet book, saying he wasn't no baby and reckoned he could teach himself just fine. In response, Evie created her own stories featuring their favorite characters from *Ivanhoe.*

Sara sent her off with a nod and leaned forward to secure her coronet of braids. It was the first time she'd attempted anything other than a tight knot of hair at the base of her neck, and her fingers felt thick and clumsy. A loose strand curled around her finger, the thick ringlet reminding her of the first time she'd put her hair up in artful curls that had taken her maid an hour to arrange. She gave a ruthless tug, forcing the errant strands back into submission and securing them with a jab of the hairpin.

She stood back to examine the effect. The gray silk shimmered around her, the bodice tight, her narrow waist emphasized by a wide satin belt and gilt buckle. There was nothing showy or overdone about the gown, yet after so many years in simple sack dresses, she couldn't stifle the fear that she looked ridiculous.

She reached up to adjust the wide, rounded neckline and

froze. In the mirror, her hands were still rough and red, and the contrast of her chapped skin against the silky-smooth fabric struck her. She wasn't Sara O'Connor, not in this dress. Nor was she the pampered girl she'd once been. She was becoming someone altogether new.

She'd lived for years now feeling as though she walked in a dark alley, unable to see the path ahead. Alone. Granny said God was with her, but Sara hadn't believed her, not until Evie Kinney had taken her by the hand. Not until she'd heard James's voice in that filthy alley in the wharf.

You'll make Mr. Kinney a fine wife . . . if ever you find the courage to be yourself. A final look in the mirror revealed a woman she didn't recognize, a woman who had worked too hard for this chance at happiness to let doubt overwhelm her. *Thank you. I see how you protected and guided me, though I thought myself abandoned. Help me to embrace this new life before me.* She straightened her shoulders.

Today, she would take her place as the lady of the house.

~~

The bouquet of hothouse roses trembled in her hands, their lush pink profusion in stark contrast to James's solemn bride. Sara stood next to him in the parlor, as prim and serious as a schoolmistress, her hair pulled sharply back from her face in a tight circle of braids. She was radiant in the gown, as he'd known she would be, the pearly gray setting off her creamy skin and bringing smoky depths to her blue eyes.

Despite the tremor in her hands, Sara's voice was clear and firm as she spoke her vows, her eyes focused straight ahead. A rush of relief swept through James as the minister pronounced them man and wife.

Mrs. Hobbes and Andrew were the only attendants. The ceremony bore no resemblance to the elaborate affair Amelia had planned, the dozens of guests she'd insisted on—though James scarcely knew their names—or the yards of French lace on her gown.

This was practical. This time he was thinking with his head, not his heart.

Then Sara leaned forward to bury her face in the flowers. A ray of sunlight caressed the graceful curve of her neck and turned her hair to pure gold. Closing her eyes, she inhaled deeply, her lips parting in pleasure, and he felt the blood pulse through his veins.

She looked up and her eyes locked with his. "I love roses," she said. "They don't last long, but I try not to let that stop me from enjoying them."

James swallowed, his mouth suddenly dry. A curl escaped her braid to brush the nape of her neck, fascinating him. For a moment, he imagined leaning down to push the curl away and kissing the soft skin. Inhaling her scent. He forced himself to turn away and sign the register, his fingers squeezing the delicate quill. This was the path to disaster.

Andrew cleared his throat, making James jump. He gathered the documents and shoved them into James's hands. "Here's the paperwork."

James took the papers. "Thank you."

"Congratulations." Andrew's lackluster tone was at odds with his words as he shook James's hand, then turned to Sara with a perfunctory bow.

"I wish you much joy, Mrs. Kinney."

James watched Sara's face, hoping she didn't recognize the undercurrent of hostility in Andrew's voice. He wanted this to be a happy day for her.

"Won't you have a cup of tea, Mr. Ridley?" She gestured to the tea tray. "I'm sure dinner is almost ready."

Andrew fiddled with the chain of his pocket watch. "Ah, I thank you, but . . . no. I must be going."

"Going?" Evie stood at the parlor door, her eyes wide with hurt. "But Mrs. Hobbes sent me to call you for luncheon."

Andrew's smile was forced. "Well, I . . ."

"She made your favorite pudding, Uncle Andrew." Evie went to his side, grabbing his hand in both of hers and tugging him toward the dining room.

Andrew reached out to tweak one of her braids. "I suppose I can spare an hour for you, princess." Avoiding James's eyes, he let Evie pull him from the parlor. James smiled despite the tension in the room. Andrew never could refuse Evie anything.

At the dining table, Sara supervised the serving of the soup in an atmosphere of tense silence. Andrew raced through his bowl and sat with barely concealed impatience for the next course. James eyed the younger man. It wasn't like Andrew to ignore the social niceties.

"Why are you in such a hurry today?" Evie turned to Andrew, her gaze direct. Trust her to ask the question they were all thinking.

"Business." Andrew didn't lift his eyes from his plate.

Evie tilted her head. "Are you working on a case?"

Andrew took his time cutting a piece of trout. "Nothing I can share with you, princess."

If Andrew had been in a courtroom lately, it was news to James. He'd all but abandoned their practice in recent weeks.

Before Evie could ask another question, Andrew turned his attention to James. "I suppose you'll prepare for the wedding visits now?" He fixed his eyes on Sara's face as though waiting for a reaction.

Sara sent James a quick glance, her eyes wide. "James doesn't entertain," she said. "I didn't think—"

"A single man can't entertain, though, can he?" Andrew said. "Always said that was my chief motivation for avoiding matrimony." Andrew laughed at his own joke.

"We won't be paying wedding visits," James said, trying to ease the look of strain on Sara's face. They had an agreement about social obligations.

Andrew shrugged. "I suppose no one would be surprised by that," he said. He raised his eyebrows with a sidelong glance in Sara's direction. "Under the circumstances."

Sara averted her face but not before James saw the hurt in her eyes. He felt a rush of tenderness at her vulnerability.

"But you won't hold them off forever," Andrew continued. "Especially Ballantine. He'll want to come and . . . look things over."

"B-Ballantine?" The color left Sara's face.

Andrew turned to Sara. "Heard of him, have you?"

Sara swallowed. "Why would Mr. Ballantine be interested in meeting me?"

"He's James's best client." His lips quirked. "Once Ballantine decides to take you on, he considers you his."

She turned to James. There was a wide, wild look in her eyes that had him ready to rise to his feet in case she should bolt from the table. "You work for Ballantine? Impossible." Her hands gripped the edges of the table. "Stephen Osgoode is his barrister."

James scanned her face, trying to make sense of her agitation. How did she know who Ballantine employed?

Andrew tilted his head, his eyes sharp. "Osgoode is his barrister. But Ballantine decided to take a hand in my affairs and realized James was the best way to get to me." He rolled his eyes. "Meddling in other's business seems to be his speciality."

Sara's head snapped back to James. "Why didn't you tell me you worked for him?"

She sounded as though he'd kept a vital secret from her. "It never came up." James searched her face for a clue to her distress. His legs twitched with the impulse to stand up and go to her side. Curl his arm around her shoulders and protect her from whatever was bothering her.

"Well, I must be going." Andrew broke the strained silence.

"Already?" Evie had disappeared after the main course to help Mrs. Hobbes serve the dessert. Now she stood at the table, a plate of steaming Essex Pudding in her hands. "But I want you to meet my friend."

"I'm sorry, princess." He looked away, a faint flush staining his cheeks. "I told you I could only stay an hour."

"It'll only take a moment," Evie said, setting the pudding down. "He's here now, right, Henry?"

Henry popped his head into the dining room. "I don't got time for a visit," he said, shaking his head in exasperation at Evie. "Told you I only come to bring a message." He cast a longing glance at the table. "And maybe get a bite to eat."

"A message?" James said.

Henry straightened. "Aye, sir. Militia come by the inn." He paused, his chest swelling with importance as all eyes in the room focused on him. "Said to have arms at the ready. All able-bodied men are to report to Parliament House if they hear the College bell ring."

No matter how often James had warned about the rebels, this call-to-arms still shocked him. *Arms at the ready.* Would it really come to that?

Andrew jumped up from his seat. "Thank you for the luncheon," he said with a hurried bow in Sara's direction. James rose, determined not to let Andrew leave before they spoke.

"Where are you going?" Evie said. "The pudding is here."

James met Sara's eyes for a fleeting moment. She gave a short nod and set to work herding the children to the table with the promise of pudding while James followed Andrew to the hall.

"Is it true?" James asked without preamble.

Andrew took his time shrugging into his coat. When he finally looked at James, his eyes were cool, his expression impenetrable. There'd been a time when they'd shared everything, but his face made it clear how much distance was between them now.

"Are the rebels really ready to attack?" James asked, losing patience with Andrew's silence.

Andrew paused, his hand on the doorknob. "*If* they are, it wouldn't be any business of yours, James. You've chosen your side . . . and I've chosen mine."

Chapter 27

It took every shred of self-governance Sara possessed to keep a smile on her face through the rest of that interminable day. James worked for her father. He might be called to the militia at any moment. He could be hurt . . . or worse. Sick panic rose in her throat at the thought.

She had to tell him the truth. Tonight.

What a fool she'd been to think she could run from the past. Her mind spun with scenarios, each worse than the last. James's trust in her would be broken. Her father would confront her and condemn her anew or he'd turn against James. His influence stretched far beyond Toronto. He could ruin James's credibility in a way that could reach every settlement in the colony.

Only one thing was certain. There was no going back, no matter how much she wanted to curl up on her bed, close her eyes and return to the way things were when she was invisible Sara O'Connor.

She left James to finish tucking Evie in for the night with a muffled excuse about wanting tea, and escaped to the kitchen.

"I moved your things to Mr. Kinney's room." Mrs. Hobbes looked up from the sock she was darning with a curious tilt of her chin. "Do you need any help with your gown?"

Sara tried to swallow, though her mouth felt like it was full of sawdust. It's not like this was a surprise. She knew she'd be married. Sharing a room. Mrs. Hobbes stared at her, waiting for a response.

"No, no, I'll be fine on my own." Sara looked around the kitchen, wishing she could pick up the mending or put away plates as she'd done only a week ago. Her lips quirked. Wouldn't Mrs. Hobbes wonder if she started doing housework on her wedding night?

She made her way to James's bedroom with slow steps. Sara looked around, taking in the walls, papered in delicate, swirling pink vines and flowers. They were at odds with the solid, dark furniture and the plain, woven coverlet on the bed. Her eyes skimmed over the long dresser that spanned one wall, empty of any ornament. A washstand in the corner was the only other furniture, displaying a white washbasin and a few shaving tools.

She reached out a finger to trace the outline of a rose on the wallpaper, the only sign left of the woman who must have once shared this room. Was Amelia's memory so painful to him that he'd removed all other reminders? Was he still in love with her? She snatched her hand away from the wall, clenching her fingers. It didn't matter. He'd given her a home and a daughter. She didn't have the right to ask for more.

Shaking off the dark turn of her thoughts, she undid the buttons on her gown and hung it in the wardrobe. At some point today, Mrs. Hobbes had moved James's clothing to one side and hung Sara's few dresses next to his. She washed and slipped into her new nightdress. It was fine lawn, gathered at the neck and flowing in voluminous folds that hid almost every inch of her body. She was thankful for that. Her old nightgown had been so threadbare it was practically transparent.

Removing the pins from her hair, she felt the blessed relief as she unwound the tight braid. Perhaps she ought to have tried a fancier style, but something in her rebelled at the thought of erasing every sign of Sara O'Connor, laundress, plain and simple.

Her hand paused as she pulled the brush through her hair. *Plain and simple.* Her past was anything but. A sickening wave of guilt threatened to overwhelm her. She dropped her brush onto the dresser and quickly braided the loose waves.

She took a steadying breath. *Give me the words to tell James the truth.*

The fire burned low, and she burrowed under the covers, pulling the quilt up to her chin. She took a moment to luxuriate in the comfort of feather ticking and sweet-scented sheets. Curling up on her side, her eyes fell on James's pillow, turning her thoughts to a more immediate uncertainty. Tonight.

Her memories of Colin were hazy now, as though they'd happened to someone else. He'd been full of life, and the girl she'd been then had taken his hand and followed wherever he led. But never once had she felt his touch down to the soles of her feet. Never once had a glance seared her and left her body humming with energy.

She'd agreed to a marriage for Evie's sake, but she couldn't ignore the way her heart raced at even the most casual brush of his hand against hers. And that kiss . . . She allowed herself a moment to remember the featherlight touch of his lips on hers and to wonder what it would be like if he kissed her again. Kissed her and didn't stop.

But it was clear he wasn't interested in her *that* way, for he'd gone out of his way to avoid her these last few days. It was a relief, she assured herself. She didn't want the complication any more than he did.

She squeezed her eyes shut, forcing her breaths to become deep and regular until the beating of her heart slowed and the frantic quivers in her stomach settled.

The sound of the door handle turning woke her later. She heard his steps cross the room and then his weight on the mattress beside her, his familiar scent of sandalwood drifting across the pillow.

She was still, waiting for him to break the silence. But he said nothing, did nothing. Her eyes, accustomed to the darkness, made out the shape of him. He sat on the side of the bed, his back to her, elbows leaning on his knees, head bowed.

Tell him. Tell him the truth. She opened her mouth, willing the words to come out.

"James?"

~~

Marriage wouldn't change anything. Sara already lived in his house and presided over Evie's education. The ceremony was a mere formality to silence Stephen Osgoode and give Evie the security she needed.

At least, that's what James told himself, right up until he walked into his bedroom and saw Sara curled up in his bed. Now he sat beside her, his body attuned to her every breath. How had he ever thought marriage would make life easier?

He closed his eyes. Would there come a day when she would accept him as a husband . . . in every sense of the word? Did he even want that? Of course, he did. Every nerve in his body strained to hold her. But a deeper worry held him back. What if he gave her everything, including his heart, and it wasn't enough?

"James?" The sound of her voice was like an electric shock, bringing every sense to life.

"Yes?" He hesitated, then turned to face her.

"I—I need to tell you something." She sat up.

His body grew still, his stomach dipping in sudden tension. Married less than twelve hours and he'd already disappointed her.

"It's about your employer. I didn't know . . ."

He relaxed a fraction. She was still worried about moving in society. "Ballantine might be one of the richest men in Toronto, but you have nothing to fear from him." His eyes had adjusted so well to the dark by this point that he could see the way she worried her bottom lip in an expression he was coming to recognize. "You'd be an ornament to any assembly you chose to attend." He was watching her as he spoke, otherwise he might not have seen the shadow that passed over her face.

"No, I wouldn't. Please don't ask it of me." There was an edge of desperation to her voice.

"I won't," he said, rubbing his thumb over the back of her hand. If anything, she looked more upset than ever. "It doesn't matter what any of these people think. Come spring, we'll head north."

He leaned forward and pressed a kiss to her forehead. It was the most natural thing in the world. Yet, in an instant, everything changed. The camaraderie between them vanished, leaving behind a crackling tension that set every nerve on edge.

Sara must have felt it, too, for the smile faded from her face. Her eyes searched his, her bottom lip still caught between her teeth. He lifted her hand and tucked it against his chest. If he tugged, she'd be in his arms.

Her body softened, swaying toward him. He wanted to reach out and touch his lips to hers. To lower her to the bed. She was so close he could feel the delicate exhale of her breath. Emotions rushed at him, faster than he could take them in. Tenderness. Desire. Love.

No. Not love.

He'd promised himself he'd never risk his heart again. He ducked his head, pressing a kiss on her knuckles. For a long moment he stayed thus while he fought to get his emotions under control. *I'd make no demands on you.* Wasn't that what he'd promised her?

She tugged her hand, and he released it. "James, there's something I need to tell you."

She was going to push him away. Tell him to stick to his promise and take himself off, and she was right.

"There's something I need to tell you, as well," James said, avoiding her eyes. "I think it would be best if . . ." If what? If he listened to every pulse of his body and kissed her? If he left the room as fast as his legs could carry him? His eyes drifted to her lips. He was so close. He'd only need to lean forward and—

His lips found hers, and in an instant, he was lost in her warmth. His hands reached out to tangle in the silky strands of her hair that escaped the confines of her braid. He deepened the kiss, pulling her close against him. Her hands drifted up, fluttering for a moment before coming to rest on his shoulders. He felt her touch, searing him through the thin fabric of his shirt. It was enough to bring him back to his senses. With a groan, he tore himself away.

"Sara. I—I'm sorry." She looked away, but not before he saw the hurt in her eyes. He was making a mess of this. "It's not that I don't want—" He concentrated on his words and not the memory of the kiss. "I want to protect you from disappointment."

"You don't need to protect me." She brought her eyes level with his. "I've loved and lost before. I understand the risks." Her voice dropped to a whisper. "If there is anyone who needs protecting in this marriage . . . it's you."

He jerked back. "Ridiculous. Protection from what?" He scanned her face, trying to grasp the meaning behind her words, but he had a hard time focusing on anything other than the faint scent of roses in her hair and the warmth of her hand on his.

"Do you hear that?" Sara turned to the door, a crease forming between her brows.

"What?" James shook his head, trying to break the spell of her nearness. A faint pounding was audible. He cocked his head. From the back door?

The pounding came again, louder this time, breaking the spell between them. He jumped up as Henry's warning came crashing back.

"Who could that be?"

Sara's question followed him out into the hall, but he didn't stop to answer. His mind had already gone to muskets and militia.

The rebellion had begun.

Chapter 28

Sara followed James down the stairs, stopping only to tie her wrapper over her nightgown and tuck her feet into slippers. Darting into the kitchen, she gasped at the familiar form at the back door. Henry danced from foot to foot, his eyes glued on James.

"Henry?" She surged forward. "What are you doing here so late?"

The boy straightened, his chest puffing out in pride. "Got hired to bring a message. From a Mr. Ballantine."

Her stomach swirled at the name.

"What did he say?" James asked, his body tense.

"He says you're to go to Montgomery's Tavern straight away. Fetch Ridley and bring him back."

"Blast," James said under his breath. "Did he say what's happened?"

Henry shrugged. "That were all he said." He leaned forward. "But I heard the grooms talking. Militia's been called from Hamilton."

James kept his eyes on Henry, his words low and urgent. "Fetch my horse from the livery."

"Aye, guv." Henry darted out the door.

James bent to pull on his boots, his face grim.

"What's happening?" Sara wondered if he might refuse to answer. But she was his wife now. She had a right to ask.

He grabbed his hat from the side table. "I don't know." James didn't spare her a glance as he shrugged on his jacket and straightened his cravat.

The tension thrumming through him told her this was more than just a meeting at the inn. "What do you suspect, then?" He hesitated and she squared her shoulders. "I need to know, James. I'm your wife."

James sighed. "The less you know about it, the better. In case the magistrate comes sniffing around."

"Magistrate?" Sara's heart pounded. "James, what's going on?"

James came to stand in front of her, so close she could see the lines of worry around his eyes. "Andrew's involved in something serious."

Sara took a steadying breath. "Surely it could wait until the morning." She studied his face for signs of the truth. "It's the rebels, isn't it?" James inclined his head a fraction. "It could be dangerous. What if there's a mob? Violence?" Sara worked to tamp down the fear and keep her voice calm and reasonable. "We need you."

James's hands came up to frame her face. "I'm not in any danger."

Sara bit her lip, distracted by the warmth of his hands. What would happen if she were brave enough to wrap her arms around him and refuse to let him go?

"I'll be fine." His thumbs moved in a slow sweep across her cheekbones, a gentle caress that made her shiver. "You don't know what it means to me that you're here. For Evie." He released a rough breath, his eyes scanning her face as though he were memorizing every detail. "And for me to come home to."

She gave him a weak smile, her throat too constricted for speech. *Why won't you open up? You trust me with your daughter, but not with yourself.* Then again, she still hadn't told him the truth about herself.

"Look at us." James gave a rueful smile. "Creating high drama out of nothing. I'll probably be back before you're awake."

Henry trotted up to the gate leading James's horse. Sara grabbed a muffler and a pair of gloves. "Here. It's cold out."

James spared her a brief smile and wrapped the muffler around his neck. He jammed his hat on his head, opened the door and disappeared into the night.

"Mama?" Sara turned to see Evie at the top of the stairs, her eyes wide. "Where did Papa go?"

"He had to go to a meeting," Sara said, her voice casual. She didn't want Evie up all night. She'd do the worrying for them both.

"What kind of meeting could he have so late at night? The courts are closed."

Sara grimaced. There were times when Evie's quick mind was a definite liability. "I'm not sure. He said we weren't to worry. He'd be back soon." She saw Evie bite her lip. "Would you like me to lie down with you? Until you fall back asleep?"

Evie brightened. "Would you?"

"Of course." Sara started up the stairs, her eyes never leaving Evie. "That's what mamas do." They snuggled under Evie's blankets, and the girl's slender arms clasped her close in a fierce hug.

"I'm so glad you married Papa." Evie whispered close to her ear. "When you were young, did you get a new mama, too?"

Sara was silent for a moment, feeling the sting of old wounds that never fully healed. "No, I never did."

"Then I'm lucky, aren't I?" Evie asked, her voice heavy with sleep. "God gave me two."

A wave of gratitude washed over Sara for this precious little girl who called her Mama. She closed her eyes, praying for James. For Evie. For all of them.

The distant clang of the alarm bells woke her sometime later. She rose from Evie's bed and pushed aside the curtains. A shout sounded down the street, then a group of men passed, muskets slung over their shoulders. Heading to defend the city?

Sara paced to the kitchen and built up the fire to make a cup of tea, her movements slow and silent. Poor Mrs. Hobbes needed her sleep.

Opening her lesson book, she tried to plan the next week but the tension that tightened her stomach refused to let her rest. The city was under threat, James was in danger . . . and she still hadn't told him the truth. Restless, she wandered to the parlor and pulled the Bible from the shelf.

Back in the kitchen, she sat by the fire with the heavy weight of the Scriptures on her lap. One of Granny's favorite verses came to her before she even opened the pages. *But the God of all grace, after that ye have suffered a while, make you perfect, stablish, strengthen, settle you.* How often had she heard those words as Granny rocked in her chair, listening to Sara's worries?

She went out on the back porch, her quilt tucked around her shoulders, and looked up at the clear night sky. *Please, let me have one more chance.* It was the same prayer she'd sent up that night in the alley at the wharf. Since then, she'd had hope she hadn't felt since childhood. The tough shell she'd built around her heart had softened. She could pray again. She could ask for guidance. For forgiveness.

Now, she prayed for James.

Keep him safe. And bring him back to me.

~~

James was tempted to ignore Ballantine's summons. Andrew had made it clear he didn't want James's help. Yet, why would Ballantine send word, so late at night, if there wasn't still a way to keep Andrew out of it? Perhaps the rebellion wasn't as far along as he feared. He might be able to talk some sense into Andrew and get him home before things got out of hand.

"You'd best head along to bed now," James said to Henry as he mounted his horse.

"Not likely." Henry crossed his arms, glowering at him from beneath lowered brows.

"It's not safe for you out on these streets." James sent a glance down Duke Street. The houses were dark, the road deserted, but he heard the distant rumble of wagons. Or was that gunfire? Something was afoot.

Henry snorted. "I know how to take care of myself. Or did you forget that night at the docks already?"

James looked down at him. "Listen, I've got to go, and I need to know you're home safe."

Henry shrugged, undeterred. "I'll follow you, no matter where you go, so you might as well give me a ride." He sent James a sidelong glance. "No telling what might happen to me on my own."

"Fine." James raised his hands in defeat. "But only so you can bring word back to Mrs. Kinney if I should be . . . delayed." He reached down and pulled Henry up behind him. "You'll leave straightaway when I tell you. It might get dangerous."

"I'm hoping it will," Henry said, wrapping his arms around James's waist as the horse sprang forward. James shook his head at the suppressed excitement in the boy's voice.

They struck out north, avoiding the main thoroughfare. After ten minutes, they left the clapboard homes and stores of the city behind them. Fields and woodlots bordered the road, broken by the occasional farm lane and the outline of a log barn in the distance.

They approached a turn in the road. He couldn't see what was ahead, but all his senses urged caution. He slowed the horse and Henry's arms tightened around him. He turned and pressed a finger to his lips and Henry nodded his understanding. They stood silent until James made out the faint sounds of footsteps and low conversation ahead. A picket to stop travellers along the road, but who had set it up and to what purpose, he couldn't be sure. He turned his horse off the road and into the thick bush. It would be slow going, but at least they'd be safe. He hoped.

Half an hour later, they emerged from the forest into the chaotic yard of Montgomery's Tavern. Men on foot held torches and pikes aloft, while a handful on horseback shouted orders and attempted to organize the confusion. A chill went through James that had nothing to do with the cold December night. More than a hundred armed men milled about the yard. Through the windows, he saw countless more inside. The rebellion was real.

They dismounted at the edge of the clearing. James turned to Henry and pressed the reins into his hands. "Stay here out of sight. I'll be back." Henry nodded, his eyes huge in his face.

James approached the milling men, scanning the crowd but finding no sign of Andrew or the big bay gelding he rode. Most faces were unknown to him, their clothing giving them away as farmers from outside of the city. Then he recognized Wilkie from their attempts to bring the land speculators to justice and made his way to the man's side.

"Kinney," Wilkie said, his eyes widening in surprise. "I . . . I hadn't thought you—"

"Good evening," James said with a nod, cutting off the man's question before he could ask it. "I'm looking for Andrew Ridley. Have you seen him?"

Wilkie's eyes shifted to the side, and he coughed. "Ridley, you say?" He took a step back and looked around. "Best ask Lount," he said, nodding in the direction of a muscled giant, barking orders to a young man who then left his side at a run.

James eyed the man as he approached. He'd heard of Samuel Lount, the well-known blacksmith of Holland Landing, and it seemed the stories hadn't been exaggerated. His size alone gave him an aura of command. "Excuse me. Mr. Lount?"

The man turned to James. "Yes?" He didn't look up from the note in his hand.

"I'm looking for Andrew Ridley. Have you seen him?"

"Assigned to the scouting party with Mackenzie. Left an hour ago." The man looked up, his eyes narrowing on James's face. "Who are you?"

"James Kinney. A friend." Lount looked James up and down. He hadn't dressed for a night battle, nor was he armed. No wonder Lount's suspicions were raised. "Perhaps I ought to follow him," James said, anxious to be out of the man's presence.

Lount reached out a beefy hand, grasping James's forearm. "Now just wait a minute. What squadron are you in?"

Two men galloped into the clearing, saving James from answering. "Ambushed!" one shouted. "Captain Anderson's been shot!"

Lount dropped his arm, rushing to the arrivals with a barrage of questions. Bile rose in James's throat. The violence had begun. He pushed closer, trying to hear as much of the story as he could. *What of Andrew Ridley?* He wanted to shout his question, but caution held him back. He'd be no good to Andrew if these men decided he was a spy.

Instead, he listened as the man sputtered his tale of ambush and the shot through the neck that killed Captain Anderson. The men grew restless as the tale spread through the crowd. At once the mood shifted from defiance to uncertainty.

The other man who'd arrived now made his presence felt. He was wrapped in a huge greatcoat which seemed to swell his size, and his voice rang out across the clearing.

"A great man has fallen," he shouted. The milling men stilled, and faces turned to the figure on the white horse. "But we will not be deterred from our fight." His voice was unmistakably Scots, and its lilting cadence captivated every man in the yard. For the first time, James felt the pull of William Lyon

Mackenzie and understood why Andrew risked his life and live-lihood for the man. "A wicked government has trampled the law." He rose in the saddle, turning as though he would look each man in the face. "We are poor, ignorant peasants, they say, born to toil for our betters." The men booed and hissed at this, joining Mackenzie's fervor. "But we have opened our eyes. Felt our strength. We will persevere!" A roar of approval echoed through the innyard. "To your posts, men. Victory awaits!"

Men rushed to ready their arms and find mounts. Lount called out orders, largely ignored as men flocked to Mackenzie's side. James plunged through the mass of bodies and weapons, heading to the edge of the clearing. His eyes scanned the face of every man he passed to no avail. Andrew hadn't returned. He'd have to find him, and soon, before he found himself pressed into a rebel squadron and sent marching into the city.

James wove his way to where he'd left Henry. No sign of the boy or his horse. He broke into a jog, his eyes scanning the woods as he circled the clearing. Behind him, a hastily formed troop was already setting out toward the city with a roar claiming victory was in sight. Surely the boy hadn't joined the rebels. Evie would never forgive him if he let something happen to Henry. He felt a tug at his sleeve and slowed to find Henry at his elbow, tears tracking down his cheeks.

"I tried to stop 'em, guv, I did. But they just grabbed the reins right away from me."

James understood in an instant what must have happened. "They confiscated my mount?"

Henry nodded, looking down. "I'm sorry, sir."

James squeezed Henry's bony shoulder. "It's not your fault, my boy."

Henry looked up, a faint glimmer of hope in his eyes. "You're not mad at me?"

In the moonlight, the red welt of a whip was visible on Henry's face. "You're hurt. Tell me you didn't try to fight them off."

Henry lifted his chin. "I know where my duty be, sir."

James didn't know how he'd acquired such a loyal supporter. If only Andrew paid him half as much heed. "We've got to get out of here, lad. Before they get more than just my horse."

Henry nodded, his eyes scanning James doubtfully from head to toe. "I reckon we'll have to walk."

James smiled, pulling the boy further into the woods as another troop approached. "Afraid I can't hack it?"

Henry grinned back. "I reckon you can make it just fine, sir."

"If they should come after us . . . if anything should happen, I want you to run straight back to the city. I need you to keep an eye on Mrs. Kinney and Evie. All right?"

Henry looked up at him for a long moment. "Who'll be keeping an eye on you, guv?"

James would have laughed if the boy's expression hadn't been so deadly earnest. "I'll be fine. I'm a barrister, remember? I can talk my way out of anything. Now, let's go."

Henry gave a reluctant nod and started through the woods. Every few moments they would stop and listen, keeping the sounds of the troops on the road to their left. Even in the dark, they could move much faster than the regimented columns of men holding heavy weapons and they soon left the lines of rebels behind. James kept an eye on the clear, starry sky so he wouldn't lose his way. Henry marched gamely beside him, never complaining as they stumbled through a marsh and icy water seeped into their boots.

"Listen, guv. You hear that?"

Across the fields came a faint tinkling sound. The city had realized the danger and the bells rang, calling men to its defense. James released a slow breath and pulled his hat lower over his ears. This was a fine kettle of fish. He'd left Sara and Evie alone, defenseless. He pictured his home, Sara curled up in his bed, and felt such a rush of longing, it almost crippled him.

At the next fence line, he turned in the direction of the road and led them back to Yonge Street. Henry trotted at his side, only his silence giving away how exhausted the boy must be. "You all right, Henry?"

"Never been better."

James felt a rush of tenderness. Henry deserved a chance to make something of himself. When they made it through this night, when life was back to normal again, James would see to it that Henry had that chance. *We are poor, ignorant peasants, they say, born to toil and sweat for our betters.* Mackenzie's words hit him anew with the force of their logic. The world wasn't right. Ballantine and his cronies weren't right, either. Things needed to change, and he wanted to be a part of it. *I'll make a difference. I'll do better.*

Henry skittered to a halt, yanking on his arm. James had let his attention wander, let down his guard for a moment. Three men stood in the middle of the road in front of a makeshift barricade of logs and brush. He'd forgotten about the picket.

James gave Henry a push. The boy slid into the ditch at side of the road and disappeared seconds before the men reached James.

"You, there. Hands up where we can see them." One of the men pointed a musket at James, and he raised his hands. "Now walk forward, nice and slow." James stepped forward, swallowing a sigh of relief as he drew closer and recognized one of the men.

"Sheriff Jarvis? Thank goodness. I've come from Montgomery's. Men are heading this way. Armed."

"So we've heard." James recognized the crisp tones of the other man though he could scarcely credit his ears. Stephen Osgoode stepped out from behind Jarvis, his face now visible in the moonlight.

"Osgoode?" James took a step forward, more confident now. He had no idea how Osgoode had ended up manning a picket, but he was glad to see another familiar face.

"What were you doing at Montgomery's Tavern, Kinney?" Osgoode's question cracked like a whip in the cold night air. "Joining the rebels?"

"Don't be ridiculous, Osgoode. Ballantine sent me."

"Ballantine's at the governor's side, doing his utmost to get every man armed and ready to defend the capital. He'd hardly send you on a fool's errand when he could use you in the city."

"I was . . . I'm sure you understand why he sent me." James sent Osgoode a meaningful stare. He hesitated to mention Andrew's name in front of the other men and implicate him without proof. After all, he hadn't *seen* his friend.

"What I understand is that we have our first rebel captive of the night." He turned to Jarvis. "What are you waiting for?"

Jarvis hesitated, looking between the two men. "Never thought you a rebel, Kinney." His gaze swung away, searching the dark road. "Though how you come to be here on foot at this time of night beats me."

"I went to check out a report I'd heard. My horse was stolen and—"

"Men were asked to report to City Hall to defend our city." Osgoode ignored James, focusing his words on Jarvis. "Kinney came north instead." He shrugged, as though there were nothing left to discuss. As though he hadn't known James for ten years. "What more proof do we need?"

The man's duplicity took James's breath away. Osgoode seemed determined to push Jarvis into arresting him. Anger coursed through him, urging him to some rash action that wouldn't help his cause.

"Come with me, Kinney." The older man grabbed James by the arm. James was so surprised, it took him a moment to wrest his arm free.

"What on earth? You can't possibly mean to arrest me. I came up here to talk some sense into them." James looked at the other two men. They were faintly familiar. Guards at the jail, he thought. No one who would vouch for him. "Jarvis, listen, I came here at Ballantine's request."

"Don't listen to him," Osgoode said. The glow of triumph lit his face. "Jarvis, you were there last week, at Ballantine's. Kinney all but acknowledged himself a rebel."

James felt his world tilt. "I'm not a rebel," he said, his words low and fierce.

"Guess you'd best save it for the judge." Jarvis tied James's hands behind his back. James thought he saw the guards smirk. No doubt it gave them pleasure to see a barrister brought low. "We've got orders to stop anyone coming down this road tonight."

"I'd like to see the warrant." James planted his feet, stalling for time, the bitter taste of betrayal in his mouth. It was futile. He wasn't going to be able to talk his way out of this.

"Warrant, eh?" Osgoode's voice was mocking. One of the guards shoved James forward and he nearly fell. "You ought to know better."

"Know what?" James said, only just staying on his feet.

"Don't need a warrant for treason."

Chapter 29

The streets were silent now, in these hours before dawn. Sara found the quiet even more unsettling than the warning bells and the distant shouts she'd heard earlier.

A sharp tap sounded on the back door, and she sprang out of the chair. Heart pounding, she peeled back a corner of the kitchen curtain. A man stood on the back step, the weary slope of his shoulders seeming to indicate that he posed no threat. Her eyes caught the sweep of black hair curling from beneath the brim of an oversized beaver hat. *Andrew Ridley. Alone.*

She rushed to the door. Andrew stood, pale and disheveled. He clutched his left arm, holding it tight to his side.

"Mr. Ridley?" She covered her mouth with her hand as her stomach dropped.

He looked over his shoulder. "May I come in?"

She nodded, moving aside as he lurched into the kitchen. She gestured toward a chair, and he took a seat at the table with a sigh of relief.

"You're hurt. What happened?"

"Bullet grazed me. I'm fine."

His pale face and trembling hands didn't look fine to her. Granny's teaching took over and she bit back her questions about James and the events of the evening. *First, tend the patient.* "Here, let me clean it." She moved about the kitchen, rekindling the stove and setting the kettle on to boil without conscious thought, her mind still racing with worry.

"It's all right. A wo—someone already cleaned it." Sara looked closer and saw the outline of a bandage under his jacket. Her eyes flew back to his face, but he was scanning the room, a crease between his brows. "Where's James?"

"James? He went after you." Sara didn't need to see the blank look in Andrew's eyes to know something was wrong.

"He did?" His brow furrowed in confusion.

"A message came from Ballantine around eleven. Said you'd gone to Montgomery's Tavern and James should fetch you back straight away." Sara searched Andrew's face for some indication of what happened to James, but the man seemed utterly confounded.

"I never saw him."

Sara tried to decide if that fact was comforting. "Start from the beginning. What happened?"

"We got word to assemble at Montgomery's Tavern. Mackenzie said it would be tonight."

"The rebellion?" Sara said, pushing a glass of water into his hands.

Andrew nodded. "Mackenzie wanted to see Toronto's defenses firsthand. I was chosen to be part of the scouting party." He leaned toward Sara. "They saw Charger, of course. Not a horse can match him for stamina." He grinned with a flash of his old boyish charm. "He doesn't feel the cold at all." His smiled faded quickly. "But then—" He broke off and took a gulp of water.

Sara wasn't sure she wanted to hear what came next. "And then?"

"There was a picket set up along the road. We weren't expecting them." He shuddered. "He shot Anderson. Right through the neck."

"Who did?"

Andrew looked at her, his face pale. "Osgoode. I saw him, clear as day. He called out my name. I thought he meant to warn me, but he . . ." His voice lowered to a whisper.

Worry for James was rapidly turning into panic. A man had died. Osgoode was involved. Where *was* James?

"He shot me, too." There was a dazed confusion in Andrew's eyes that Sara understood. Why would Osgoode shoot a colleague, and Ballantine's godson at that?

"How did you get away?"

"I kept my seat when Charger bolted through the woods and he eventually found his way back to the road." His forehead crinkled in worry. "I don't know where Charger is now. I must have lost consciousness and fallen off at some point. Next thing I knew, I woke up at the side of the road." He broke off with a self-conscious glance at Sara. "I came here thinking James could help me figure out what's to be done now." He glanced around the room as though he expected James would step out from behind the cookstove and save the day.

"We have to find him." Sara stood.

"I can't. I was recognized." He ran a shaky hand over his face. "I need to disappear for a while until this all dies down. James will be home soon. Tell him I'll send word when I can."

"What if James is hurt?" Sara turned on Andrew, her fear making her lash out. "Why didn't you heed James's warning? He told you to stay clear of the rebels, didn't he?"

Andrew winced. "If I could go back, I would, but . . ."

The sight of his stricken face stilled the angry words on Sara's tongue.

He rose and Sara moved to follow him to the door. "If James isn't back, you must go to Ballantine."

Sara froze. *Ballantine. Not a chance I'll be going there for help.* "How could he help? He's not a magistrate."

Andrew studied her face for a moment. "He's a powerful man." His eyes narrowed. "But whatever you do, don't go to Osgoode." His brows contracted. "James never trusted him, and he's got a good nose for that sort of thing. Stay clear of the man."

Sara nodded her agreement. If Andrew only knew. A distant musket shot echoed through the silence that had descended on the kitchen, making Andrew jump to his feet. "I've got to get out of the city." He set his hat back on his head. "I'm serious about Ballantine, Sara. He's got influence. Go to him if you need anything."

She was the last person Ballantine would help. Sara forced a nod, following Andrew to the door. She'd think of something.

"Andrew, wait." Turning back to the kitchen, she shoved

a loaf of bread and a chunk of cheese into a sack and pushed it into his hands. He looked down, his hands flexing on the bag.

"Thank you." He met her eyes. "I'm sorry for the way I acted this morning." His eyes were dark with regret. "You'll be a good wife to James. A better wife than I am a friend."

Sara nodded, watching as he slipped out and disappeared into the darkness. Her mind was whirling, her hands shaking as she gripped the edge of the table.

James, where are you?

～～

Henry arrived at the back door at dawn, shaking with cold and fatigue.

Sara ushered him into the kitchen where Mrs. Hobbes was bustling about as though her breakfast alone would be enough to bring James home.

"What happened? Where's Jam—er, Mr. Kinney?" Sara said, plunking him down in a chair next to the stove and wrapping a quilt around his shoulders.

"I tried to help him." The words burst out of Henry. His eyes filled, and he blinked, his lower lip trembling.

Sara had never heard Henry at a loss for words. Suppressing her worry, she knelt in front of the boy, placing her hands on his shoulders and giving him a squeeze. "Of course, you did."

"They nabbed 'im."

Sara was well enough acquainted with the language of the slums to know exactly what this meant. "He's in prison?" The words caught in her throat. At least he was alive.

Mrs. Hobbes let out a gasp and turned from the counter, a fork suspended in her hand.

"Aye. On the way back, they was waiting in the road, just like they knew we'd be coming. Guv tried to talk his way out of it, but they said it's treason." He shook his head. "Ain't no way to get out of that."

"It's a mistake." Sara jumped to her feet, pacing to the door and back again. "He only went to help Mr. Ridley."

Mrs. Hobbes sat a heaping plate of eggs and toast in front of Henry, but for once the boy wasn't interested in food.

"It's my fault. I oughtn't to have brought that message last night." Henry picked up his fork and pushed the eggs around on his plate. "Knew there was something funny about that man."

Sara stilled her flying thoughts. "What man?"

"Ballantine. Only, that's not his name. Osgoode, that's what guv called him. He's the one who gave me the note to deliver." Henry looked up, his eyes full of tears. "And he's the one who nabbed guv. I shoulda known it was a trap."

What game did Stephen Osgoode play? It grew deeper and more forbidding with each new revelation. "Henry, you did just as you ought." She reached out and smoothed a rebellious lock of hair from his forehead. "Without you, I wouldn't even know Mr. Kinney was in prison."

"Why would anyone put Papa in prison?" Evie entered the kitchen in her nightgown, hair askew, her sharp eyes taking in the occupants of the room. For a moment, the kitchen was silent, for none of them knew how best to answer her. Evie turned to her with trust in her eyes, as though Sara could solve every problem. "It's not true, right, Mama?"

"It is so true." Henry dropped his fork and crossed his arms. "D'you think I would lie about something like that?"

"I don't believe it." Evie took a step forward, jutting out her chin and looking Henry in the eyes.

Sara moved to Evie and put an arm around her shoulders. "If your papa is in prison, it was a mistake." Sara injected optimism into her voice that she was far from feeling. "I'll go right now and clear it up."

Evie turned. "I'll get dressed."

Sara stopped her with a gentle hand on her arm. "No, my love. You can't come."

Evie froze. "Papa might need me."

"*I* need you to stay right here, with Henry and Mrs. Hobbes. In case your papa sends word." Evie crossed her arms, looking her most stubborn. "The warden might not even let *me* in, never mind two of us."

"But—"

Sara placed a finger over Evie's mouth. "It's what your papa would want. You know it. Come, help me get some supplies together to take."

Evie shrugged off Sara's hand but went willingly enough to fetch paper and ink. After the long night of worry, it felt good to do something and Sara's spirits lifted as she worked. She repeated Granny's verse to herself. Surely, she'd finished her suffering. *Let this be my last trial. I'm ready to settle, to find joy in life again.*

A curl of hope unfurled in her heart, spreading until a quiet smile formed on her lips. She was strong, determined, capable. If they wouldn't let her see James, she'd go to the magistrate.

She'd go to the lieutenant governor himself. She wouldn't let them take this family away from her.

~~~

It wasn't until he entered his cell that the true danger of his situation hit James. *Treason*. The heavy iron door closed with a thud that echoed through the room. He was alone in a cell in the basement of the courthouse. Reserved for gentlemen prisoners, the warden had said with a smirk.

It was damp and cold, the stench of waste so strong he had no desire to look closely at the dirty straw strewn on the floor. A faint murmur of voices was audible from the common prisoners in the next room, and a barred window high in the hall outside his cell let in the growing daylight and a draft of frigid air.

He needed to get home to Sara and Evie.

His hands clamped on to the iron bars of his cell until his knuckles turned white. He was powerless and he hated it. Resisting the urge to shake the bars, he loosened his fingers one by one, dropping his hands and shaking his arms to warm his numb hands.

He sat on the rough wooden bench that was the cell's only furniture, forcing his mind to sort through the jumble of faces, dates, and alibis. James leaned back, his brow creasing in thought. Nothing settled him like forming a solid argument.

The sound of footsteps in the hall woke him sometime later. He sat up and swallowed, his tongue thick in his dry mouth.

"Right this way." The warden spoke over his shoulder as he approached James's stall. "Mind, only five minutes."

The door opened and Sara entered. He would have pinched himself to make sure he wasn't dreaming, but he knew she was real by the way his heart tripped and the blood surged in his veins. He came alive in her presence, like a man who had only ever seen the world in black and white suddenly exposed to all the colors of the rainbow.

She stood before him, wearing her simple navy dress, a warm shawl draped over her shoulders. His eyes traced the movement of her hands as she set down a basket and reached up to untie the ribbons of her bonnet with jerky movements.

"Sara." He took a step forward and reached for her. She came straight into his arms, squeezing him tightly around his waist. Tension drained out of him at the contact. Her presence absorbed his worry and filled him with new strength.

"I was so worried," she said, her voice muffled against the wrinkled lawn of his shirt. "Henry said you'd—" Her words caught on a sob, and he leaned down to press his face into the side of her neck. He breathed deep, letting her fresh scent block out the stench of unwashed bodies and human waste.

He pulled back, the first thrill of her presence fading. "What are you doing here alone? It's not safe. There's a rebellion afoot."

"They haven't reached the city. Foiled by a group of twenty volunteers, according to the jailer, but that seems an unlikely story."

"Twenty men?" James remembered the unorganized group of farmers he'd seen last night, most without arms or training. No wonder they hadn't managed to inflict a blow. Still—"The situation could change at any moment."

She pulled away with a jagged sigh and turned to the basket. "I knew you'd be difficult. I brought some things you might need." She peeled back the cloth and he saw bread and ham, a jug of water. Pen, ink, and paper.

It had been so long since anyone had taken care of him. "Thank you." His throat was so thick with emotion that he could barely force the words out. "Evie?"

"She's well. She wanted to come . . ." She pressed her lips together, but he saw the telltale tremble.

"Tell her I'll be home before she knows it." He attempted confidence he was far from feeling. He hadn't even managed to track Andrew down. "I'm worried about Andrew," he said. "I couldn't find him yesterday. Have you heard anything?"

"Andrew." She took in a deep breath. "Yes. He came by early this morning."

"He did? Thank God." He hadn't expected that. Some of his worry subsided, knowing Andrew was well and back in the city. Perhaps he'd come to his senses and left the rebellion before it was too late. "They told me he'd gone off on a patrol and not returned. I was worried he'd—"

"He was shot." Sara came to stand at his side. "He said it wasn't serious, but . . ."

"Shot?" Guilt sliced through him. He should have been there. He should have stopped him. "What happened?"

Sara recounted the story of Andrew's ambush and James realized he'd been stopped by the same picket that had held James at gunpoint. Thanks to Osgoode, they'd both been identified. They were in deep. He, Andrew, and by association, Sara. If she'd been seen helping a fugitive . . . His stomach gave a sickening lurch. She was alone and unprotected while he was trapped in this infernal cell. He needed a plan. "I'll have to contact Ballantine. With his influence, I should be able to get someone to hear my case right away."

She gave a decisive shake of her head. "There's more." Sara perched on the edge of the rough bench, pleating the skirt of her gown with one hand. "Henry told me about the man who'd given him the message for you last night." She looked up and he saw the fear in her eyes. "It wasn't Ballantine. It was—" Her voice caught.

James sat beside her. "What? Tell me."

"It was Osgoode."

The breath left James in a rush. He clasped his hands together, trying to hold on to calm. Forcing his mind to push past the anger and betrayal, to look for the pattern. The common thread. Osgoode. He stared, unseeing, at the toes of his boots. Osgoode sent the message, Osgoode shot Andrew. Osgoode convinced Jarvis to arrest him.

"I know he's a Tory through and through," Sara said, her voice low. "But what if it's more than that?"

James rose and paced to the cell door. Osgoode's resentment had simmered for years, but would he purposely plan to ruin James in such a public way?

Sara's words chased him across the cell. "Osgoode set you up. Sent you on a wild goose chase, knowing you'd be caught." She was at his side in two quick strides. "Didn't he?"

Of course, Sara had figured it out. "It wouldn't be the first time he's tried to discredit me." James thought back to the snide comments and sabotaged cases. "But never anything like this."

"It's because of me."

James swung around to face her. "What?" Where had she come up with that?

"I'm not the woman you should have married." She inhaled with a shudder "I—"

"No." He couldn't let her take the blame for his shortcomings. "This has nothing to do with you. Osgoode blames me for taking Ballantine's business away from him." He pulled her close, but she stood stiff in his arms. "I'll write Ballantine straight away. He'll help me. This will all be cleared up by supper."

"What if he doesn't?"

"He will. I'll write him right now."

He pulled ink and paper out of the basket and sat on the bench, using the space beside him as a makeshift desk. Knowing the guard was bound to return soon, he wrote quickly, explaining the situation as succinctly as he could while Sara paced the cell. He jumped up as soon as he finished, taking her shoulders in his hands.

"Don't worry. It will all be well." He forced his voice to remain steady and deliberate. "You are to keep Evie safe and as far away from this as possible. I'll handle it."

"Do you really expect me to abandon you?" Sara stepped back and crossed her arms, chin jutting out, looking as though she'd take on the whole of Her Majesty's militia for him.

Her support washed over him, covering his anger. He wasn't alone. She believed in him. There wasn't a flicker of hesitation in her eyes, nor did her stance waver. He could only thank God for putting such strength and loyalty in his life. He hadn't thought they existed.

"Sara, I—" He broke off, stunned by the words that almost slipped out of his mouth. He loved her? His hands came to her face, his fingers tracing the lines of her cheeks, the curve of her chin, memorizing every detail. He lowered his head, his lips touching hers gently, softly. She didn't pull back. Instead, her lips clung to his, her hands creeping up between them to twine about his neck.

He broke the kiss, leaning forward so their foreheads touched.

"You can't distract me, James Kinney," she whispered. "You need my help."

He sighed, the breath leaving his body in a long sweep that carried with it the last shreds of his resistance. "I know."

She took a small step back, just enough to meet his eyes. "Then tell me what I can do. Who should I talk to?"

"Have this delivered to Ballantine, then stay safe at home until I return." He ignored her murmur of frustration. "I'll sort this out." He tipped her chin up, forcing her to meet his gaze. "And when I am freed, I'll treasure you all the days I have left, Sara Kinney."

He didn't know where the vow sprang from, but he didn't wish the words unsaid. He was ready to face the truth. She was necessary to him. Precious. He savored the thought even as he buried his face in the silky strands of her hair and breathed deep of her scent until the heavy footsteps of the jailer forced them apart.

She stepped back and stared at him, her eyes huge in her face, and reached trembling hands up to tie her bonnet. Her eyes never left him, and he read in them the shock he was feeling. It was as though the threat of loss had stripped away every barrier between them, leaving only two souls whose parting he felt like a wrenching, physical pain.

"Come on then, Mrs. Kinney." The jailer looked back and forth between the two of them with a smirk, his eyes traveling down Sara's body in a way that had James's hands closing into fists. He couldn't protect her from the man's insolence, and he hated it.

"Sara," he said. She looked back over her shoulder. "If you should need anything, ask Ballantine."

A shadow passed over her face and for a moment her eyes were filled with a stark anguish he couldn't understand. In the next moment, it disappeared, replaced with a mask of calm and a brisk nod. "We'll be fine. Just come home." She looked at him, long and deep, until the door clanged shut in front of her, leaving him alone.

Chapter 30

Sara jerked her arm out of the jailer's overfriendly grasp and bolted to the street. She drew in a breath of the cold morning .air, her fingers tightening around the letter that weighed like a brick in her grasp. She'd wanted to tell James the truth, but that could jeopardize everything. If her father found out, he could very well turn his back on them both and James counted on his aide. She had to get the letter to Ballantine.

Henry emerged from a nearby alley, full of news. "Militia's arrived from Hamilton on the steamer. Forming companies. Going to march north to meet the rebels, I heard."

Sara chewed her lip, knowing she hadn't much time. Her father would certainly join the defense of the city. She looked down at Henry who danced from foot to foot. A sleepless night hadn't slowed him down. "Do you know where Thomas Ballantine lives?"

"Up on Palace Street? In one of them estates?"

Sara nodded. "You must deliver this into his hands. He could save Mr. Kinney's life."

Henry straightened. "Don't you worry, Sara. I won't let you down."

～～

The streets were quiet as Sara turned up Duke Street. Too quiet. The busy traffic to and from the wharf had disappeared. No gentlemen of business were to be seen, nor servants loaded down with packages. Blinds were drawn in the windows of every house she passed. The city waited, holding its breath for what would come next.

Exhaustion pulled at her, turning every step into an effort. When she opened the kitchen door, Mrs. Hobbes took one look at her face and hustled her off to bed as soon as Sara had soothed Evie's worries with a rosy picture of James's prison cell and the assurance that his release was imminent. Although she was certain she wouldn't be able to sleep for worry, she dozed off almost as soon as her head hit the pillow.

It felt as though she'd only just closed her eyes when Evie woke her.

"Henry is here," she whispered into Sara's ear. "He says he needs to see you."

Sara raced down the stairs to the kitchen. Henry stood next to the fire, holding out his hand to the blaze. His fingers trembled and her heart sank. It wasn't good news.

Henry looked up and she realized it wasn't fear or worry that had him trembling. His eyes blazed and there were two spots of color on his cheeks that she suspected hadn't been caused by the cold.

"That Ballantine fellow wouldn't even read it," he sputtered. "Took one glance and tossed it into the fire."

Her heart sank. They were too late. Osgoode must have informed her father of her identity. Her father had decided to wash his hands of James. She'd known this might happen. Yet she'd continued blithely on, building a castle in a cloud that was bound to come tumbling down.

"Did he say anything?"

Henry's frown grew fiercer. "He did. He said he weren't going to read the words of a traitor like Kinney."

"Papa's not a traitor," Evie said. She'd been uncharacteristically quiet since James's arrest, but this accusation roused her spirits.

"I know that," Henry said. "So, I says to him, *How dare you talk about Mr. Kinney like that. He isn't no traitor.*"

Sara's eyes flew open. "You said that? To . . . Mr. Ballantine?" She had a fleeting image of her father being taken to task by a child from the slums and it was almost enough to make her smile.

"I did." He crossed his arms. "Didn't do no good, though."

"Sara, what are we going to do now?" Evie looked at her as though she were their last hope. Maybe she was.

"You are going to get a good meal into you. And then Henry needs to sleep." Henry started to argue but Sara swept aside his protest that he wasn't a bit tired. "When you wake up, I'll have our plan ready."

The false promise made her feel slightly ill. She met Mrs. Hobbes's eyes over Henry's head and the older woman came forward to take the children in charge. Sara slipped out of the room and down the hall. She closed the parlor door behind her, dropped into a chair, and lowered her face into her hands.

A lone tear trickled down her cheek, then another. Soon, she could barely catch her breath for the sobs that wracked her. A familiar wave of helpless anger washed over her, the same anger she'd felt when Papa had locked the door in her face and bade her never return. The anger that had coursed through her when she'd placed a handful of wilted wildflowers on top of Colin's grave.

It had happened again. She'd given her heart to a man, come to trust in his love. Not the dreamy, giddy love of a girl. She'd come to love James with a woman's heart, deep and true. She'd dared to dream that she'd found a true partner in life. That she was following a path laid out for her and guided with love.

But this path only led back to heartache.

Then she remembered the desperate prayer behind that grimy inn. The pure joy she'd felt when she'd heard James's voice. She hadn't been alone then.

She felt a hand on her shoulder and raised her head. Maybe she wasn't alone now, either. Blinking away tears, she turned to see the ample form of Mrs. Hobbes beside her, her face creased with concern.

"You mustn't carry on so."

Sara sat up, wiping her face. "Where are the children?"

"I put Henry in the chair by the fire. Evie's telling him a story. I reckon they'll both be fast asleep in five minutes." Mrs. Hobbes sat down beside Sara, her forehead creased in worry. "You don't look much better yourself." Sara bit down hard on her bottom lip, but she was too late to stem another wave of tears. "I suppose a good cry never did anyone any harm." Mrs. Hobbes rubbed a comforting hand across her shoulders.

"Ballantine won't help him," Sara said between sobs. "And it's my fault." Mrs. Hobbes passed her a handkerchief. Sara took a shuddering breath and mopped her tears before she said too much.

Mrs. Hobbes gave her an approving nod. "That's right, you dry your tears. You'll need all your energy to figure out how to get that husband of yours back home to you."

"I'll go back tomorrow, see if I can see the magistrate. That's all I can do."

"All you can do? Are you sure?"

Sara avoided the older woman's eyes. "What else is there?" She folded the handkerchief into a square, wondering how she could get away from the probing questions. "No one will listen to me."

"They might not listen to you, but they'd listen to your father."

Sara froze. Her heart seemed to stop beating for a long moment before resuming, pounding through her veins so loudly that she half expected Mrs. Hobbes to hear it. "My father?"

"It took me a while to place you, but I knew from the beginning I'd seen you before. Just couldn't figure out where."

Sara moved her head from side to side in a slow shake. "Impossible."

"You're Sally Ballantine. Leastways, that's who you used to be."

"I don't use that name." Sara tried to rise, but Mrs. Hobbes's hand on her shoulder became insistent, pushing her back to her chair.

"Not anymore you don't, but you did, once upon a time. My sister worked for the Ballantines when you were just a little thing. I used to come and visit the kitchen. Catch up on all the gossip. Must be ten years since I last saw you. From a distance of course. That's why it took me so long to place you. I knew you weren't a laundrywoman, though, from almost the first time I laid eyes on you."

"I have nothing to do with my father," Sara finally conceded. "Or, rather, he has nothing to do with me."

"What a dustup that was, you running off with the stable boy." Sara's face burned, words of explanation bubbling to her lips, but Mrs. Hobbes shook her head. "It wasn't all your fault. I always said that Thomas Ballantine was his own worst enemy."

"It doesn't matter who was in the right. My father won't help James because of me." She hung her head. "I'm a disgrace to him."

"Time has a way of changing people. Mellowing them."

Sara shook her head. "Not my father. He told me he never wanted to see me again." The day was engraved in Sara's memory. Stephen Osgoode had somehow convinced her father that she was on the verge of eloping with Colin. They concocted a plan between them to marry her off to Osgoode as soon as could be arranged.

She'd risen from the dining table in a passion, declaring she'd rather die.

You'll be as good as dead to me, my girl, if you leave with that stable boy.

She left anyway, packing her bag, and escaping out a window in the middle of the night, fueled by a sense of injustice and the romance of it all. She'd had no idea of the hardship ahead of her.

"Hmpf." Mrs. Hobbes raised her eyebrows. "Said that, did he? Wouldn't be the first impulsive act Mr. Ballantine lived to regret."

Sara bit her lip. The very idea of approaching her father seemed impossible just a week ago. But now that everything she'd come to care for was about to be wrenched from her hands, now that she had a little girl to think of, something shifted.

As good as dead to me. Those words had held her prisoner for so long. She took a deep breath, pushing the words away and replacing them with Evie's voice, high and sweet. *I'm lucky, aren't I? God gave me two.* Mothering this girl was the most beautiful gift she'd ever been given.

Thomas Ballantine's repudiation still burned sharp in her heart, but her father's rejection wasn't God's rejection, as much as she'd conflated the two. She'd clung to the past instead of focusing on the little girl who brought her so much joy and the man who had taught her to love again. They were worth fighting for. Was she brave enough to try?

～～

A noise at the window startled James awake. He sat up, stretching the stiff muscles of his back. Through the bars of his cell, he could see two shadowy figures in the window. Then a face appeared. A face as familiar as his own.

"Evie?" he said, all the color leaving his face. "What on earth are you doing here?"

"I came to check on you," she whispered. "Are you all right?"

Her pale face peered down at him in concern. He opened his mouth, but he had no words of comfort to offer her. No words at all.

"Told you," came a voice behind her. In the next second, Henry's dirty face joined hers in the window. "What've you got to say now, milady?"

Evie only stared at James, her eyes filling with tears. Oh, Lord, he had to get her away from here.

"Hey, now, you promised no waterworks." Henry gave her a gentle shove. "Knew I shouldn'ta brought her." His eyes met James through the window. "Sorry, guv."

"You'll be more than sorry when I get out of here. Shouldn't you be cleaning out stalls right about now?"

Henry flushed and looked down. "I . . ."

"It's not his fault. I told him I'd come without him if he didn't help me." Evie swiped the tears from her face with her sleeve. "I didn't really believe him."

"Does Sara know where you are?"

A flash of guilt spread over her face. "Um . . . not exactly."

"She went to talk to that old mort," Henry added helpfully. "Him what burned your note."

"Mr. Ballantine?" James froze, his mind unable to comprehend Henry's words. He swallowed. "He *burned* it?"

"Said he weren't going to help a—" Henry broke off with a quick glace at Evie. "Sara's gone to straighten it out."

James ran his fingers through his hair. Nothing made sense. Ballantine knew where James's loyalties lay. Didn't he?

Now Sara was traipsing across the city alone when any crossroads could become a battlefield. He trained his gaze on Henry. "Henry, I need your help."

Henry straightened. "Aye, sir." James wouldn't have been surprised to see him salute.

"Your first task will be to get Evie home. Then, you're to follow Mrs. Kinney to Ballantine's home."

"Aye, guv." He elbowed Evie. "C'mon, you heard him."

Evie had a stubborn look that boded no good. "Evangeline Kinney, go home this instant. It's not safe for you in this part of town."

Evie dismissed his worries with a toss of her head. "I need to know what happened, Papa."

James ground his teeth. "*I* need you to get home."

"How can I help you if I don't know why you're here?"

"I don't need you to help me. I need you to stay home where you're safe." James forced himself to lower his voice. "I don't want to worry about you on top of everything else."

"What's the point of being safe?"

"What?" James slowed his racing thoughts and tried to grasp her question. Wasn't it obvious?

"Well, if you're gone, there's not much point in us staying safe at home. There won't be anything for us there."

"You'll have Sara."

"Oh, Papa." Evie looked at him with an expression he could only call pitying. "There won't be anything for Sara there, either. Don't you see? You're worth the risk."

James stood still for a long moment as her words sank in, past all his logical objections. They lodged deep in his heart, cutting him with a pain that was half sweet. Love was courage. Love was risk. Why hadn't he seen that before now?

A strident voice called out from the street above. "You there, get away from that window. Don't you know those are dangerous prisoners?"

The faces disappeared and he heard Henry's voice. "Aw, we don't mean no harm."

"Run along now, before I call the constable."

Evie ducked to offer him a jaunty wave and then disappeared.

James gripped the bars of his cell. Evie and Sara were in danger. Frustration at his powerlessness rose like bile in his throat.

His hands came up to cover his face, the regret sharp and biting. Strange, what stuck out to him now wasn't the decisions he'd made, but what he hadn't done. He hadn't confided in Sara, not really. He hadn't called out Osgoode's machinations or refused Ballantine's offers, even when he knew he could do more with his life.

He'd tried to orchestrate every moment of every day and avoid any risk that might endanger his family. He thought he could keep them safe through sheer force of will. Of course, he'd never once thought the person who would need rescuing would be himself.

Chapter 31

The gray gown buoyed her as the carriage swept up the curving drive of the estate on Palace Street. Bordered by elms, the drive ended at an elegant Georgian home with tall, symmetrical windows on either side of an imposing oak door. Sara named the rooms as the carriage approached, picturing them in her mind. The parlor. Papa's study. The knot in her stomach grew, making her breath quicken. It was so familiar, at once linked to every memory of her childhood, and yet synonymous with rejection and loss.

Even the butler who answered her knock was unchanged. He paled, his eyes widening at the sight of her. "Miss Sally?" His voice was faint, unbelieving.

"Hello, McBain. May I come in?"

McBain snapped to attention, stepping aside for her to enter. He faltered, his eyes darting between the library and the small family parlor in the back as though he were wondering just where one placed a prodigal daughter who'd disappeared for over a decade.

"Is my father here?"

"Yes," he answered quickly, then seemed to recollect himself. "Ah, that is, I will see if Mr. Ballantine is at home." He led the way to the library. "Follow me, please, Mrs. O'Connor."

"It's Mrs. Kinney, now, McBain," she corrected gently.

For a moment, the older man appeared perplexed. She could almost see the wheels of his mind turning, trying to figure out why the name Kinney was so familiar. His eyes widened, and she saw the moment when the truth clicked into place.

Sara moved further into the parlor, her eyes lighting on the familiar furnishings before coming to rest on the portrait above the hearth. Her mother as a young bride, dressed in the flowing, high-waisted fashion of a quarter century ago. Sara had spent hours curled up on the sofa, staring into that face for a clue to the woman she couldn't remember. The soft, dreamy eyes and whimsical smile were just as she'd remembered them, but now she noticed the tightly clasped hands, the way her brows drew together as though she were pondering some deep truth. *Help me, Mama. Help me find the words to save my family.*

"McBain!"

The gruff voice in the hall brought a flood of memories so sharp that she took a step forward. *Papa.* The years fell away, and she heard the voice of her childhood hero, the man she'd tried so hard to please. The man who had rejected her and pushed her out onto the streets. This last thought checked her steps, reminding her of everything that had happened since she'd left this house. She drew in a deep breath.

"You have a visitor, sir." McBain moved to the door, blocking her view of the hall.

"Nonsense. No time for a visitor now. Told the governor I'd be back by noon." Her father's voice drew closer, and her heart started to pound.

"It's Miss Sally."

Silence greeted this pronouncement. Sara held her breath.

"Sally?" His voice was different, hoarse, and tinged with disbelief. The gentleness of it gave her the courage to step around McBain.

His hair was fully gray now, and the lines across his forehead and around his eyes more pronounced. His frame was bent where before he had always stood so straight and proud. She felt the weight of his eyes on her and steeled herself to meet his gaze.

"Sally. You've come home."

She'd prepared herself for his anger, his indifference, even. But his gentle words, uttered so softly, shocked her into silence. Then she remembered why she'd come. She cleared her throat. Her future depended on this conversation.

"I—I hope you don't mind."

Her father handed his cane and hat back to McBain, his eyes not leaving her. "Not at all, not at all." He seemed to recollect himself, and some of his usual bluster returned to his voice. "Sit down." He swept an arm out in front of him, indicating a seat on the sofa. "Refreshments, McBain," he called over his shoulder, before taking a seat in the armchair.

His chair. She remembered climbing onto his lap while he sat, gazing into the fire on a rare evening he spent at home. Sometimes he'd smoke his pipe, looking up at the portrait of her mother. He didn't talk much on those nights, but she'd been content to curl up in his lap and feel the strength of his arms around her.

The rush of tears surprised her. She thought she'd long ago ceased to mourn her father, her heart taken up with bigger sorrows. But here, in this room, she was a child again, desperate for any attention that came her way.

He cleared his throat, startling her out of her reverie. "You . . . you look well." His gaze swept over her fine silk dress and stylish half boots.

What would his reaction be if he'd seen her scrubbing dirty linens in a courtyard? Would he turn away, pretend he didn't know her?

"Colin died." She hadn't meant to start there but suddenly it seemed important that he hear it all. Her father paled, his mouth pinching together at the mention of her first husband's name. "Seven years ago."

"Seven *years*?" He straightened. "Why am I only hearing of this now?"

"I went to live with his family," Sara continued, ignoring his question. "I worked to support myself. I took in laundry." She met his eyes, daring him to take exception to her choices, but she could find no trace of the scorn she expected. Instead, his eyes softened. He looked down, but not before she saw the faint shimmer of tears.

"I looked for you." His voice was so quiet, she leaned forward in her seat to hear him better. "I made inquiries, put Osgoode on your trail, but there was no trace of you." His hands tightened on the arms of his chair. "You just . . . vanished."

She was silent, unwilling to contradict him. She'd never been more than two miles from him, but Osgoode had probably worked diligently to keep her hidden away. A reconciliation while she was married to Colin would have spelled the end of his plans to inherit her father's estate.

Her father turned his head and Sara followed his eyes to the woman in the portrait above their heads, watching them both with her inscrutable eyes.

"On Monday, I remarried." Sara wasn't sure who she was talking to, for her eyes remained trained on her mother.

Her words seemed to snap him out of his fixation on the portrait. "Married? Well, that's something, I suppose." The hint of sarcasm under his words reminded her of the man she remembered. Assuming the worst, never listening to an explanation. Never willing to bend. She remembered how he'd used that biting tongue on her, laying her emotions bare before banishing her from his house.

Sara pushed the memories aside and focused on the reason for this painful interview. James. "I need your help, Papa."

His brows lowered and a faint tinge of red dusted his cheekbones. "How much?"

How perfectly like him, to assume that every problem could be solved with money. She rose, reining in her temper with a quick turn about the room. Papa hated tears. She needed to be calm and rational if she wanted to win his support. "It's not money I need," she said when she had her voice under control. "My husband is James Kinney."

His jaw dropped and it took him long moments to reply. "What? How can this be? He got himself tangled up with his governess, but I put a stop to that . . ." She saw by the widening of his eyes that he'd put the missing pieces of the puzzle together. "You're the governess."

"I'll tell you about it later," she said, "but first I need to get him out of prison. Those charges aren't true, I know they're not."

He looked away. "Your loyalty does you credit, but I doubt you know the whole story."

"He went for Andrew Ridley."

Her father shook his head. "That's what I thought at first, too. But I had a visit from Osgoode last night that lifted the scales from my eyes. Turns out Andrew *and* James were up to their necks in rebellion. I was duped."

"Duped, yes, but not by James."

He ignored her words. "Puts me in a blasted uncomfortable spot, I can tell you. My lawyer and my godson suspected of treason." He rose, pacing to the window. "James was seen at a meeting down at Davies' Tavern, you know. And then that governess—" He broke off, sending a quick glance at Sara. "Made me doubt everything I knew about him."

The hint of vulnerability on his face gave her pause. "He's innocent, Papa." She hesitated. Once before she'd tried to get her father to see the truth about Osgoode and he called her a liar. Why did she think this time would be any different? She took a breath. She had nothing to lose. "The real villain here is Stephen Osgoode."

He was silent for a long moment. She expected him to argue, to throw Osgoode's distinguished pedigree in her face. *Descended from a viscount. Haven't you heard of Lord Osgoode?* Instead, he seemed to shrink into his chair.

"James got a message late at night summoning him to Andrew's rescue. From you."

"I sent no message," her father said, instantly on the defensive.

"I know that now. Osgoode sent it. Osgoode manned the picket on Yonge Street, too. He identified James and made sure the sheriff arrested him."

"There's no love lost between Osgoode and Kinney, I know that, but he wouldn't deliberately target him. It's ridiculous."

"Osgoode set James up. Pushed him right in the middle of the rebellion, knowing he'd likely be arrested, or at the very least, discredited. Please, Papa," she said, not even trying to mask her desperation. "You have to believe me this time." Memories of that other day came rushing back, making it impossible to continue.

Ballantine leaned forward, his hands running over his face. He was silent for a long moment. "I suspected Osgoode wasn't the man I thought him. Started to turn things over to James and Andrew. Osgoode must have noticed the work I sent their way, but . . . I never thought he'd go this far." He settled back into his chair, frowning, his gaze far away.

Sara stifled the urge to tap her feet. This was not the time to settle into a brown study and reflect on Stephen Osgoode's treachery. They needed to *act*. "James is a good man. I love him." It was the first time she'd said the words aloud and she lingered over them, feeling her heart soften and ache in her chest. She swallowed, forcing herself to continue. "He has a daughter, and we need him." Her voice broke. "The magistrate probably won't even speak with me. You've got to help us."

"Don't cry, Sally." The use of her long-ago name only caused the tears to fall harder. Sara wiped them away, feeling the hope that had sustained her ebb away in the face of his continued silence.

Then her father sighed, all the air leaving his lungs in a great gust that left him deflated. Smaller. "It's my fault he's involved, but I had to do something," he said suddenly, his gaze drifting over her shoulder and focusing on the family crest of arms displayed on the mantel. "Imagine the scandal if a Ridley got caught up in the rebellion." His eyes moved back to her, and she was surprised at the grief they held. "Promised his father I'd look out for young Andrew, but he'd moved beyond my reach. I asked James to steer him out of trouble. Nice, solid lad, James Kinney."

"You know James is innocent." Sara prodded. "You can tell them he was only trying to protect—" She broke off, hearing voices in the front hall. Her father's gaze strayed to the door. They couldn't afford any delays. "Let's go right now," she said, forcing his attention back to her.

The door to the parlor swung open to reveal a harried McBain, attempting to block entry to the room.

"Let me pass." The voice was familiar, as was the shock of red hair that barreled into the room.

Sara didn't have time to wonder how Henry came to be here. McBain grabbed him and Sara intervened before Henry's flailing legs made contact with McBain's shins.

"He's with me. Please, do let him go."

McBain released the boy, taking a cautious step back. Henry righted his clothing with a withering glance at the butler and stalked into the room.

"You again?" Ballantine stared at Henry beneath lowered brows.

Henry was uncowed. "Mr. Kinney sent me to keep an eye on the missus." He jerked his head in Sara's direction. "See her home."

Sara was still trying to find words to explain Henry to her father when Evie marched into the parlor.

"Evie?" Sara sat down on the settee with a thump. Evie was supposed to be home under the watchful eye of Mrs. Hobbes.

The girl avoided Sara's eyes, seeking out her father instead. "Mr. Ballantine. How do you do? I'm Evie Kinney."

Her father nodded, looking stunned at the rapid turn of events. Sara understood how he felt.

Evie looked up into Ballantine's face, her eyes clear and focused. "You have to help my papa."

Thomas Ballantine, political maven and man of business, looked helplessly from Evie to Sara, his eyes begging Sara to rescue him. "They won't free him on my say-so alone."

"Of course not," Evie said with a wave of her hand. "We need to find proof."

A strain of defensiveness seeped into the older man's voice. "If you think I can snap my fingers and procure a witness out of thin air, let me tell you, young lady, the law requires—"

Evie had no time for a lecture. "Henry can do it." She grabbed Henry by the arm, dragging him in front of Ballantine. "He delivered the message. He was with Papa all evening."

Ballantine straightened, shooting the boy a keen glance. "The entire time?"

Henry nodded. "Aye, sir."

"And who might you be?" Her father's glance took in Henry's ragged clothes.

Sara rose and placed her hand on Henry's shoulder. "He's our friend. Thanks to him I know what happened to James."

Her father stroked his whiskers, weighing her words. "Still, a young lad, uneducated." He waved a hand at Henry, encompassing everything from his unruly mop of hair to his boots, one of which was held together with a piece of string. "Irregular."

Sara wondered how she could convince her father to take a chance on Henry, but she needn't have worried. Evie stepped up, her hands on her hips.

"Henry is not uneducated. He can read and do some letters. And he knows more about what goes on in this city than anyone, Papa said so." Her little chin jutted out in a way all too familiar to Sara. Thomas Ballantine had no idea who he was dealing with.

"Yes, well." His fingers drummed a tense rhythm on the arm of his chair and his eyes narrowed in thought. "Osgoode sent the message to James, eh? Pretending he was me?" He rose and paced the length of the room before turning to Sara. "Impossible to prove, though." A new urgency had entered his voice.

Evie stepped beside him and tugged on his sleeve. "Not impossible." Her head whipped around, and she pinned Henry with her eyes. "Who was there when Osgoode gave you the message?"

Henry's brows pulled together. "I reckon the groom beside me heard. And Pauly, the other stable boy. He wanted to take the message, but I were the one who knew where James Kinney lived, so he picked me."

Ballantine stared at the children for a long moment, his brow furrowed. Then he smiled, patting Evie on the head. "Clever girl. Run along now, children, and tell McBain I'll be needing the carriage instead of the horse, after all."

He turned to Sara and rested his hands on her shoulders.

"I'll make it right, Sally. I shouldn't have let it happen in the first place."

She wasn't sure if he was still talking about James, or about her departure all those years ago, but it didn't matter. She saw the love in his eyes, felt the question underlying his words. "Thank you," she whispered, reaching up to kiss his cheek. They still had work to do to put the past behind them, but she sensed that healing had begun. For both of them.

His eyes closed, and his hands tightened on her shoulders. "I didn't know if I'd ever get a second chance. I heard about the cholera epidemic, had Osgoode make some inquiries. The name O'Connor came up more than once and he could find no trace of you—" He broke off.

She shook her head. "I never stopped thinking about you, Papa. I hated how I left. And after Colin . . ." she shuddered.

His brow creased with concern as he looked down at her. "If you needed something, you should have come to me. You should have come home."

"You said you never wanted to lay eyes on me again."

"And you think everything I say in a temper is the gospel truth? I told you I tried to find you, but Osgoode . . ."

Stephen Osgoode had destroyed so much. She couldn't bear to think he'd destroy James as well.

"He has a lot to answer for," she said over the lump in her throat. "You're the only hope I've got left."

Her words seemed to inspire him, for the fire returned to his eyes. He turned, bellowing at McBain to bring his hat. "I won't let you down, my girl," he said over his shoulder. "No son-in-law of mine will be accused of treason. Not if I have anything to say about it."

Chapter 32

The first clue James had was the water. A steaming jug of warm water for washing. A cup of lukewarm coffee, too, and something resembling a biscuit. The warden passed him the tray without his usual smirk and inquired if James was needing anything else. Perhaps they'd decided to skip the trial and proceed directly to the hanging.

He'd just finished washing when a voice boomed down the corridor.

"Bring him up, then. What are you waiting for?" Ballantine's voice was full of a familiar irritable impatience that bolstered James's spirits.

The warden returned with a jerk of his head to indicate James should follow him. Hope bloomed in his chest as he mounted the stairs. Surely if he were still a prisoner, his hands would be bound.

Ballantine strode forward and clapped him on the back. "You're free, man."

James swallowed, scarcely able to believe the man's words. "Thank you, sir."

"Don't thank me. That wife of yours is mighty determined when she sets her mind to something. Daughter, too." James cast a quick glance around the upper chambers of the jail. "No, no, they're not here. Convinced them to stay home, have a welcome ready for you when you get there."

His thoughts were spinning. He was free because Sara and Evie had convinced Ballantine? He didn't have time to dwell on this improbability, for another figure caught his eye.

"Henry?"

The lad came forward, with a cheeky grin. "Aye, guv."

"What are you doing here?" His eyes swept the room again. "Tell me Evie didn't sneak—"

"Not a chance. She's tucked up safe at home, just like you said."

"Then what are you doing here?"

"Got me a new job, I does." He stood straighter, a proud tilt to his chin. "Page for this one." He jerked his head in Ballantine's direction.

"Errand boy," Ballantine corrected, with a shake of his head. "'Twas that daughter of yours who called him a page. From some fool book she's reading."

James hid a smile. If Evie wanted to make Henry a page and Ballantine a knight, straight out of *Ivanhoe*, who was he to argue? He'd been rescued, just like Isaac of York. And, like Isaac, it seemed he had his daughter to thank . . . and his wife.

Henry sidled up to him. "Guv, I thought you was good at

spinning words, but I never saw anything like this one." He jerked his head in Ballantine's direction and lowered his voice. "That magistrate didn't know which end was up by the end of it."

Ballantine snorted. "You did your part, too." He turned to James. "Likely lad and wasting his talents down at Cooper's stable. 'Twas his testimony that turned the tide." Henry swelled up like a peacock, earning him a gentle cuff from Ballantine. "Be off now, make sure the carriage is ready."

Henry tugged his forelock, though his eyes were far from repentant. "Aye, sir."

James looked from Henry to Ballantine, wondering if two days in prison had rendered him not quite lucid.

"Decided to take him on," Ballantine confided as they moved toward the exit. "Don't find loyalty like that every day. Magistrate tried to trip him up, practically bribed him to sell you out, but the lad didn't falter." Ballantine shook his head. "Sally told me he was a sharp one."

"Sally?"

"Er, Sara, I mean." Ballantine looked away, a faint tinge of red staining his cheeks. "Never been good with names."

James let himself smile for the first time in days. "She talked you around, did she? I assume that means you've come to appreciate my choice of a bride?"

"That daughter of yours had something to do with it, too." Ballantine shook his head. "When those two join forces, you'd best give in straight away and cut your losses."

"My daughter is mighty persuasive, but I'd still like to know how you managed to avoid charges."

"Yes, well, all in good time." Ballantine turned toward the

door. "Let's get you home. Unless you've developed a liking for this place?"

James gave a reluctant chuckle. "I'm ready to go home."

Home. The word had never sounded so beautiful.

Ballantine led him to the carriage and went on to detail the interview, a process James would normally find fascinating. Today, though, his mind had room for only one thought as they trundled down King Street. *Sara and Evie. Home.*

~~~

Sara smoothed her hands down the front of her gown, the same soft gray she'd been married in. The table was set and James's favorite, steak and kidney pudding, ready to serve. Mrs. Hobbes was bustling about the kitchen, fussing with apple pastries, a wide smile on her face.

Sara joined Evie where she stood at the parlor window, watching the road with anxious eyes, her tense little body straining toward the street. Sara understood how she felt. She wouldn't relax until she saw James with her own eyes.

The sound of carriage wheels had Evie racing to the gate. "It's them!" she called back. "I can see Henry up beside the coachman."

Sara hurried to join her as the carriage rolled to a stop. Henry jumped down and opened the door and James stepped out. Unshaven, disheveled, with dark circles under his eyes and new lines etched into his face, he was the most beautiful sight she'd ever seen.

Evie rushed forward to embrace him. Over her head, his eyes sought her out. *Thank you,* he mouthed. He widened his arms and she stepped into the embrace, sandwiching Evie between them. His hands came around her, warm and real.

Evie began to squirm, and they drew apart.

The carriage pulled away, James and Evie calling out their farewells. Evie grabbed Sara's hand, pulling her along with them as they walked up the path to the house. "Supper is ready, Papa. It's your favorite."

James smiled at Sara over Evie's head, his eyes roving over her face with such care that it was almost a caress. She attempted a smile in return, trying to ignore the thread of unease that ran under her joy. He still didn't know the truth about her. She'd asked her father to hold off, let her tell James tonight.

James kept Evie entertained over supper with glossed-over details of his arrest and time in prison. Mrs. Hobbes bustled in and out of the dining room, swelling with pride when James complimented her supper.

"The best pudding this side of the Atlantic. Mrs. Hobbes, you are a treasure." James smiled, his eyes sliding back to Sara. They hadn't had a chance to speak privately yet, but she felt like they were having a conversation all the same. *If I am freed, I'll treasure you all the days I have left, Sara Kinney.* She dropped her eyes into her lap, where her hands twisted together under the tablecloth. Would he still feel the same when he knew everything?

"We should have a celebration with all of us," Evie said. "Mr. Ballantine and Henry can come. Uncle Andrew, too."

Sara's eyes flew to James's face. At the mention of Andrew's name, James's smile faded. "Uncle Andrew had to travel out of town."

"He'll be back. Has he written you?"

"I—I haven't heard anything." James rallied, forcing a laugh. "Knowing Andrew, he's gotten himself embroiled with some fair lady and forgotten all about us."

Evie giggled. "Oh, Papa, Uncle Andrew doesn't have a sweetheart."

James waggled his eyebrows. "That's what you think."

When Evie was finally tucked in bed and Mrs. Hobbes had retired for the evening, they had a moment to themselves. Sara reached out to clasp his arm.

"James, I—"

"I've been waiting all evening for this." James reached for her and then grimaced. "Let me bathe first and get the last of the stench of the prison off me."

Sara nodded, in an agony of anticipation and dread. "Yes, of course." He leaned close, pressing a gentle kiss to her brow, then her cheeks.

Sara couldn't stop herself from leaning closer and tilting her face, sealing their lips. He was gentle at first, his lips sliding over hers like a caress. Warmth spread from where their lips connected until her fingers tingled with the need to be closer. Her feet crowded up against his, pulling closer to the strength of his body.

James broke away. "At this rate, I'll never get that bath, and trust me, I need it. I don't want to . . . come to you with the dirt of the prison on me."

Sara stepped back, running a shaky hand over her skirts. "I'll just wait in the parlor."

James's smile was hesitant. "Why don't you head straight to bed? I won't be long."

She nodded, too nervous to speak. He wanted her. The

thought was terrifying and wonderful all at once. Once she told him everything, he might change his mind.

She took her time preparing for bed, brushing her hair with long strokes, all the while her heart pumping, rehearsing her confession in her mind. Her face in the mirror was flushed, two spots of color on her cheeks, her eyes large and bright. Scared. She heard his step in the hall and whirled about, tucking herself under the covers just as the door opened.

She forced her eyes to take him in, standing in the doorway in only an open shirt and breeches. He pushed the door shut with a backward kick of his leg, all his attention focused on her, his eyes devouring her as he walked closer. She scrambled up to sitting.

"James, wait. We need to talk."

~~

Talk? He'd thought of little else than this moment since they'd tucked Evie in for the night, and not because he wanted to talk. But it didn't follow she would feel the same, no matter what he'd thought her kiss told him.

"Yes, of course," he managed. He took a seat on the edge of the bed, trying not to notice how her nightgown revealed a crescent of pearly skin across her collarbone.

"There is something you need to know."

The serious tone of her voice brought his eyes back to her face in a flash. "What is it?" The hum of dread replaced the anticipation low in his belly.

"I'm not who you think I am."

He'd always known there was more to her than met the eye.

How strange that now, when she was finally going to tell him, he wasn't sure he wanted to hear. They loved each other. They were going to be happy. *Don't change the story now.*

"I'm not a laundress. Well, I am, but that's not all."

He couldn't help the smile that twisted his lips. "That much I figured out already." A schoolmaster's family, he'd guessed, or perhaps even a vicar's. A family with access to learning, but whose credibility couldn't survive a scandalous marriage.

She continued without acknowledging his comment. "My family was—is—quite wealthy."

This he hadn't expected. *Wealthy.* He would never be wealthy. If they left the city, their circumstances would be even less promising. "I'm afraid I don't understand." He cleared his throat, hating the unsteady throb in his voice. "You said you didn't have anyone but Granny."

"There wasn't anyone. At least, not anyone who would acknowledge me."

"That's splitting hairs." James tried to make sense of her words, but they danced about his mind, refusing to settle in any logical pattern.

"Well, you're the lawyer. You would know." Her voice was sharp.

An uncharacteristic flush of anger surged through him, making him ball his hands into fists. "Sara, just get to the point."

"I—I was born Sara Ballantine."

James was still for a long moment. He only knew one family named Ballantine in the city and that was—"I don't understand."

"Thomas Ballantine is my father." James shook his head and she continued, a thread of impatience in her voice.

"Oh, surely you've heard the story of Ballantine's disgraced daughter."

"You're Sally?" Hints began to fall into place. Her insistence on staying away from society. The look on her face when she discovered he worked for Thomas Ballantine.

"Papa wanted me to marry Osgoode." James gave a sharp intake of breath, but she refused to look at his face. "I refused, and he told me I was no daughter of his. If I left with Colin, I was never to darken his door again. I didn't see my father again until this morning."

"You mean to tell me that Ballantine, one of the richest men in Toronto, let his daughter scrub laundry at Cooper's Inn?" James crossed his arms. The story was incredible, unbelievable. Yet what motivation would she have to lie? He remembered the strange hesitation in Ballantine's voice when he'd said the name Sally and the flush on his cheeks.

"He didn't know any of that." Sara looked down at her hands, her fingers rubbing against the remains of a callus. "They'd arranged my marriage to Stephen Osgoode. I was afraid, if I went back, I'd have to—" She met James's eyes. "You know what Osgoode is. He'd find some way to trap me into it, I knew it."

James's hands clenched at the fear in her voice. He took a step toward the bed, and then another, feeling her anguish down to his soul. "Yet you went to your father this morning. What did he say?"

Tears filled her eyes. "He said he was sorry." She barely got the words out before a sob shook her. James closed the space between them in one step and sat beside her, gathering her close in his arms.

"Hush, my love. Hush."

Sara wrapped her arms around him, pressing her face into the nook between his neck and shoulder. He breathed in her scent, pulling the soft curves of her body close. Her hands crept around his waist, returning his embrace, and sending a shock of awareness through him. His hand soothed the supple line of her back until her sobs subsided and she took a steadying breath.

"I never thought I'd hear him say those words. I thought I was alone."

"I wish you had told me." How could she ever be happy with the life he offered, when her father could give her so much more? She'd grow unsatisfied, just like—

"James, look at me." The touch of her hands on his face brought his attention back to her with a snap. "I'm sorry. Had I known you were so intimately connected to him, I would have told you before we wed. After, when I found out . . . well, I thought it could damage your career. What if he refused to acknowledge me? Or punished you, though it was no fault of yours?" Her voice broke.

"You thought all that, but you never thought to trust me with the truth?"

"I was afraid I'd lose you."

"But that's not what happened. You can't lose me, Sara Kinney. You're stuck with me now." The thought made his stomach dip.

A hint of a smile curved her lips. "I didn't believe I'd ever be this happy." He sucked in a breath. Did she really have no regrets? "There's no one else I'd rather be with. Granny said you were the one, but I never believed her."

What Sara needs is a family. I reckon that's what you need, too.

He smiled. "She told me the same thing. I assured her she had the wrong man."

Her fingers twisted in the linen of his shirt, her eyes wide and warm. "Granny's never wrong. I love you, James. Forgive me?"

"There's nothing to forgive." The joy he'd felt earlier, coming home to her, returned, stronger than ever. She loved him. She wanted to be with him. "I think I might be the happiest man in Toronto tonight."

She smiled and there was a subtle shift in the air about them. James's hands on her back slowed, tracing the fine bones along her spine in a delicate swirl. She drew closer, her breath cool against his neck, making him shiver.

He closed the remaining space between them and touched his lips to hers, softly at first, then more firmly as her arms tightened around him. His hands cupped her face as he deepened the kiss. They fell back on the bed and her arms moved up to wind around his neck, her fingers buried in his hair.

With a groan, he broke off the kiss. "Sara?" he gasped. He tore his eyes from her lips and forced himself to focus on words. "Are you sure?"

She smiled. "I've never been more confident about anything in my life, James Kinney."

Epilogue

DECEMBER 1838

"They're here!" Evie came running into the kitchen. She'd kept watch at the front window for the past half hour, her eyes trained on the street while she traced designs into the frost that coated the panes.

The house was full of delicious smells. Ham and roast turkey and Christmas pudding. Every dish Sara could remember from her childhood. Mrs. Hobbes had been busy for a week, enlisting Sara and Evie in all the chopping and mixing required to prepare the feast.

Sara rushed to the front door in time to welcome her father and Henry as they entered in a rush of frosty air. James was already shaking Papa's hand and taking his heavy wool coat to hang in the front hall.

Henry stood behind him, wrapped in a new navy coat with

shiny brass buttons. "May I take your coat, Master Henry?" James said, turning to the boy.

Henry crossed his arms. "I'll keep it on, if it's all the same to you."

Sara hid a smile. "I don't blame you. What a handsome coat."

"Christmas present," Henry said, straightening his shoulders.

Ballantine glanced down at the boy and shook his head in mock impatience. "Nonsense. Can't wear a coat in the house." His voice held a gruff fondness that warmed Sara's heart. "Best take it off."

Henry hesitated another second before carefully peeling it off and handing it to James. His eyes followed the coat to the hooks on the side of the hall as though he didn't want to let it out of his sight. In the year since he'd gone to work for Sara's father, he'd evolved from errand boy to something closer to godson. He spent his mornings with Ballantine's secretary, copying ledgers and deciphering contracts, before summarizing the day's business for Ballantine over luncheon.

Evie grabbed Henry's arm and dragged him into the parlor to show him the contents of her Christmas stocking.

"And we've got a present for you, too," she said.

This distracted Henry enough for him to forget the coat. Sara returned to the kitchen to help Mrs. Hobbes get the meal on the table. The excited voices of Henry and Evie filtered back, underscored by the deep rumble of her father and James. Sara paused, a spoon full of dressing in her hand. She'd never dared hope to have such a Christmas, all the people she loved together in one place, the bonds of family growing stronger with each week that passed.

They'd decided to stay in Toronto, and she was grateful.

Thanks to her father, Osgoode's role in James's downfall was made public and the man had fled the city in disgrace. Though her father urged James to take over Osgoode's wealthy clients, he'd stayed true to his decision to help the poor and spent his afternoons at a tiny office in Irish Town.

Henry's eyes bulged at the table full of delicacies as they sat down to the Christmas feast after sending Mrs. Hobbes off with a basket of treats for her family. Finally, it was time for the pudding. Sara carried it to the table and reached for a taper.

"Wait!" Evie cried. "We must all make a wish. You start, Grandpapa."

Silence fell over the table. Sara met James's eyes across the table, an amused glance passing between them. It hadn't taken Evie long to adopt Sara's father and it warmed her heart to see the bond growing between them.

"Well, I . . ." Ballantine cleared his throat, and Sara was shocked to see the sheen of tears in his eyes. "I suppose I wish I could convince this stubborn son-in-law of mine to move house, but I don't expect that to happen anytime soon."

Ballantine had tried to convince James and Sara to move in with him. Sara's hand crept to her middle under the table and she smiled a secret smile. The move might happen sooner than he thought.

Henry wished for fine sledding weather, and James prayed the proposal he'd presented to the assembly would move swiftly through Parliament.

Then it was Sara's turn. "I don't have a wish," she said softly, looking around the table and meeting the eyes of each dear member of her family in turn. "Little more than a year ago I was alone in the world. I though I'd been abandoned by God and family." She swallowed back the swell of emotion that threatened to clog her throat. "Now I'm blessed beyond anything I could have imagined." She sent a misty smile to James, deciding to wait and share her news with him in private later. "I suppose I must be Rebecca after all," she said. Evie perked up at this mention of a character from her beloved *Ivanhoe*.

Evie nodded wisely. "Because you healed me when I was sick."

Sara's smile widened. "Yes, but also because I am *like the herb which flourisheth most when trampled upon*. I couldn't see then that there would be an end to my time of trouble, but now—" She swept her arm around the table. "Now I'm blessed beyond measure." Her gaze fell on Henry and she passed him the taper. "Why don't you light it, Henry?"

Instead of grabbing the taper, Henry frowned, his eyes darting from the taper to the pudding with suspicion.

"Why do we want to start it on fire? Won't be no good charred to a crisp."

Evie leaned closer to Henry. "I used to worry the same thing," she confided. "But don't you worry, only the brandy burns off, and no one would want to taste that anyway." Evie made a face to signify her distaste. "Go on, light it."

Henry reached out a hesitant hand and touched the lit taper to the pudding, which burst into low, blue flames that lit the darkened room, illuminating the faces around the table. Henry's eyes grew wide with wonder, Evie laughed and clapped her hands together. Papa watched the children with fond indulgence, and James watched her, a slow smile spreading across his face.

I love you. He mouthed the words and Sara felt her heart swell with so much love, she thought it would burst.

Sara served the pudding, drizzled with sweet, dark sauce.

"Can I have more?" Henry asked, as soon as he could speak.

Papa cleared his throat and Henry straightened in his seat. "That is, may I have another serving?"

"Or we could move to the parlor," James suggested, his eyes dancing. "I heard there might be presents."

Henry looked so torn that Sara took pity on him and gave him a small second serving before promising he could also take some home. The party rose to move to the parlor, where Papa had left a gift for Evie. James had brought down their gift for Henry as well, a handsome edition of *Ivanhoe*.

As they settled into the parlor, James stood at the window, his gaze far away in the twilight. Sara slipped her hand into his. He turned his head and pressed a surreptitious kiss to her brow.

"It's almost too much, isn't it?" she said.

James gave her a rueful smile. "How do you guess my thoughts?"

Sara leaned into his side and brought his hand to her belly. "There's something I want to tell you."

"Papa, Mama, come on," Evie called from the hearth. "We're waiting for you."

Sara turned back to the cozy scene. Her father sat in the armchair before the parlor fire, watching Evie and Henry with a contented smile. She tugged at James's hand to pull him with her, but he stood unmoving as a boulder, staring at his hand pressed against her.

"James?"

"Does this mean what I think it does?" he said, his voice hoarse.

She nodded.

James wheeled about, tugging her to the privacy of the kitchen, and Sara knew a moment of sickening doubt. Perhaps she should have waited until they were alone to tell him. Amelia's labor had been a horrible tragedy. Perhaps he didn't want this baby.

Then James's voice, incredulous, broke through her fear. "A baby?"

Sara nodded, her lips pressed together. She'd promised herself she'd be content with the blessing of James and Evie for as long as she lived and hadn't dared to ask for more. The promise growing inside her was a gift beyond her wildest dreams. But perhaps James wouldn't see it that way. She cleared her throat. "I've known for a week or more. I just didn't know how to tell you. I was afraid . . ."

His arms came about her, warm and solid, cradling her head into his shoulder. "I'm afraid, too," he whispered into her ear. His arms tightened around her. "But more than that, I'm hopeful." He pressed a kiss to her temple. "What did Granny tell you?" he said after a long moment. *"A time to weep and a time to laugh . . ."* He stepped back to look into her face.

"A time to mourn and a time to dance." She sighed and nestled back into his arms with a smile. Granny had been right all along.

A Note from the Author

Although the characters in this story are my creation, the Upper Canada Rebellion was a real event, and its leader, the clever, fiery, and forthright William Lyon Mackenzie, is a larger-than-life figure in Canadian history.

On December 5, 1837, a group of some one thousand citizens organized under Mackenzie, a printer-turned-politician who railed against the restrictive and self-serving policies of the colonial government. They met at Montgomery's Tavern to begin an ill-fated march on Toronto that quickly disbanded in the face of loyalist opposition. Two days later, a volunteer militia marched north, defeated the remaining rebels, and burned Montgomery's Tavern to the ground.

Mackenzie and many of his followers fled to the United States. Authorities arrested others, including my relative, twenty-six-year-old Duncan MacPhedran. After a short prison term, he was released and returned (chastened, I imagine) to the family farm. He was lucky. Many men who played key roles in the rebellion were deported and several were hanged.

In 1849, William Lyon Mackenzie received a government pardon and returned to Toronto from New York. He reentered political life and was elected to the Legislative Assembly, where he served until his retirement. Although his legacy still invites controversy, many consider Mackenzie to be the founder of responsible government in Canada, and his grandson, William Lyon Mackenzie King, became Canada's longest-serving prime minister.

Acknowledgments

First, I would like to thank my agent, Rachel McMillan, for your hard work, encouragement and enthusiasm . . . and for loving this obscure bit of history as much as I do. I am forever grateful to Stephanie Broene at Tyndale for seeing the potential in this story and taking a chance on a new author. Thanks also to the entire team at Tyndale, who gently guided this newbie through the process of publication. Special thanks to Kathy Olson and the editing team for smoothing all my rough edges, to Libby and the amazing cover design team, to Wendie for your warm welcome to the Tyndale family, and to everyone who helped introduce me and my story to readers.

Over the years, my critique partners have provided hours of valuable feedback. Thank you, Erin, Michael, Amy, Joanna, Alisha, and Jessica, for taking the time to read, comment, and most of all, encourage me to keep going. A special thanks to my lifelong friend and first reader, Maria. Without our brainstorming sessions and your careful eye for plot and pacing, this story would never have seen the light of day.

Finally, I thank my parents for instilling in me the faith that sustains me, my husband for believing in me and my dreams, and my children for their encouragement and patience. The hours spent at museums, cemeteries, and historic sites will pay off someday, I promise. I love you all so much.

Discussion Questions

1. At the beginning of the novel, Sara feels rejected by God and has turned away from her faith, while James—who has also faced adversity—continues to seek God's guidance and provision in his life. Why do people react so differently to life's hard circumstances? Which comes more naturally to you when you face challenges?

2. Mrs. Hobbes suggests that Sara's father might regret the impulsive words he spoke in anger. Did this seem realistic? Have you ever experienced something similar, either as the speaker or the recipient of words spoken in anger?

3. Granny tells Sara, "There's a time to mourn and a time to rejoice, says so right in the Scriptures. Mayhap your time of mourning is done. Might be time to live again." Was Granny was right to suggest this? How can we know when it's time to start living again after a tremendous loss?

4. The poverty of Irish Town stands in stark contrast to the extravagance of Ballantine's mansion or even James's comfortable home. Have you ever been in a situation where you saw wealth and poverty right next to each other? How did it make you feel?

5. Sara thinks the portrait of Evie's mother may bring Evie comfort, and James says he thinks it would make her sad every time she sees it. Do you enjoy seeing photos of loved ones who have died, or do they make you feel the loss all over again?

6. Granny urges Sara to go in her place to help the sick Leary child. She tells Sara, "It's time you were using the gifts God gave you." Why do you think Sara is hesitant to believe in herself and her gifts? Do you sometimes feel hesitant to step forward confidently and bravely?

7. James and Andrew were once very close but have grown apart. Have you ever had a relationship drift apart like this? Did you try to do anything about it? Do you agree with the way James handled it?

8. Granny tells Sara, "You figure God abandoned you, but you know deep down that's not true. He was there all along, holding you up until you was ready to stand again." Have you ever felt like God had abandoned you, but you realized later he had actually been holding you up the whole time?

9. Was there a certain point in the story where you began to suspect who Sara really was? How did you feel about that revelation?

10. The historical novel *Ivanhoe* is read and loved by several characters in this story, inspiring them to bravery and adventure. Are there any books you loved as a young person that have stayed with you and inspired you?

About the Author

CHRISTINE HILL SUNTZ knew she wanted to write as soon as she finished *Anne of Green Gables*, and she's been lost in her imagination ever since. Her love of language led her to study French and German and to pursue a graduate degree in comparative literature, before finding a home teaching high school French.

In 2022, she won the ACFW Genesis Contest and the West Coast Christian Writers Goldie Award for best fiction writing, and she was a finalist in the 2023 ACFW Genesis Contest. She lives in Ontario on a hobby farm with her family, a flock of nosy hens, one attack rooster, and a herd of entitled goats. When she's not writing or teaching, she loves to try out historical recipes on her (mostly) willing family. Follow her adventures in writing and historical farming at christinehillsuntz.com or on Instagram at christinehillsuntz.

CONNECT WITH CHRISTINE ONLINE AT

christinehillsuntz.com

To keep up with the latest, subscribe to her newsletter, get book updates, or follow her on:

 christinehillsuntz

 christinehillsuntz

CP2039

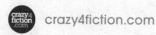
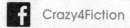